MAX LAGNO

ABSOLUTE ZERO

You're the
chosen one!
Max Lagno

ADAM ONLINE
BOOK ONE

MD
BOOKS

MAGIC DOME BOOKS

Absolute Zero
Adam Online, Book One
Copyright © Max Lagno 2019
Cover Art © Vladimir Manyukhin 2019
English Translation Copyright © Alix Merlin Williamson 2019
Published by Magic Dome Books, 2019
All Rights Reserved
ISBN: 978-80-7619-038-2

ALL BOOKS BY MAX LAGNO:

Adam Online LitRPG Series:
Absolute Zero (Book 1)
The City of Freedom (Book 2)

Level Up: The Knockout LitRPG series
(with Dan Sugralinov):
*The Knockout (*Book 1)

TABLE OF CONTENTS:

Chapter 1
Death and Oblivion

A RED MESSAGE appeared on the projection screen:

Radiological hazard. K-coefficient — 20%%%%%
Assessing radiological environment...

At that the system froze, displaying a spinning wheel. Either the readings were too complex, or the on-board computer had failed.

My traveling companion put aside the tablet on which he had been watching idiotic stand-up shows for the whole flight. For a full hour and a half, I'd been forced to listen to loud cackling and jokes in Tatar, Russian and Chinese. They were just as bad in every language. I even started getting annoyed that the cabin's soundproofing shielded us from the sound of the rotors. Their whirring would have been better than those attempts at humor.

My traveling companion stood up and opened a cupboard. "Size?"

I stood up too and grabbed a radiation suit for myself.

He smirked. "You soldiers give yourselves away with details like that."

"I don't know what you mean."

"The fact that you didn't trust me with the choice."

I unfastened the suit. Within twenty seconds, exceeding the standard time requirement, I'd put it on and checked it was functioning.

"My dad taught me not to trust strangers. Sorry, but this is the first time I've met you," I sat back down, keeping the controls in view.

My traveling companion followed my gaze. "And you always keep an eye on the controls."

"Maybe I've never seen a combat helicopter piloting itself."

"You've seen it all," he zipped up his suit (almost making the standard time). "And you know full well that if we're shot down now, your best bet is taking the controls."

"Isn't the chopper equipped with reactive defenses?"

"Of course, the defenses will shoot down a missile in flight, but that's why they have gamma emitters built in. After the missile explodes, the EM pulse knocks the computer out of action. It won't be able to perform an emergency landing. That's why you're sitting there ready to jump into the pilot's seat. Anyone who's served knows that."

By the last sentence, I was listening through the earphones of my radiation suit. I wanted to answer that the on-board computer would crash even without an EM pulse, but I kept silent. The conversation was pointless enough as it was. We were swapping obvious facts, feeling each other out to find out who was hiding more about themselves.

He picked up a tablet and brought up the map on the projector panel. "Beginning descent."

The symbol of our Mi-200 SU moved through an area crosshatched in yellow and black. Formally, the land belonged to Chinese Kazakhstan, an autonomous republic incorporated within China. In practice, it belonged to nobody. It had been several decades since the last nuclear bombing. The place would be highly radioactive for centuries to come.

There was no better place to set up an unregistered access point to Adam Online. Even if they followed the signal, it would lead them to the edge of a deserted zone. Then no electronics would determine the precise location of the pod: too much interference.

The map disappeared from the projector panel and the lower camera came up on the screen. It showed the remains of a ruined town, with broken streets like cut veins. The sun had not yet risen, so the camera was in night mode, making the ruins seem even more lifeless.

"Don't tell me the pod is on the surface."

"Relax, bro," my companion replied. "It's so deep underground, you can hear Satan knocking from hell."

The beginnings of dawn barely tinted the lifeless sky. The city ruins drowned in blue. I stood on the ground by the helicopter's open cargo hatch.

"Look over there, under the bricks," my companion said from the depths of the cabin.

People like him were called "landlords." They owned "landings," buildings containing unregistered log-in systems for Adam Online. And people like me, who wanted to steal their way into the virtual world, were called "squatters." Or, considering the quantum nature of the extranet — QUANTers.

Beneath the pile of bricks was the end of a hose with a fluid transfer mechanism. The hose pulled easily from a hole in the ground. The landlord brought a second, similar hose out of the cabin. We connected the ends to the two tanks of dissociative electrolytes occupying half the helicopter's cargo compartment. On the sides of the tanks, apart from inscriptions in Tatar, Chinese and English, were stickers bearing the crest of the Kazan People's Republic.

The contents of the tanks began to pump into underground vats.

"Grab your things and follow me," the landlord told me.

I took my backpack from the helicopter cabin and got my pistol from the side pocket.

"Who are you planning to shoot out here?" my escort asked over the radio. "Everything's under control."

Hesitating a little, I put the pistol back. I placed my backpack in a protective bag. The backpack was shielded against radiation too, but I didn't want to risk it. If my injection syringes took a dose of radiation, I'd never return from the taharration.

I threw the backpack onto my shoulders and hurried to the ruined store building. The helicopter remained on the town square, surrounded by an overgrowth of yellow thorns, its cargo doors wide open, the hoses stretching out like lines for an intensive care patient. No wonder it was such a mess inside.

The landlord and I climbed through broken windows. The store was completely overgrown inside with thorns and twisted trees reminiscent of saxaul[1]. The scraps of an ancient coca cola advert hung limp. A cloud of insects rose into the air. There were no animals in the radioactive zone, but there were bugs, hornets and butterflies aplenty, pollinating who knows what and how.

Walking through a swarm of gnats as if through mist, we reached the wall. The landlord cleared away some creeping plants and opened a disintegrating door, revealing a stone wall. He grabbed a protruding stone and pulled at the wall. It opened like an ordinary door. Behind it, a dark corridor with steps leading down.

"Took me and my partners three months to build this landing," the landlord said, walking down the stairs. "Then I lived here alone for a month with the building droids. Cobbled together the infrastructure for connecting to the extranet."

A bulb came on in the corridor, illuminating the cage of a lift. The landlord tapped a code into a tablet to unlock the doors.

I looked back. The insects had settled back down onto the branches. Pink clouds hung in the

---

[1] Saxaul: a desert shrub common in Kazakhstan

triangle of the broken storefront as if in a picture frame. My last glimpse of the real world for a long time. Even if it was a sad world with high background radiation, like these abandoned lands of Chinese Kazakhstan.

We took off our suits and left them in the airlock after we went through the radiation scrubber. The landlord walked into the dark emptiness and pulled a switch with a loud crash.

The lights came on slowly, those that came on at all. Pumps and air vents spluttered into action along with them. The air in the underground room filled with dust.

"See, brother, the air is filtered and purified," he barely held back the urge to sneeze. "We... we refine oxygen from water we get from a well. The hydrogen left over from producing oxygen goes to the power system. Like on a lunar station, bro."

"What's up with the electricity?" I pointed at the blinking lights. "My pod going to work like that?"

"Please. The computer and pod have a separate generator, and the battery can last two months in emergency mode."

Along one wall stood two gyroscopic cells; orbs of yellowed plastic three meters in diameter. The brand looked to be LG. Hmm. Who needed gyrorbs these days, apart from the underage and the crippled? And besides that, why keep them in a landing? Medical cupboards and valves for dissociative electrolytes lined the other walls. Building droids gathered dust in the corners.

There was a separate cabin at the room's center. The landing itself. It stood out with its bleach-white cleanliness. Thick air ducts stretched up to the ceiling. I looked through the square window and examined the taharration pod covered in a plastic sheet. An old droid started crawling into the room.

A message appeared on its screen.

Sterilization: 34%.

"What do you think?"
"Pod looks great."

The landlord approached the door of the landing. At its center was a projection screen. He waved his hand, opening the computer interface. I approached and called up the system information.

— NELLY —
Quantum Computation Platform

20445 MgQ-bits (Last date checked: never)

Model Name: QCP
Model Identifier: QCP 6.2
System Release: 100.07
(Server upgrade unavailable. Please check firewall settings. Reconnecting 3… 2… 1…)
Hardware UUID: 8D9DBA65-21FA-5629-8A59-46ECF5708B77

…

7

"Six-two?" I exclaimed. "Seriously? This computer is ten years old."

The landlord took offense as usual. "Look here, brother. How old are you in standard years?"

"Thirty-six."

"Why were you sent for this, instead of a twenty-year old kid? Right, because you're experienced. A major? A captain? Maybe even a general, huh? You guys in Moscovian Rus rank up pretty quick."

"What are you driving at?"

"New doesn't always mean better. And 'new' doesn't necessarily mean 'reliable.' Alice here has sent so many people to the other side that you have nothing to fear, she's the most experienced around. She's amassed so many human consciousnesses that..."

"Computers don't keep binary arrays of human consciousness."

"Eh, nah, bro, even the scientists that invented taharration technology can't explain all that confusing quantum stuff."

"They can, you just don't understand it. No offense. Never mind, relax, six-two it is."

I decided not to annoy the landlord. For the next few months, my body would be floating in a pod of dissociative fluid. If the landlord decided to throw it in the garbage, my consciousness would have nowhere to come back to.

The droid signaled the end of the sterilization process and exited the pod room.

The landlord pointed out a cabin in the corner. "It's time, brother. There's a shower and a changing room in there. I'll prep the injection."

I nodded toward the backpack. "I have my own. In the pocket next to the pistol.

"See, that's just what I'm talking about, brother... You won't even trust me with the injections. Why do you guys — CIA, NSA, FSB, or whoever — even need us landlords? Even ones as high-class as me."

I shrugged, entered the cabin and started to get undressed. The landlord droned on behind the door, rummaging through my backpack. "Why, I ask? When the details of the hundred-year story of the Mentors broke, you all bolted into the extranet to find them. That's no secret. They talk about it in all the Rims. The one who finds the Mentors may be able to achieve digital immortality. So you hide from each other. Try to infiltrate the extranet under the guise of petty criminals. But you can't fool me. I'm no tech support droid, heh."

I turned the valves. The pipes coughed, spluttered out some dust onto me.

"Oh, that's right, I forgot. There's a pump on the wall there, pump the water yourself. Couldn't make a normal water pipe. Like I said, was building on my own."

Taharration[2], the copying of human consciousness, was a complex operation. The human body was

---

[2] Taharration: from the Arabic word *Tahara*, the ritual cleansing of body and soul

immersed in a pod of dissociative electrolytes and put into stasis. All life functions were frozen. The dissociative molecules melded into every cell of the body, creating its digital copy, which was then scanned by the QCP, the quantum computing platform. A virtual model of the individual, sometimes called a 'binary array' (although there was no binary code involved) was processed and forwarded to the extranet. Usually to Adam Online, the largest virtual world.

Adam Online was better than reality in all respects. The air, the food, the entertainment. The work paid better and was more fun. After all, a quest to seek out some item was more alluring than the manufacturing of real items at a real conveyor belt in a real factory.

According to the statistics, over seventy percent of the planet's population was in stasis at any given time. They floated in pods or in their own homes, or in a district MTC department: a Municipal Taharration Cluster, a pathway to Adam Online for the poor. A building full of tightly packed torpedoes, in each a naked and bald human being.

People lived in a virtual reality, earning virtual millions, or roaming the endless zones of Adam Online, imitating trade, and earning billions through it. They traded user-made skins, upgrades, weaponry, and gear.

The place used fake money in a fake economy, creating real added value that could be used to produce an even greater number of artificial objects: new skins, new weapon modifications, new structures. The gigantic flywheel of the digital economy encompassed almost the entire population of the planet.

To bring it back to reality, the QCP converted the consciousness back again and rewrote it into the body via the dissociative electrolytes. The old consciousness was overwritten with the new version, the one that had lived in Adam Online.

Ordinary dissociative fluid preserved its conserving properties for between five and eight thousand hours, depending on its quality. If one failed to return to the body in that time, then the decay process began and prevented reintegration. High-quality dissociative fluid, such as the fluid in which my body now floated, could support stasis for almost a year.

But a year is an unattainable time.

The limitation was not in the electrolytes, or the powers of the QCP. It was in the human consciousness itself.

It could not exist in a virtual world for an unlimited length of time. It could never truly let go of the fact that it once had a real body.

After eight thousand hours, people gradually began to lose themselves. Their consciousness was subjected to so-called informational entropy. All memories of life before entering the pod began to disappear. They would lose the ability to think logically, would confuse cause and effect. All the symptoms of schizophrenia began to set in.

Those subjected to this entropy ignored the fact that Adam Online was an artificial reality. They forgot everything that happened to them before taharration.

They believed that they had always lived in Adam Online. They fought, died and were reborn in respawn towers. They refused to accept tales of the real world. Laughter was their only response to those that insisted that their bodies actually lay in some pod somewhere. In the end, the consciousness of these people decayed and melted away in the virtual universe.

Death reached humanity even in an attempt to trick it by hiding in a digital copy.

That's what happened to my Olga. That's what happened to all those too weak to face ultimate annihilation. They preferred infinite virtual rebirths, which, in the end, all led to the same unavoidable point: death and oblivion.

You cannot cheat death by digitizing your life. But everyone wanted to.

As more and more people failed to return, QCP software was updated with a forced log-off mechanism. In addition, when the game session reached 7900 hours, the player received debilitating debuffs. Living in Adam Online became harder with each passing hour. Even a gust of strong wind could kill a character at the maximum level. The threat of losing all one's accumulated resources and experience was stronger than the threat of losing one's life. Adamites returned to their bodies before being forced to log off.

A pleasant side effect of taharration was an increased lifespan due to stasis. People aged roughly five months per year. The body's expiry date was pushed back. This led to decreased birth rates, solving the problem of overpopulation and insufficient resources more effectively than the last nuclear war.

Why hurry to have kids if you have two hundred years full of adventure ahead of you?

Living two hundred years is good. Living forever is better. But informational entropy prevented that. If the Mentors had truly found a way to neutralize it, then everything would change. For the sake of immortality, we would kill each other both online and off. Just like we once killed each other over land, over oil, over the neighboring tribe's livestock.

Man has always been able to find a reason to strike his neighbor before his neighbor strikes first.

Don't you think?

Completely naked, I sat on the edge of the pod. It was filled with a thick blue liquid. It was warm. The scent of pine overwhelmed the stench from the tub. My face and bald head were covered in a neurotransmitter net. The landlord's tablet was on the chair in front of me, showing the progress of the scan. ALICE was calculating how much space and time the digitization of my existence would take up.

The landlord brought in the last bucket and poured it into the pod. Even the dissociative fluid had to be added manually! What did he even build in those three months?

"Done," the landlord said, wiping sweat from his brow. "Gonna inject yourself too?"

"Nah, you do it." I presented my arm. I had to show him that I did trust him after all.

He took the syringe from the box, put it against my vein, waited for the green light and pressed. I felt drowsy right away. I could barely move my lips. "There's a card in the other pocket in the backpack... Bring it here, please."

The landlord left, then returned looking at the card. "Wife, daughter, sister?"

"None of your business. No offense. Put it on the chair. Switch off the animation."

The landlord placed the card next to the tablet. He switched the animation mode off. Olga froze, strolling to somewhere in the distance, above the lens.

ALICE blinked through the tablet.

Process complete. Ready to taharrate.

I turned, easing my legs sluggishly into the pod. The dissociative fluid gently cooled them. The landlord took the neurotransmitter net off my head. "From here on, we do it like we agreed. I'll stay here a week. If you show no signs of resurfacing, then I'll pack my bags and head home. I'll destroy the lift... and fill the shaft with sand. Haven't changed your mind?"

"I need safety. Who knows who might be wandering around here? There could be nomads."

"I'll launch the defense system here, in the hole. Three fully equipped Cassies will be in the building. They'll be the ones that dig you out after the mission is over."

"Which Cassies exactly?"

"CAS-4-M, the M is for modernized. Old machines, but again, reliable. One even has a flamethrower. So don't you worry. They're all already configured to detect your voice and appearance. In other words, they'll recognize you, don't fret. There's a Cassie buried at the surface too. It'll destroy the whole building if there's a threat of infiltration. Then you'll be really covered up, no digging you out. But how you'll get out isn't my problem, got it?"

"Okay."

"Good luck, brother."

I lowered myself into the pod silently. The dissociative fluid seeped into my lungs, sank into my stomach in a chilly blob. I resisted the urge to come back up. I wasn't used to sensations like this. For some time, I watched the world through a blue fog. The blurry face of the landlord flickered above me. Something loud struck the bottom of the pod, probably the droid checking the hermetic seal. It would do that every forty minutes for days, months...

The dissociative fluid flowed through my veins, working its way through my body, seeping into every cell. My metabolism slowed, and my sense of time along with it. I saw one of the lights flicker: it slowly went out, turning red.

I went out with it.

Chapter 2
Good Time of Day

I OPENED MY EYES. The blue haze quickly faded.

Another second and the force of gravity came crashing down. I stood on the ground. My ears filled with the noise of wind. The wind itself gently touched my cheek, bringing the freshness of rain. I stood in a field of bright green grass, almost up to my shoulders. The sun glowed softly behind a veil of cloud.

I wore a standard grey vest and jeans. I had a ten-shot Glock X5 in a holster and a knife at my belt. A lighter and a paper map in my left pocket. In my hands were three booklets: *Guidebook on Rim Zero of the Adam Online Universe*, an advert for the Tenshot weapon store, and *Adam Online Version 101.45 Update Information*.

I had a small uncomfortable bag on my shoulder. In it was a tablet, a flat box of rounds and a Small Medkit.

The standard set of the new character.

But since my spawn point wasn't standard, and instead of a name there was a line, a message lit up before me, complete with a triangle with an exclamation mark:

Something went wrong, %Username%.
Please exit your account and log back in. If the problem persists, please contact tech support.
Error code: unknown.
Additional information...

I threw away the booklets and walked toward a semicircular white cottage, almost disappearing in the grass. The system message hung before my eyes. A second message layered on top of it:

How do you rate our tech support service?

I pressed five stars just to get the message out of the way. It wasn't just annoying, it was alarming; would a tech support bot be closing in? There were no instructions about that.

I'd almost reached the white cottage when a booklet appeared in my hands again: "Information on Adam Online Interface Updates." It looked like it wouldn't disappear until I read it to the end. I quickly skimmed through the booklet and threw it into the grass. But then it rematerialized in my bag. Alright, fuck it.

I reached the cottage. Remembering forgotten skills, I gazed along the cottage walls, expecting to read its stats, but saw nothing. *Oh, right. I'm at level zero. All the info is through that dumb tablet.* I took it out, switched it on and aimed it at the tent. There it is:

Improved Tent.
Structure class: shelter.
Structure type: temporary accommodation.
Owner: %?????????%.
Access: public.

Level: 5.
Defense: 300,000/300,000.
Durability: 100,000/100,000.
Dimensions: %???% by %???% square meters.
Capacity: from 1 to %???% guests.

Effects:
Partisan Trap. The tent may disappear from other players' field of view. Effect range: 50 meters.
Unknown Effect. Requires 20 Knowledge.

Note: temporary dwellings can be created by a player in any area, regardless of ownership or permission for construction.

A hacked tent, too? Now I could definitely expect the tech support bots...

I put away the tablet, pushed the low door of the white cottage and went in. The system message disappeared immediately.

I saw a figure in a bot's overalls in the gloom. He stood with his back to me. Instinctively, I reached for my holster. The bot turned and I recognized Major General Makarov, my superior.

"Hello, Anton," he said. "You should know that this is just my image uploaded into a bot. It's programmed to only answer questions on the mission. If you want to hear about my fishing trips and other trivialities, we'll have to catch up in real life. As always, you can visit any time."

The Major General imitated the habits of the original. From time to time he patted his chest where he normally kept cigarettes, but then remembered that there weren't any here.

"You are aware of the primary goal," he began. "Let me tell you what they didn't tell you at your pre-flight briefing. The Mentors exist. That's a fact. But more importantly, the consciousness of Nelly Valeeva exists too."

"What? She digitized herself a hundred years ago."

"Exactly. She exists in the extranet, fully conscious, not subject to informational entropy.

"Why are you so sure her consciousness hasn't degraded?"

"We don't know exactly how, but we suspect that her binary array was fully saved somehow. That's one of your intermediary goals: find Nelly Valeeva, or rather the digital copy of her consciousness, and learn her degree of entropy."

The Major General called up a projection interface. "Memorize her face."

A video came up showing the presentation of the

first taharration complex in the world. This video was just as momentous as the Moon landings or the surrender of the Chinese in their war against us.

"Look, it was almost a hundred years ago," Makarov said. "And practically nothing has changed: a pod of dissociative fluid and a connection to a quantum computing platform."

"Only it was crap, Sir. It was all jury-rigged, like the first exoskeletons."

The speaker came into view. A beautiful, strict face. She was a little over thirty then. An aggressive twist of her lip showed that this legendary woman was no rose. As far as I remembered, she even died alone, at her desk. She continued working on the taharration technology deep into her old age. A line of affordable quantum platforms was named after her: NELLY.

There's something mystical about the fact that I was sent into the game through precisely one such platform. "What's the point of searching for her by her appearance, Sir? Was it really possible a hundred years ago to digitize an individual to the same detail as we can now? How do we know she looks like that? Does she show up at all in Adam Online? Doesn't tech support wipe her, thinking she's just another bug or hacking attempt?

"That too is a problem you're going to have to solve."

"Sorry, Sir, but the mission looks like I'm supposed to find something without knowing what it is. Adam Online has millions of users and trillions of NPCs at all difficulty levels. It takes half an hour just to go through the list of zones..."

The Major General interrupted me. "A year ago, during a random scan of Adam Online traffic, we caught something."

He swept away the presentation video and dragged in a new one.

Two washed-out female figures stood opposite each other. The image twitched, turned to static. Corrupted snatches of dialog came through.

"Who are you?"

"Just like you. A copy of a copy."

"Who created the Darknet?"

"The Mentors from Do..."

The image blurred. It came together again and started over. I recognized Valeeva as one of the figures. The second was younger, in a vest bearing some kind of emblem, upon which the word Darknet was visible.

"We don't know who she's talking to," Makarov said, anticipating my question. "This isn't even a video, it's a three-dimensional reconstruction of raw data caught at random in Adam Online game traffic."

"Maybe it's the start of some porn scene?"

"The fragment has a date field. The same day that Nelly Valeeva tested out taharration technology: she digitized her consciousness and sent it to the Adam Online version of that time.

I nodded. "I agree, it's an anomaly. What makes a hundred-year event in new traffic? On the other hand, what's so special about it? Adam Online isn't just on servers, it's in the consciousness of the users connected to it. We could have caught anyone's nonsense."

"The analysis department concluded that Nelly's companion was an avatar of the Mentors. That's what we're going on."

"I see, Sir. Now another question..."

A knock at the door interrupted me.

"Good time of day, players!" the tech support bot said. Without waiting for permission, it opened the door and came in. A standard blue-eyed, broad-shouldered blond.

Arild 23-003.

Adam Online Asian Cluster Tech Support Bot.

<< Disclaimer: a majority of users in the Asian Cluster voted for the bot Arild's appearance. If you consider that your race or gender has been discriminated against, please change the bot's appearance in your account settings >>

I moved my hand to my holster, ready to draw my weapon.

Smiling broadly, Arild approached us. "The dispatch station received a notice that there have been bugs in this zone. Will you allow me to begin a scan? Yes-No? In the meantime, please familiarize yourself with the new additions to the interface."

Some of those idiotic booklets appeared in the hands of Makarov and myself. I didn't throw them away, just skimmed through them and put them in my bag.

The bot turned toward me. The smile changed to concern. "We cannot fix the bugs in your account, Username. The error code reports that your taharration system is the cause. Your location cannot be Unknown. Please contact your taharration service provider."

I shot him in the face. After thoroughly coating the walls in blood, Arild fell to the floor.

"Hm, you couldn't bump off tech support in Adam ten years ago."

"The users voted for the ability," Makarov chuckled. "You can even fuck them now."

I searched the bot, but apart from a pack of booklets and a nametag with its serial number, I found nothing. The habits of a seasoned adamite were slowly returning to me. I put the bot's nametag in my bag. Then the tablet beeped. I took it out and read:

Quest available: Fair-Haired Beasts.
The owner of the All-Seeing Eye chain of stores invites you to cull bots like Arild. Bring the bot's nametag to any All-Seeing Eye store and you can swap it for money or upgrades.
Let's show the fair-haired beasts who's boss in the Asian Cluster!

Please note, each nametag reduces your Reputation with the authorities of Rim Zero: -1.

Makarov closed the tent door. "In short, a piece of data containing Valeeva was captured from the traffic. We narrowed its source down to Rim Six. It was generated relatively recently. Players are only just starting to take those regions. Actually, they're only just planning to take them. Nobody has opened a way there yet.

I whistled. "I'll need to level up a lot to get there."

Makarov approached the wall of the tent and summoned a projection panel. "It's all been done for you. The bravest warriors of Adam Online have worked on leveling up this character. Meet your new virtual body. We used your old name."

The name Leonarm lit up on the panel, and a diagram of the character started loading. Even in this form, it was clear that the character had been leveled to the max. The UniSuit list of skills and upgrades took up most of the panel.

"Leonarm? I'd rather forget that name..."

A user of Adam Online could choose any name, whether it was already in use or not. The log-in system used a unique 1024-symbol identifier instead of the name. I remember Adam's locations being full of Fire Demons, Crushers, Reality Distorters and Supernoobs. Even my Olga had the name Dark Angel. Along with millions of other Dark Angels."

"Alright, Leonarm is fine. How are the stats?"

"We chose the Human race for you," Makarov said. "Not because you've always worked for them, but so that Nelly won't be frightened at the sight of a bizoid or mechanodestructor.

"Um, I remember the mechanodestructors, but who are the bizoids? Sounds scary even to me."

"One of the new races. In the years you lived in

reality, a few things have changed here. Your achievements and skills are out of date, Anton, so try not to mess up with Leonarm in Rim One. But don't worry, I'm going to be here for two more hours to show you what's new in the world..."

"Why only two hours?"

"After that, the controllers will pry me out of this tech bot. They're doing it right now, actually."

"Who are the controllers?"

"They're designed to deal with hackers like me. If tech support bots are ordinary NPCs designed to fulfill one task — to eliminate bugs — then the controllers are here to neutralize cheating players."

The walls of the tent shook. A notification lit up on the panel. A missile strike had eaten through half the defenses. I couldn't help but smile: I was unused to a tent withstanding a missile strike just because it had been upgraded with a force field. A tent! Not a bunker, a tent. I wasn't at all used to the way things were here.

"That's it, Anton, they've found us. I'll hold them off, you get elsewhere."

Makarov waved the image of Leonarm onto me, confirmed the character transfer and fled the tent. As he ran, a heavy Nevsky infantry exoskeleton formed on his body, almost the same as the type used in real military theaters. The real military preferred realistic equipment even in a virtual world.

Then I felt myself changing. My vision flickered out and appeared again, now equipped with neurointerface data.

✳

I opened up the character tab.

My head span from the abundance of data. To go from level zero to three hundred was stressful even for a digital conscious.

Name: Leonarm.
Player: %Username% (Error! Check taharration system settings).
Race: Human.
Level: 322.

Classes: Gunner, Technolord, Stalker.

Why all these classes? Don't they conflict with each other? It seems the people that leveled up Leonarm disagreed on what was most important for him. Or more likely, they didn't know who they were leveling him up for and for what, so each went by their own opinions.

I didn't even open the Skills tab. I could imagine what that list was like! I moved to the equipment description. Humans were capable of expanding their battle abilities via one method: UniSuit upgrades.

The Universal Suit (UniSuit) looked just like a level one or two suit after buying it in the store. After installing the right upgrade in one of the slots, the UniSuit turned into both armor and neurosuit for controlling combat machines, and an exoskeleton like Makarov's.

You could either buy the upgrades or make them yourself...

The number of slots depended on the UniSuit's level and could be increased again by the upgrades themselves. A Multislot upgrade could fit in one slot without issue. After which you could put not one upgrade in it, but three or five. The upgrades themselves could be components too. They were made from the corresponding expansions. For example, radiation protection plus infrared, plus vision, plus perception upgrade. In other words, the range of combinations was huge. The UniSuit of a single adamite was rarely similar to the UniSuit of another.

I scrolled through the list mindlessly. Most of the upgrades told me nothing. There was a time when I knew them all. Damn, what could "Defense Against Bizoid Seed" mean? Or "Leap into the Unknown"? Or "Angelic Shepherd"? Out of interest, I expanded the description of the last:

Angelic Shepherd.
Allows you to capture angels and bend them to your will as long as their level is lower than yours.
Duration: 5 minutes.
Cost: 1,500 energy per minute.

So much was new to me. What kind of race were the angels? Fallen ones too. Back in reality, I avoided news about Adam Online. And that was hard. Most people that are forced to spend time in their body to get back into a pod talk about nothing but Adam Online.

I was afraid that Makarov had entrusted this

mission to the wrong guy. I was starting to doubt myself.

"Player Name Hidden is calling you. Action?" the voice of the personal assistant in my head rang out unexpectedly.

"Accept call."

Chapter 3
First Damage

ANTON, Makarov's voice said. *It's worse than I thought. Someone knows our plans. Used to your new body yet?"*

The sounds of shots and explosions accompanied the question.

"Um... Ah.... Not quite..."

There's no time for a tutorial. You'll figure it out in battle.

I opened the inventory and selected a machine gun based on its size and fearsome appearance. I noticed that the UniSuit was equipped with a Stalker Dimensional Compression Backpack. The number of items in it was off the scale. Apart from heaps of weapons, ammunition, medkits, expansions and upgrades, a box depicting an armored car came to my attention. A toy, or...

Not trusting my guess, I expanded the description. There it was:

Tiger.

Armored Vehicle.
Level: 69.

Speed: 55.
Acceleration: 14.
Maneuverability: 22.
Economy: 49.
Reliability: 102.

Durability: 102,000/102,000
Fuel Supply: 49,000/49,000
Fuel type: energy units.

Armament:
Left Side: Twin Nagata Machine Guns.
Right Side: Twin Nagata Machine Guns.
Turret: Arena Plasmagun.

Upgrades:
Toyota Transmission: +5 Maneuverability.
Gorilla Front Glass: +1 Perception.
...

And another dozen lines. But it was the backpack itself occupying one of the UniSuit's upgrade slots that interested me. From reading the description, I realized that it compresses items to an identical size and weight: within it, an armored car and a chocolate bar took up the same weight and linear size.

The past hit me like a punch in the gut: Olga invented a backpack like that many years ago. She even sent the idea to a contest for improving the Adam

Online world...

I unfolded the map. It turned out that we were far from Town Zero, the starting point of all new players in Adam Online. Then I examined the weapon I'd chosen. The model was unfamiliar. The so-called "Automatic Salinger Rifle". It used magazines with a capacity of ten *eus*. One *eu* (energy unit) was equal to one gold. I was basically shooting currency.

I didn't have time to read the long list of this gun's characteristics. After making sure I hadn't forgotten anything, I ran out of the tent.

Makarov stood tall, blocking the entrance to the tent, and shot from the same Salinger rifle. So I made the right choice. To his right and left, fifty meters away, there were machine gun turrets. Spinning around, they emitted long volleys of covering fire, cooled down for a couple of seconds and opened fire on the enemy again.

Two huge spiderlike robots meandered through the tall grass. I aimed at the first and read:

Grisha, Mechanodestructor.
Guild: Black Wave.
Classes: Pilot, Defender.
Level: 332.
Health: 42,439/59,000
Armor: 7,865/9,000.

When a volley from the turret hit Grisha's mechanodestructor, its protective field glowed blue, and blue damage numbers tumbled out into the air:

-230.
-106.
-643.

Grisha launched missiles at us in response. They tore away from the shoulder-mounted missile launcher and drew a complex trajectory in the air, dodging the anti-air defenses we didn't have. They flew into the sky and turned back, dropping onto us from an unexpected angle. The explosion dissipated across the dome of the force field, reducing its power.

I aimed my sight at the second mechanodestructor:

Fortunado, Mechanodestructor.
Guild: Black Wave.
Classes: Engineer, Defender.
Level: 340.
Health: 40,000/40,000.
Armor: 2,336/16,000.

I addressed my personal assistant:

"Why are players of this level in Rim Zero? You can't come back here after reaching level five."

The assistant answered instantly: "Initialization err..." and cut out.

Fair enough. Strange to ask the game assistant about a non-game situation. I readdressed my question to Makarov:

"How did they get here?"

"Someone hacked the block, like we did," Makarov replied. "That's why you're here, and these high-ranked players."

"What's the Black Wave guild?"

"A brigade of high-rank mercenaries. Their interests include contract killing and fighting wars for other guilds. Their HQ is in Rim Four, at the Black Wave military base. Grisha[3] and Fortunado are the guild leaders, twin brothers."

Makarov sent two identical photos of men aged around twenty. Judging by their perfect appearance, the photos weren't real.

"Handsome guys," he continued. "They've headed up the leaderboard for the coolest adamites for two years now. Only you caught up to them sometimes. Or rather, the people that were leveling up your Leonarm."

I summoned my personal assistant. "Show leaderboard."

"The leaderboard consists of three billion six hundred twenty million three hundred thousand entries. Estimated time to display list: eleven minutes. Continue?"

"Just show me the top ten."

Adam Online Ranking Leaderboard (Asian Cluster)

1. Fortunado — 340 (Mechanodestructor, Guild:

---

[3] Grisha is a pet form of the Russian male name Grigory

Black Wave).

2. *Grisha — 332 (Mechanodestructor, Guild: Black Wave).*

3. *Jamilla — 329 (Fallen Angel).*

4. *Most Ancient Evil — 327 (Bizoid, Guild: Black Wave).*

5. *Leonarm — 322 (Human).*

6. *David Kronenberg — 319 (Bizoid).*

7. *Nika — 301 (Android, Guild: Black Wave).*

8. *Crusher — 292 (Angel, Guild: Black Wave).*

9. *HyperNoob — 284 (Mechanodestructor, Guild: Langoliers).*

10. *Evil Transformer — 277 (Mechanodestructor, Guild: Golden Horde).*

An interesting spread. The mechanodestructors dominated in the top ten. One human and one android. Two bizoids. One angel and one fallen angel. I didn't know the difference between them.

I had other things to deal with. Time to fight.

The turrets had torn up the entire field before them. The grass no longer hid the fact that apart from the two gigantic mechanodestructors, a dozen or more smaller enemies now approached us. A couple of tall, thin androids towered over us.

They were all player-controlled. There were no NPCs or procedurally generated soldiers. All of them were between level 200 and 300, and all from the Black Wave guild. I could see several red squares in the sky. That was my neurointerface marking air targets: one Eurofighter, two MiGs and one empty target, which my combat system stubbornly lit up, but didn't describe.

My personal assistant came to my aid:

"That is an angel. They are invisible to the naked eye, but your level allows you to at least be aware of their presence."

Strange that they brought androids onto the battlefield. That race stood out for the fact that it couldn't attack or use weapons against any players or characters.

But I quickly remembered what androids did on the battlefield. One android approached the spiderlike mechanodestructor and placed its long fine fingers on its force field. The Defense scale instantly rose.

"Makarov!" I yelled. "Switch the turret fire to the androids! They're healing the spiders."

"Take care of it yourself, son," Makarov replied. "I know nothing about these games."

A message appeared in front of me:

Obtained:
Automatic High-Caliber Ellen Turret (x2).
Damage: 200-600.
Cost: 1,000 eu per 10,000 shots.
Upgrades: barrel cooling (10 sec.), King force field generator (+2,000 Defense, 25 meters), intelligent target search.
Attention: second turret Durability at 450/5,000.

I opened my equipment and selected a Nanoid repair kit. I sent the nanobots to the turret — the device's Durability scale crept upwards. Great, my skills as a seasoned adamite had almost returned. I was acting automatically, without having to waste time thinking.

The repair finished and a message popped up:

Urgent Repair skill increased: +10 XP.

Having given me time to get my bearings, Makarov rushed forward. Two missiles launched from his back and flew toward our enemies. But a beam of light came down from the sky, cutting the warheads in half. At the same time, quiet music descended from the sky and dispelled my doubts: this was an angel at work.

I opened the turret control interface and reconfigured the targeting to aim for androids. The first volley took down the android restoring the shield on Grisha's mechanodestructor. The android exploded in a flurry of damage notifications, which instantly filled up my progress bar.

Leonarm (Human) killed Digerati (Android, Guild: Black Wave) using: Automatic High-Caliber Ellen Turret.

A second android lost both legs and fell into the grass. Damage numbers fell off him for a short while longer, but quickly stopped.

Congratulations, Leonarm, you leveled up!
Your level: 323.
Attention: you have unused stat points (1) and skill points (1). Spend them wisely!

"Keep it up!" Makarov encouraged. His Armor

meter floated around two thousand. Health: around five thousand. Just as I was about to grab a medkit, he stopped me:

"Don't waste it on me. The controllers are already here. Stay focused. They don't meddle in player affairs unless they're cheaters like me, hacking a bot or another account. That's it, Leonarm, you're on your own now. My advice: don't try to take them all out. Break through and run to the respawn tower in Town Zero. You have more than enough money on your account to go straight to Rim Five. From there, move to the most distant and unexplored zones. The Mentors are somewhere where there are no players yet..."

Before I could speak, the Major General shut off the radio and ran at the enemies. The rain of fire cut through his defense. His health bar began to drop. Aside from the mechanodestructors, the angels were shooting at him too: fiery arrows fell from the sky with a piercing whistle, drowning out the angels' song.

The figure in the exoskeleton was covered in a cloud of fire, columns of dust. But all the same, Makarov reached the enemy. He detonated a powerful explosive. The explosion threw tons of earth into the air. The turrets' force field shuddered and rippled as if in fear.

Small explosions tore through the sky. The Eurofighter and the MiGs lost control and went down. They all exploded before hitting the ground, struck down by Makarov's superweapon. It seemed to be a unique bomb assembled by an experienced and high-ranking weaponsmith.

The shockwave hit me. It knocked out the turrets

and blew away the tent.

Damage taken: -945, shockwave from Wiper Swiper photon mine.

Automatic High-Caliber Ellen Turret (x2) destroyed, cannot be repaired.

A list of players killed by Makarov stretched out before my eyes. I didn't know how they'd all gotten into Rim Zero, but I guessed that the fines for dying in such a low-level zone would be huge.

Two mechanodestructors remained among the enemy's ground forces. Not only were their force fields destroyed, but their Armor had been halved. Their health bars also showed less than eighty percent. They were defenseless against the full-fledged power of Leonarm.

Chapter 4
Damned Angels

"LEONARM CALLING Black Wave," I said over an open frequency. "How's it going? Hanging in there?"

"Get lost," Grisha's avatar replied.

Fortunado's avatar just sent a picture of an ass.

"What do you want from me? How did you hack the protection in Rim Zero?"

Fortunado answered this time. "Nothing personal, Leonarm. We got an order, we're carrying it out."

"As for how we got into Zero, that's none of your business," Grisha added. "Give up now. You can't escape."

Their words were booming, frightening, spoken through a speech modulator.

I aimed down my sight: a few surviving soldiers stirred in the churned-up earth. A legless android crawled to them on his hands and began to heal them. I aimed for the android's head and fired. The white-blue stroke of the energy charge took out half the skull. The burnt edges of the head's remains glowed. A blue flame burned to the android's shoulders. Damage numbers fell off it as it burned, adding to my XP bar.

Leonarm (Human) killed Nika (Android) using: Salinger Automatic Rifle.

Why was that so easy? These are top players. Why are they so slow, and why do they die so quickly? Maybe it's because of the hacking?

The mechanodestructors continued toward me. Suspecting that they were attacking out of sheer stubbornness, I calmly picked off the remaining soldiers, gathering experience points. I tried to tease more information out of the brothers about their customer:

"You're about to die and respawn fifty percent weaker. Want to make a deal?"

"It could be a hundred percent," Fortunado said.

"We're bored of being at the top all the time. We'll level up again."

Were they bluffing? I checked the contents of my Wallet. Wow! 5,345,700 g.

"Then I'm officially offering the Black Wave guild a job. I need bodyguards."

"Don't be an idiot, buddy," Grisha said. "Firstly, there's a conflict of interest."

"Secondly, we were paid so much that you wouldn't be able to save it up in a hundred years," Fortunado added.

I aimed my sight at Grisha and shot out one of his left legs. The spiderlike mechanodestructor reeled. Another bunch of experience points flew into my progress bar.

Grisha opened fire with all his guns. My Armor

slowly lost durability. But when Grisha's guns quietened, cooling down, my automatic repair bots kicked in and my Armor rose just as slowly.

Fortunado's mechanodestructor reared onto its hind legs. The upper section transformed into a turret. Now its four front legs turned into guns: two machine guns and two cannons.

I had to finish them off, I decided. Since I'm their target, they'll keep getting in my way. After death, their level would be so low that they wouldn't be able to follow me to Rim Five.

The earth shook, tossing the broken turrets around like toys. A few meters from me, the soil rose into a mound.

"What's that?"

In answer to my question, the top of the mound broke, revealing a huge eyeless creature. A worm's face with a round mouth that could consume ten Leonarms. The mouth was full of thick rows of teeth the size of two-handed swords.

Most Ancient Evil, Bizoid.
Guild: Black Wave.
Class: Slug.
DNA Modification: Earthly Tremble.
Level: 327.
Health: 67,000/67,000.

I had no idea what bizoids were capable of, or how best to fight them. They hadn't existed in my day. Time to follow Makarov's advice and escape. I decided to get out of the mechanodestructors' fire and activate my armored vehicle. I'd barely made it ten meters before the earth around me rose in a ringed hill. How big was this bizoid?

Pretty big, as it turned out. I was surrounded by its long body.

Then I leapt up, activating the jet pack built into the lower part of my UniSuit and flying over the bizoid. I'd almost gotten over him when a thick beam of light lanced down from the sky toward me.

That damned choral singing! Damned angels.

My jet pack cut out. Waving my arms and legs as if trying to fly like a bird, I spun head over heels in the air. The light beam pressed down from above. With a crash, I struck the ground, sliding several feet ahead.

Damage taken: -34,555, fall from height and strike from angel's light beam.

Just like that, in a second, I'd lost half my Health.

Left arm injured. Gunner skill reduced by 50%.

Upgrade slot #4 destroyed. Urgent Repair skill lost.

Upgrade slot #6 destroyed. Sprint skill lost.

Upgrade slot #7 destroyed. Capacity of Stalker Dimensional Compression Backpack reduced by 70%.

A list of lost items stretched out after the message that my backpack was damaged. The first to go, of course, was the Tiger armored vehicle. Then I saw a message that I was bleeding, but it was quickly replaced by another:

Automatic healing in progress (upgrade slot #13).

I climbed out of my UniSuit-shaped hole and looked skyward. The only air target remaining was the angel. But it was still impossible to determine its location. The highlighted target square just hung in place, showing the angel's possible presence.

I opened the Character tab.

Angelic Shepherd skill increased to level 3.
I see angels, mom!
Now you can see the location of all angels whose level is below yours.

A name appeared above the empty square in the sky:

Crusher, Angel.
Guild: Black Wave.
Level: 292.

All this happened in mere seconds. Bullets continued to rain down on me from the mechanodestructors. My UniSuit's armor was now going down faster than it was recovering. The round face of the bizoid closed in on me from the left while the circle of his body tightened. The angel's beam continued to press down on me, making it hard to move.

I switched from my rifle to a one-handed Uzi machine pistol and unloaded an entire clip into the bizoid's round maw. Not the most fearsome weapon against the Most Ancient Evil. But it had an Electroshock upgrade. Each bullet hit the target with an extra electric shock, so the damage was high. A thick stream of numbers fell from the bizoid's maw, along with blood and scraps of flesh.

The bizoid Most Ancient Evil turned and fled underground. For some time, I could track its movement using the damage notifications which continued to appear from the electricity.

That gave me time to concentrate on the angel. I had no time to read how Angelic Shepherd worked. I just activated it. To my left appeared the image of a man, holding the angel by the wings and shaking him from time to time.

Attempting to catch angel. Chance of success: 74%.

But a blinking red message covered up that hopeful sign.

Damage taken: -12,460.

I reeled.

The mechanodestructors were getting too close. I unloaded another magazine at Fortunado. It knocked out his cannons and machine guns. But the cannons weren't even firing. Perhaps the artillery gear on both mechanodestructors had been damaged after Makarov's suicide bombing.

The mechanodestructors retreated and took

cover behind a mound left by the bizoid. All three would probably be healing up and repairing.

Link to angel established.
You have five minutes to play God.
Attention: not enough energy (need 4,500 more)
to maintain connection. Time left: 25 seconds... 24...

Twenty-five seconds? But the skill promised five minutes!

I immediately took the magazine out of my Salinger rifle, took out the energy rounds and converted them into energy units. That gave me more than enough. I took control of the angel.

I was dragged out of Leonarm's body and thrust upward.

Chapter 5
From the Sky to the
Earth

THE ENTIRE WORLD of Rim Zero spread out at my feet. Space contorted strangely to display its entire area. That said, it wasn't large: at the center was Town Zero, and around it were familiar old zones. Firefly Swamp, Mercurian Ruins, Mechanodestructor Heap...

One of the angel's skills was the ability to see every player. All I had to do was focus on a zone for it to expand, rotating before me like a globe. It seemed that angels didn't fly. It was as if they hovered in place, turning the world beneath them. It was a stunning sensation of omnipotence.

I could see the name Amy McDonald roaming through the Mechanodestructor Heap. I could not only see her stats (human, level four) but also her current quest: Find the First Mechanodestructor Core. The piercing gaze even penetrated her equipment: a novice tablet with a couple of upgrades and booklets. No medkits left. She'd swapped her Glock X5 for a Lefaucheux revolver, the best weapon of all the pistols available in the Rim Zero stores.

Several mechanical spiderbots hid behind a hill in the girl's path on the heap. They were the weak but numerous denizens of the heap. The girl hadn't seen them. Alas, Amy, you won't complete this quest without a medkit.

I examined the stats of the character I'd taken over:

Crusher, Angel.
Guild: Black Wave.
Class: Patron.
Level: 292.

Strength: 100.
Perception: 42.
Agility: 30.
Knowledge: 97.
Spirit: 65.
Luck: 23.

Reputation: 45 (Friendly).
Angelic Aura: 31,544/65,000.
Mana: 9,560/97,000.

Instead of Health, angels had Spirit, whose level determined the amount of their Angelic Aura. Crusher's was lower than its initial value due to his getting involved in a battle as a soldier.

The mana value for angels was calculated the same as for magic characters: Knowledge multiplied by the player level, plus skills increasing mana.

Crusher's low mana level was because he'd spent it on creating a Blessing, a special buff that he gave to his guildmates. However, his mana was slowly rising.

I cast my gaze to the battlefield. My Leonarm was frozen in a strange pose: on his knees, hands clasped and raised to the sky as if in prayer. So that was how controlling angels worked?

The mechanodestructors and the bizoid still hid behind the cover of their mound. Their health and armor were continually increasing. A little longer and they'd begin their attack. I had to hurry while I had them in the palm of my hand. Or rather, an angelic hand.

Alright. Time to get back to earthly affairs.

I skimmed through the angel's skills. Most of them, naturally, were meaningless in the current situation.

Angelic Patience, level 10.
The more you give, the more you receive.
You bestow Blessing upon all players on the ground:
+10 Stamina.
+10 Strength.
+10 Health.
In exchange, you receive an increase in Reputation.

Or:

Divine Messenger.
In a difficult situation, a player can summon the angel using a Prayer (prayers are obtained in

Temples).

Attention: there is a fine for failing to answer a prayer:

Angelic Aura: -10,000.
Reputation: -20.

That was the downside of angels: if you use your skills to harm another player, regardless of race, your Angelic Aura dropped. It dropped quickly and irrevocably. Nothing could restore the Angelic Aura bar. It was permanently reduced.

Since they had no Health, angels were immortal... How could they be destroyed?

Oh, right: once the Angelic Aura dropped to zero, the angel becomes a fallen angel. He fell from the sky to the earth, taking on physical form, transforming into a simple human with wings. Then he could be killed.

Hmm, this angel was an interesting character... But it wasn't suitable for everything. Sex, alcohol and drugs made the Angelic Aura drop like a stone. Even bad language damaged the aura with every word. Having taken over the angel, I could drop its Angelic Aura to zero merely with a long stream of swearwords.

Angels fulfilled the role of scouts on the battlefield, and something like bards, supporting their allies with buffs. They were omniscient, capable of perceiving other players' equipment, but were limited from directly interfering in earthly affairs.

Alright. What could I send down on my enemies? The beam of light that forced me to the ground turned out to be called Stairway to Heaven. It was actually intended for quickly moving a praying player from one zone to another. But it could also be used as a weak weapon.

The angel had few weapons: an angelic sword, a bow, something called Krishna's Pistol, which didn't kill, but fired a powerful blessing pulse, the Trumpet of Jericho, and Solar Pillar.

The timer counted down. Enough studying. Time to use this conquered angel for its purpose. I didn't know whether my Angelic Shepherd skill would block the player completely, or if he could still talk to his guildmates. Even if it did block him, they'd quickly figure out that something had happened to their comrade if he stopped responding.

The symbol of the Solar Pillar spell had been hanging in front of the angel for a while. That meant that Crusher had been planning to use it against me.

I span the battlefield beneath me, focusing on the bizoid, Most Ancient Evil. I had no idea what the new race was capable of, so I feared the worm most of all.

I don't know how it all looked from below, but from above the sight was magnificent. Clouds gathered around me. The airflows formed something like a pattern with bright yellow rays lancing through it. At the center where I was, the blue sky disappeared and the vastness of space opened up. A vague flow of energy fell down onto the bizoid, filled with flashes of light reminiscent of human bodies.

The bizoid stopped crawling under the ground. The strength of the spell forced him to the surface, held him in the air for a moment. I looked at the gigantic worm's body. It was as big as a train. Tentacles, legs and pincers grew across its entire body. The entire mass writhed, covered in mud and a yellowish slime, which probably helped it slither its way through the earth. I didn't know which advantages the bizoid species had, but beauty certainly wasn't one of them.

A white spot grew at the center of its ringed body, quickly absorbing its flesh. The damage increased as the spot grew. I checked: all the damage was attributed to me, meaning Leonarm, not Crusher, the angel's owner.

Attention: you have attacked a creation of God.
Angelic Aura reduced to 21,544.

Attention: you have deliberately and treacherously attacked a member of your own guild.
Angelic Aura reduced to 16,544.
Reputation reduced to -32, disgust.
Good NPCs will try to avoid conversing with you, will ignore you, and if you are persistent, they will call the police. High chance of refusal of service.

The effect of the Solar Pillar ended. The sky cleared. The bizoid transformed into a salted mummy and fell to the earth, covering the mounds with a white layer of salt.

Attention: you have taken a life that was not yours. God perceives that you are unworthy of the role of divine messenger.

Angelic Aura reduced to 6,544.

Reputation reduced to -44, strong disgust.

Only bandit NPCs will talk to you, or police during an arrest. Most legal merchants will refuse you service. No access to services of Projectoria and Respec-T stations. You will be automatically blacklisted.

My time was coming to an end. I had forty seconds until I was sent back.

"***** ****!" I cried in my trumpeting voice. "F...*** a...***!"

Angelic Aura reduced to 2,147.

Twenty-five seconds. Did I have time? I couldn't remember enough swearwords. Then it hit me:

"There is no God!"

Attention: you have crossed over to the path of evil. The heavens have never seen such an unworthy angel. Descend to where you belong.

Angelic Aura reduced to -7,853.

Special skill gained: Apostate.

I didn't bother reading what the skill did. I leapt from the falling angel and returned toward Leonarm's body in a dizzying fall. I cleared the warning messages from my view: while I was soaring through the skies, Leonarm had taken a dozen new hits, and his Health bar was dangerously low.

There was a flash in the sky. The outline of a man appeared. He started to fall, folding his scorched wings behind him.

I aimed down the sight of my Uzi and fired.

Leonarm (Human) killed Crusher (Fallen Angel) using: Uzi Machine Pistol.

While in the angel's form, I'd memorized the location of the brothers behind the mound. I chose the most powerful grenades I still had left after my compression backpack broke, then asked my personal assistant to calculate the best angle to throw them.

Wait a bit, it replied.

After a few seconds, an overlay appeared in front of me. The height of the mound, wind speed, distance to the target and strength of throw. A crosshair appeared at the center of the overlay. By moving my head, I aimed the crosshair over the second one on the overlay. Swinging my arm, I threw the grenades one after another.

All four exploded on the other side of the mound. Numerous damage notifications flashed in the cloud of dust and salt left by the bizoid. During the battle, my experience bar had gone up by several hundred points at least. Various achievements popped up in the notification windows I'd moved to the edge of my vision.

Before the twin brothers had a chance to

recover, I started limping toward them. I reloaded my Uzi on the way. But a new notification made me stop:

Fortunado (Mechanodestructor) killed Grisha (Mechanodestructor) bare-handed.

I switched to an open channel.

"Have you gone mad? Why the fratricide? Couldn't wait for me to finish you both off? Think a little pre-death leveling will help you?"

You're way off the truth.

"But I'm very close to you," with those words, I climbed the mound and saw the two mechanodestructors. They lay awkwardly, covered in earth and salt, legs akimbo. And didn't move. The fragment of leg that I'd shot off still moldered with a blue flame. Neither of the mechanodestructors moved as I approached.

Fortunado continued talking. "We know that strong players leveled you up. But you're not bad either. You almost finished us off alone. Although it's all because of the hack. Players at our level aren't meant to be here, so nothing works like it should."

"Now I'll deal with you once and for all..." Then I lowered my weapon.

Hexagonal holes yawned in the bodies of both mechanodestructors. Both Grisha and Fortunado were already gone from the battlefield.

The lower level mechanodestructor was a small, hexagonal robot about the size of a nightstand. It moved on a wide monowheel. Instead of eyes, it had one black-and-white camera. At the sides of the nightstand were hands with clumsy claws that couldn't even pick up a bottle without breaking it. All its equipment is kept in a body that opens to the front, like an ordinary oven. Or like a nightstand.

That little robot is called the 'Mechanodestructor Core' and serves as a base for further upgrades. The core is set inside a structure made specially for it. It transforms from a nightstand into a gigantic six-legged robot spider, a human-like transformer, a giant armored self-propelled gun, a flying machine... The mechanodestructor is the apparatus overlaid on the core. Without the core, it's just a heap of scrap metal. By the same token, without the apparatus, the core is nothing but a harmless nightstand on a monowheel. A nightstand capable only of nipping at the enemy with its pincers.

From what I remembered, characters of the mechanodestructor race were the most expensive to maintain. They need a garage to keep an entire zooload of add-ons: for swimming, flying, walking and so on.

I examined the smoking mounds as if trying to glimpse a nightstand joyously rolling away from me on a monowheel.

"But why did you kill your brother?"

"His core was damaged. He couldn't move on his own. Better I get the experience from killing him than you."

"Little early to celebrate. I'll easily catch up to you, pipsqueak."

"Good luck, Leonarm," Fortunado continued. "I don't know who put a price on your head. But since the client gave us a nuclear bomb, you can come to your own conclusions." "A nuclear... What?"

A flash of white light filled the air. I had just enough time to notice a mushroom cloud rising behind my back, where the mechanodestructors' frames had been left behind. Next I heard a mighty roar, and then darkness fell, with hundreds of scrolling lines:

Fortunado (Mechanodestructor Core) killed Leonarm (Human) using the 2.9 kiloton Big Pulowski atomic bomb.

The unfortunate facts followed:

Damage taken: -12,120,000.
Attention: you died in Rim Zero.
Penalties for dying in a low-level zone:
-50% to all achievements.
-75% capital.
Your new level: 161.

Not the end of the world. I could get back to level three hundred in two or three months. But a new message appeared:

Attention: the Big Pulowski nuclear bomb is a weapon of absolute destruction. You did not survive the explosion. All your achievements have been reset, all your skills have been reset, all your stats...

Little early to celebrate. I'd forgotten that the default Adam Online interface had an awful feature: it showed all messages, even those that had lost all meaning due to following messages.

"I got it, I got it!" I shouted helplessly into the darkness.

How would you rate your gaming experience?

(All data are processed and stored in accordance with the rule Processing Confidential Data in Virtual Reality Extranet Systems adopted by the UN in 2099. Article 3, Paragraph 14-2. Please contact support if you have any questions).

I pressed five stars just to get the message out of the way.

The darkness faded. The sensation of a weightless body returned. All the parts of the neural interface that Leonarm's UniSuit generated had disappeared. Gravity kicked in, and I fell into the center of a bright square.

Another second and I stood on the dusty stones of Town Zero's central square.

I wore a standard grey vest and jeans. I had a ten-shot Glock X5 in a holster and a knife at my belt. A lighter and a paper map in my left pocket. In my hands were three booklets: "Guidebook on Rim Zero of the Adam Online Universe", an advert for the Tenshot weapon store, and "Adam Online Version 101.45 Update Information".

I had a small uncomfortable bag on my shoulder. In it was a tablet, a flat box of rounds and a Small Medkit.

The standard set of the new character. But no: the tablet in my bag showed a series of new notifications. New characters don't usually get anything like that.

Chapter 6
All and Nothing

I TOOK THE TABLET out of the bag. I also found the nametag of the bot I'd killed and the booklets that I'd received when I logged in to Adam Online. If things kept going like this, my bag would fill up with garbage.

A green indicator flashed on the tablet, and the dark screen showed a deliberately pixelated message: "New Achievement." I pressed the on button and waited for Leonarm's stats to load.

Using a tablet as the game interface was the heavy burden of every beginner. That was why those that wanted to level up a soldier made it their first concern to upgrade the interface. They at least upgraded from the tablet to augmented reality points. The end goal, of course, was to equip yourself with the same neurointerface that Leonarm had.

I read:

Achievement: All and Nothing.
You have lost everything. You are at absolute zero. You are nobody. You had the luck of being in the epicenter of a nuclear explosion, Leonarm. To ease

your task of full suicide from Adam Online, you have been given a complimentary Glock. Your choice: a bullet in the head or a new fight for the top of the leaderboard.

Obtained:
Complimentary Glock X5 pistol.

Radiation Resistance skill (level 1).

"I was there first" vest.
500 g.

I dragged the icon of the vest onto myself. Instead of a simple grey vest bearing a small Adam Online logo, I saw myself wearing a black vest with an image of a nuclear explosion and the phrase "I was there first." It gave no bonuses and was designed a "Collectible Rarity". It wasn't worth much, somewhere around three thousand five hundred gold.

I opened the Weaponry tab. The tablet did its job of loading the data painfully slowly. I'd have to get used to its built-in lag:

Complimentary Glock X5 pistol.
A pistol that everyone has.

Ammunition: 10 mm round.
Magazine: 15 shots.
Damage: 40.

Rate of fire: 0.6.

Scatter: 0.5.
Weight: 2.
Value: 8,000 g.
Attention: you received this weapon as an achievement reward. Selling or losing the weapon will lower your Reputation by 1.

A great starter weapon. Compared to the default Glock, it held five more rounds in its magazine. It had heightened accuracy due to its low scatter. I drew the weapon from my holster and examined it. The handle was engraved: "Leonarm, for insanity and courage."

I could get a bunch of money for it, but selling it would lower my Reputation.

Alright, onto real problems. Or virtual ones. I was stilling standing in Town Zero's central square. It was a clear midday. The sun burned down on my head. A short blue shadow fell from the respawn tower.

Characters kept appearing all around me: some had only just logged into the game, others were respawning after dying during missions.

Little mechanodestructor cores scurried around my feet. Beginner angels fluttered a few feet above the ground. They looked like translucent figurines of little naked humans with wings.

The level one bizoids just looked like big clumps of white slime. They moved slowly, like legless cripples, tentacle-shaped growths emerging from their bodies. I wondered which advantages the bizoid species offered for people to be willing to play them. The mere sight of them turned my stomach.

Androids began the game in the form of pale,

thin creatures. Their long arms hung at their sides, and they wore no clothing. This caused no embarrassment: they were genderless creatures. They had identical rounded pubic mounds instead of genitals. The lack of sex and any sensation at all from narcotics or food was the race's main disadvantage, and what drove most players away from it.

On the other hand, high-level androids could install a Humanity Chip in their heads that allowed them to experience all the joys available to humanity, but at half the strength. The Humanity Chip also unlocked the Transformation process. Artificial hair could be grown on the android's bald head, and it could take on secondary sex characteristics: barely noticeable breasts or an even less noticeable penis. Androgynous nature allowed no choice between genders, so androids had to get breasts and a penis at the same time. Also, androids couldn't kill anyone, neither directly nor indirectly, which many would see as too negative a quality. In exchange, androids had almost an instantaneous learning ability, which was reflected in the fact that all their achievements and points were doubled, and in some skills even tripled. All they had to do was complete a couple of missions in Rim Zero to level up to five and go to Rim One. The real game started there, at One.

Humans, men and women, appeared in identical grey vests, with identical bags on their shoulders. They grabbed their tablets and aimed them at each other, or at objects, reading their characteristics. Some focused on my expensive vest and nodded respectfully. Many moved to the side, sitting on stone benches arranged around the edge of the area in several rows, and immersed themselves in their tablets, distributing stat points.

Time for me to do the same.

The system had already distributed all available points among my stats, all I had to do was press confirm. But the default values aren't my style. I had to figure out my strategy. I reset all the points and thought:

Leonarm, Human.
Class: not chosen.
Level: 0.

I opened the list of classes and scrolled to Tracker. My task was to find the Mentors, right? And find Nelly Valeeva, find an answer to the question — how did they manage to escape informational entropy?

Class: Tracker.
Your step is swift, your gaze sharp, and your movements accurate. You are a tracker.
You are capable of seeing more details in the environment. To others, trampled grass may just be trampled grass, but to you, it is a clear track left by a person. But not you.
The tracker leaves no tracks.

Attention, this class requires: Strength of at least

3 (distributed automatically).

Perception of at least 5 (distributed automatically).

Agility of at least 4 (distributed automatically).

Knowledge of at least 2 (distributed automatically).

Rifles and Shotguns skill (selected automatically, 1 free skill remaining).

On the other hand, Stalker isn't a bad class either. But best to be a Tracker at first. Most of the Stalker skills wouldn't be available at low level. Although... Who knows what could have changed in all these years? I opened the Stalker sheet to check:

Class: Stalker.

You are the lone explorer of numerous zones. You heal radiation wounds with vodka and feed only on canned meat. Your backpack will hold a ton of one and a ton of the other. Unfussy and low-maintenance, you survive where the bizoid insects perish, the androids break down, and the mechanodestructors' electronics fail to withstand the anomalies' influence.

Your philosophy is simple: if it's day, there's food. What else do you need at night by the fire, when the crackle of the Geiger counter mixes with the crackle of burning logs? Except a guitar for a good song...

Attention, this class requires: Perception of at least 8 (distributed automatically).

Agility of at least 8 (distributed automatically).

Knowledge of at least 4 (distributed automatically).

Strength of at least 8 (not enough points! Need 28. You cannot select this class).

Ooh, stricter than it was. The Stalker class was probably still one of the 'easy' classes. Everyone wanted to pick it, messing up the game balance. After selecting Tracker, I had five points left, and Leonarm's stats looked like this:

Strength: 3.
Perception: 5.
Agility: 4.
Knowledge: 2.
Health: 1.
Luck: 1.

Knowledge was a strange and undefined stat in Adam Online.

Olga, being a fanatic adamite, read materials on the history of its creation. I learned from Olga that a long time ago, when gyrorbs had just been released in the virtual world, this stat was called Intellect.

The invention of taharration changed the fundamentals of character control. You became the character. The game character's Intellect stopped influencing anything.

After all, people in a virtual world have their own intellect. It could not be modified by anything in the virtual world. A character's body could change as much as you wanted, changing the signals sent to the digitized brain. You couldn't forcibly write the ability to shoot, play the violin or successfully perform all the

Kama Sutra poses into the binary array of the human consciousness. All you could do was give the virtual body more strength to lower spread when firing. Or more agility to move the bow faster. Or more health to complete all the sexual poses in one sex act.

The control systems could change only what they created: the parameters of weaponry, zone physics and item characteristics. This created equality between players. If you were a crack shot in real life, then in Adam, your knowledge didn't exactly disappear, but was corrected by the guns. You could aim as well as you liked, but your accuracy would be the same as that shown in your character sheet. The weapons behaved accordingly. Low skill meant fewer hits. The fact that you could wing a fly in real life didn't matter.

Knowledge was the main stat for people who wanted to craft their own weapons, equipment and other items. I usually put a few points into Knowledge when starting a character. But now I doubted myself. Did I really need it in the low levels? Fast leveling seemed more important right now, and Knowledge leveled up more slowly than anything else.

But that didn't mean I'd completely ignore the stat. Leveling it up unlocked complex armaments and UniSuit upgrades. Just right now, in the very beginning, Knowledge could be neglected.

I put all five points into Health, increasing it to six. I didn't have to worry about the spiderbots at Mechanodestructor Heap killing me in the first few hits now.

I chose Automatic Weapons as my next skill,

which included the Uzi machine pistol that I liked so much. I liked the fact that it had such a high rate of fire at a low level. It gave the enemy's Armor no time to recover.

I got the Tenshot Weapons Store booklet out of my bag and found the Uzi. I didn't delve into the upgrades yet. I made sure it was for sale in Rim Zero stores.

I decided that I'd limit Leonarm's leveling to firearms. Energy weapons were expensive and slow. When I played for myself, that's what I chose, but right now I didn't have the time. I wasn't playing for myself, I was playing for my country.

Actually, for all mankind.

I rose from the bench. I pressed Apply Changes on the tablet. The surrounding world froze for a couple of seconds, me along with it. Everything began to move again. I stopped feeling the weight of my bag and holster. My increased Strength was working.

"Shit! Shit Shiiit!" I heard next to me.

A girl appeared in the square. She wore a torn light armored vest on top of the standard vest. She held a Lefaucheux revolver, smoke still rising from the barrel.

"Shit fuck," the girl summarized.

She opened the cylinder and shook out the smoking shells.

I didn't have to look at her with the tablet to recognize

Amy McDonald. I'd seen her from above when I was controlling the angel.

"You won't survive a spiderbot ambush with gear like that," I said.

"Fuck! How do you know where I was?"

"I guessed."

"And what am I supposed to do, since you're so clever, dickhead?"

"Stop swearing for one thing."

"Fuck off, bitch."

Amy haughtily walked by me. She stopped and turned:

"Sorry, I was an angel for so long that I really missed swearing."

I looked at the girl. Like everyone in Rim Zero, she had a real appearance, slightly embellished by the control systems. For example, all blemishes like moles, pimples and scars had been removed from her skin. Changing your appearance completely was a perk reserved for players over level thirty. In the initial levels, only cosmetic corrections were possible: hair and eye color, skin tone. And three hairstyles to choose from. Long, short and bald. Everything else cost money. And not in-game gold, but real dollars and cents that had to be sent to the provider before immersion in the pod.

I didn't know how bizoids could be changed. The number of tentacles, the color of the slime they left behind?

Amy had short hair dyed to a lilac color. Her face was round, with a sharp chin. She cast an appraising gaze on me as well:

"Awesome vest. That from the nuke mentioned

on the radio?"

"Probably," I answered evasively.

"Where'd you get it?"

"It's second-hand."

"Liar."

"Of course I'm lying, Amy McDonald."

"How do you know my name?" she sounded surprised as I hadn't pointed a tablet at her.

She took her own tablet out of her bag. It was already upgraded with Processing Speed, shown by the large fan in the casing, lit with a lilac LED, the same color as her hair. She aimed it at me:

"Uh, Leonarm. So many Leonarms now, damn."

"Want to complete the Heap together?"

"There'll be less experience that way."

"I'm at level one, every little helps. And for you, it's a chance to finally get to level five."

She thought a little. "No, f-f-fu... Not worth it for me. I have an awesome revolver, armor, a tablet with an upgraded personal helper. I even have a backpack instead of a bag. I mean fuck, all you have is a cool vest. You'll be killed at the entrance."

I pointed to the graphic of the nuclear explosion on my vest. "Look, I was at the epicenter. I can deal with spiderbots."

She twigged it right away. "A hidden achievement, right? Awesome. Which?"

"Not telling. So are we going or what?"

"Alright. But don't expect me to sacrifice myself to protect you. Dickhead."

Why did I invite her along?

"Sonny," Makarov had said to me. "You're a

former champion in the game, right? So please, act like a normal player. Socialize, accept duels and join groups. Your behavior shouldn't differ from that of other players."

Of course, the Major General hadn't given me any instructions on how to behave after losing a character. Such a scenario probably wasn't even considered. Who could have known that top players would attack me? And in the sandbox, no less!

In other words, if I had to socialize, then why not start right away?

Chapter 7
Collapse Shmollapse

THE HQ OF THE BLACK WAVE guild stopped being a simple military base a long time ago. After getting a geographical marker on the Adam Online world map, it became one of the zones of Rim Four. Fortunado even built a village around the base to promote it, calling it Shoreline, even though there was no sea or lake nearby. Although later, using the user location editor, he added a lake too.

Shoreline wasn't just home to the NPCs designed to imitate normal life for added realism. Plenty of players bought homes there too.

At first people settled there who had business with Black Wave: merchants, crafting masters and new recruits wanting to join the guild. Since the brothers had a strict selection process, some new recruits lived here for four to six months of their game shift. They completed little errands and earned the experience necessary for initial selection into the guild. The neuronet generators noticed the increased number of players in this area and doubled the generation of quests and random events.

The village became a place where you could earn a good living. But thanks to the brothers' elitism, it never turned into a large population: they couldn't stand black marketeers, drug dens or public houses. And without them, any human village, even a virtual one, stayed a boring village.

Patrols from the Black Wave recruits regularly held raids to clear Shoreline of entertainment establishments, not caring who they belonged to, player or NPC. The verdict was the same for all: shoot on sight. Nobody knew why the brothers wanted it this way, and they weren't talking.

Shoreline maintained a reputation as a place for serious combat characters.

Here you could outfit your UniSuit with custom-made upgrades crafted by human master craftsmen. In contrast to the procedurally generated upgrades, custom-made goods had a more useful multiplier from expansion combinations.

For example, if you wanted to increase your Armor stat. In the Divine Armor or Human Factor store chains, you could get a set of upgrade expansions:

Chest armor upgrade + helmet upgrade + intricate skin (+10 to attractiveness to NPCs).

One might be forgiven for wondering why the hell that skin was there. But the procedural algorithms stubbornly added something useless to all upgrades. If it wasn't an Intricate Skin, it'd be something like Block Bizoid Tentacle Capture. An upgrade that might come in handy in one situation out of a thousand. Not every bizoid had tentacles. Not everyone using them tried to grab with them.

The human artisan, on the other hand, carefully assembled a set like this: Chest armor upgrade + helmet upgrade + Strength upgrade.

Or filled all three expansions with the same Armor upgrade.

High-quality upgrades like that could be found for any race. Mechanodestructors were served at the Depot. People worked there, not NPCs who could suddenly refuse a repair, asking you to take on some dumb quest first.

The Angel Temples were also staffed by angel players that knew exactly how to endow a spell with the greatest effect. Such rarities as Solar Pillar and the Trumpet of Jericho were made there.

The biolaboratories sold Nutrient Packs and DNA modifiers for bizoids, carefully crafted by other bizoid players.

Upgrades and items created by Shoreline's artisans were highly priced, so only people who knew exactly what they wanted bought them.

All user zones in Adam Online had a respawn tower that also acted as a transition point from Rim to Rim.

Sentry mechanodestructors, humanoid robots with missile launchers and plasma guns instead of arms that protected the respawn point at Shoreline, were surprised to see the naked core of a mechanodestructor appear on the respawn point. Any level one hundred player could kill the defenseless nightstand just by poking it.

"Stop staring like idiots!" shouted the core, trying to scurry between the legs of the sentries. "Get out of my way!"

They were even more surprised when they read the player's name:

Fortunado, Mechanodestructor.
Level: 165.

"Sorry, boss, didn't recognize you in that setup... and with that ranking."

Angrily spinning his monowheel, the nightstand careered clean across Shoreline and disappeared into the Depot building.

Ten minutes later, Fortunado emerged, shrouded in a humanoid transformer — everything that his low level allowed.

Less than some of the new recruits that were trying to get into his guild.

The leading members of the Black Wave guild gathered in a meeting room: a tall domed building. It was large enough to fit huge mechanodestructors and the no less huge bizoids.

A hexagonal table occupied the center, with a gold statue of a mechanodestructor core sitting on it. A projector panel covered an entire wall. It showed events from all the Rims of Adam Online, news from the real world, news from the virtual world. Stock market data, the state of all guild members and the progress of all the guild's operations on all levels.

Fortunado spent a lot of time leveling up his Architect skill to build that structure.

The android Nika sat on a sofa, legs up. She folded up her thin two-dimensional body dressed in a white jumpsuit. Pulling her sharp knees in to her chin, she gloomily scrolled through a projection of the Adam Online leaderboard in front of her.

Tousled black hair like obsidian knives fell onto her face. She swept it back angrily, but the blades stubbornly fell down again.

The bizoid Most Ancient Evil had lost his Earthly Tremble DNA modification after he was transformed into a pillar of salt. He was no longer a colossal worm that could move under the ground, avoiding fees when moving from Rim to Rim.

He was the only one that had no need of a respawn tower.

Now he looked like a three-meter hairy monster, half bear and half monkey. This DNA modification, called 'primatebear', had a few skills thanks to the player's personal inventions. Most Ancient Evil once earned a decent amount from selling the DNA modification for 600,000 g per test tube. Now he felt he'd have to return to biocrafting.

Crossing his furry paws on his chest, the bizoid walked bowlegged from Nika's chair to the giant screen.

He stopped and wrinkled his monkey nose. "The brothers are arguing again."

"No wonder," replied Crusher the fallen angel. "We won, but it feels more like we lost."

Nika switched off the projection. "I went down to level one hundred fifty. I'm not even in the top hundred anymore. Five thousand hours of leveling down the drain."

"You're talking as if you didn't get anything in exchange," muttered Most Ancient Evil. "With money like that, we won't have to worry about pod fees for a whole five years."

"I lost my advertisement contracts because I fell off the leaderboard," Nika hissed. "Who needs adverts from a player at level one fifty? I had a stable income from my ads."

The bizoid turned his face toward a column casting a dark shadow. "What about you, Crusher? Did you have corporate contracts?"

The fallen angel emerged from the shadow. He was shrouded in a chlamys, which he was unable to swap for anything else. His white wings with their scorched tips were folded behind him. He had a stately body, a beautiful pale face. His eyes were all black, with no whites. It gave him a demonic air.

"Yes, I worked for the Jehovah's Witnesses. But they don't care what level I am as long as I give out their booklets."

Slapping his bare feet on the hexagonal tiles, the fallen angel walked to the table and sat in an armchair. He had to lift his wings to sit down.

"You're not angry because you lost your contracts, Nika. You're angry because Leonarm killed us all solo."

"Oh, please," Nika rolled her eyes. "That char is like a revolving door. One player in it one day, another the next."

"No-o-o," the bizoid cried. "Something tells me that Leonarm's rightful owner is back. There was a champion under that name ten years ago."

"You don't remember anything that happened ten years ago."

"Who needs memories when you can search?"

"God, you're such a drag," Nika slid out of the armchair and stretched her wire-thin body. "One good thing, at least: the nuclear explosion took him back to zero."

"By the way," added Crusher the fallen angel, "why didn't we use the nuke right away? Why were we sent into battle first?"

"Don't you get it?" Nika snorted. "The twins were saving the a-bomb. They didn't want to waste it. They hoped we could take care of it. And look how much we've lost to their frugality."

The gate in the wall swung open, letting in Grisha and Fortunado. Grisha was in his core. The tiny robot was entirely lost against a backdrop of gigantic characters.

"What are you droning about?" Fortunado asked. "Are you dissatisfied?"

"We're plenty satisfied, boss," answered Crusher and Most Ancient Evil.

"I am dissatisfied," Nika said. "As a temporary participant, I joined only for the raid to Rim Zero. I'm leaving the guild."

"Are you sure?"

"Then scram, get out of here!" the little Grisha squealed. He began to roll toward the android. He nipped a thin leg with his claws: "We won't call you again. Go complete some NPC quests."

Nika carefully pushed Grisha back with her foot. "Unlike you losers, I do real scientific work."

"Real scientific work is done outside, beyond the pods," Fortunado replied skeptically. "This entire place is an imitation. Thank you for the help, Nika. The mission was more challenging than we initially expected. We have decided to give you an extra fifteen percent on your reward."

"Oh, that's good!" Most Ancient Evil thundered.

"I wouldn't have given her anything," Grisha muttered, trying to get to Nika again to bite her.

After checking that the money had reached her account, Nika nodded. "Thanks, Fortunado. Pleasure doing business with you."

"Not with you, not at all!" Grisha said, waving his pincers and escorting her to the exit. But then he stopped and whispered to Nika: "I'll come see you tonight."

When the door closed behind her, Fortunado stood at the head of the table. Grisha rolled himself to a chair and stretched out his claw arms in expectation:

"Someone give me a lift, dammit."

Carefully, knowing that he could critically harm the little thing just with a touch of his claw, the furry bizoid lifted him up and put him in the chair.

"Friends," Fortunado began. "My brother and I have held counsel. We have decided that..."

"You decided, you did," Grisha said, waving his

pincers. "I was against it."

"Very well. I have decided to inform you of our relationship with the client that commissioned us to kill Leonarm. After the losses we've suffered on the leaderboard, this is the least we can do for you."

"Come on, boss," Crusher said, flapping his wings. "We earned a fair amount. But thanks for the trust."

The primatebear growled in agreement.

"This isn't just a question of trust," Fortunado continued. "As the leading guild members, you must be informed of all events. And we need your advice."

The bizoid Most Ancient Evil opened his maw in a grin. "I do wonder what client could craft a nuclear bomb."

Grisha tapped his pincers on the table. "We don't know who our client is exactly. It could be the US government, or the Chinese, or ours, or the Russians, or even the Kazan People's Republic. But there is no doubt that these people are all-powerful."

The fallen angel shook his wings. "Are they the ones that gave us the passage to Rim Zero?"

Fortunado nodded.

"But how did they do it? It should be impossible."

"Why?" the bizoid muttered.

"You can hack individual objects, weapons, even characters... and the controllers will come down on you and kick you off the game. But the game itself doesn't just exist on the servers. It exists in the players' heads as well."

"Woah, crazy..." the bizoid scratched his head. "Right inside my noodle?"

"Yours, mine, his, everyone's," continued the fallen angel. "Take at least a little interest in science. Read some books on quantum consciousness theory."

"You read 'em."

"Adam Online isn't just a server cluster, it's a kind of imagined reality that is being created by the players themselves."

"But there are servers, right?" Grisha asked.

"They're used to store data that hasn't yet been perceived by any Adam Online players. Damn, how am I supposed to explain this kind of thing to people that don't even know what a wave function collapse is..."

"Collapse? Huh?" the bizoid clenched a clawed fist. "Don't make fun of me. Collapse shmollapse. Explain things properly before I collapse you down to your glands."

"Well, imagine that we all got together in real life in one big room and started imagining a virtual world. While we're imagining it, while we're involved in it, it exists. I'm looking at you, you're looking at me. It's as if we're both creating each other."

"So why the servers?"

"The servers store information about us in case we stop perceiving each other. Nika just left the zone, but she didn't disappear into thin air, right? The servers are the room where we're imagining this virtual world. The CSes, the control systems, generate new maps and quests, then insert them into the consciousness of the player that requested them.

"Ugh. I don't feel like playing after hearing all that."

"The servers also store data about NPCs, gear,

weapons, zones, number of players..."

"Right!" Grisha exclaimed. "The zones are on the servers after all. So they can be hacked?"

"No. The game rules can't be violated. We all agreed to them. That's what the voting system is for, changing the rules. All adamites decide whether it's possible to do this or that in the game. Think about it, why do you think there's a ban on returning to Rim Zero?"

"Well, so that high-level players don't waste scrubs."

"Exactly. That's just common sense. We all agreed to that. In the same way, you can't go from Rim Five to Rim One without lowering your level. The game couldn't exist without basic rules. And while all three billion of us believe that high-level players shouldn't be messing around near noobs, that's how it'll be."

"Wait," The Most Ancient Evil frowned. "Theoretically, I could imagine myself up to level one thousand?"

"Theoretically? Hell, to level one million. Practically, of course not."

"Why not?"

"Your will alone isn't enough to become a level one-thousand player. The other players also have to agree to it. And they won't. So you have to level up in the same conditions as everyone else. Up to four hundred and no higher."

"Shame. Then tell me why..."

"Friends, whoever wants to familiarize themselves with the theory of Adam Online's functioning should read the manuals," Fortunado interrupted. "I... We gathered you here to talk to the client. She's already on the line."

A video chat window opened on the projection panel. A girl appeared on the screen with blonde hair gathered into a ponytail. Her blue eyes literally smoldered on her face like two little flames. She was wearing a vest with a graphic of the word Darknet.

"Hello, Fortunado. Why are these people here?"

She spoke without emotion, making an emphasis only on the word "people", which was also strangely unemotional. It was hard to tell whether she was indignant or surprised.

"Where do you see people?" grumbled Grisha the mechanodestructor.

The bizoid and the fallen angel giggled warily.

"Hello, Mariam," Fortunado said. "We won't be able to continue the operation without them."

Mariam held her blue eyes on Most Ancient Evil and Crusher for precisely one second each. "Very well."

Chapter 8
New Victim Leaderboard

MARIAM SPOKE unhurriedly. The pauses between her sentences could have been measured with a stopwatch.

"You failed to kill Leonarm without attracting attention. But we are satisfied with the result. No, we are not entirely satisfied with the result."

Fortunado listened carefully, while Grisha clicked his pincers thinking: *A nuclear explosion in Rim Zero sure does draw attention.*

"We have analyzed the course of the operation," Mariam continued. "We cannot give you another nuclear bomb."

"Shame," Grisha said, clicking his pincers.

Fortunado nodded. "I understand. Too much noise. The explosion is the talk of the town. The atomic bomb was an urban legend in Adam Online, but now everyone knows that they actually exist."

"We cannot give you another nuclear bomb," Mariam repeated for some unknown reason.

It wasn't that she had no facial expressions, but it was as if she was following a certain rhythm.

Crusher couldn't help himself. He messaged Most Ancient Evil privately: *This girl bothers me.*

She scares me too, the bizoid answered.

Grisha tapped his pincers on the table, demanding attention.

"Then we'll have to increase our fee, Mariam. Killing high-level players costs a lot in ranking points. Sometimes those players take us out, after all. Our guild is already off the top ten."

Fortunado nodded his agreement with his brother.

After a pause that seemed unnecessary, as if the girl was imitating a pause for thought, she asked,

"How much?"

Fortunado examined his guildmates inquiringly, then turned to the screen. "Another five hundred million."

Holy shit, Crusher and Most Ancient Evil said to each other.

Now there's a demand.

"The world of real business and big bucks."

Mariam shook her head. "Too much. We are forced to request services from the Golden Horde and Langoliers guilds. Thank you for your collaboration..."

Grisha waved his pincers. "Hey, hey, ain't ya heard of haggling?"

"Haggling?" Mariam said pensively. It seemed to everyone as if something like arrogance appeared in her blue eyes. "We already pay a lot."

Fortunado stretched his mechanical mouth into a smile. "No harm in trying. Alright, Mariam. How much extra can you give us?"

"Another hundred million for every level three hundred player. The amount will reduce in direct proportion to reduced level."

Grisha and Fortunado exchanged glances. *Still a hell of a lot*, Crusher messaged Most Ancient Evil privately.

Yep. We're rich. Even in real life, after converting it into money.

What's the exchange rate right now?

Sixty-two thousand gold per buck.

Fortunado brought a document up on the projection panel. "Agreed. Who's next?"

"Any player from the leaderboard with an obvious intention to explore the borders of Rim Five," Mariam signed the contract. "Or even if he's trying to approach it."

"What are our orders for Leonarm?"

"None."

"But he'll level up again. Wouldn't it be simpler to camp him in Rim Zero?"

Mariam took another artificial pause, then finally explained,

"He would simply exit his pod, wait another rotation and enter a new ranked character. The MSB constantly levels them up for their purposes. We do not need that. We cannot give you another nuclear bomb. Any questions?"

The guildmates exchanged glances. "I don't think so," Fortunado said.

"Get started, then."

Mariam disappeared.

Grisha gleefully rattled his pincers on the table.

"Five hundred million!"

Even Fortunado smiled indulgently. "Don't take it for granted. We need to level back up to three hundred. And keep others from doing the same. First let's figure out what to do with the people at the top of the leaderboard right now."

Fortunado pulled up the current leaderboard on the projector panel. The top ten now looked like this:

Adam Online Ranking Leaderboard (Asian Cluster)

1. Jamilla — 331 (Fallen Angel).
2. David Kronenberg — 322 (Bizoid).
3. HyperNoob — 290 (Mechanodestructor, Guild: Langoliers).
4. Evil Transformer — 280 (Mechanodestructor, Guild: Golden Horde).
5. Knight_Ivan — 266 (Human, Guild: Viatichi[4]).
6. Your Mom — 253 (Super).
7. Slippery Joe — 250 (Bizoid, Guild: Golden Horde).
8. Blondie Lee — 245 (Fallen Angel).
9. Henrich Saidullaev — 240 (Mechanodestructor).
10. Alan Kachmazov — 231 (Super, Guild: Langoliers).

Crusher the fallen angel skimmed through the

---

[4] The Viatichi: a Dark-Age kingdom of Eastern Slavs, predecessors of the Russians

champions' profiles. "Boss, the trouble is..."

"Yeah, I know," Fortunado said, shaking his mechanical head.

"I don't," admitted Most Ancient Evil. "Why's everyone so down?"

Grisha pointed at the leaderboard. "To knock down at least Jamilla, we need at least five of us."

"And even then, it might be tough," Crusher said.

The bizoid retracted his head and snarled. "I'll tear her apart right now for five hundred million. I don't care about the levels. I need cash."

"So does everyone," Crusher replied. "But that's not the only problem."

"What else?"

"The ranked players are in some guild. What do you think will happen when we start knocking them out?"

"Guild wars? Haven't had those in a while. The Black Wave will show who rules Adam."

Fortunado and Grisha were silent. The mechanodestructors' facial expressions were primitive: their smile was grimace-like, and an attempt to knit their brows (or what they had in place of them) lead to such a deformation of the head (or what they had in place of it) that it was hard to follow what was going on.

"Nobody is tearing up anybody!" Fortunado snapped. "We're too weak to start a war against the other guilds. We need to prepare."

"Agreed," Crusher said.

"What if this Jamilla heads out to the border with Rim Six, to get into unexplored zones?" Grisha objected. "That's exactly what Mariam is afraid of, as I understand it."

"That's why we need to be as fast and level-headed as possible." Fortunado brought up a list of Black Wave guild members on the projection panel. "Let's plan our work for the next five days. We need to bring in all members above level two hundred."

Fortunado, Grisha and Crusher looked at the cards, noting the zones with the highest level black wavers in. Most Ancient Evil was the only one that didn't understand the tables. He just opened the description of the Jamilla character, thinking that he'd need to level up to destroy the super-strong fallen angel.

"As commanders, we have to not only get back to level two hundred, but also strengthen our battle skill leveling," Fortunado summarized. "If you see strong upgrades, DNA modifications or spells for sale, buy them all up, don't haggle. The more we buy, the less the people we have to kill can buy. We have plenty of money. Buy it all up. You'll have access to the guild budget."

Most Ancient Evil grunted contentedly.

"Each of you will create a group of ten of the best warriors," continued Fortunado. "Each group will pick a target from the leaderboard. We'll figure out who gets who as we go along. Make the groups based on who complements who. Meaning you, Crusher, shouldn't just pick angels or fallen angels. You should have a couple of each race..."

"But nonetheless, put an emphasis on mechanodestructors," Grisha interrupted. "They're expensive to maintain, but effective. Also, our guild

Depot will maintain them for free."

"Question," Most Ancient Evil raised a paw. "Do we accept anyone, or only guild members?"

"Anyone. Moreover, I'll start by trying to lure the best warriors from other guilds to our side. Then we won't have to kill them. The main thing is not to mess around with Rim Six or any zones after Rim Five. I'll also increase recruitment. We need to expand the guild and help our warriors level up."

The bizoid scratched his furry chin. "Hey boss, what's in those secret zones? And who is this Mariam person anyway?"

Crusher also pricked up his wings waiting for Fortunado's answer.

"I don't know who she is or what her endgame is."

"Right, but all the same..." the bizoid said, lowering his voice. "What if she's one of those... what do you call 'em, Tutors?"

"Mentors," corrected Crusher.

"I don't believe in the Mentors," Fortunado spoke decisively. "More likely the special forces of Moscovian Rus and the Kazan People's Republic are plotting against each other again. Or China against India. Or the south against the north."

"But don't you wonder what's in those new zones? What if..."

"It's irrelevant to our commission," Fortunado interrupted. "Let's get to work, boys. I'll expect lists of your group candidates in twelve hours. In twenty hours, we need to drop Jamilla down to level one hundred."

Grisha pointed his pincers at the map. "Hmm,

she's heading straight for Rim Five..."

Fortunado gestured for Crusher and Most Ancient Evil to leave. "Good luck. Keep in touch."

After the newly promoted guild bosses left, Fortunado turned to Grisha. "How long you planning to walk around naked?"

"Patience, bro. Nika is making me a mechanodestructor body the like of which nobody in Adam Online has ever seen. We're going to crack players like nuts."

"All the same, put yourself in a tank or a mech at least. Anything could happen, someone might step on you. And by the way, the group stuff applies to you too."

"But not you?"

"No. I'm overseeing all of you. Or do you think you could do better than me?"

Grisha leapt off his chair, clanging his monowheel. "Nah, bro, I'm a bad organizer."

Fortunado approached the projection panel and brought up a log of the battle in Rim Zero.

"Can't get Leonarm out of your head either?" Grisha asked.

"He's a dangerous enemy. He fights as if barely thinking about it."

"So? He still went down."

"Anyone would have gone down to a nuclear blast. It's as if Leonarm doesn't take Adam Online seriously. That ease is what makes him dangerous. We need to keep an eye on him."

"But we don't have anyone in Rim Zero, or even in Rim Three. Nothing but scrubs there."

Fortunado turned. "Alright, I'll do it. You fulfil your duty."

Grisha rolled to the exit. "Then I'll head over to see Nika. I'll try to convince her to rejoin the guild."

"Don't forget to get changed!" shouted Fortunado at his retreating back. "You're tempting fate to take you out."

Chapter 9
Teenagers Online

THE TWINS Grisha and Fortunado were humble citizens in real life. And not because they were anti-social jerks. Unsociability became the norm of reality, to compensate for excessive socialization in the virtual world.

Life was such that the majority of the planet's population had no employment in life. There was no work that demanded full attendance, or even real-life entertainment. Robots did all the work, and the wealthy people of the west had all the fun. They owned all the land that wasn't irradiated. They invented, did research, built factories where robots manufactured new robots. They sailed the oceans, flew into space. They risked their real lives to build a station on the Moon. It was them, the heirs of rich families, who died in the first landing on Mars. And the second, and the third, before attempts to colonize the planet were finally abandoned.

At least, that's what the news said.

The rest of the population had been forced to sit in grey apartments, first donning a virtual reality helmet and then stepping onto a gyroscopic sphere. Rotating under the user's feet, the gyrosphere imitated bodily movement across virtual worlds, conveying other information through the neuronet on the body. On gyrospheres, people felt real sensations in a virtual world: pain, orgasm and a thirst to kill others.

Living in virtual reality had become the norm even then.

The invention of taharration didn't wipe out the border between reality and invented fantasy. On the contrary, the difference between grey, narrow reality and the beautiful, endless virtual worlds became even more glaring.

Integration into virtual reality began in school. Sometimes the schools themselves were virtual, accessible through a headset or a gyrosphere. It was called Klein-Method Distance Learning. It was used in regions with dangerous environmental factors. This tuition method was the only way onto the social elevator created by rich western society to add to their supply of lackeys.

Talented children were sent to special schools built after the manner of classical schools. There they wore a school uniform, took gym classes and read plenty of high-brow literature. There were also certain special classes about which little was known. The citizens that finished this special school were sent to universities that took up most of Australia — a continent that had completely avoided the ravages of nuclear war. None of them ever left Australia again. Fewer and fewer of them even maintained a connection to their parents, affording them only sparing messages.

The remainder of the young students had a choice to make after finishing school: continue their studies in a college or begin their 'adult life'. Which means: get a certificate of adulthood, settle down in a grey new build and take on the millstone of debt to buy a standard Ocean-3S taharration pod connected to the municipal QCP mainframe. They paid off the debt using money earned in Adam Online. But although gold, the currency of Adam Online, had high purchasing power in the virtual world, when converted to dollars it turned into a paltry sum.

The system worked without fail. Ninety percent of graduates wanted one thing: to plunge into a taharration pod as soon as possible and leave the drab real world behind.

Grisha and Fortunado studied in an ordinary school in the city of Omsk. Siberia was considered a relatively safe region of the planet, so the students attended school in real life, not resorting to Klein's crippling methods. But all their studies were focused on preparing for a life in virtual reality.

Taharration had a detrimental effect on growth, so underage players entered Adam Online through a gyroscopic sphere. The user's movements were transformed into movements in the virtual world. The neural connection network provided a rough, but accessible method of conveying signals created in virtual reality to the human brain.

The twins Grisha and Fortunado, as so often happens, were very different in their characters. It wasn't that one was better than the other, or that they had a jealous rivalry. They added to their outward similarity with their internal contradictions.

The brothers became stars of virtual duels even as children, defeating opponents in gyrosphere games. With age, their differences shone through even stronger. Grisha preferred fast-paced shooters and beat-em-ups. Fortunado liked strategy games or worlds that had the player build competing virtual states, like Civilization.

When the twins united in a game that required both action and thoughtful strategy, then they had no equal. The Black Wave guild began back in the world of DotA 5, the most popular game among the underage.

The twins were fourteen when their dreams came true and they made it into the incredible and forbidden world of Adam Online, not through a gyrosphere, but through a taharration pod. Like adults.

After waiting for their mother and father to go on their rotation in Adam Online, Grisha and Fortunado fled the boarding school that housed the children of such parents. They converted their virtual funds earned in DotA 5 into dollars and bought a two-month pass from a landlord for a pod in one of the underground landings on the outskirts of Omsk. One for two.

Their rotation in the game was short, but the brothers not only reached level 90, they also earned enough money to cover the landlord's rent. Before leaving the pod, they transferred their capital to the control of a credit organization in Liberty City, the capital of Rim One. The organization lent money to players who wanted to buy expensive weaponry and equipment.

When they returned to the boarding school, the twins were met with punishment and a penalty from their parents, but glory among their peers. Along with sweet calculations that by the time they came of age, their investment would grow by six hundred percent.

Aside from the fruits of fate, they also took a blow. There was a reason that it was forbidden for the underage to enter a taharration pod. The dissociative electrolytes blocked the growth spurt that normally occurs in teenagers during puberty. The brothers stayed scrawny and small, and their skin was blue as if the dissociative material had stained it forever. They both likely experienced some other issues too, but neither spoken of it.

Grisha and Fortunado weren't unique cases. Many teenagers used black market landings. It was this that made the authorities step up their fight against the landlords. They forced them to move their pods from cities to radioactive zones, making it much harder for simple citizens to access the landings. And the landlords, for their part, had found a reason to raise their fee.

On the day they came of age, Grisha and Fortunado, like everyone, got apartments and Ocean-3S pods on loan. In their first rotation, the twins visited an organization in Liberty City and learned some sad news: the outfit was controlled by some NPC playing the role of a mafioso. Of course, as the years went on, this NPC had become a central figure of certain quests. Players regularly robbed his organization, fulfilling requests from the city authorities in the fight against bandits. The honest NPC sent investors regular notifications about the need to urgently withdraw funds, but since the brothers didn't log into the game anymore, they couldn't read them.

When they logged into Adam Online on the day they came of age, they found no increase on their investment, only mere remnants of their initial sum.

The brothers had to start from nothing. They worked their way up to the required level and created the Black Wave guild, recruiting some of their friends from the boarding school. Nika was among them.

Time went by, rotation after rotation. The guild grew significantly, got its own headquarters and moved it to Rim Four. Fortunado grew the economy in the town of Shoreline, enjoying his hobby of strategic construction and development. Grisha arranged the continuous completion of NPC quests. Neither of them was rushing anywhere. Both knew that after the dissociative material became part of their bodies, their place was here, in Adam Online. Exiting the pod was an inconvenience that had to be weathered.

In reality, the twins lived in different homes, in different parts of the city. Grisha worked as an operator on a production line for synthetic soy sausages, and Fortunado as a manager of some warehouse at a nuclear power plant. The roles were not difficult, as they consisted in regulating the operation of systems that worked just fine even without human regulation.

Fortunado didn't even know what it was that the warehouse stored. But he remembered perfectly what was in the Black Wave guild vault.

Grisha used his real name in Adam, but Fortunado chose a nickname that ended up replacing his name even in real life. It was even on his ID papers: Fortunado Ivashin.

In real life, the brothers met only before their rotation began. They rented a special office in Omsk where they set up the very best taharration pods, controlled by the latest QCP technology. The money they earned in Adam was enough to buy medical droids that kept an eye on the twins while they were in stasis. They also bought the very best dissociative material, allowing them to spend eight thousand hours in Adam Online.

Nike logged into Adam Online in the same office. She was the best and only friend of both brothers.

They became an inseparable trio back in the boarding school. Nika helped the brothers find a black market landing. According to the plan, Nika was supposed to go with them to occupy the second pod, but after the winter exams, an unexpected message informed Nika that she was being sent to a special school. Even then, she was an outstanding student.

However, after a few months she was sent back from the special school to ordinary school. Even her parents weren't told why, and Nika herself was so full of obviously imagined stories that she was immediately dubbed a 'crazy girl'.

Nika spent all her years in Adam Online solo, on and off at least. She entered a guild to complete profitable quests, then left without explaining herself. This annoyed the brothers, but Nika was almost a sister to them.

Their crazy sister, to put it simply.

In addition, she was one of the most skilled manufacturers of handmade weapons, upgrades and add-ons. Always better to be friends with such people than enemies. Even if that friendship is accompanied with regular messages like "Player Nika has joined the Black Wave guild", followed by "Player Nika has left the Black Wave guild" the very next day.

Fortunado treated her with professionalism when she joined the guild, as if she were any other guild member, and with even greater professionalism when she left the Black Wave.

Grisha spoke to her with the same ease as he had in his school years. Even though Nika had returned from special school a little touched, it didn't change their friendship, which stood on a strong foundation of sarcasm and jokes.

In Adam Online, the path of Nika and the twins diverged because she permanently chose the path of the android. A creature completely independent of humanity. Mechanodestructors, oddly enough, experienced all the joys and sensations of life. According to Adam Online legend, they were a 'mechanical form of life' born in the depths of space as an alternative to biological life. Moreover, some mechanodestructor sensors allowed the human consciousness to experience feelings that cannot be experienced in the real world.

Instead of warring against other players, Nika leveled up boring skills like Armorer, Android Expert, Mechanomaster and others. Everything linked to crafting weaponry, items and upgrades. These crafts took up a great deal of time. Having chosen to level these skills, the player spent entire days creating weapon parts from components, then tediously attaching one piece to another. Success depended on the number of attempts. One could spend an entire game day (eight hours) assembling just the frame for a Plasmashock pistol attachment. The other ninety-six parts of the attachment took no less time. It took a long time of effort to level up Knowledge, too, the stat that allowed you to see exactly which parts had to be pieced together. It was the same story for Luck, which slightly reduced the number of fruitless attempts.

But all the same, even after finally assembling an item or upgrade, there was a chance that the item simply... wouldn't work. Strict though the limitations in the crafting process were, items crafted by players were also very powerful. This meant they demanded a high price.

Nika earned enough to buy her own zone in Rim Three. Using the Terraform skill, she created an unassailable territory surrounded by cliffs. Above it, she placed a magnetic anomaly that disabled all means of flight, except flying bizoids. For them, she had a flak cannon.

The zone became known as Dimension X.

Dimension X became a kind of challenge for adamites. Everyone tried to attack it, testing the fortress's defenses. The space around the zone was littered with the corpses of the permanently dead: Nika's turrets had a random chance of absolute annihilation. Although rare, there was a chance that an attacker would lose their character after death.

The graveyard of brave souls served as the best possible advertisement for Nika's weaponry.

Cutting herself off from the whole world, she continued to hammer together weapons and upgrades, outfitting entire guilds, not even giving a discount to Black Wave. She gave discounts to no one. There were few people in Adam Online willing to devote thousands of hours of play time to crafting.

Nika left the guild as soon as she sniffed out a big opportunity to sell upgrades to an enemy guild. Knowing this, the twins tried to buy up everything she produced before anyone else. Her weapons, add-ons and upgrades weren't the main reason for Black Wave's domination, but they made a significant contribution to maintaining the status quo.

Nika knew better than anyone that no known resource in Adam Online had in its description "required for the creation of a nuclear bomb."

Chapter 10
Foul Insinuations

FIRST OFF, Amy McDonald and I added each other as friends in the Adam Online social network.

> *Amy McDonald, Human.*
> *Player name: Hidden.*
> *Class: None.*
> *Level: 4.*
>
> *Age: 25 standard years (total years hidden).*
> *Hometown: Guangzhou.*
> *Political views: Socialist.*
> *Religious views: Indifferent, i.e. — Buddhism.*
> *Studied theoretical automation at Guangzhou University.*
> *Personal motto: "I will find you and kill you."*

Interestingly, Amy didn't seem like your average Chinese girl. An Asian girl, yes, but clearly one born of assimilated Russians in Kazakhstan or Siberia.

"Hey, that's not fair," she said. "You haven't filled out anything in your profile. First time on Adam?"

"Just haven't been here in a long time."

I opened my profile and filled it out.

Leonarm, Human.
Player name: Anton Brulov.
Class: Tracker.
Level: 0.

Age: 36 standard years (total years hidden).
Hometown: Bryansk.
Political views: Russian patriot.
Religious views: Orthodox.
Studied programming for quantum computing platforms at Moscow State University.
Personal motto: "In search of digital immortality."

As I was wondering whether that motto was too cliché, a message covered the page:

New achievement: Open Book. +10 XP.
You filled out more than half of your personal information. Keep up the good work and make sure everyone knows everything about you. Especially scammers. Don't forget to enter your bank account PIN.

A growing progress bar flashed up in the corner of the screen. This was Rim Zero, where you got progress points every time you farted. All to make players level up faster.

A second message appeared as if to confirm the above:

New achievement: Open Book. +10 XP.

You have a new (and only) friend. Don't lose her.

"Strange motto. What does it mean?" Amy McDonald asked.

"Nothing special. Just have to put something there."

I opened my map and found the nearest All-Seeing Eye store. "How much money do you have?"

Amy hesitated. "Twenty-five gold."

"I have six hundred. Let's go check out the electronics store first, then go to Tenshot. We'll upgrade your armored vest and get some ammo while we're at it."

"Thanks. Shit, those spiderbots killed me so many times that all my savings went on penalties. I also got Radiation Exposure. Minus one to Health. Had to buy pills."

We left the zone and walked onto one of Town Zero's streets.

Town Zero was deliberately built in an antique style. Stone bridges, dilapidated buildings made of stone covered in moss. The architecture was reminiscent of the advanced Medieval period common in fantasy.

As far as I remembered, one could find some useful things in those artificial ruins. But that would take too much time. And it would be boring. The basements were full of rats that you could shoot for experience. The upper floors were home to rare NPCs that could give you a quest: they'd ask you to shoot X number of rats in the basements, or take out another NPC for made-up personal reasons.

A reflection on the paving stones drew my attention.

I bent down and picked up a 10 mm round. My tablet beeped.

I read:

Eagle Eye skill increased to level 1: +50 XP.

Get used to seeing things that others don't want to see.

That's what boosted leveling on the tracking skill meant, a full level right away.

I immediately saw a new light a few feet away. This time I picked up a 5g coin. Another twenty feet and I found a second coin, 10g this time. On the way to the store, I found: four .44 rounds (I gave them to Amy), another 2g, three 10 mm rounds and a strange tool that looked like a bottle opener. No matter how many times I scanned it with the tablet, the description never changed:

Some sort of metal item that looks like a bottle opener. Maybe it's a bottle opener?

"Amy, I don't have enough Knowledge. Will you take a look at this description?"

She took out her tablet but covered the screen with her hand. "We might be friends, but I don't want you to see all my stats."

She aimed the tablet and read,

"Cortaperillas. A device for cutting the ends off cigars. Worth five gold."

I put the cigar cutter into my bag. While I had space, I could store any old garbage.

The All-Seeing Eye store was on the first floor of a temple. There was an angel statue on the roof. Wings outspread, he extended his hands, blessing those below. Anyone who entered the store passed through its rays, getting free health.

The temple was dilapidated, like all the buildings in Town Zero, but it was active. Tiny angels flew into it. There was probably a spell store there for them.

"Did you say you were an angel?" I asked Amy. "Why did you switch to human?"

"I want to become a super."

The supers were another species in Adam Online. You could only become one by leveling up special human skills that transformed you into a superperson. Incidentally, that wouldn't be a bad option for me. Supers had lower sensitivity to pleasure, but advanced battle skills.

I wasn't interested in sex and drugs in the virtual world. I wasn't there for that.

"What happened to your angel?"

"I don't want to talk about it."

"We're friends, aren't we?"

"For clearing the heap."

"As you wish, friend."

I pushed open the door to the store.

Several humans walked along the long half-empty counters, as did one sad-looking android. His bald head reflected the dim light of the yellow bulbs. Salesmen stood on the other side of the counters, dressed in identical checkered shirts.

One poster advertisement stood out more than the others. It showed a dead tech support bot like Arild — with crosses instead of eyes — and the header 'Fair-Haired Beasts'.

"Holy shit," Amy said, reading the quest conditions. "Why haven't I heard about this? I'd take out those bots with pleasure."

I pulled out the bot nametag and put it on the counter. The salesman turned it in his fingers and threw it into a basket under the table.

"Thanks for taking advantage of our special offer. For your first tag, you get one free tablet upgrade or the equivalent value in gold. The next stage is to bring five nametags."

The tablet beeped about a few messages.

I walked away from the counter and Amy unceremoniously looked over my shoulder, but I covered up the tablet screen like she had:

"You said it yourself, we're only temporary friends."

She walked away, and I read:

Fair-Haired Beasts: +10 XP.
Murdering defenseless tech support bots pays well. It's their own fault, they should work better.

Obtained:
100g.
+1 Reputation with the All-Seeing Eye store chain. They won't give you discounts, but they'll let you jump the queue. Maybe.

I closed the window and saw a second under it:
Class: Hired Killer.
No qualms with killing for money? That feeling when every shot counts. For your bank account.

This class provided a few interesting skills. Cold-blooded Precision improved firing from weapons equipped with any kind of sight: optical, thermal or a laser sight. A great compliment to Eagle Eye. There was also Target Localization — the ability to mark your target in a crowd from a great distance. If Nelly Valeeva still had a human form, this skill would be a lot of help. The class lowered my Reputation by one with the legal authorities in all zones, but increased it among the criminal authorities. I finally had access to the Blacklist, a kind of notice board where hit orders were placed against players or NPCs.

Unfortunately, all that required a UniSuit, which I didn't have yet.

I saved the class selection to my notebook, then expanded the list of available tablet upgrades. I chose three of the ones I found most important.

Processing Speed.
Is your tablet freezing? Tabs opening slowly? Personal helper crashing halfway through a sentence?

This powerful 3000RPM cooler from LG will cool your graphical and central processors. Your tablet will open windows at the speed of thought.

The fan comes with a red and highly necessary LED which will give away your position in the darkness.

Price: 1,000g.

A good upgrade, it would save time. But the LED! What moron thought of putting LEDs on gear to make it shine like a Christmas tree? On the other hand, not everyone in Adam Online wanted to fight. The peaceful population liked electronics to glow with all the colors of the rainbow. Things like that hadn't been made in the real world for a long time. It wasted resources.

Lightweight Apple Battery

The tablet should weigh no more than a handgun. Replace the heavy standard battery with the lightweight revolutionary Apple Long Life battery. Forget about recharging for 48 hours.

The tablet's weight is reduced to 300 grams.

Price: 1,400g.

Now that's news! In my day, tablets didn't have to be charged. Nobody wanted that level of realism. I still didn't. I checked the tablet data. It still had eight hours of charge left.

My choice narrowed to the battery. I didn't plan on hanging around in Rim Zero to find places to charge my tablet.

I thought a little on the third option.

Application: Google Maps.

All Adam Online in your tablet. Place markers, set routes, swap location coordinates with other players. All this in the Google Maps application.

Please note, this application contains premium content.

Price: 900g.

After reading that the 'premium content' were Google Maps advertising functions, I chose the lightweight Apple battery and pressed confirm. The tablet disappeared for a second. When it appeared again, it no longer weighed down my hand.

We walked to the weaponry store in silence.

Amy McDonald wasn't as talkative as me. I felt an urge to ask her about angels, about their hidden abilities. But talking doesn't just mean asking questions, it means answering them. Which I didn't want to do.

The Tenshot weaponry store was in a building just as dilapidated as the All-Seeing Eye. It was light inside. I heard dull shots behind the wall: someone was practicing target shooting on a range.

My mood fell when I examined what was on offer. In my head, everything cost just as much as it did ten years before. Back then, my seven hundred gold would have made me a rich man in Rim Zero. Of course, it still meant something now, but not as much as I expected.

An android stood behind the counter. He was painted in the Tenshot livery.

We started by buying two Light Armored Vests. The one Amy had equipped could have been repaired, but neither of us wanted to go to the outskirts of Rim Zero in search of a We Fix It! workshop, where they could fix everything from torn vests to stuck grenade launchers. So we sold Amy's armored vest for two gold.

I chose the option that gave plus one to Agility.

Then I bought myself a Simple Backpack. It couldn't connect to the UniSuit, which meant it was an unrecoverable expense. But I was sick of carrying a bag on my shoulder. We planned to fight spiderbots, and a knapsack hanging at your side only got in the way.

I moved all my items into my backpack and then threw the bag in a trash can full to the brim with the same bags.

I pulled my complimentary Glock from my holster and handed it over to the android. He placed it on the surface of a scanning table. The projection panel on the wall lit up with the available upgrades.

There were many, but I only had enough money for Double Magazine. Now I had a whole thirty shots instead of fifteen. Of course, against spiderbots it would have been better to get a Plasmashock attachment. It provided bonus damage against all races and double the bonus damage against mechanodestructors.

I tore myself away from the upgrade descriptions with some difficulty. Making my own weapon modifications used to my favorite hobby back in the day. But I had no time to learn the required skills for crafting weapon components. I'd have to rely on money for everything. It's always quicker to buy something than make it yourself.

I bought one pulse grenade using what I had left. They were designed for knocking out mechanodestructor electronics and reducing the processing speed of android brains. I also took a few boxes of ammunition for myself and Amy.

"I have nothing in my account," I said.

"I have enough money for two bus tickets to the Mechanodestructor Heap," said Amy. "If we hurry, we'll get there before the next batch of players sets off."

We left the store. The tablet emitted an alarm signal. I took it out of my backpack's special side pocket and read:

Open Book: +10 XP.

Generous Spirit. Thanks to you, your friend isn't in rags. Maybe you'll start carrying her around everywhere too? So that her shoes don't get dirty.

A little further and I'd reach level one. What should I do? Amy looked at me expectantly.

"Undress," I ordered her.

"What?! I might have been a sexless angel for years, but you can't be so forward."

"You like my vest? We can swap."

Amy pulled off her grey vest right away and gave

it to me. Female characters weren't given a bra, so she covered her breasts with her arm.

The android salesman came out of the store and shook his head.

"You are behaving improperly. I will call the police."

"You guys leveling up Sex in Public?" a player shouted from the end of the street. "You have two minutes before the police come. I checked."

"If I join in, the Group Sex skill will unlock," another player echoed him. "The more people, the more XP."

Amy turned to the wall and put my vest on. She turned back. She looked so pleased that I doubted whether it was the vest or the other players' suggestions.

Open Book: +10 XP.

Those who have nothing are always willing to share with their friends. Are you so close to death, Leonarm, that you've decided to give all your stuff away?

Congratulations, Leonarm, you leveled up!
Your level: 1.
Attention: you have unused stat points (1) and skill points (1). Spend them wisely! Not like you're doing now, giving away collectible rares to anyone you meet.

"Are you sure you can spare it?" Amy asked.

I pulled her narrow vest over my head. It quickly

took on my size.

"Not really. But I have bad memories of that gear."

I actually wanted to get rid of an item that would make passersby curious. The later the Black Wave notices me, the better.

Amy's tablet squawked. She took it out and looked at the screen, then at me.

"Since we're friends, I'll tell you. I unlocked the Collector skill. If I collect another five rares like this, I'll get a reward. Do you not have that skill?"

"No... Probably because of my low Knowledge. And it's not a skill, it's an achievement. You're confusing two concepts."

"Shame."

"What's a shame?"

"That you're such a bore. What damn difference does it make whether it's a skill or an achievement?"

I didn't bother answering my aggressive companion. I was only trying to be social.

Chapter 11
Cortaperillas

AMY MCDONALD and I bounced along in the bus. Leaving a trail of dust behind, it careered across the steppe separating Town Zero from the zone known as Mechanodestructor Heap.

There were five people in the bus apart from us. Three people, one bizoid who had already found himself the Shell DNA modification. Now he looked less like a defenseless ball of slime and more like a bipedal turtle. His tentacles had turned into hands with three fingers. The humanoid turtle was armed with a katana that he constantly spun around, cutting the air with a whistle. A mechanodestructor core sat next to him, equipped with a small laser cannon bolted onto his hexagonal body.

Everyone on the bus was at least level four. The Mechanodestructor Heap was a hard zone, so people leveled up a little before visiting it.

A fat NPC sat in the driver's seat, dressed in a worn vest soaked in sweat. His fat body wobbled over the bumps. Rolling a cigar butt in his mouth, he pontificated endlessly.

"Those spiderbots gonna kick your ass soon,

darlins. Especially you, Leonarm. Where do you think you're going, weakling? You should go shoot some rats like the other noobs. Or fumble around in the Mercurian Planes and find a couple of artifacts. 'Cos damn, you're gonna get into a lather in the Heap."

The driver — an old acquaintance of mine — hadn't changed in ten years. The same cigar butt, the same vest. The same muffled radio station, Free Adamite, blaring out music through broken speakers.

I chuckled. "Say, why do you always have a cigar butt in your mouth instead of a whole cigar?"

The question made the NPC "Mechanodestructor Heap Bus Driver" glitch out. He froze, continuing to turn the wheel. After calculating all his dialog options, the so-called creative circuit kicked in. All NPCs in Adam Online had it, apart from mindless beasts.

"Because you only see me on the bus. In the morning I wake up at home, eat my eggs, drink my coffee and walk to work. On the way I smoke my first cigar of the day."

Of course, the NPC had no home, no bed to wake up in, no breakfast or coffee. The creative circuit helped them appear more human. It generated a biography, memories, new behavioral features. When necessary, it added 'internal conflict', a certain life-changing event in the past that supposedly formed the NPC's character: the death of a loved one, a psychological trauma, unrequited love and other things in the same vein.

Naturally, if I'd asked the driver where he lived, and visited the place in the morning, I'd find that he does have a house and coffee. The life of an entire person would have been generated specially to satisfy my passing curiosity. And that life would exist for only as long as I was observing it. As soon as I left the "Driver's Home" zone, it would disappear, moving to archival storage on one of the servers.

My tablet squawked.

Sometimes it's better to be quiet than speak. Your Reputation with the bus driver has gone down: -10 (Suspicion).

That's what I got for playing a seasoned adamite. I'd set an important NPC against me! I tried to fix the situation.

"Sorry, I didn't mean to offend you. It's just that your cigar smells so nice that I'd like to know what kind it is. Cuban? Vietnamese, Brazilian?"

The driver puffed on the foul-smelling cigar. He took it out of his mouth, opened the window and spat into the eddying dust. He put the cigar butt back to his mouth.

"You know, Leonarm, I've been driving passengers to the Heap for years. But I never recall meeting an asshole like you."

"Wha..."

"What's your beef with my cigar? I'm just a driver. I'm poor. I can't smoke Cuban or Brazilian cigars. I've been chewing on this butt for three days now. Ordinary Chinese shit."

My tablet beeped again.

"The most important thing for a young man is to establish a credit — a reputation, character." — John D. Rockefeller.

Your Reputation with the bus driver has gone down: -20 (Alarm).

The driver will now drop you off at the farthest entry to the Mechanodestructor Heap. Keep your nose out of other people's business and you won't harm your own, Leonarm.

Shit.

I panicked a little. How did that happen? Was I really so out of practice at living in Adam? Would this put the whole mission in jeopardy? I had to do something, and fast. I wanted to prove to myself that I hadn't lost my skills...

I stuck my hand into my bag and grabbed the cortaperillas, the cigar cutter I'd found on the bridge in Town Zero.

I stood up and, holding the handrails, walked toward the driver.

"Sorry, my bad. I want to give you something useful to apologize. It's called a cota... corta... perillas. It's designed for cutting the ends of cigars..."

The driver shot a glance at my hand.

"You're a real piece of work, aintcha? Get away from me, asshole. I don't need your handouts! Stick your perillas up your ass. I'm poor, but I have my pride."

I was struck dumb. I went back to my seat and grabbed my tablet nervously.

Okay, Leonarm, you really don't know when to

stop and accept life for what it is without trying to fix what is irrevocably broken.

Your Reputation with the bus driver has gone down: -25.

The driver will now not only drop you off at the farthest entry to the Mechanodestructor Heap, but also at the most dangerous. Keep your nose out of other people's business and... actually, there's no point repeating myself. You're incorrigible.

I quickly closed the message so that Amy wouldn't notice. I tried to look relaxed. I glanced at her sidelong.

She was looking at her tablet. She kept replaying the intro to the quest Find the First Mechanodestructor Core. The video clip was sent to your tablet when you got on the bus. But nobody watched it. Everyone was sure they'd find the core quickly.

The video showed a rusty old mechanodestructor with a white chin stylized as a beard. It stood with the Heap at its back and spoke.

"Many, many years ago when I was still a new and shiny core, I had an older brother. He was the legendary First Mechanodestructor, the progenitor of our species, our model range. I am just the second. But my brother was lost in the Heap, and since then I have heard nothing of him. My operating life is coming to an end, but unfinished business prevents me from pulling the plug. Therefore I will give all my fortune to the one who brings me my brother's core."

"Why are you watching that?" I asked.

"The intro has a clue about where to look."

"Did it help?"

"Yes, actually. Last time I almost got there, but I died from a spiderbot hit and a radiation injury."

"What's the clue?"

"You see those rags hanging on the ruins sticking out?"

"Sure."

"The wind changes direction and the rags point to one side, then the other."

"Alright."

"Every third time, they show the same direction. That's where we need to go."

"Perfect."

"But shh. I figured this out myself."

"Well done," I whispered. "But haven't you completed the Heap before, don't you know that you have to search the south side? The algorithm always hides it there."

"Umm, no... I was an angel, remember? All we have to do is hover over the Heap and send Blessings to players. We leveled up Reputation and got the levels we needed without fighting the spiderbots."

"The biggest threat in the Heap isn't the spiderbots."

"Then what is it?"

"Other players. If we find the core first, then all these people..." I pointed at the other passengers. "...will be our enemies."

"We're here. The southern entrance to the Heap!" the driver shouted. "Everyone off. Apart from you two, you're going further."

"Shit, why?"

The driver closed the door behind the departing passengers and spat out of the open window. "Because I say so."

"Dickhead," Amy grabbed her revolver.

The driver quickly pressed a button on his instrument panel. A shield of bulletproof glass came down over the driver's seat. At the same time, all the bus's windows went down and locked. The driver hit the gas and Amy and I were thrown back in our seats. Iron restraints sprang out of the seat backs and held us fast. Amy dropped her revolver.

"What the fuck is happening?"

I avoided her gaze.

"Maybe it's... a random quest? It happens."

"What the hell are you talking about?" Amy frowned in realization. "This is your fault. You pissed him off somehow."

"I lost a little Reputation with him. Not on purpose. It just kind of happened."

"Noob."

Though bound to her chair, Amy McDonald somehow managed to turn away from me pointedly and face the window. The bus carried on at great speed, careering even harder over the bumps than before. The driver was doing it on purpose.

The high concrete fence of the Heap stretched out beyond the windows. Piles of compressed technological garbage slowly drifted by behind them.

Amy stared wistfully at those rags hanging off the ruins that she'd seen in the intro. The bus took us further and further to the west.

"Sorry, Amy, my bad."

"Why did you talk to him at all?"

"He started it."

"Dumb excuse."

"I haven't played for a long time. I didn't think an NPC that tries to troll every other passenger would have a creative circuit supported by a whole cluster, not just a neuronet node. He was analyzing my behavior and coming up with a way to entertain me."

Amy McDonald looked at me curiously.

"I have no idea what you're saying."

"The neuronet control system algorithm works roughly like this: since I started a conversation, that means I was bored. As in, time to add some excitement to things."

"Huh, so these neuronets analyze our actions?"

"Something like that. The CS, the control systems, react to player action and inaction. Try going to a deserted part of any zone and standing still. See what happens."

"What would happen?" Amy asked. "I've never thought to do that."

"Stuff will start happening around you after a while. Maybe a rat will run up to you, or an NPC will appear and ask you for help, or some other creature roughly around your level will turn up."

The bus braked suddenly. The iron restraints dug into my body. Amy cried out as well.

"Damn it, take it easy or I'll shoot you!"

We stopped by the northern entrance: a huge gate with a smaller door at its base. It was gloomy. Occasional rain drops fell onto the windows.

The driver lifted the glass shield and stood up. He walked toward us, puffing on his cigar and scratching his crotch.

"Overload your circuit," Amy snapped, "And untie us, fast."

I watched the NPC's actions in silence, unable to help but admire the precision of the character's engineering. While we were driving, the control systems likely recreated his life down to the smallest details. Right down to the childhood memories and psychological inclinations that made the driver stare in lust at the tied-up Amy.

"Ah, what a woman."

At the same time, keeping his gaze fixed on her, he began to feel me up. That was too much... But he stopped at reaching a hand into my bag and pulling out the cortaperillas:

"This is for the emotional distress."

He returned to the driver's seat and lowered the protective glass. Then the restraints came off and slid back behind the seats. The first thing Amy did was draw her revolver and shoot at the glass. The ricocheting bullet ended up in my seat's headrest.

"Sorry," Amy put the revolver away.

"Final stop, Mechanodestructor Heap," said the driver dully. "We're here."

Walking past the glass shield, Amy jabbed a finger at it. "I will find you and kill you."

The driver chuckled in response.

While getting off the bus, the dashboard caught my eye. It had a photo stuck to it: a woman and a boy smiling and waving at the camera. Behind them I could see an angel statue, the same one that was above the All-Seeing Eye store.

I didn't notice that detail when I'd approached the driver before. Crazy. NPCs even had families invented for them.

The bus doors clanged shut, catching my elbow. The driver laughed. The bus turned and left, spraying up a cloud of dust. My tablet beeped insistently.

Eagle Eye skill increased: +10 XP.
Eagle Eye skill increased to level 2.
Get used to seeing things you haven't seen before.

And then a second message:

Quest available: All My Children.
That bus driver was a strangely nervous type, right? Don't you want to find out the dark secrets in his soul?

I thoughtfully moved the quest to my logbook.

If I were an adamaddict, I'd have immediately started investigating the character's plot line. But my interest in the virtual world had faded... Right? It had, hadn't it?

A measured knock pulled me out of my revery. Amy was already standing at the doorway and was hitting the rusty lock with the handle of her revolver.

"Get back!" I shouted. "Don't open it."

Too late. The lock broke off and Amy stared at me dumbly.

"What's wrong now?"

That's when the trouble started.

Chapter 12
All Thumbs

THE DOOR FLEW OPEN from a strike from within and fell down on one hinge. The front of a hairy spiderbot appeared in the gap. It was much larger than an ordinary spiderbot — twice the size — and was covered in fine gleaming metallic spikes reminiscent of hair.

"Run to the side!" I shouted at the girl, drawing my pistol.

The ends of the creature's spikes crackled with electricity: it was planning to attack. Amy, still holding her revolver by the barrel, ran to the left of the gates.

"Get down now, get down!"

She hesitated but complied. She fell hard into the withered grass and dust. I did the same. A crack rang out and I pressed my face into the dust. The wave of an electrical discharge pulsed from the spiderbot. My hair stood on end. I stood up at once and began to shoot before the enemy could regain strength for a second strike.

Since I was standing quite close, none of my bullets missed. I aimed right at its flat head covered in its short spikes. Those didn't gleam: they were rusted from blood. He'd gored more than a few players on those spikes.

The enemy desperately pulled with its body, shaking the gate. In trying to chase after Amy, he'd dumbly got himself caught in the door. Only the front of its body with its two thick paws stuck out. He waved them, clawing the ground, thrashing around like a dog trying to get out of its collar. But he was stuck firmly.

The spiderbot must have taken significant damage. All the data was now displayed in full detail on the tablet I'd dropped before I fell. A squeak came from the spot where it lay, notifying me of achievements. I'd most likely leveled up my Pistols and Revolvers skill, one of the default Human skills.

My pistol clicked fruitlessly.

I pulled out the magazine and put in a second. Amy's haste meant that we'd had no time to prepare. My magazines were filled for the ordinary Glock, meaning 15 shots, not 30. I'd need to hurry and get a UniSuit, which solved the problem of filling magazines with rounds.

While changing the magazine, I looked around for my companion. Her hair stood up on end from the electricity too. The girl's head stuck out of the grass like the back of a purple porcupine.

"He's stuck," laughed Amy, standing up. "He got stuck, the idiot. Dickhead."

"Shoot, what are you waiting for? He'll put the second charge through the earth, then we're toast."

Amy aimed, holding her gun with both hands. The Lefaucheux revolver shots were loud, low-frequency. The girl's hands went up with the recoil after every shot, and she was pushed a step or two back.

"I see you economized on Strength," I said.

Only two of the six shots hit the target. One of them tore off part of the spiderbot's head, the second pierced and immobilized one leg. The mechanical monster had now clearly decided to crawl backwards, but it couldn't.

"Hehe, can't get out, can't get in." Amy emptied her revolver's chamber, grabbed a clip and loaded in the rounds.

"Shoot on my command!" I shouted.

"Alright, commander."

"Go in from the left, get twelve steps closer."

I myself approached from the right. I had a perfect view of the blue sparks gathering on the ends of the beast's spines.

"Aim carefully. If you hit the head even once, we're saved. Ready. Aim... Fi...

Bang bang bang! Amy was nearly thrown onto her back.

"Fire..." I muttered pointlessly.

This time Amy broke her previous record: not a single hit. She looked at her revolver's barrel in amazement.

"Is it broken or something?"

I pulled my trigger with the speed of a sewing machine. I had to fire for two. I don't know what rate of fire I had, but it felt at least as fast as an automatic Uzi. At first, the furry spiderbot's head smashed into pieces. Then the scraps still hanging off its neck attachment fell off.

The spiderbot emitted a weak charge, making

our hair stand on end again, and then — it died.

We approached the defeated spiderbot.

It stank of machine oil, warm metal and burnt plastic. Amy kicked a battered leg.

"How do you wanna share the loot?"

"First we need to talk. Have you ever fought in a group? You need to coordinate your actions, not rush straight in."

Amy frowned.

"Look who's talking. Remember whose fault it is that we're here, instead of at the south entrance?"

"That's not what I'm talking about."

"It's what I'm talking about. Dickhead."

"Let's agree not to do anything without talking about it first, alright?"

I returned to my tablet and quickly viewed my messages: the Pistols and Revolvers skill had leveled up, as I thought. I'd earned ten points for killing the furry spider.

I aimed my tablet at it:

Furry Spiderbot, Mechanodestructor.
Class: Scavenger.
Level: 5.

Knowledge. Rare beasts for the Mechanodestructor Heap in Rim Zero. It is unclear how it got here. But if there's one, maybe there's a second?

Or a third? Or even a hundred? Who knows.
Unknown property (requires Knowledge 5).

We didn't get anything particularly special from the spiderbot. I picked its corpse open with a knife and found ten energy charges. We split them equally.

Amy wasn't happy. "I heard that spiderbot corpses are full of useful UniSuit mods."

"Our Knowledge level is too low to extract them."

The spiderbot hull had a special compartment, its 'belly', or synthesis chamber. If I were leveling up weapon crafting, the chamber would be a useful find, since it served as a basis for building a primitive weaponsmithing machine. The spiderbots themselves kept swallowed objects in the chamber: garbage, the debris of other spiderbots, even stones and grass. They disassembled them into components and synthesized parts for their structure, replacing damaged parts.

However, even if I didn't need the chamber, someone else would. I could sell it. I tried to unscrew it from the frame with my knife, but I broke both the knife and the fragile chamber connectors. Without them, it was useless.

My tablet bleeped.

Achievement All Thumbs completed: +5 XP.
Completed: 1/1.
Break a few more mechanodestructors when opening them up to get a consolation prize. Although... would you even be able to hold it with your butterfingers?

"Time to move on." I rose from my heels. "But let's get ready first."

I grabbed a box of rounds and filled all three magazines. Amy, of course, didn't bother getting ready. She was tugging the spiderbot by a leg.

"How will we get through the door with this thing blocking it?"

We tried to pull it together, but it was useless; the corpse was stuck fast in the narrow doorway. The gap above it was too narrow to get through.

"We'll have to walk to the western entrance."

"God dammit."

"Agreed."

But as so often happens in life, our problem was solved by a still greater problem. The frame of the dead spiderbot shuddered and moved a few inches forward. Then a little more, and more. Someone was shoving it from behind.

"What's happening?"

The pushes sped up, making the huge gate shake.

"Nothing good," I sighed. I drew a pulse grenade.

The corpse of the furry spiderbot was pushing through the doorway faster and faster. I signaled to Amy to get back. I switched off my tablet and put it in my backpack.

"You switch off yours too."

The corpse of the furry spiderbot popped out of the doorway like a champagne cork. Behind it stretched out a line of standard spiderbots. They all had identical bodies, flaring out to their bellies with the synthesis chamber inside. They varied from six to ten feet tall. In contrast to the furry spiderbots, they had no eyes. Their heads contained mandibles that they constantly clicked, creating a monotonous cracking.

A few spiderbots descended on the furry spiderbot's corpse. After a minute they divided, leaving a few parts and a tangle of wires. Having sated themselves on the parts of the furry spiderbot, four spiderbots stood up and pressed their bellies against each other, forming a cross. That's how they multiplied. In a few minutes, the four spiderbots had produced a fifth.

"What are you waiting for? "Fuck... Mess 'em up with that grenade."

"I know when to throw it, thanks. And enough swearing, okay?"

I looked at the crowd, trying to identify the leader, the spiderbot that took decisions for the whole cluster. That Target Localization skill would come in handy right now.

I couldn't figure out which was the leader, but I noticed that a few of the ones at the front had wounds from bullets and laser burns. Considering the spiderbots repaired minor damage quite quickly, I had no doubt: they'd recently been in a skirmish with our fellow passengers from the bus. Which meant that they'd made a lot of progress through the Heap before we'd even gotten inside!

Amy couldn't wait. She started shooting. The spiderbots hadn't shown us any interest yet, but now they changed their mind. Since they were standing in a crowd, all six of Amy's shots landed. She even tore an arm off one spiderbot, launching it over the fence of the Heap.

"Oh, Amy, what about coordinating actions, strategy, the guerilla tactics of small groups, all that good stuff?"

"I got scared," she answered, reloading her revolver efficiently.

I tried to adjust to her fire to avoid us both having to reload at the same time. Our Pistols and Revolvers skill was still low, making reloading a tortuous process.

But there was no point trying to teach Amy. She went from shooting all six of her rounds in ten seconds and hitting whatever she hit, to aiming carefully... and missing completely.

The blind mechanodestructors reacted to sound and surface vibrations. It didn't take long for them to triangulate our position and begin to surround us. By then, our shots (mostly mine) had thinned their ranks a little. Several spiderbots stood in a group of four, joining together to birth reinforcements. Others surrounded them to protect them against bullets, and still more rushed toward us, forcing us to redirect our fire.

Waiting for Amy to reload her revolver, I threw my grenade into the center of the reproducing cluster. The pulse charge worked as usual: a bang, a flash. Lightning-like charges emanated from the epicenter. The spiderbots it hit fell onto their backs, fitfully and chaotically clenching and unclenching their arms. They cowered in convulsions like drug addicts in withdrawal. Their mandibles cracked even louder.

Soon all was quiet.

"Are they dead?" Amy McDonald asked.

"No, they're disabled for a while. Now we start the genocide."

Amy and I began to walk among the twitching spiderbots, finishing them off.

"Don't shoot them in the head," I said. "Aim center mass, where the belly connects to the chest."

"Why?"

"That's where the core is."

"Then why did you tell me to shoot them in the head before?"

"Because they were standing on four legs. It would have been hard to hit the core. Now they're lying belly up."

The spiderbots began to come round. One stirred, then another, then a third. True, there were only a few left. We'd exterminated the rest. I shot one in the belly while it was trying to turn onto its legs, then turned to Amy...

Just in time.

The girl sat in front of the shell of a dead spiderbot, trying to work it open with her knife. Just as one of the rising beasts loomed over her, drunkenly staggering on its shaking legs. Opening its mandibles, it aimed at Amy's neck.

"Look out!"

Amy turned around in fear. She aimed her revolver ahead.

I shot several times in a row. The spiderbot dodged, grabbing the girl's arm in its mandibles. Amy dropped her revolver and screamed.

Walking quickly, I shot on the move. The spiderbot shut down but didn't release its mandibles. It fell, dragging Amy down with it.

"Oh fuck, it hurts."

I reached her and rammed in my last magazine. Three more were already shuffling toward us: the last survivors of the cluster.

Sitting on the ground, Amy tried to kick the mandibles off with the heels of her boots. I reloaded and carefully took out the rest of the spiderbots.

I picked up Amy's knife, put the blade in the hinged joint of the spiderbot's jaw and twisted.

Amy rose, holding her arm. She was covered in blood: it dripped onto her armored vest, the grass, the spiderbot's corpse.

"Ugh, it hurts so bad... But my kicking skill leveled up."

"Stand up straight," I ordered.

I turned her back to me and jerked at the lock of her backpack.

"Hey, don't rummage through my stuff."

"Heal yourself then."

"There's a medkit in the side pocket. I'm not an idiot, I read the Survival Manual. I keep it close specially.

I got the medkit. It contained the same syringe that the landlord had used to inject me with dissociative fluid, and two packs of bandages.

The injection stopped the bleeding and reduced

the pain by fifty percent. While waiting for me to bandage her wound, Amy stubbornly took the knife and sat in front of the spiderbot.

"Why does it hurt anyway? We're in a game, damn it."

"Firstly, it's not a game, it's virtual reality. Adam is only as much a game as you want it to be."

"You're so damn clever, ain't ya? And secondly?"

"Secondly, if there were real pain here, you'd have already lost consciousness."

"Still, why the pain?"

"Pain, sex, narcotic highs, adrenaline, fear, laughter — all these are feelings. They're the reason we come to Adam Online. Switch off pain and you switch off sex too. Sense of taste. The feeling of joy you get when you smell a sea breeze."

"How poetic."

"Without sensation, there's no point in virtual reality. Actually, virtual reality is nothing but pure sensation."

While I was talking, Amy continued to take apart the spiderbot, hoping to get the energy charges inside. She finally took the cover off the belly and spoke with disappointment.

"Empty. Fuck."

"You could have asked me. There's nothing for us in the little spiderbots. You have to have the right skills."

I'd already stopped getting annoyed at Amy. She was clearly no warrior. It was strange that a former angel had decided to become a super. Her true nature didn't match her chosen race.

Chapter 13
Arachnophilia

AMY LEARNED from her mistakes. She stopped running off headlong to God knows where.

Before we entered the Heap, she reloaded, straightened her backpack. She gave herself another injection. She even retied her shoelaces and fixed her hair.

Then we took out our tablets and spent a couple of minutes reading messages.

Achievement Arachnophilia completed: +5 XP.
In some countries, people believe that spiders bring luck and should not be killed. You're clearly not from any of them.
Kill 5 spiderbots.

Unlocked achievement Arachnophilia I.
Kill 50 spiderbots.
Completed: 11/50.

Battlefield Surgery skill increased: +10 XP.
You won't always tell a fracture from a nervous

breakdown, but you can stick someone with a needle and sort of bind a wound.

   Open Book: +10 XP.
   A friend helped a friend. Thanks to your courage, your friend is alive and you don't have to tend her gravestone every year, crying drunken tears and blaming yourself for her death.

On top of everything, I'd killed eleven spiderbots, earning a point for each. Not bad for someone ten years out of the game.

Stepping carefully, we walked through the door. A labyrinth of mostly metal compressed garbage spread out before us. Amy took out her tablet and swallowed.

"The radiation here is high."

"I have radiation resistance. Only level one, but that's enough."

"By the way, aren't you going to tell me what that nuclear explosion was?"

"No clue."

"What were you doing at the epicenter?"

"Wrong place at the wrong time."

"Are you lying to me?"

"Of course."

We walked along the paths among the scrap metal for ten minutes. We found dead ends, sidestepped puddles of chemicals, climbed over small trashdrifts.

From time to time, my improved perception identified lone spiderbots amid the metal. They didn't rush to attack. It seemed we'd destroyed the cluster that controlled this part of the Heap. It'd take some time for them to form another and pick a leader.

Of course, it was a shame that I'd spent a pulse grenade. It would have come in handy for the time after we found the core. A flood of spiderbots would come then. Any experienced adamite starting with a new character took a pulse grenade into the Heap.

The deeper we went into the labyrinth, the more distant shots we heard. Our competitors weren't wasting time.

"Haven't you thought about going back?" Amy asked.

I sighed. It seemed she'd figured out that I was no simple player, and that I was in Adam Online illegally... Almost failing my mission by losing my boosted character. Going back to real life, leaving the pod — that would be the logical decision.

"Where to?"

"To Town Zero, where else? Don't you think we're already behind the others?"

"What do you think?"

"I'm stubborn. I won't go back until I reach the core."

"What if someone gets to it first?"

Amy waved her gun. "My Pistols and Revolvers skill is up to level two. I'll find them and kill them."

"I'm stubborn too."

"That's good. Our friendship works well."

"Sure, but you're a re-e-ally bad team player."

"That your way of complimenting my distinctive personality?"

We ran into the remains of a second furry spiderbot. The damage told us that it had been hit with a laser and ran off, and was then devoured by the small spiderbots. Their leader decided that disassembling a senior ally for spare parts was better than repairing it.

"If there's a leader, that means we're in the territory of another cluster. Stay sharp." I looked around and pointed to a heap of garbage. "Let's try walking along the top."

"The radiation is higher up there, I could die."

"You have around ten minutes with the tablets before you get any irreversible changes. We'll be able to skip a few turns of this maze."

I climbed up first, examining every edge of the garbage heaps. I gave Amy a hand up from time to time. Due to her low Strength stat, she got tired quickly and slowed down.

During my climb, I noticed two ammo boxes. One had .44 caliber rounds, and the second, unfortunately, had .416 rounds for a sniper rifle like the Barnes. Amy stopped at the top of the hill, unwound the bandage on her hand a little and checked which way the wind was blowing. She checked some numbers that only she could see and pointed confidently.

"That way."

We'd just started to descend when I noticed movement below. Two spiderbots were scurrying around, stretching their blind heads upward and clicking their mandibles. Another five joined them.

A new cluster. And they knew we were there.

✳

"Do we fire?" Amy whispered.

"Thanks for asking. No, we don't. Let's try to get away quietly."

As slow as if I was stoned, I shifted my feet, helping with my arms to push myself up higher. I crept a few feet back, toward the top. I expected to learn the Stealth skill, but it didn't happen. That means I wasn't moving stealthily enough. Amy tried to follow suit, but some scrap iron soon slipped out from beneath her foot. Crashing loudly, it skittered down the pile and fell with a crash onto a spiderbot's head.

"Damn, Amy, how'd you manage that?"

"I don't know... Maybe it's a side effect of high Luck?"

We stood up and started running along the top of the pile. The spiderbots detected our location and split into two groups: the first climbed upwards, the second followed us from the ground.

The beasts approached interminably. They deftly gripped the parts protruding from the piles of garbage with their feet. Like monkeys on branches, they bobbed along one ledge and swung to the next.

Amy suddenly fell onto all fours. "I feel sick."

I lifted her up by the arm and dragged her along. "There's no time be sick."

"Need to go... down..."

"No. We need to go higher."

"I'll die."

I dragged her to the rusty cabin of a truck

crowning the garbage pile. My Eagle Eye stubbornly told me that something was shining in the cabin. It could have been some more useless ammunition or another cigar cutter. But I knew the game — there should be unusual things to find at such a dangerous height.

I pulled open the rusty cabin door and put Amy on a seat... next to the skeleton of a man dressed in the silver UniSuit of a scientist. Paying no attention to this discovery, Amy moved across to the opposite door and bent out the window like a drunken college grad on the way home in a taxi. Wiping her mouth, she muttered,

"Fuck... this realism."

"It's alright," I said, trying to calm her. "The sickness will pass soon, and you'll get covered in radiation sores. Now pull yourself together, girl... And give me your revolver."

"What am I supposed to do?"

"Look around the cabin, check the skeleton. He has a UniSuit!"

Amy handed over her revolver and several magazines. Then she took out her tablet and aimed it at the dead man.

The first spiderbot appeared on the edge of the heap. A shot from the Lefaucheux took its head clean off. The second shot pierced its breast. The spiderbot's legs collapsed and it clattered its way down the heap.

"How much Knowledge do you have?" Amy asked.

"Three."

"Sucks to be you. The UniSuit needs at least

five."

"Any upgrades?"

"One. With the alluring name Arachnophilia. There's also a pack of radiation and chemical poisoning meds, a shielded tablet with a Geiger counter... that's the second piece of bad news. The radiation..."

Two more spiderbots appeared.

They climbed onto the platform our cabin was on and quickly split off in different directions. I managed to shoot a leg off one — it teetered and then fell face first into the iron. It tried to dodge my second shot, but its mandibles had snagged on some scrap. The spiderbot turned onto its back. I pinned it down with a shot to keep it there.

The second managed to approach me and grabbed me by the leg.

I put two bullets into its hull. Fortunately, one made it to the core. The spiderbot begrudgingly unclenched its jaw and fell at my feet as if asking forgiveness. I kicked it away.

"Well? You were saying? What's the other news?"

I turned and saw Amy's naked back. Gathering her purple hair, she zipped up the UniSuit.

"The background radiation here is so high that we need at least three Radiation Resistance. So you're the one that'll be covered in sores. My new UniSuit can withstand it. That's all the news."

Amy stuck her tongue out, put the clear glass helmet on her head and fastened it.

"Is the Arachnophilia upgrade what I think it is?"

Amy became absorbed in her tablet. "I don't know what you think it is, but yeah. It lets you tame a spiderbot and ride it. It takes on the status of a means of transport. Mechanodestructors can use a trained spiderbot as a sexual partner. People can too, actually. You can upgrade it... Ugh, wow. The main thing is... Watch out!"

I turned around, grabbing my pistol with my right hand. Five spiderbots at once had climbed onto our platform.

"Hurry, into the truck," Amy swung the door open.

I climbed into the cabin, kicking the skeleton out behind me.

"The truck didn't save that guy."

The spiderbots hesitated, looking for their lost target. They started combing the whole platform, feeling every outcrop and part with their mandibles.

"I think I get how it works," Amy whispered, her voice barely audible through her helmet.

She crawled across me and I swapped places with her. Amy aimed her tablet and I saw the unfamiliar Arachnophilia interface. Capturing first one spiderbot in the square brackets, then another, the tablet displayed some data. Some percentages stood out: 62%, 47% and so on.

I grabbed my medkit and bandaged my leg.

"Looks like that blueish one is the most vulnerable to taming," Amy whispered.

"They all look gray to me."

"I can see the colors in their hulls now. That one over there at the edge has a beautiful swirly pattern on it."

"Must be the leader. Would be nice to tame that one."

"Fifty two percent. Not a high chance."

"What's the cooldown on the upgrade?"

"Thirty minutes."

"I'll die from the radiation. Got any pills?"

Amy hesitated, then begrudgingly handed me a pill from her pack."

"I need them too. Or will. Later. Probably."

"Greedy. I gave you my collectible vest."

"Not greedy, just careful. If you're going to die from radiation anyway, why waste expensive medicine?"

We silently observed the spiderbots shuffling around the platform. One, probably the blueish one, approached the cabin and thoroughly investigated it with its mandibles, pushing them through the broken glass. We backed off, sinking into our seats, sucking in our stomachs. It was a purely instinctive reaction; the hitbox of a human player took up the same space regardless. You could pull in your tummy all you liked — your volume in the game didn't reduce.

"How high is your Luck?" I whispered to Amy after bluey left.

"Five."

"I don't remember the multiplier, but I think it increases your taming chance by a few percent. Come on, try taming the leader."

"Why that one?"

"I have an idea... Let's see how right it is."

Amy picked out the spiderbot standing at the edge of the platform and not taking part in the search. The tablet magnified the spiderbot and showed an indicator to confirm the action. Amy looked at me. I nodded. She pressed 'Yes'. A progress indicator appeared above the image of the lead spiderbot. The 52% started dropping quickly. Already 43%... 37%... If it reached zero, that meant we'd fail to tame the spiderbot — we'd have lost.

My gaze locked on the leader. At first, it didn't react at all. Then it raised its head as if sniffing something out.

33% — it made a few steps toward us, then hurriedly turned back.

29% — it ran chaotically along the side of the platform, knocking into the other spiderbots. It extended its legs down, then backed off like a dog afraid to leap into a pool after its master.

21% — it ran toward us confidently. I aimed my pistol...

18% — it hit the cabin with its legs at a run, knocking out the remainder of the glass. The cabin shook, almost overturning. The remaining spiderbots, bowing to the will of their leader, also rushed the cabin.

11% — the leader stuck its head into the cabin and grabbed my shoulder in its mandibles, but somehow uncertainly. I threw my pistol into my left hand and was almost ready to take off the leader's head when Amy shouted,

"Done, it worked!"

A victorious signal from the tablet confirmed it.

The leader carefully released my shoulder, dropped off the cabin and stood nearby. The other spiderbots dispersed across the platform and froze. Their task — seek and destroy — was canceled.

I climbed out first. "How long does the taming effect last?"

"It doesn't say."

"That means until it dies."

Amy looked at her tablet. "He's my pet now."

I chuckled. "Not just him — the whole cluster."

"Ooh, so that's why you chose the leader for taming? Clever Leonarm."

Amy approached the spiderbot and stroked his square head, tickled its mandibles rusty with dried blood. "I'll call you Swirl."

Chapter 14
The Dichotomy of Luck

THE SPIDERBOT'S smooth hull made an uncomfortable seat. The slight forward lean made me slide down to the neck flange, which threatened to pinch my testicles in the clanking space between the hull and the head. I managed to find a comfortable hold on the stationary sections of the legs starting at the body. Our iron horses strode quickly along. They leapt and skidded, but their gyroscopes corrected their body position and we barely felt any jolts.

The cooling processor in the spiderbots' core made their hull temperature lower than the surrounding air. They were even more comfortable to ride than horses, which I'd ridden on the Bryansk estate belonging to Major General Makarov.

Amy rode Swirl at the head of the cluster. I was somewhere in the center. Amy said that my spiderbot was the selfsame Bluey. I took her word for it. Before she rode forward, she said that one of her pet's perks was the ability to find the shortest paths in any zone. She showed me her tablet with a map of the Heap. It had a circle marked on it.

"This will take us to the core before anyone else gets there. We don't even need to search for it ourselves."

And so it was. The spiderbots not only confidently ran into inconspicuous alleyways in the labyrinth, they also often climbed up onto hills, cutting the path short along the peaks. That was the hardest part. Not only did the background radiation increase, but it also became difficult to hold on to the slippery hulls.

The cluster suddenly stopped next to a pile of fresh electronic waste and fanned out. After investigating the veins of electronic garbage, they started gulping down the components they needed to repair and recharge. Amy and I dismounted to stretch our legs.

"We got pretty lucky, right?" Amy asked.

"The fact that we got a fancy UniSuit isn't luck, it's 'game balance'."

"What do you mean?"

"We began the quest with unfavorable conditions. Those difficulties have to be balanced out with benefits. The balance is that there are dangerous enemies and high radiation at the northern entrance. The CSes are kind of giving us a choice: either go where it's easier, but there's high competition between players, or go where there's a high chance of death, but lots of perks."

"Hmm, I get that. It's the same in life."

"Only life doesn't have CSes that give you a choice."

"Who knows, who knows..." Amy responded

mysteriously.

My vision darkened and I felt that I was just about to fall. I shook my head.

"Give me another pill. Must have gotten too much radiation while we were riding on the mounds.

This time Amy gave me the whole pack. I swallowed two pills and watched the spiderbots grazing peacefully.

"I'm sure there are a lot more options for progressing through the Heap that we don't know about."

"Why?"

"There was no trigger for starting additional scenarios."

Amy laughed.

"You're trying to make excuses for your fuck-up with the bus driver. Trigger, choice options... don't try to bullshit me."

"Not bullshitting you. Something will happen soon and you'll see for yourself."

"What?"

"I don't know what. But we've been standing here and chatting for a while now."

"That bother you?"

"Of course. When we don't act, it's like we're handing our fate over to the control systems. You never know what they could throw at us."

Amy thought for a moment.

"But when we do act, then our fate still depends on the damn control systems, right?"

I scratched my head. "Strictly speaking, yes. Action and inaction on the part of the player are two different states that the CSes react to differently."

Amy took out her revolver and checked that the cylinder was full. She did that all the time now. As if hinting at me: look how fast I learn. Always on guard! It seemed my words about her inability to work as a team had had an effect on her.

"I guess Adam Online bores you when you know how it works, huh?"

"You can't be completely sure of any of it. Most of the code for the QCPs is generated automatically by the QCPs themselves. And the code has been continually generated for hundreds of years now. Humanity can no longer figure out even a single line of it. In fact, there aren't even actual lines."

"Then what is there?"

I waved my hand at the environment around us. "This. An imitation of reality in which we're forced to live so that we don't see the horror beyond the comfort of our pods."

The spiderbots suddenly stopped chowing down on electronic garbage and froze. Another second and they went into a battle formation, backs to each other, ready at any moment to create reinforcements.

Swirl ran to Amy, helping her mount him. I had to find Bluey myself. Since they all looked the same to me, I tried to mount the wrong spiderbot a few times. They threw me off until I climbed onto the right one, which had been waiting patiently.

"What happened?" Amy shouted at me. "One of your damn triggers?"

"We're in another cluster's territory. Its owners have arrived..."

Several spiderbots emerged from cracks in the compressed garbage as if to confirm my words. Another dozen or more descended from a hill. I had another opportunity to appreciate how thoroughly the control systems produced such scenarios. The Heap was split between clusters that punished their rivals for trespassing. They may even fight wars for dominion over the Heap. Of course, all this happened only when a player appeared who was capable of understanding what was going on.

And this is what happened.

Swirl left the defensive ring of his cluster. Amy sat astride him cowboy-style, holding her revolver barrel-up. Another spiderbot separated from the enemy cluster. Both leaders slowly approached each other, clicking their mandibles.

"What are they doing?" Amy asked.

"How should I know?"

"You're a programmer."

"So? The spiderbots are just doing what they do."

"God dammit."

Both leaders approached and touched mandibles.

"How cute. They kissing or what?" Amy lowered her revolver.

"Maybe it's a type of handshake."

The leaders continued to feel each other with

their mandibles. Too long for a handshake. Finally they stopped scratching and disentangled from each other. I felt Bluey's hull relax.

"I think they've agreed to let our cluster through their territory."

"Clever boys."

Then, when Swirl turned around to come back to us, the enemy leader jumped and latched onto his belly. Amy fell to the ground, swearing worse than ever.

Our spidersbots and the enemies rushed toward each other. I barely held onto Bluey's back. And immediately regretted it; it would have been better to fall. Now I was in the center of the skirmish. Identical spiderbots crowded around, grabbing each other with their mandibles, striking with their legs. A rusty dust rose. Shards of hulls and broken limbs rained down around me.

"Shoot, shoot them!" Amy shouted.

Pulling up my legs to escape bites, I reeled on the hull. "They all look the same!"

Through a haze of dust, I saw another spiderbot grab my own by the neck. I felt Bluey's the junction of Bluey's neck crack behind my back. I held on and fired several shots. The enemy fell back. I heard the deep rumble of the Lefaucheux revolver, along with Amy's "die, bitch".

The enemy spiderbots were too busy with the battle to pay us any attention.

Every time Bluey grappled with another spiderbot, I supported him with my fire. I heard my tablet beeping through the rumble and scraping. Even if we lost, we'd level up a little.

But our fire support helped Swirl's cluster withstand the foe, even outnumbered. The sudden attack subsided, we started to steadily push the enemy back toward the garbage piles. Then the dust settled. The crowd of attackers quickly thinned out. Some sank away into crevices, others scrambled up mounds, where our shots quickly brought them back down.

The battle ended as quickly as it began. All the spiderbots froze as if processing information on the outcome of the skirmish. Bluey's hull, which had overheated during the battle, quickly cooled down.

Swirl victoriously dropped the bitten-off head of his enemy from his maw, then latched onto its chest. Covering himself in drops of oil and sparks, he tore out and victoriously swallowed the enemy's core, which then immediately fell through the broken synthesis chamber in his belly.

Our spiderbots, those still able, descended on the enemy corpses. After consuming one, they approached a damaged comrade and begin to repair him. They resynthesized broken limbs, replaced smashed mandibles, reset neck joints and screwed heads back on. The newly repaired spiderbots joined in with repairing the rest.

In some cases, the repair involved taking a whole part off an enemy and using it to replace an ally's damaged part.

Swirl was missing two legs. He hobbled up to

Amy.

"Poor thing, did that traitor hurt you?"

Swirl was quickly equipped with new legs, and a synthesis chamber from the enemy leader.

I climbed off Bluey and sat on one of the corpses. I picked up a piece of mandible. Using it instead of a knife, I cracked open the belly. I tried to pull out the synthesis chamber. It was damaged — the controller was at it again. I moved to the next one and repeated the procedure. Nothing, of course. I moved to another, pushing away a spiderbot trying to repair an ally. I unscrewed the panel on the belly. Without even trying to be careful, I began to unscrew the synthesis chamber.

Like in life, in Adam Online luck came unexpectedly and right on time. I'd wanted to upgrade my All Thumbs achievement, hoping for a reward. Instead, the chamber easily separated and fell into the sand.

I aimed the tablet at it.

Synthesis Chamber.
A valuable item for people who, unlike you, Leonarm, have arms that grow from their shoulders. The main component for building a CAM (Component Adaptation Machine).
Value: upwards of 7,000g.
Weight: 10 kg.

CAM... I felt a rush of memories that I'd suppressed in real life. I remembered how Olga and I had built our first adaptation machine. We'd spent whole days and nights trying to craft weapons. The first pistols we made would hit anything but the target. Sometimes they rewarded the shooter by falling apart at random. We gradually gained experience and increased our Knowledge. The pistols got better. People bought them willingly, and we got rich. Life seemed great (even if it was virtual). Dozens of years of enjoyment in the worlds of Adam Online stretched out before us...

I tapped on the image of the synthesis chamber and it moved into my backpack, significantly increasing its weight. I checked my Carrying Capacity, which for a human was set at Strength multiplied by ten. Of course, if I picked up a little more than my Carrying Capacity allowed, I wouldn't be stuck in place, but I'd move a lot slower.

Trying not to think of the past, I took apart a few more hulls. I found another synthesis chamber and gave it to Amy. I hoped I'd get a reward for Open Book, but my tablet remained silent. I'd need to try harder.

After breaking another chamber, I got a new message.

Achievement All Thumbs: +10 XP.
Keep up the good work.

Is that it? Where were the goodies that everyone in Rim Zero gets? Either my memories were corrupt, or the game was harder now... or maybe I'd really lost all my skills as an adamite.

On the other hand, all this got me to level two. After a moment's thought, I put plus one into Strength.

I needed to make sure I had space to put loot.

"Had enough playtime?" Amy asked impatiently. "Time to move on."

She was already sitting astride Swirl. Bluey grazed nearby, eating scraps of devices in the compressed garbage.

"Have you ever thought that the Luck stat is a very strange one?" I asked, climbing onto the spiderbot.

"Why?"

"All our adventures are the result of my low Luck. That's what lowered my Reputation with the driver. But at the same time, it was our bad luck that gave us so many unexpected finds. You got the rare UniSuit and an ability. You ended up controlling a whole cluster of pets. With allies like this, we're a force to be reckoned with."

Amy laughed woodenly in her helmet. "You mean your low Luck value is helping my high one?"

"Something like that. Everything I do leads to problems, but those problems turn into advantages for you. And indirectly, for me, since we're a team. Luck is like a dichotomy of two mutually exclusive factors.

"Cool. Now I see a point in teaming up with you." Amy paused, then added: "And I'll make like I understand what a dichotomy is."

She dug her heels into Swirl's sides, and we started careering across the Heap again. After half an hour of wild riding across the hills, skidding down narrow alleyways and crossing high radiation zones, we arrived at a structure that looked like the remains of a huge spaceship.

It was usually in decorations like this that the algorithm hid the core.

As soon as we dismounted from our iron horses, a pulse grenade landed at my feet. The flash blinded me. One of the electrical discharges swirled around me like a tentacle and went into my backpack. My tablet squawked.

That was that... now it would be knocked out for twenty-four hours.

It's a good thing I hadn't spent any money on that Google Maps upgrade. An EMP returned the tablets to their factory settings, wiping out all their software upgrades. Good bye, loyal personal assistant. You were alright.

Surrounded by lashes of electricity, our spiderbots contorted and fell onto the backs Bluey reared, fell and pinned me to the ground.

Amy managed to leap off Swirl as he fell. A rain of bullets fell down on us, along with the flashes of lasers.

It turned out we weren't the first to find the crashed spaceship.

Chapter 15
Numbers After the
Decimal

I LAY ON THE GROUND, pressed against the spiderbot's hull. I had already freed my leg from underneath it, but I didn't risk standing up. An unseen enemy followed us, punishing any attempt to act with shots. Bluey's hull throbbed weakly with electricity, shuddered from the effects of the pulse explosion, sometimes twitched when a bullet hit, or heated up from a laser beam. Even if Bluey woke up, he wouldn't live long: the damage was too great.

Amy lay not far from me. She was in the same situation, the only difference being that around the girl — or rather, around the fallen Swirl — was a crowd of spiderbots that had avoided the explosion. But without the leader, they didn't know what to do. They passively took shots to their sides and aimlessly span around, trying to connect to each other, but then separating. Without the command of the leader, they couldn't reproduce.

First one and then another reeled, falling onto

their tucked front legs; they were taking critical hits. Two had already fallen with their cores shot to ribbons.

"What do we do?!" Amy shouted.

"We wait."

"What for?"

"Until the enemy runs out of ammo. Or until they flank us and shoot us. Or until the spiderbots pick a new leader, if we aren't all dead by then."

"And what then?"

"Then they'll attack us first, as their closest target."

"Did you forget? I have the Arachnophilia skill."

"Did you forget? The pulse grenade knocks out all active electronics. Our tablets are dead for twenty-four hours. Or until we die and respawn."

"I don't feel like dying."

"There are two options in any fight: retreat or attack. You can also hold your current position, but that always leads to a choice: attack or retreat."

"God dammit, Leonarm, why are you so tedious? Let's attack, what are we waiting for?"

"Sure. But do you see the enemy?"

"No."

"Me neither. Judging by the fire, there are two of them. One is a mechanodestructor with a laser cannon in its belly. The other is a human armed with twin standard Glocks."

"They've teamed up?"

"And very successfully. While the human fires, the mechanodestructor can fill magazines for him. His hands are free after all."

The fire thinned out noticeably. The enemies no

longer shot at us, hidden behind the spiderbot hulls. Instead they switched their attention to the living spiderbots and the ones that were gradually coming round.

My Bluey twitched, trying to turn over onto its legs. But Swirl still wasn't moving. That meant his core was shot. The living spiderbots froze. A sign that they'd begun to choose a new leader.

Amy lifted the glass in her helmet... I caught her bewildered gaze. The helmet... The UniSuit...

"We're both idiots," I shouted. "You have a second tablet you got from the scientist."

Amy hurriedly took it out of her backpack and switched it on.

"Yes! It works. The battery is low. Enough for a couple of minutes..." She performed the necessary actions to add another user to the tablet. "Done. Now it's my tablet."

"Wait for the leader to be selected and tame him."

Amy lifted the tablet over the spiderbot's frame. Bullets cracked around her, preventing her from aiming it properly.

"Wait. I'll distract them."

I stood up from cover and ran behind the frame of another dead spiderbot. I saw a stirring by the remains of the starship's engine. The stirring was accompanied by a laser flash. The mechanodestructor! That meant the human was somewhere nearby too. My Eagle Eye tracking skill was fully operational.

Around thirty feet away, a giant piece of metal from the starship stuck out of the sand. After measuring the distance, I made a second run. This time shots fired my way. The human was obviously a bad shot: the bullets landed a long way behind me. But the mechanodestructor's laser hit me in the leg. Twice.

Screaming in pain, I rolled under a piece of metal and held my burning wound. Even my jeans were on fire. I beat out the flames and grabbed my medkit.

Injection. Injection. Bandage. Injection. Injection.

The sharp pain subsided, turned into an annoying itch.

Even without the tablet, I knew that my Battlefield Surgery skill had leveled up. I threw away the empty medkit. All gone. Now I had no way to heal. The next wound would lead to bleeding out and dying.

However I sliced it, I had to increase my Luck. Otherwise every skirmish would leave me maimed.

Now the enemy was forced to divide their fire between me, Amy and the spiderbots. There were six remaining. Two were so badly damaged that they couldn't stand properly. They leaned to one side as if drunk. As soon as they finished choosing a new leader, they'd quickly escape to cover or repair each other in place without running... I hoped that Amy would be able to tame the new leader faster than she tamed Swirl.

I assessed my condition: due to my injury, my Agility had probably fallen a point, and my Perception had likely gone down due to the large amount of painkillers in my system. Although a tracker's skills should compensate for that, right? All this knowledge had faded so quickly.

I shot a quick glance around the corner. The enemies changed their strategy. Now they stood next to each other. The human slowly moved toward Amy, hiding behind debris and shooting. Amy answered him once or twice with her Lefaucheux. She missed both times. These two were a perfect match in marksmanship.

The mechanodestructor had more cunning. He started focusing his laser beam on the spiderbots' legs. A few seconds and a leg fell off. The spiderbot tried to correct for it, balancing poorly on the remaining legs.

I stopped firing, calculating that Amy would soon take control over the remainder of the cluster. Plucking up my courage, I ran straight to the starship's entrance, to the position my enemies had left.

They saw me halfway there. Many make a mistake in such situations: they start to weave in the hope of being difficult to hit. But that doesn't work with mechanodestructor lasers. They can set their firing mode; instead of a concentrated beam of energy, the ray turns into an uninterrupted line, burning all in its path. The more advanced the laser cannon, the longer it can support an uninterrupted beam. If I'd started to weave, my Speed would have gone down. The laser would have caught up and cut my legs off, just like the spiderbots.

All hope was on the agility of my virtual body.

I even forgot that Adam Online is a collective illusion created by its participants out of despair and an inability to live in the real world. I was a living creature trying to save myself from a deadly beam, not a binary array sent to the abyss of the QCP. My non-existent muscles were working as hard as they could. My imaginary legs dug into imaginary burning sad. The illusory radiation pierced my body, smashing against my Radiation Resistance (I dearly hoped)... The bright sun cast a short blue shadow ahead as I ran, as if encouraging me: "Run, Leonarm, run..."

If none of this was reality, then what *was* reality anyway? A lifeless body immersed in dissociative fluid?

I ran onto the starship's entry platform and rolled behind some containers. It seemed the aliens were trying to unload cargo, and something got in their way. The laser beam hit the containers and burned right through them. What was going on? Did this mechanodestructor have infinite energy? As soon as the thought came to me, the beam flickered out. There, now the mechanodestructor would need time to recharge his energy banks.

I took a breath and looked out from behind the containers. The human stood over Amy, aiming both Glocks at her. He said something. I heard fragments of malicious laughter. Amy sat on the ground, covering herself with the tablet. The idiot was savoring his victory. Which, as everyone knows, is the beginning of defeat.

I raised my pistol and took careful aim. Don't let me down now, Eagle Eye. And you, increased critical chance on the complimentary Glock. And you, Luck, sorry for neglecting you. I promise to level you up to ten.

One dull shot from my Glock combined with the twin shots of my enemy's pistols. At that moment, Amy rolled to the side, knocking the tablet with her fist. I wondered whether her high Luck had helped me with my precise shot. Actually, how did Adam Online solve for things like that? If the opponent had the same Luck as Amy, would that help him dodge my tracker's accuracy?

Whatever the case may be, the human dropped his pistols along with bright red chunks of flesh. He fell face down in the sand, his head shot clean through. It was a shame I had no tablet. I couldn't see the name of the player I'd sent back to the spawn point, nor how much experience I'd earned. I should have received more for a player than for an NPC.

Amy put her tablet aside and reached out to search the corpse. The spiderbots stopped passively awaiting execution and rushed at the mechanodestructor. He hopelessly tried to escape from them. Thirty feet later, his monowheel stuck fast in the sand. The cluster descended on him, covering him completely, then moved off again, leaving a monowheel in the sand alongside the remains of a black hose, like a mourning ribbon on a grave.

I approached Amy.

She threw the tablet she'd found on the enemy. "Catch. Your reward for saving me."

I pulled my old tablet out of my backpack and

threw it away. It was a shame to lose the lightweight battery. But such was life. Or rather, such was Adam Online.

My regret passed quickly. I added a user to make the tablet mine and noticed that the device was better than mine had been. It not only had a lightweight battery and the High Speed cooler, but also two applications: Google Maps with the option to set routes to quest locations in Rim Zero, and the Adam Online Wikipedia.

When I pressed the button, nothing appeared but a description window:

Adam Online Wikipedia.
+1 Knowledge.
Why think for yourself when you can look it up on Wikipedia? Your tablet has a full and detailed guide for rims One, Two and Zero. (Purchased separately.) In addition, by spending just 100,000g, you will unlock a closed section with a list of secret locations. (Each list purchased separately.)
Buy Wikipedia addons?

No thanks.

Alright, time to check out the rewards. Under the protection of the spiderbots, which had managed to bulk their number up to ten, we were safe.

Leonarm (Human) killed IOI655321 (Human) with a complimentary Glock.
+10 XP.

Open Book: +50 XP.

Are you sure you chose the right character? You should have been an angelic protector. You saved your girlfriend again.

It was funny how Adam Online found character traits in players that they never knew they had. There was a reason that some politicians and journalists said that Adam Online was a reflection of ourselves, without the distortion that our own egotism creates.

Battlefield Surgery skill increased: +10 XP.

You've fixed yourself up so much that you can now heal others. Although after your treatment they'd better go see a real doctor.

My old tablet didn't show achievement levels. It was probably disabled by default. The deceased IOI655321 didn't have time to configure it. The captured tablet didn't even show the level progress as a whole number, but as 3.79. And I thought I was a dork once.

The thought came again: had I become another person? There was a time when I'd have spent hours configuring a tablet. I used to install nice fonts, change the color scheme, change the mode for displaying stats. Now I couldn't care less. As long as it showed me what I needed to see. I couldn't give a damn how many fractions of a percentage I'd progressed in some imaginary achievement.

That's what it means to have a specific goal. You focus, you stop noticing the numbers after the decimal point.

Of course, Pistols and Revolvers and Eagle Eye had leveled up. All together, I had one stat point and I'd reached level three. Just as I'd promised to who knows who, I put it into Luck.

I found a medkit with two syringes and a bandage among the dead man's things. I took them. Along with a box of ammo. I gave one Glock to Amy and kept the other myself. IOI655321's armored vest was in good condition, but in contrast to mine, which gave me plus one to Agility, his gave plus one to Strength. I read Agility. I could have sold it to second-hand merchants in Zero Town, of course, but I didn't want to fill up my backpack.

After all, we had a whole spaceship to loot.

Chapter 16
Corridor Shooter

THE SECOND AIRLOCK led into the alien vessel, and it was shut. There were no locks on the wall next to it, nor any signs of how to activate it. Classic case. That was probably what had delayed our competitors. They weren't ready for such a variation of events. Or they hadn't had time to solve the puzzle to open the door.

"What do we do now?" Amy asked.

"I've completed the Heap a few times. The algorithm varies the scenario. Instead of an alien ship, sometimes you have to find the core in an underground science lab. Sometimes it's in a military base captured by mutant aliens. Sometimes it's in the Heap itself in a lair of furry spiderbots. The algorithm usually puts a huge spaceship here."

"Doesn't the story of the world have to be the same for all players?"

"The storyline is the same: we have to find the core and bring it to our employer, discovering on the way that the mechanodestructors are the descendants of an alien civilization. All the options invariably lead to that fact. The different options are added for variety.

Instead of a locked door, we might have found a forcefield that we'd need to disable by finding a generator. Or we might need to find a way through the ventilation system, or another way through the ship's sewage system. There are lots of variants."

"Alright, but how do we open this variant of the door?"

I examined the huge space of the cargo department. There wasn't enough light from the open airlock to show what hid in the dark corners. The nose of a small shuttle stuck out on our right. On the left were containers marked with alien text. I pointed at the containers with my pistol.

"I bet there's an alien corpse somewhere over there with the activation key on it. Come on, I'll go right, you go left."

"What if there's no corpse?"

"Then the key will just be lying around somewhere. Trust me, all you have to do is show your willingness to understand the world. The CSes will put the key where it needs to be, you won't miss it."

Amy walked into the darkness between the crates. I headed for the shuttle. I put my hand against the lock and the door lifted up silently. A red light blinked in the cabin, revealing a mess and signs of a fight. There were scratches on the walls and burns from a laser gun.

If you believed the legend that the alien ship crashed a hundred years ago, you might wonder why the red light was still blinking. But I know that as soon as I asked myself that question and started to look for the reason that several of the ship's systems still functioned, I'd find that the starship's reactor was still working and powering them. Or some sort of quantum-positron tank. Or a Calabi-Yau space generator. Or some other pseudo-scientific sci-fi bullshit.

A trail of dried blood led from the shuttle door to the door of the pilot's cabin. It disappeared into the darkness beyond the red light. I checked a box on the wall. I'd hoped to find an alien flashlight in it. Those were useful for dungeons: they worked for a few days, then all they needed was half an hour to recover. But the box was empty.

There was a time when I'd have celebrated increased difficulty, but right now I had no time for games. The CSes weren't in a hurry. They could generate infinite plot branches. But I had no desire to wander through them.

I even felt a desire to ignore the mysterious blood trail, but I hoped to find something...

I took out my lighter and, stepping carefully, walked into the darkness. In the flickering light of the lighter I saw the twisted corpse of a humanoid on the floor. The remains of a torn spacesuit covered its fine bony limbs. The head looked at me: huge slanting eye sockets, a sharp chin, a small mouth. The CSes used all the dramatic touches and compositional flair they had to make it as creepy as possible.

I carelessly moved the corpse with my foot, expecting some sort of parasite to crawl out of it and jump at my face. But nothing like that happened. Too predictable?

I crouched down and pulled the heavy corpse closer. My intuition hadn't let me down: the dried-out long fingers gripped a laser rifle. Just what I needed.

Amy and I got back to where we'd started our search at the same time. Amy held the arm of a humanoid with a bracelet on it.

"I couldn't take it off, I had to cut it... What did you find?"

"An alien energy rifle. It's weak, but it has infinite ammo. It takes energy from the air by transmuting nitrogen isotopes. Nonsense in real life, but it'll do for Adam."

We reached the door.

"Do you always live in the past?" Amy asked.

"Meaning?"

"Well, you're always comparing reality and Adam Online as if it's so different, or as if it's important to you to point out that difference."

"Isn't it?"

"The only difference is that you remember that you're lying in a taharration pod. You remember that there's some real reality. If the moment of moving to the virtual world wasn't so clear, you wouldn't notice any differences between the real world and this collective fantasy, as you call it."

"But I do remember, and I know about the differences."

"Don't you see, dumbass? Reality is what other people have been telling us since childhood. If it weren't for them, we wouldn't know what's real and what's not. We wouldn't split our lives into reality and virtual reality."

"I'm not convinced. There are so many flaws and mistakes in your logic that I don't even know where to begin correcting you."

"You don't have to correct me. The reality that exists beyond the pod is a deception that humanity hands down from generation to generation."

I looked at the girl in amazement. "What's gotten you all philosophical?"

Amy shook her head as if trying to snap herself out of something. "Nothing, it's just... I'm afraid of the dark. So I started thinking while I was looking for the key."

"There are lots of dark corners in the spaceship's corridors. You aren't going to philosophize every time, are you?"

Amy placed the cut-off arm on the door. It screeched and squeaked, then opened halfway and jammed.

I crouched down and crawled to the other side first. Amy crouched down too, holding the arm with the bracelet between her knees.

She looked at the spiderbots crowding the airlock entrance. "Are they not coming with us?"

"As you can see, the spiderbots can't come onto the ship."

"Why not?"

I shrugged. "If you want to waste some time, you'll find an explanation in some log on an alien computer. It'll say that the ship's security system stops all external mechanisms from functioning. Or we'll run into another dead scientist that was supposedly researching the mystery of the spaceship before us and discovered that the spiderbots are remnants of the ship's security system that rebelled against the central computer, took on a primitive consciousness and somehow managed to live in the Heap. It all depends on which story we're most likely to believe. The CSes just want to weave our emotional investment into the storyline."

"See ya, Swirl the Second." Amy waved the severed limb. "I'll be back soon, don't go anywhere."

She crawled to my side and we moved along the tubular corridor. Illuminated lines stretched out along the floor and ceiling. They often went out, plunging us into total darkness, then came back on again.

I raised my alien rifle and pulled the lever on its side. A green stripe lit up on top of it, showing it was ready to fire.

"Get ready, Amy. We're going to have to shoot a lot."

"At who?"

"We're about to find out. Could be alien mutants, or people turned into monsters by some unknown pathogen, or any number of other things."

The corridor forked off to the right and left. Both branches led to locked doors. And on the wall hung the second alien corpse, nailed to it by something like a long, crooked claw.

The dead humanoid had nothing valuable on it, but the claw itself was no simple object. I read the description on my tablet:

Knowledge. The unusual claw of an alien creature, a rare collectible.

Unknown property (requires Knowledge 10).

I had to give this one to Amy too, increasing my Open Book.

"I think you'll get all the rare collectibles you need on this spaceship. Keep an eye out."

The light blinked again, interrupting my words. Both from the left and right, I heard a hard knocking sound... Claws scrabbling over metal! Both doors opened by themselves, revealing a dark emptiness. After a dramatic pause, several creatures rushed out of the darkness. Their short front legs ended in large claws. They reminded me of women in stiletto high-heels. The creatures were somehow able to crawl along the smooth concave walls of the corridor, sticking to the ceiling. A couple had already climbed up and were preparing to attack us from above.

Amy and I stood with our backs to each other. "Remember, when you see a creature with outstanding design features, those very features will be its weakness," I warned her.

"Meaning?"

"Shoot off their legs, it'll slow them down."

To confirm my words, I shot at the nearest monster. The rifle's beam cut off a taloned leg. The creature itself fell from the ceiling and ran off into the darkness. A few more appeared to replace it.

Amy and I got to work.

Since my rifle was more effective than Amy's revolver, I had to turn from time to time to help the girl shoot the monsters emerging from the doors on her side. Then turn back to my own door, then back to hers again. I was fighting on two fronts.

Amy herself shot more accurately than before. It was easier at close range. I even managed to shoot off two clawed legs in one shot. Deprived of its weapons, the monster rolled toward me on pure inertia, trying to grab me with the stubs of its legs. Paying it no attention, I continued to shoot the monsters coming out of the Darkness. Then, when things got a little easier, I finished off the one wriggling around at my feet.

The attack lasted a long time, but we shot around a dozen monsters. The floor before us was covered in corpses and severed limbs. Some stirred weakly, scratching the floor with their claws.

The doors closed and didn't open again.

"Ugh," Amy said, emptying the shells from her revolver. "I need a rifle like yours."

"We need to search in small rooms like armories. Or root around in dark corners to find a humanoid corpse."

After reloading, we moved toward the door on the left. As I expected, both doors led into a large room. At the center was a bar of energy confined in a transparent column. The column first lit up, lighting the distant corners of the room, then went out, but never fully.

I took out my tablet and aimed it at the light.

Knowledge. An unknown construction of alien design. Maybe it's for making food?
Two more unknown properties (requires Knowledge 5).

"Amy, I don't have enough Knowledge."

The girl took out her tablet and read aloud. "A power core for performing hyperquantum jumps. Required for space travel. But as for how it works... I don't know. You have to be a scientist. And have at least ten Knowledge."

"I thought so. We're in the engine compartment. That means we need to go to the other end of the ship, to the bridge. The core is probably there."

"How do you know?"

"Life experience."

"Wait, don't we need to look for something valuable here?"

I moved toward the far door. "I wouldn't waste the time. Do you want to be a scientist? Want to craft weapons or devices? Want to explore space?"

"No. I want to be a super, you know that."

"The spaceship in the Heap is designed for people leveling up those skills. Like, decipher an alien language and find out how a fake hyperdrive works. There's no point looking for anything here. There's nothing useful for either of us. You might get some diagrams for assembling a primitive laser pistol. Or the coordinates of another crashed spaceship somewhere in Rim Zero. After searching for a long time, you'll unlock some scenario which tells you there's some infinite war going on in the universe, and these aliens came to Earth to share the secret of interstellar travel, but their enemies shot them down. A pointless story, in other words. If you level up Space Explorer, you'll become the captain of an intergalactic cruiser and fight in a boring war and trade stuff. Only instead of stores, there'll be planets with monotonous landscapes and monstrous aliens."

Amy hurried after me. "That's right. I just remembered about Hyperion City in Rim Four. It has a spaceport and the Space Marine Academy."

"It still exists?" I asked in surprise.

"Yes, but it isn't very popular."

"It was the same in my day. Not many wanted to spend time learning how to build a spaceship and all its upgrades. Nobody likes space sims."

Amy nodded thoughtfully. "Hmm, you're right, only one guy from my class wanted to be a space explorer. And he ended up becoming a space marine."

"The entry threshold is too high. And for anyone who wants to be a space marine and kill monsters on unknown planets, they can always do it without a bunch of boring physics study. To be honest, that would have been boring even to me, a former nerd."

We reached the door. Amy placed the severed hand against it. The door opened with a screech, revealing another round corridor. A shadow flickered along the wall, and I heard scratching and growling.

Amy raised her pistol, but I stopped her. "If the corridor looks as if something is just about to attack you from around a corner, that means they won't attack."

"When will they attack?"

"When it looks quiet and peaceful. All these shadows and noises are psychological warfare."

"Fuck, Leonarm, you've told me so much about Adam Online that I'm not sure I'll be able to ever come back."

"What do you do in real life?"

Amy went quiet. "I don't want to talk about it."

"I understand. Reality is grey and dumb."

We walked to the end of the corridor. The rustling, growling and scratching of claws along the floor accompanied us to the next door. Behind it was an unexpectedly well-lit room. It was full of tables and sofas, their absurd shape showing their alien origins. Music was playing. Along the walls were screens with changing images of extraterrestrial landscapes. Some tables held unusually shaped glasses and pitchers.

We stopped.

"Hmm, it's very quiet and peaceful here," Amy said.

Chapter 17
Non-Game Character

THE FLOOR SHOOK. A bulge appeared in the wall from a hit from the other side — something big had struck it. The bulge got bigger, then broke. A monster flew into the room. It had the same clawed legs as the last monsters, but was twice the size. It opened its round mouth, roared and fired several spear-like claws toward us. We barely managed to take cover behind the nearest sofa. One crooked spear pierced the sofa, the point coming through between Amy and me.

"Well, what are your orders, commander? It's some kind of... Clawthrower!"

"Let me think. While we're in cover... We need to try and flank the clawthrower. Maybe this species' weakness is in its back?"

"Oh!" Amy screamed.

She fell onto her back and shot into the air several times. It turned out that the clawthrower decided not to wait for my orders. It had crawled onto the ceiling and was firing at us. A stockade of crooked spears grew around our cover. But one of them still struck me in the left leg, pinning me to the floor. Why had I even bothered raising my Luck?

I wrenched myself free, pressed a button on my rifle and held it until the green stripe turned blue. That showed that the next shot would be powerful, but then the weapon would take two minutes to recharge.

As soon as I aimed, the clawthrower dropped from the ceiling and vanished into the hole in the wall. The blinding blue beam from my rifle hit the spot where he'd just been. A wave of hot air hit us. It crackled with electricity and smelled of heated metal. Drops of molten metal splattered the sofa, burning round even holes in it.

"Oh!" Amy cried again. One of the drops had landed on her head and left a trail of scorched purple hair.

The spot that my rifle's beam hit sparked and burned for a few more seconds. Amy peeked out carefully.

"It isn't coming back."

"Smart bastard," I said. "He hid to restore his supply of throwing claws."

I pulled the claw out of my leg. I felt no pain. I realized why: a loss of sensation was a sign of poison. I grabbed my tablet.

Something has poisoned you.
-1 to all stats.
The effect of this unknown poison will increase by 10% every 30 minutes, continuing to reduce your Strength and Stamina.
You must find an antidote as soon as possible.

Under this was a previous message:

188

Energy Weapons skill learned.

Pew-pew-pew! Burn enemies with lasers, cook them with plasma, incinerate them with Tesla coils, blow them up with magnetron cannons. Discover the rich world of energy. But first, at least learn to keep your eyes open when you fire.

After injecting myself and bandaging my wound, I rose, keeping hold of the claw that I'd pulled from my leg.

Amy was already keeping watch on the hole in the wall. "How long do you think it'll take the clawthrower to recover?"

"Not long, I think. I've never seen that monster before, but there are similar creatures in the swamps of Rim Two."

I approached Amy, sensing that my Speed had reduced significantly. I moved as if underwater or as if I'd just left stasis: slowly and sluggishly. My body couldn't keep up with my thoughts.

Amy scratched the end of her nose with her revolver barrel. "What do we do now?"

"If we go straight, the clawthrower will shoot us as if he's playing a corridor shooter. He's probably set up shop around a corner in the corridor."

"So we'll find a way round?"

"Yeah. But first, we need more firepower. Your revolver is completely useless in here."

Amy noticed that I was holding the claw. "Another rare collectible?"

I put the claw in my backpack. "I need to

synthesize an antidote, and for that I need to keep some source material."

"How do we synthesize it?"

"In some lab on the ship... I hope."

"What if there isn't one?"

"There has to be."

"Shit, your cockiness is annoying."

"Your swearing is annoying. I suggest we turn back and go around the engine compartment along another corridor. It'll probably be blocked, and the corridor with the clawthrower will be the only way to the core. But we'll definitely find something that will help us defeat it."

"And if we don't?"

"Then I was wrong and we'll die to an even more dangerous monster."

"Nice prospects. Fuck."

We turned around and went back. Along the way, we diligently pushed open all the doors and checked all the nooks and corners, looking for something that would help against the clawthrower. Amy even nicknamed it Bully and asked me:

"Do you think we can make it our pet?"

"Taming a monster like that would cost you a dozen respawns. It'll take you a month to get out of Rim Zero. And to make it trust you, you'd have to feed it an undetermined number of players or NPCs. Luring players into a trap is tough."

"Yep, that's Bully. He's a difficult one." Amy looked at me playfully. "What if I feed you to him first?"

Since I was moving slower, Amy constantly ended up ahead. She remembered that I was slowed down, came back, tried to keep my pace, but then overtook me again.

"So you say the CSes adjust to fit us and all that stuff," Amy said. "But what if we, as in humans, adjust to fit them? Know what I mean?"

"Let me say right away: don't assume you're the smartest person here. As if no one before you has experimented, checked the CSes' reactions to non-standard user behavior. All that was done at the dawn of the development of virtual taharrated worlds. We aren't pioneers, we're enjoying some very carefully developed technology. The CSes, and the game itself — they aren't our friends or enemies, they're like indifferent gods that don't adjust to suit us to make things easier for us, but adjust to make things as hard for us as possible without making things impossible."

"How does that work? And what the hell is a demiurge? Some kind of monster?"

"It ensures that every situation appears hopeless, but there's still a solution to the problem. As for 'demiurge', it's an Ancient Greek word, it means 'creator'."

Amy shook her head thoughtfully.

"You make it sound as if the CSes just create the appearance of difficulty."

"The CSes create the appearance of everything in Adam Online. Don't forget, their main task is to make our time in Adam as rich as possible. That means they have to hold our interest. They give us a goal, an achievement that interests us."

"Hmm, so what's your goal? Obviously not just life in Adam, not the game?"

"Not telling. My goal isn't in the game. But I can guess why you stopped being an angel and decided to be a super. You liked being an angel so much that they somehow took away the option."

"Don't think you're the smartest one here," Amy said, imitating me. "You don't know shit about my motives."

"Whatever they are, I'm sure the CSes had a role in creating them. While my goal doesn't depend on them."

Amy scratched the tip of her nose with her revolver again. She also bit her lower lip, making her even cuter. There's a certain kind of girl that really suits a thoughtful look.

"But shit, players die when they complete quests, right?" She continued another thought as if from nowhere. "Stronger NPCs take them out, or they fall into traps or anomalies."

"You won't believe it, but according to statistics, players are most often killed by other players. There's an emphasis on it. The people that come to Adam Online to play, not just to have a happier life than in the real world, get just what they want. A game. And the difficulty of a game depends on the opponent. The best opponent, it turns out, is another person. No NPC can compare.

"Are you sure?" Amy snapped. "Lots of NPCs

will be better than people."

"In what sense?"

"In all of 'em! As if you don't know?"

The sharpness of her objections surprised me. She looked at me so strangely, as if she expected an open answer. Something hid behind that expectation. I made as if I hadn't noticed the changes in her tone. As if nothing had happened, I continued.

"Of course, there are leveled up NPCs that are tough to kill. But beating one of those can't compare to beating a person. Surpassing another human being creates completely different feelings than defeating a string of code."

Amy stopped.

"I'm not talking about fights, or levels or skills."

"What then?"

The girl spoke slowly, syllable by syllable as if for an idiot.

"I'm talking about how there are NPCs no worse than people. They're so advanced that you can't tell them apart from... from you, for example."

"Even the most complex non-game character whose behavior is controlled by a whole farm of quantum computers wouldn't be able to imitate a human."

"How do you know? The Mentors, for example..."

"The Mentors are a myth."

Amy angrily waved her revolver.

"Ugh, I'm sick of this. You think you know it all. Maybe you're just a figment? Think about that, dickhead."

She rushed forward and I shuffled after her, slow as jelly sliding off a plate.

I suspected that Amy had asked those questions to solve some personal issue, not wanting to admit what was worrying her. I knew her well enough. Not a minute had passed before she turned to me and asked me with a tone as if she wasn't angry:

"What if, let's say, someone doesn't want to play? Will the CSes still pull them into some kind of interaction? Can that happen?"

"Refusing to play is just another way of playing," I answered vaguely. "The CSes act as a kind of middleman, creating a background for interaction for us. The game is the same — the genres differ."

"First you say the control systems create everything, and everything depends on them, then you say that it's the other way around, that we're in charge and they're just middlemen."

"Consider it a quantum uncertainty," I chuckled.

"I won't. I don't know what that is."

"Quantum..." I began.

"Damn it, Leonarm, you're messing with my head. No quantums. I'm not one of those people that comes to Adam Online to play or level up dumb skills. I just want to enjoy a happy life."

"Uh-huh, and angels have a happy life, right? They can't even swear. Don't you see how you're contradicting yourself, Amy?"

"Have you been an angel?"

"No," I lied.

"It's like being... I don't even know how to explain it. You don't have to rush anywhere, or defeat anyone, or achieve anything. Absolute calm, with a sense of complete control."

"I heard something like that," I answered, remembering scraps of sensation from my short stay in an angel's body. "But you can achieve the same state with all kinds of drugs."

"An angel can melt into the surrounding world, become a part of it. Going back to reality from being an angel is doubly harsh."

I stopped answering. Billions of people suffered stress from the need to return. If it weren't for the threat of death, none of them would leave the pod. Even death didn't stop them sometimes. All that kept humanity from extinction was the short expiration date of dissociative electrolytes and the forced exit.

Although my Olga once managed to get around the forcing mechanism...

Once and for all.

For all...

I walked the last stretch of the corridor leading to the engine compartment with even greater difficulty. The poison's effect was increasing. I didn't just not hurry after Amy, I walked slower and slower. My backpack's weight increased. I'd be damned if I had to throw out items.

I heard the familiar terrible knocking of claws on metal. The corridor exit was guarded by several ordinary... what would they be called? Clawlegs?

Clawwalkers?

Amy stopped suddenly and aimed her revolver at them. I grabbed my rifle as quickly as I could. This meant that I moved about as quickly as someone high as a kite.

It was all up to Amy in this fight. Before I could aim my rifle, the clawwalkers had already left my line of fire. Which wasn't saying much: my reaction speed was so low that a blind and legless zombie could have gotten out of the way.

Amy displayed wonders of accuracy and agility. She shot off legs, making every single bullet count. Incredibly, all six of her shots hit their targets. The crippled clawwalkers fell prey to my rifle. Even as slow as I was, I had the time to aim and fire. My sloth-like pace made me hold the rifle trigger down a little longer than necessary. That made the beam so powerful that it burned up the creatures.

The corridor filled with smoke from the burning corpses. Amy and I crouched down to get below the smoke. After making sure there were none left, we moved on, listening out for the scratching of claws.

Chapter 18
Pick Your Poison

IN ONE OF THE smaller rooms, which looked awfully like a kind of futuristic storeroom, we found a laser pistol. Unfortunately there were no charges for it. Amy had around ten energy rounds, but to transform them into charges suitable for the gun, we'd not only need the right equipment, but also the right skills. Apart from the pistol, there were several other unknown items in the storeroom. Both my level of Knowledge and Amy's defined them as "Mysterious Trinkets of Unknown Value and Origin". Their weight varied from a couple of pounds to twenty.

"Maybe we should risk it and take a couple?" Amy asked. "We can sell them in Zero Town. The merchants will know what they are."

"Risk it, but you'll be annoyed when you find out that you brought some twenty-pound scrap of a lunar tractor worth two gold."

"Right," Amy sighed, putting aside the item she was looking at.

The doors to the side sections were often closed and didn't react to the bracelet on the alien's arm. Amy insisted there were mountains of loot behind those doors, but I asked her not to waste time and ammo on trying to shoot off the locks or opening mechanisms. She called me a "boring nerd".

My skills had gone down due to the poison and all the medicine I'd been taking. Nonetheless, my Eagle Eye skill noticed a suspicious detail under the door of one compartment. Slowly, like an old man, I dropped down to my knees and took a closer look. There it was: a brown stain. I aimed my tablet at it:

A bloody fingerprint.
Eagle Eye. Judging by the shape and partially detectable ridge pattern, this is a fingerprint from a human hand. Judging by the degree to which it has dried, the fingerprint is between one and five years old.

A smaller message covered up the information on the tablet:

Eagle Eye skill increased: +10 XP.

I rose, aimed my rifle at the door and held down the trigger, letting the charge build up. Amy stepped back and hid behind me.

The rifle's beam ripped open a section of the door, throwing off shards of burning metal. But that wasn't enough. I made more cuts at the top and bottom of the door. Before the cuts cooled down, I pulled the door toward me, opening the entrance to the cabin.

A narrow bed and a row of strange statues took up half of the room. The cupboards on the walls were wide open, and the floor was covered in crumpled alien clothing. Amy sat on her heels and started rooting through it all without a moment's hesitation.

I walked further. The floor was slightly angled, like it was all through the ship. That's why I didn't find the corpse right away. It had slid into a corner. He was a scientist dressed in the same kind of UniSuit as the one we found in the truck on the Heap. With one difference: he was torn to pieces. A claw protruded from his leg, and the blade of a second stuck out of his chest. The skull had fallen from the decaying corpse and lay some distance away, looking at me with eye sockets full of garbage.

Amy pulled a red shirt out of the pile of clothing and pulled a metal badge shaped like a star from it. "Bingo! Another rare collectible."

"Good for you," I turned the corpse onto its back and took off the backpack. I could feel bones and remnants of flesh beneath the UniSuit.

Amy walked over and we ransacked the backpack together. We found a box of energy rounds branded with an alien emblem, and a second laser pistol. Amy took both pistols and held them like a cowboy.

"Now I'm armed and dangerous."

"With your aim, you're only a danger to yourself. Don't forget, energy weapons ricochet more often than firearms. And some surfaces make the charge bounce back, with around a quarter of its initial strength. If it hits you, you'll get a bad burn."

"Alright, dad," Amy said, deftly spinning both pistols in her fingers.

"That was cool," I said. "Where'd you learn that?"

"My Agility and Knowledge levels unlocked the Pistol Tricks skill. Practically useless, but it looks cool. I don't even have to try, I just start spinning them and it happens by itself."

"Don't be silly. Learning new tricks lets you reload your pistol with one hand. Could be useful if you get wounded."

We continued our looting. The scientist's tablet was the Protected Tablet version, but the screen was broken and the battery was dead. It also didn't have any valuable upgrades to transfer to ours. We found another Glock with a silencer and flashlight. The silencer wasn't particularly valuable. We could sell it at Tenshot for scrap. But the flashlight under the barrel was a welcome surprise. It wasn't particularly rare, but right now it'd come in handy. There were some pamphlets at the bottom of the backpack: "New Data on Spiderbot Fauna at the Mechanodestructor Heap North Entrance in Rim Zero", "Hypothetical Principles of the Operation of the Hypothetical Hyperquantum Jump Drive", and another couple that I didn't bother looking at.

"A pamphlet about spiderbots — that's for you," I said, handing it to Amy. "If you manage to get through it, you'll teach your pets to get into forbidden zones."

"You mean they'll follow me everywhere, even outside the Heap?"

"Yep."

"I'm going to be a super, I don't need an escort like that."

"About that, Amy. You understand that a super is a tough character to be, right? You don't just have to level up your human to two hundred, you also have to level up certain branches of skills. Only that unlocks the ability to transform a human into a superhuman."

"You're too long out of the game. The toughest character right now is the bizoid. You're not wrong though. I have the branches written down. And stop with the unsolicited advice. Talking to you is like playing through an endless tutorial."

I found two large flasks reinforced with metal in the backpack's side pockets. One was full of a cloudy reddish liquid, and the label on the glass read:

Test Sample #6

There was little liquid in the second flask, and it was transparent, light blue, and nothing was written on the bottle.

The last item at the bottom of the backpack was a dictaphone. Just like the one the scientist in the truck had. The dictaphone had enough charge to listen to a message.

"There are three of us left out of the whole group..." the speaker breathed heavily. Distant shots rang out in the background. "The spiderbots wounded my colleague and the expedition commander ordered us to leave him in the truck. We all felt awful to abandon a comrade, but now we've been properly punished."

The scientist coughed. There was a noise as if he was crawling across the floor. I heard the hiss of a door opening.

"It is now clear that our colleague in the truck has a better chance of surviving and being rescued than we do..."

"No, buddy," Amy laughed. "Your colleague didn't get rescued."

"We've reached the spaceship's engine. We couldn't study its specifications... My tablet has all the necessary diagrams not only to repair this ship's engine, but also to create one like it. This gives us, humanity, a path to the stars... But an engine alone isn't enough. In the navigational cabin in front of the main deck, there are maps of all the star systems that this extraterrestrial species has explored..." He coughed. I heard a strike from something heavy. It was accompanied by the familiar scratching of claws along the floor. The scientist screamed and the recording cut off. Then it continued again. There were no more shots. The scientist spoke quietly. It was clear his strength was failing.

"We studied the alien spaceship all day. It took a lot of time to map out the corridors and find out what the rooms were for. In the room that we deduced was a laboratory, we placed our own lab. We moved all the alien corpses we'd found into there. None of the aliens survived, which surprised us. All showed signs of a violent death. But what killed them? That forced us to take safety measures. We began to carefully check the entire ship, room by room, until one of our groups of soldiers ran into a nest belonging to some kind of creatures with long claws instead of legs. We don't know whether those creatures are a product of the Heap, or if they arrived here with the aliens... Most of our soldiers were killed. Two came back wounded, with claws in their body, but the others managed to shoot one and dragged it into the lab for study..."

During a pause in which the scientist had another coughing fit, I glanced at Amy. The girl listened, her mouth open and breath held.

"This is what our biologist found out," the scientist continued. "Their claws inject a venom into their victim's body, and it does more than just slow you down. The poison works as a preservative. The victim's blood slowly starts to thicken, and the patient first falls to sleep, and then into a coma. After some time, the victim dies and turns into jelly suitable for absorption by the monsters' digestive systems... Incidentally, we have called these beasts..."

The scientist broke off to cough again.

"Oh no, Leonarm, you're going to turn into jelly?" Amy said in all seriousness. "How am I going to handle this alone? Who's going to give me boring lectures?"

The scientist finally stopped coughing. "Our biologist managed not only to synthesize an antidote, but also to create a new venom based on it: something that affects the clawed creatures just like their venom affects us. It slows them right down, then kills them. That was a good find, since our soldiers came to the conclusion that the creatures are tough to kill. Killing just one requires several men and lots of ammo. And we were already struggling with ammo... We decided to hit the creatures. We planned to produce plenty of poison to take them out with their own weapon, as it were... At the same time, we tasked our engineers with crafting several tranquilizer rifles that would shoot darts containing the poison... But the creatures were too quick for us. They attacked at the same time. They didn't strike from the corridors, where we'd built solid barricades. They broke right through the lab walls. We didn't expect that... We saw similar damage in the corridors, but we didn't understand what it was. The ship had crashed from space, right? Who knows what damage it sustained. I barely managed to escape the lab, bringing both these vials with me. I don't know what I was hoping for. Of course, the antidote would help if I'd just been hit by a claw, but I've been impaled... I'm dying... I don't know why I'm saying this into this dictaphone... As if someone will hear me... Ugh... Tell my wife... And my kids..."

I paused the dictaphone. "I see. We need to choose. One vial has the antidote, the other has an even stronger venom."

Amy, as she often did, answered in a completely unexpected way.

"Why did they have dictaphones? Couldn't he record his messages in a bottle on his tablet?"

I stared at her. "What are you talking about? Do you get that I have to choose between life and death? Or respawning, at any rate."

"Still though, why the dictaphones?" she repeated stubbornly.

"How should I know? Maybe the scientists had to keep logs on separate devices."

"Right, right. Let me hear the message, there was gonna be something sad about his kids and wife."

"Amy!"

"God dammit, why do you always gotta be so boring? Don't worry, I'll make the choice for you."

"Why?"

She took the vials from me. "I have higher Luck."

"What does Luck have to do with it? We have to think about this logically..."

She offered me the vial with the red liquid. "Drink this."

"Why?"

"Why not? The chances are fifty fifty. But my Luck-"

"Now let's try some logic," I interrupted her. "If there's more red liquid than blue, that means that was the one developed to fight the clawthrowers. They planned to fire it from those tranquilizer rifles, so there's more of it."

Amy shook her head. "Yes, but the red vial is labeled Test Sample Number Six, and that means it was tested on someone, right? The dead scientist didn't say anything about testing the poison on the clawthrowers, but there were definitely injured and poisoned people in the squad. They tested the antidote on them."

I barely kept a poker face. Was the poison starting to eat away at my mind? The girl was right. To preserve the image of a man who knew what he was doing, I first grabbed the tablet and aimed it at the vials. Neither my Knowledge nor my Eagle Eye gave me any details. I weighed both vials in my palm again.

"Hurry and decide, god dammit."

"If I drink the poison, you'll be alone," I reminded her. "I doubt you'll reach the core."

"But if you're not wrong, then the second vial will be useless anyway. What will you shoot at Bully? We have no tranquilizer rifle. The engineers didn't manage to craft them."

I unscrewed the lid of the red vial and sniffed it. "I have a plan."

"Going to ask Bully to drink the venom?"

I opened and sniffed the blue vial. "Almost."

The red vial smelled like shit, the blue like dishwater. Not much of a choice. Well, time to decide.

I took the vial of red swill and raised it. "Cheers."

"Hurry and drink it, that stuff reeks."

I screwed up my eyes and lifted the vial to my lips. I didn't know what dose I needed for the antidote to work (or, if it was poison, for it to kill me completely). I trusted my instincts.

I took a gulp and belatedly thought that I shouldn't have risked it with my low Luck. Better not to waste the time, to just find the core and go back to Zero Town. They'd definitely have been able to heal me there.

Chapter 19
More Wood

GRISHA, AS USUAL, ignored his brother's advice and did not put himself in a tank or a Eurofighter. He just took a guard of two guildmates. One was a mechanodestructor, a transformer tank, the other a human. Although the human had such a sophisticated UniSuit that from afar, he looked like a small transformer.

After paying the toll for each, they moved to Rim Three, to a location known as Brooklyn Forest, not far from the village of Brooklyn, named after a real New York district destroyed during the war.

Then they walked down the road a long way. After twenty minutes, a bizoid attacked them. It was half made of wood, half of living flesh. They were called 'treegorgers'. Grisha hadn't been in the woods for a long time and had forgotten about them. The guards dealt with the treegorger pretty quickly, but Grisha felt a sharp fear, suddenly aware that he was standing in a forest full of monsters with a completely defenseless core.

"Hah, boss," the human said, gathering the loot. "This player thought you were an easy mark."

"What level?" Grisha asked. "I don't have a neurointerface."

"Hundred and ten. From the Langoliers guild, if that matters. Looks like they have a base here. As long as they don't..."

"Forget about it, we'll reach Nika, then we'll be safe."

"What about getting back?"

"On the way back I'll be able to take out the whole guild myself. Hopefully, anyway. Got a locator?"

"Yeah. It says there's something like a base around six miles to the north. Looks like there's another one to the south."

"So the Langoliers have decided to expand, huh?"

"Black Wave got knocked out of the top ten, everyone is getting more active. They all want to take our spot."

They moved down the road again. There was a tank ahead. Grisha was in the middle, the human was at the rear. He put his UniSuit's locator up to full power and left it there. It took a lot of energy to work, but now nobody could approach unnoticed. Apart from bizoids with the Earthly Tremble DNA modification, or angels.

"Why are we walking around on foot, boss?"

"Nika doesn't let any military vehicles close to her borders. You'll have to stay outside too, by the way."

"That's why you're going to see her naked?" the human asked.

"Not just that. She asked me to 'simplify' things."

"What does that mean?"

"Be the person I am by default in Adam. A naked core."

"Why the hell...?"

"Says it'll kind of reset my habits. Keep me from relying on my level."

"Why though?"

"She crafted some sophisticated mechanodestructor add-on. But its controls are so unusual, she claims, that I need to forget all my old habits and behavior patterns."

"Behavior what?"

"I don't know. That's what she said."

"She smart?"

"Yeah. She got sent to a special school at twelve. The social distribution neuronets predicted a science career for her. She studied in the special school for half a year. Then she went back to our normal one."

"How come?"

"Don't know that, either. That's when she started going all loopy. She won't talk about what happened there."

"They say, boss, that in special schools they do the same with people as we do here with our characters. Train up their stamina, strength, agility. Only in real life, not online."

"I heard that. Bullshit."

The human suddenly slowed his pace. "Careful, three targets detected. They're moving from that base in the north. Looks like all three are treegorgers. They'll reach us in ten minutes.

Grisha twitched unhappily. He kept forgetting

that he had no neurointerface, no access to chat, nothing at all. Even his vision was black and white. Damn Nika and her ideas. There was probably no basis to the need to forget habits.

"Alright, you and I will run to Nika's zone, the tank will sacrifice himself."

The tank couldn't speak aloud, and Grisha couldn't see the chat.

"He says he doesn't wanna die," the human said, conveying the tank's words.

"We're all being fairly compensated. Three hundred thousand for one death."

The tank silently turned around and drove down the road, then turned into the woods, heading directly for the enemy. Huge fantastically shaped trees bent and broke under his weight. A flock of multicolored birds took flight. Two drones accompanied them. They were designed to give the tank a bird's-eye view of the battlefield - right up to the moment when two tree treegorgers set trees alight to create a smoke screen or threw caustic sap at the drones.

The human in the UniSuit could run at great speed. Grisha couldn't keep up with him. The human picked him up and kept running. He occasionally reported on the radar readings.

"Alright... our tank is moving into the contact zone with the treegorgers. Damn it..."

"What?"

"Two are dealing with him, the third is heading toward us. He's already close."

But Grisha didn't need a locator to see the tops of the trees shaking. Occasionally, first one and then another tree would shake and slowly drop, falling to an invisible sawblade. The treegorgers converted wood into energy. That meant they couldn't survive long out of the woods. But in their homeland of the forest, they were fearsome opponents whose strength was only limited by the availability of wood.

Soon the woods began to thin out, then ended. The road took them through hills filled with explosion craters and fire-melted cliffs. Broken mechanodestructor frames stuck out from the ground here and there, alongside long burnt-out tanks and bizoid skeletons. The background radiation increased sharply.

A barrier blocked the road, with a sign reading "Do not enter. Private land". Next to it was a billboard with a symbol and a sign reading "Dimension X". It was covered in bullet holes and laser burns.

The treegorger stopped at the edge. His body of flesh and wood looked like a centipede. It was half buried in the earth. It seemed to suck in trees, starting from the roots. One, another, a third...

"It's storing up energy to attack," Grisha said.

"Level two hundred... Judging by his size, he's grown a second stomach for wood. That gives him half an hour of time beyond the forest," the human said hopelessly.

Grisha leapt from his hands. "Well, you know what I'm going to suggest."

"I don't need money, boss. I'll do anything for the sake of the guild."

"We'll give you a Hero's Star."

"Thanks."

Drawing his Salinger rifle from his backpack, the future hero crouched behind the melted hull of a gigantic mechanodestructor. Grisha rolled further down the road, getting tangled up in the remains of some barbed wire.

After filling up on wood, the bizoid left the forest zone. Rapidly pulling himself along with its arms, he rushed forward. His body crackled and screeched, bending around craters and wrecked vehicles.

Grisha was having trouble with potholes. Just in time he remembered that Nika regularly mined the approaches to her zone. He just noticed the edge of a mine sticking out of the sand. He barely avoided getting blown up. He had to turn sharply, losing speed.

The mine was behind him, but now he had to move more carefully...

Continuing his movement, Grisha turned his hull back, watching as his guildmate activated a jetpack and flew above the treegorger, firing from his rifle. The monster, losing bark and blood, darted to the side at random. And hit a mine. The explosion didn't kill him, but severely maimed him. Trying to escape the fire, the bizoid plunged into the nearest crater. He quickly oriented himself and responded to the human's fire by throwing up a multitude of burning firebrands and smoke, covering himself from view. The bizoid was losing the battle against the highly augmented human, although he was fifty levels higher. But that was because he wasn't in his usual forest environment — he was conserving energy.

The fuel in the human's jetpack ran out. Taking advantage of his last few seconds of air superiority, he threw several grenades into the smoke. It wasn't clear whether he hit the bizoid or not. No damage notifications, no intel from the chat...

Hmm, Grisha thought. *The world really does look different when you don't rely on neurointerfaces and personal assistants. It's weirdly more realistic.*

He drove further and further on.

The last thing he saw was a mine flying out of the smoke screen. It hit the human and exploded. The jetpack deactivated and he fell. The treegorger had managed to use the anti-infantry mines by throwing them at his opponent.

Necessity is the mother of invention, Grisha thought.

The road ended in front of a monolithic concrete fence covered in holes and melted scars from lasers. The fence, like a dam, partitioned off a ravine between two cliff walls. There was a deep ditch in front of the fence, and at its floor were the remains of those who had previously tried to force their way into the factory complex where Nika produced her goods: weapons, extraordinary mechanodestructor add-ons and speed chips for androids.

Rows of Ellen turrets suddenly emerged from the ground. A projector panel appeared on one of them, displaying Nika's face.

"Hello, Grisha."

"I nearly died getting to you."

"Imagine what it's like for me. Every day another treasure hunter comes to attack my factory and get fabulously rich."

"Fabulously idiotic."

One section of the fence lifted. A bridge extended through the gap. Grisha turned: three Eurofighters had appeared in the sky. Even if his guildmate had defeated the treegorger, he wouldn't withstand the aircraft alone.

"Don't worry," Nika said. "They won't come in here. I have a non-aggression pact with the Langoliers. And the anomaly will protect us too."

The brothers had always wondered what it was that Nika did in that huge zone of hers. If all of Dimension X was occupied by weapons factories, then Nika should have been producing almost as much as the corporations. But her weapon batches stayed relatively small.

Once, the brothers tried to buy intel from a third party to learn the secrets of Dimension X. But nothing could penetrate the anomaly protecting the location from above. And nobody went beyond the defense perimeter, not even NPCs. They quickly abandoned their attempts to gain intel.

Two months prior, during a rare conversation in real life, when all three were preparing to climb into their taharration pods again, Grisha couldn't help but ask:

"Damn, are you ever going to tell us what you do there?"

Nika sat on the edge of her pod. Her body was just as thin as that of her android, only a lot shorter. As usual, she dodged the question.

"I'll tell you something one day."

Neither her nor the twins were shy of nudity. Living together in the boarding school left no room for false modesty. Nika and Grisha had already shaved their heads. Fortunado was still buzzing his in the shower room.

Nika suddenly rose and approached Grisha. "But I do have something for you," she whispered. "Come to Dimension X when you have time."

Grisha glanced sidelong at the door to the shower room. "And Fortunado isn't supposed to know?"

Nika pursed her lips. "I've created a special mechanodestructor frame. You can tell him that."

"Wow, what have you made? An arachnid? A humanoid mech? An armored vehicle? A fancy Eurofighter?"

"You'll see. Nobody has made anything like it before."

"Will you tell me your secret?"

"The secret of Dimension X has nothing to do with Adam Online, and even less to do with the guild."

Fortunado stopped his buzzing.

Nika quickly returned to the edge of her pod and offered her legs to the medical robot. It extended some tools and started clipping her toenails, filing them and covering them in a protective coating to keep them from degrading. For some reason, dissociative fluid damaged the nails of people who were regularly immersed in it. If you didn't get them treated, you could return to reality to find your nails floating around in the pod with you.

"When I come see you, will you tell me what you do there?"

Nika hesitated to answer, listening to Fortunado fidgeting in the shower room. "Maybe."

Chapter 20
Monetization

GRISHA ROLLED after Nika and span his hull all around, staring at the surroundings hungrily. The first thing he noticed was that Dimension X was covered in windowless buildings. Tall concrete boxes of various sizes. Something akin to factories. At the zone's center stood the largest box, almost as high as a mountain. The anomaly shimmered above it, protecting the zone from aerial attacks.

Secondly, Grisha felt that all the buildings in Dimension X were real, not just filler like many structures in Adam Online.

In the virtual world, everything served the purpose of entertainment. Everything had to astound the imagination of the user. For example, thousands of skyscrapers rose miles into the sky in Capital District, disappearing into the clouds or the blue sky. Billions of NPCs filled cities like that. They did nothing until a player came along, which prompted them to action as if the player was starting their life.

It was the same story with the giant industrial complexes of City 18. Factories with arcane mechanisms stretched out over thousands of square miles. Complex conveyor belts producing parts unsuitable for any device or mechanism in Adam Online. And if more users than usual came to the location, the procedural generators created even more miles of factories.

All that filler served only as a background for quest NPCs and rare item searches. And just for shooting monsters for anyone who wants to level up.

The relatively small zone of Dimension X obviously served the purpose of meaningful manufacturing. But what did it manufacture? Was Nika secretly creating more weaponry than the Black Wave knew?

It was a shame his core had no function for recording a video, or at least taking a photo...

"I get it," Grisha laughed. "You asked me to come here naked so I couldn't record anything, right?"

Nika walked slowly, matching Grisha's speed. "You need to forget everything you knew."

"How come?"

"The new frame doesn't need any of your old knowledge. None of your previously learned habits will be any use. I've created a truly revolutionary mechanodestructor frame. But you'll have to figure out how to use it in battle on your own."

"It's obvious you've been advertising the corporations' goods. You're drumming up interest. Aren't you worried that the new body won't be as cool as you've promised?"

"Heightened expectations? No, Grisha. Your expectations are more likely too low. The capabilities you'll have are going to drive you crazy."

"Alright, alright, shut up and take my money, as people used to say."

"Oh yeah, you're going to need a lot of money," Nika replied.

They walked along a concrete track. Grisha realized that it stretched through the entire zone. Paths to the grey cubic factories split off from the main track. Some bore signs with huge letters: Apartment, Playground, Schoolyard. Then there were the nameless cubes. They had numbers instead: World 0.2, World 0.3, World 0.3+, World 0.3++...

"Can I ask you what those are?"

"No, I'm not ready to talk about that yet."

"Umm."

"Not because I'm hiding it from you. You know I don't even hide my impending death from you, Grisha."

"Yeah. But..."

"I'm not ready to tell you about it because even I'm not sure what I've made here yet. Or whether I managed to make it. I need another couple of months to check."

Grisha sped up to draw equal with Nika. "You're not talking about an add-on right now, huh?"

"No."

"Then what...?"

Nika stopped next to the turn to a cube called Experimental Models. She beckoned Grisha to follow.

"I'm looking for a way to cure my sickness."

"Medicine, then?"

"No. There's no medicine for it. I want to defeat death itself."

"Oh... O-kay..."

"Enough about that," Nika cut him off. "When the time comes, you'll be the first to know. If the time comes."

She placed her hand on the lock sensor. The wall of the concrete block slid aside, letting the visitors in. Floodlights lit up automatically to light the empty space. At the center hung... a black cube around the size of a car.

Nika has some passion for strict geometric shapes, Grisha thought.

Nika crossed her arms and looked at Grisha, then at the black cube. "I call it LeCube."

"Great. Don't tell me that obelisk is the frame that can defeat them all. I mean sure, it looks like a great tombstone."

Nika sighed. She approached LeCube and laid her hand on its surface. A hexagonal opening appeared at the bottom for a core.

"Get inside."

Grisha rolled over to LeCube. When he reached the hexagonal opening, a magnetic force gripped him and pulled him inside. So far, the process was just the same as it usually was for inserting a core into a frame. Only the frame looked kind of stupid.

On top of everything, Grisha found himself in total darkness and silence. He had no visual or sensory information. Nothing at all. He tried to tell Nika, but the core's voice port was firmly pressed to the walls of LeCube. Grisha heard his voice muffled as if he was speaking into a pillow.

He wanted to get out, but the strange frame

wouldn't let him.

"Hey, I'm stuck in here. How do I disconnect from this shit? Huh? Do you hear me? Nika? This isn't funny..."

Grisha's voice was barely audible. It was impossible to hear what he was shouting about.

Nika walked into the corner and deployed a large semi-circular projector panel. "Wait, it's loading."

Columns of code appeared on the projector screen on a simple black background. None of the diagrams, spinning graphics, blinking icons or other nonsense that Adam Online used to imitate a 'scientific interface'. With Nika, everything was strictly functional.

She entered a command and waited for the system to respond. "Do you hear me?"

"And see you!" Grisha replied. His voice could now be heard loud and clear from LeCube. "Cool neurointerface. But I still don't understand what to do. What do I do now I'm in this thing? What are its combat capabilities? How do I kill my enemies? Hit 'em over the head with this box?"

Nika stood opposite LeCube. "First you need to understand how to work with this frame. It has no shape at all. I set the template to cube based on my own aesthetic preferences. I love geometric shapes and simplicity."

"I noticed."

"In Adam Online", Nika continued, "all items,

weapons or other add-ons for Mechanodestructors consist of so-called 'components', like particles of the global constructor."

"Probably... I don't know."

"I'm not asking you, I'm telling you," Nika waved dismissively. "I see. Do go on."

"The components," Nika continued in a stern voice, "are the smallest units of Adam Online world. The real world consists of an infinite number of particles, the amount of which is still being determined to this day. The virtual world of Adam Online, however, consists of objects that can be split into components. Components can't be split into smaller particles. Although there are constituent components. Like how the 'tree' object consists of the components 'Trunk — Crown — Roots'. In turn, a tree trunk consists of the components 'Bark' and 'Wood'. The roots consist of 'Wood — Tree Sap'. And they, by the same token, consist of components too. The deeper you go, the more components. If you were into biocrafting, you'd know all the plant components. The whole world of Adam Online is consists of components like that. They're the bricks and mortar of the virtual universe. That happens to be the main difference from the real world, too — because we still don't know what the final 'God Particle' is there."

"My dear Nika, all this is really boring. That's one. And two, there are crowds of enemies beyond the gates of your base. Just tell me: how does LeCube work and how much does it cost?"

Nika scratched her nose. "Fine... Alright, what makes all upgrades, add-ons and levels for all characters special?"

"I have no idea, stop asking me stuff!"

"It was rhetorical, I'm trying to explain. The special thing about them is that they all cover one side of abilities. A frame in the form of a spider-like robot allowed you and Fortunado to carry lots of different types of weapons and ammunition, but significantly slowed your movement. The Eurofighter and MiG let you fly, but they're vulnerable to pulse weapons. The bizoids..."

"Yeah, yeah. I get all that. You mean they have their strengths and weaknesses."

"LeCube doesn't."

"Meaning?"

"It can take on any form or design to perfectly suit the chosen target. LeCube can reconfigure itself into a form with whatever parameters you require."

Nika spread her hands, stretching the projector panel across the whole wall. A map of Rim Three appeared, the part containing Brooklyn Forest.

"I'll use a specific example to explain. Imagine that you just got the ability to equip any upgrades that could help you defeat an enemy in your current zone."

"Hmm," Grisha's metallic voice sounded doubtful. "Just me against the treegorgers, and in the woods too... Let me think. Treegorgers eat trees to get energy. In the forest they'd be able to regenerate constantly."

"Right. And?"

"Our guild fought some of them recently, in another forest. True, they were NPCs, not players. Before the raid started, Fortunado ordered us to replace our cannons with big saws to cut down the trees as we advanced. The treegorgers can only get energy from living trees."

"Did you win?"

"With difficulty. We cut down half the forest. But we didn't have enough firepower to completely and quickly destroy the weakened treegorgers."

Nika dragged an image of the Giant Spider frame onto the projector panel. That was the one used during the attack on Leonarm.

"When you use LeCube, you don't have to choose between a cannon and a saw. Your limbs will take on the form that you need at any given moment."

"Cool. Does it make ammo out of thin air as well?"

"Thin air has nothing to do with it. You buy ammo wherever you want, as always. You can buy it from me. But no discounts. You just don't need to think about which frame to take for each mission anymore. LeCube has the potential to be any possible mechanodestructor frame."

"It's like a transformer then?"

"No. The transformer can only take on two states. Either a means of transport or a humanoid mech. LeCube has no, I repeat — no — limitations on its transformation."

"And I repeat: shut up and take my money."

Nika hesitated, then minimized the projector

panel. "As for the cost... For you, a friend's discount. LeCube will cost you five hundred thousand."

"Not much... What's the catch?"

"The cost of the configurations."

"You said it's all built into LeCube."

"No. I said it can take on any config. But as for which — that has to be programmed in. The programs are what I'll sell you. A million each. Some will be two or three."

"How the hell did you come up with that?" Grisha shouted in displeasure.

Nika laughed. "At the end of the last century, Sony used to manufacture some games consoles called Playstation. It didn't cost much for the console, but the games were sold on separate discs. Some of them were a quarter of the price of the console itself."

"Wisdom of your ancestors, huh, money grubber?"

"It's not wisdom, it's a monetization model."

"One last question. How many LeCubes do you have?"

"One. It took me several game sessions to create it."

"When is the next one coming? A few more game sessions?"

"I'm afraid there won't be one, Grisha. After all, soon I'll be gone."

Both were silent. Nika approached the black monolith at the room's center.

"LeCube is made from modified nanobots, which are used to regenerate Armor. At first glance it might seem like a hack for Adam Online, but it's technically within the limits of this world. The control systems won't view LeCube as cheating. I used..."

"Enough, Nika, I'm not going to understand the science. If LeCube works as promised, then that's fine. Now show me which programs LeCube already has. I'll buy a couple."

Chapter 21
Enemy at the Gates

FORTUNADO'S human avatar lit up on the screen of LeCube's neurointerface yet again. The brother was openly angry and repeated:

"Damn it, Grisha, why aren't you answering? I see you online, why the silent treatment? Why did you switch off your geolocation? Where are you? Answer me right now. We have trouble. Do you hear me?"

Fortunado sent him the map of Rim Five again, with a marker at the edge of the zones still mostly unexplored by players.

"I don't know what you're doing, but you need to get here right away. The guys from your squad are tracking Jamilla. She's headed for the forbidden zones. If we don't stop her, Mariam will refuse to work with us. She'll give all that money to our competitors. Then the Black Wave will be their prey! Do you hear me? Huh? You're a moron, Grigory!"

But Grisha did not answer, for several reasons.

The least important, but most fun, was that he wanted to annoy his brother. Recently he'd begun to treat Grisha too much like a subordinate, although they were equal in the guild. Fortunado tried to teach him, give him jobs, and most offensively — control how he completed them. As if Grisha was a moron and needed a supervisor.

Grisha enjoyed seeing his brother panic. Heh, the brother at least understood that without Grisha's skills, his talents as an organizer were of little worth.

Grisha minimized Fortunado's window and switched off the sound. Another reason for his radio silence was a lack of confidence. He didn't want to start trying to convince Fortunado of LeCube's value too soon. After all, if Grisha failed, Fortunado would think even more highly of himself. He'd say, "I knew I couldn't let you take decisions without consulting me."

Grisha wanted to kill that damn Jamilla himself, to prove he was on an equal footing with his brother.

Grisha and Nika were still in the Experimental Models hangar in Dimension X. Nika transferred LeCube to Grisha's ownership, leaving herself with temporary admin rights. Now Grisha was trying to get to grips with the controls and the neurointerface.

LeCube's controls were complex. The digitized consciousness didn't know how to send signals to control the limbs — after all, there were none. Any frame, even a jet fighter or a tank, had control functions that were transferred to the user. Of course, it felt strange to feel as though a jet engine was a part of your body. Or that rotating a tank turret felt a little like moving your arm in a real body. But users quickly got used to it, found pleasure in being reborn in the form of a vehicle of destruction.

Nobody had yet decided to be reborn in an immovable object. In LeCube, Grisha felt nothing apart from being a cube. He had edges, had a sense of surfaces, a floor. That was it.

With Nika's help, Grisha steadily got to grips with it.

For example, LeCube had two 'basic shapes'. The first was the cube itself, which floated above the ground. In that shape, he moved a little quicker than a running human. But the cube had very low energy requirements. For example, the cheapest standard mechanodestructor frame, called the LG Humanoid Robot, consumed around 10 energy units per hour while moving. It could require even a hundred per hour during heavy activity. Even just standing still cost one energy unit.

"LeCube costs only one energy per hour," Nika explained. "Just because it doesn't cost much energy to maintain the shape of a cube. When it moves fast, it eats as much energy as a standard frame in active mode. So the high cost makes up for itself by saving you energy."

"You don't have to sell it to me," Grisha grumbled. "I already bought it."

The second form was called the Disk. And it felt like... a disk. Still nothing to provide bodily sensation, Grisha still felt nothing but a cold black surface and a round circle. The disk could also fly. Grisha took a test flight through the open roof of the hangar in Dimension X. The feeling of flight was added to the feeling of being a disk. That was it. Grisha's consciousness didn't feel any engines, like in a Eurofighter-type mechanodestructor, nor any wing muscles like a bizoid with the Flying Reptile DNA modification would feel.

Nor anything else that should be required for flight.

"Damn, Nika, I'm not sure I like this," Grisha said. "It all feels very strange."

Nika answered calmly over the radio.

"It's hard to trust anything new. That's enough altitude, don't get stuck in the anomaly. I'm transferring the first battle config program."

Grisha, still feeling like a plate thrown into the air, stopped and hovered. A downloading process popped up on the neurointerface.

Obtained: LeCube_000234(ver2).qcapp
Begin installation?

"You need to work on your product marketing," Grisha said, allowing the installation. "What are these dumb names?"

"Think of something better and I'll rename it."

After the installation, a message popped up.

Accept program configuration LeCube_000234?

Grisha accepted it... and nearly crashed into the hangar.

"Holy shit! Now that's more like it!"

Just when he was getting tired of the lack of control, from his brain having nothing to feel except the facets of a cube or the thickness of a disk, suddenly a range of new sensations crashed down on his consciousness. LeCube had transformed into a flying battle machine. The neurointerface started to display scanning data on the area, radar, combat system state, amount of ammunition available... true, it was all at zero. He had nothing to shoot just yet. But the potential arsenal was impressive. Two self-piloting drones that would assist him in battle... And plenty of everything that one would expect on a highly advanced MiG or Eurofighter.

Grisha checked himself and focused on controlling the thing. Stopping its fall into the hangar, LeCube sharply gained altitude. The system also marked several targets. Enemies from the Langoliers guild crowded the gates of Dimension X. A dozen humans leveled up to two hundred in impressive battle UniSuits, one super, two bizoids whose DNA modifications Grisha didn't recognize. There were probably treegorgers hiding in the woods. There was nobody in the sky, but Grisha didn't doubt that if necessary, additional air forces would appear.

They were waiting for Grisha to come out. They knew that Nika wouldn't let anyone use her respawn tower.

"Well, what do you think?" Nika asked. "Just two seconds and you have a highly powerful frame under your control."

"Impressive..."

Grisha circled above his enemies. They began to get worried. The super jumped into the air and began to fly, leaving a jet trail behind him, trying to catch up to Grisha. But he went back into Dimension X and the super turned around.

Grisha pulled up his stats on the screen.

Grisha, Mechanodestructor.
Frame: LeCube.
Guild: Black Wave.
Classes: Pilot, Defender.
Level: 167.

Strength: 29.
Perception: 38.
Agility: 91.
Knowledge: 35.
Health: 42.
Luck: 29.

Additional stats:
Balance (Pilot): 12.
Indestructibility (Defender): 6.

Grisha merely glanced at the frame's stats, just to confirm that they were as high as other flying vehicles at his level. He wanted to make sure that his pilot skills were compatible with the frame. They were, for the most part. Most of the list was green, but there were a few inactive lines. The Close-Range Aerial Combat line in particular worried him. That one was important. He'd invested a lot of time in leveling up that skill...

"What does this mean? Why aren't all the skills active?"

"What did you expect?" Nika answered. "What

works with a MiG doesn't work with a Eurofighter. They're different frames."

"But you promised that LeCube would be able to turn into whatever I wanted..."

"And it can. But think about it. A single pistol can't fire different calibers, right?"

"Actually, some can."

"Don't be pedantic!" Nika interrupted. "What I'm saying is that LeCube can turn into any pistol for the caliber you need."

"I get that. But if I want to activate Close-Range Aerial Combat, then Long-Range Aerial Combat will be unavailable?"

"Of course. Just like if you switched from a Eurofighter to a MiG."

"Got it, but with LeCube I can switch, like, instantly?"

"Well, not instantly. Transforming takes between two and seven seconds. Depends on your stats and the complexity of the config program."

Grisha thought for a moment. He flew in circles above Dimension X, looking at the roofs of numerous hangars. When he approached the gates, the system showed him the number of ground targets. It looked like there were more Langoliers. Two mechanodestructors had joined them in humanoid mech frames. If he waited any longer, the whole guild would be there!

"Now let me guess," Grisha said. "During that two to seven second transformation window... LeCube will be vulnerable, right?"

"Well..." Nika answered after a pause.

"Everything has its weakness."

"You said that LeCube could take the form of any known frame, right? But this form isn't a MiG, or a Eurofighter, or a Rafale, or any other known brand."

"This is something I made, specially designed for LeCube. It has the optimal ratio of setup time and configuration complexity. But if you really want, you can buy and download anything you like."

"No, no, I like this one... Just the name is stupid. Let's rename it."

"You're the first and only customer of LeCube, so you decide."

"Let's call it Nika."

"Very original. When I made my first frames, I named them all after myself. Until it started to get confusing. Believe me, numbers are better. Or name it after yourself."

"Umm, Multifunctional Flying Military Apparatus Grigory? Doesn't quite do it for me. Hey, let's name it after that guy that we blew up with the A-bomb. Leonarm is a good nickname."

"There are tons of Leonarms around."

"True... I got it! Grenika! We'll combine our names."

"If you like," Nika answered indifferently.

"Assault Aircraft Grenika. Sounds alright. Or is it a fighter? Or multifunctional...

Nika interrupted him.

"Grisha, LeCube can be whatever you need it to be. You still haven't abandoned your familiar concepts. You're trying to fit it with the classes and parameters that you know."

"I'm trying..."

"That's why it's easier for me to give my inventions numbers. A name is always a label. I understand your doubts. You're unsure of LeCube's capabilities, right? Then here, take this.

Obtained: LeCube_000102.qcapp
Obtained: LeCube_000002(ver4).qcapp
Obtained: LeCube_000201.qcapp

Grisha installed the new configuration programs. He quickly read their descriptions. Some sort of humanoid mech of unknown design, another flying machine...

"These are demo versions with a limited duration," Nika continued. "Your training targets are outside the gate. Start your test drive."

"What about ammunition?"

"You have two options. One: use standard ammo designed for your chosen battle configuration."

"Not very convenient."

"Yep, you'll have to stick to one set of ammunition. I developed a universal ammunition layout for that. It works only with LeCube."

"Let me guess. It's a kind of mega shell that transforms into any other kind of shell?"

"Basically, yeah. A component mass of the modified nanobots that LeCube itself is made of. It's used to create the right amount of ammunition."

"And you have to buy that mass..."

"Yes, from me. But you'll get the option to create all kinds of ammunition on the move! Need a rocket?

Make one. Need a supersonic homing missile? Easy. But in extreme danger, you can use LeCube itself to make ammunition. With the side effect of reducing its size, of course."

Grisha made another feint toward the enemy group at the gate. This time a mech fired two rockets at him. He barely had time to get back within the range of Dimension X's anti-air guns. Enough risky maneuvers. He'd gotten to grips with controlling the Grenika now.

Grisha returned to the hangar and hovered above it. He saw Nika standing, looking up and tracking his flight.

"I won't ask what you were smoking when you invented a weapon that fires itself. How much of that nanomass does it use?"

"You'll figure it out as you go. LeCube currently has an excess amount of components, enough to create a whole arsenal. Bullets will cost one amount, missiles or heavy bombs another. Energy weapons and charges for them are created using the same principle. Here..."

Unlocked access to Component Nanomass (CN).
Obtained: 11,000 CN.

Grisha glanced at the unfamiliar interface.

"Alright, so I got some CN, what next? How do I use it to make missiles or air cannon shells? And the air cannon itself, actually. And a plasma gun."

"Check out the Craft section."

"Craft? Oh no! Anything but crafting! I don't want

to craft anything, I just want to shoot and blow stuff up."

"Simmer down. I prepared some command templates in advance. Just pick what you need, LeCube will sort out the rest."

"Nice, crafting ammunition during a fight. What a good idea."

But Grisha was only complaining about the look of the thing. He quickly figured out the interface and realized that he wouldn't need to do anything but confirm.

Spent: 500 CN.
Crated: Viper Air-Land Homing Missile (x24).

Spent: 400 CN.
Created: Marinen Synchronized Aircraft Cannons (x2).

Spent: 1,800 CN.
Created: Arena Plasmagun (x1).

Spent: 3,750 CN.
Created: BunkBust Bunker Bomb (x50).

Spent: 2,000 CN.
Created: Marinen Ammunition (x2000).

Spent: 500 CN.
Created: Energy Units (x500).

Remaining: 50 CN.

After ensuring that all his weapons were combat-ready, Grisha shot upwards, leaving the hangar. He climbed, made a small turn and began to dive toward his enemies at the gate.

"Hold on now, assholes, I'm about to show you what right angles are capable of!"

Chapter 22
About Face at the Gate

THE LANGOLIERS were so sure of their numerical advantage that they didn't bother with protection from force fields. They didn't even get what was happening at first. They couldn't accept the thought that Grisha was trying to attack alone. Why would he do that, if not for a heroic death?

Grisha's next run with his unknown flying machine was taken as another feint. But when the bunker bombs fell on the Langoliers, killing the bizoids hiding under the ground, they got the message and tried to shoot down the Grenika with missiles. The flying machine continued to head straight for them, ignoring the missiles. Could the pilot have decided to sacrifice himself to kill his enemies? But then, in flight, the machine suddenly lost its shape. For a second it transformed into a black cube, and in another second the cube stretched out, became smaller, grew arms and legs. A third second and it transformed into a humanoid mech. Braking engines kicked in on the soles of its feet. Its landing threw up earth and dust, and Grisha threw a few smoke grenades along with it.

The battlefield was temporarily hidden in an impenetrable cloud.

Steel arms grabbed one of the supers and tore him in half. The second managed to dodge a giant foot, but then was crushed by a mighty fist.

The two enemy mechanodestructors - also giant robots - finally saw Grisha through the smoke using their thermal vision and rushed toward him. One waved a gigantic hammer, the second fired a machine gun on the move. Grisha froze for a while, as if wondering whether to run. But then he suddenly split into identical black cubes. The cubes span for a moment, then split into two groups, approached each other and gathered into two identical black spider robots.

The first rushed the enemy with the hammer, grabbing him with its legs. The ends of its legs first turned into saws that tore into the enemy's body, cutting it into pieces. Jumping off its opponent, the black spider aimed one leg at his head and the saw at the end of it turned into a barrel. A shot — then the shattered head of the mechanodestructor rolled across the ground and fell into a crater left by a bunker bomb.

The second spider jumped, extending its legs straight ahead. They turned into thick rotating drills that pierced right through the enemy, drilling into its mechanical body and spitting out debris. The limp enemy fell to his knees, then tragically fell head-first into the ruined ground. His machine gun fired for a while longer but stilled when it filled with earth.

The remaining Langoliers, the humans in UniSuits, scattered throughout the field, hiding behind the hills left by craters, and opened fire on Grisha with their energy rifles. When a beam hit one of the spiders, fragments of black mass fell from it.

Grisha's neurointerface reacted to each strike with a message.

Lost: 3266 primary CN.
Lost: 2497 primary CN.
Lost: 6543 primary CN.

Attention: unable to maintain current configuration; not enough CN. LeCube will take its primary form.

The two spiderbots dispersed into cubes and drew together into one large monolith. Then Grisha turned LeCube back into the Grenika and ascended. A couple of seconds later, he released a hail of fire on the surviving soldiers. Grisha fired his plasmagun, air cannon and missiles all at once. The dust that had had time to settle once again rose, almost to the sky. When it settled again, it was all over. Not one enemy soldier had survived. The field was full of the fragments of weapons, torn off arms and legs, and scraps of UniSuits. The earth was covered in blood, and a greenish slush seeped out of the earth from the dead bizoids.

Taking on the disk form to conserve energy units, Grisha descended and hovered over the field, trying to comprehend what had happened. The neurointerface was full of messages about killed opponents and points earned. He'd taken out enough enemies for a full level up.

"Well, how was that?" Nika asked over the radio. "Good product?"

"I just defeated half of an enemy guild," Grisha answered. "Sure, their levels were lower than mine, but there were lots of them. And now they're gone." "Heh heh, they're all scratching their heads at the respawn point, and they're trying to figure out what happened too. The dumbest of them will be reporting the player Grisha to tech support for apparently using some kind of cheat."

"Let me ask again: LeCube isn't a hack or a cheat, right?"

"I haven't used anything like that for a long time. I run an honest business. If LeCube contradicted the rules of Adam Online, the Controllers would have already impounded it and banned me. LeCube is no cheat, it's the result of genius crafting."

"Hmm, but if you can make something like this, then others can too, right?"

"They could, if they spent enough time as I have. And they'd be geniuses too."

Grisha ascended higher and headed back to the hangar.

"By the way, Nika, what's 'primary CN'?"

"The component mass that LeCube consists of. There's around two hundred thousand units of it. But that's an excessive amount. Even if you lose up to a hundred and forty thousand, LeCube can still take on a complex and large shape."

"What if it goes even lower?"

"Lower than that you'll get a big drop in capabilities. If you get to that point, you're better off taking on a form that will help you get away from your enemy as fast as possible."

"Bah. Everything has its limits."

"What do you expect? Don't get cocky and assume you're the strongest in this sandbox of ours. I've been tracking your actions. If your opponent had known about LeCube's weaknesses, they would have killed you while you were transforming into those spiders. You were almost defenseless."

"Alright, thanks for the warning. And get ready to sell me a few more configs and plenty of component mass. It's time for me to complete the guild's mission: take out that damn Jamilla, before my bro goes totally nuts."

Humans are perhaps the only creatures in the world that dream of being something other than themselves. And they have persisted in making that dream a reality. At first with words. They invented stories of dragons, werewolves, a son of God resurrecting after his crucifixion. When film and three-dimensional graphics arrived, it became possible not only to see these stories in paintings, but also to watch as they moved.

It became easier to imagine that you are not you, but a dark elf or an anime girl with a three-dimensional saber.

The first computer games allowed people to control these fairytale beings, creating an illusion of reincarnation. Humanity strove for a time when they could finally cease to be what they were.

The keyboard and the game controller first turned into a helmet and virtual-reality headsets. Then the gyrosphere came along, reducing the sensation of the physical body, although not entirely. Even if your character was a fire-breathing dragon, you still remained a person, walking inside a rotating sphere after covering your body with a network of neural transmitters.

Spin it any which way, you were still *imagining* that you were a dragon. You imagined with the help of technology, but all the same, the transformation was happening inside your head, which was kept in an ordinary physical body entirely unlike a dragon.

Taharration changed all that. It erased the border between the body and the mind. All that remained was pure consciousness, which was capable of fitting into any form. Or... not capable?

Back in the years when taharration pods were initially spreading, there were arguments about how human consciousness was affected by being reborn in a non-human body. Would a human consciousness relocated into a tiger actually be a tiger consciousness? Or would the human not lose the sensations of their body after all? Even in the form of a tiger, would he try to walk on his hind legs? Or if he adapts, what would happen to him after he leaves the tiger's body and transforms into, say, a dwarf? A tardigrade? A protoss or a zerg? Or that butterfly that the philosopher Zhuang Zhou saw in a dream, not knowing whether he was dreaming the butterfly, or the butterfly was dreaming him. Or were they both dreamt up by someone else?

To add to the chaos, you can't read another man's soul. Some people would undergo taharration and slip right into any body, be it a tiger or a robot that transforms into another robot. Others couldn't feel comfortable even in a virtual copy of their own body. It would take a long time for them to get used to it, they had to learn to walk and talk all over again.

Many felt discomfort from the fact that their ordinary physiological functions had disappeared. The fact that they no longer had to eat or shit or sleep drove people crazy... But since the virtual world could copy the real world to infinity, those 'naturalists' were given defecation, baldness, fingernail growth, whatever they needed.

But people adapted quickly, and then there were fewer and fewer 'naturalists'. In a single generation, all of humanity learned to accept digital reincarnation.

And people went much further. It was no longer enough to wander virtual worlds in one's own body. Or even as an anime girl. Or even a dark elf or an orc. Experiments began with introducing the most fantastic of races.

For dozens of standard years, the CSes generated various creatures and gave them to players for testing in Adam Online. It soon became clear that the more outlandish the body, the more fun it was for the digitized consciousness to take control of it. And so appeared mechanodestructors and androids. Initially they were a whole range of different classes, but standardization did its thing and they were reduced to two. The mechanodestructor became a character with a huge range of potential frames, while the android could install various chips in its head.

The plastic human consciousness incredibly learned to meld with any shape, though naturally not without the help of the control systems. After all, the problem of the connection between the body and the consciousness had stopped being a problem. It turned out that the connection didn't have to be broken, it was enough to replace it. That meant that bizoids and angels became the next step in this strange evolution of dehumanization. People didn't just get used to not being themselves, they began to find it pleasurable.

After stepping into the world of Adam Online, people transformed into fantasy dragons or mechanisms without a moment's thought. They felt those bodies as if they were their own. And so it was: their bodies became virtual vessels for the digitized soul.

Of course, people who wanted to turn into a gigantic worm, a genderless android or a huge robot for several months at a time were far fewer than those who just wanted to enjoy a virtual world in their own form. Eighty percent of adamites hadn't even tried out anything but their own body. After reaching the next level and saving up enough money, they invested in their skills and improved their appearance. The ugly became beautiful, the old became young, the infirm became healthy. And there were plenty of people born ugly and infirm — the result of radiation and a corrupted environment. People especially liked to decorate their virtual bodies with fantastic haircuts. In reality, they were usually bald, white and almost as emaciated as androids. All those decorations required money: in-game gold that had to be earned in Adam Online's virtual economy, then exchanged at a pathetic rate into dollars. All the skin stores belonged to companies managed by the heirs of the first world.

But nobody complained. There was nobody to complain to, and anyway, everyone was happy.

Adam Online maintained an illusion of equality: everyone came into it in a grey vest, jeans, with a bag at their hip. Who you became after that depended only on you, while in the real world, nothing depended on you.

Even adamites that died of old age were cremated in the same taharration pods in which they spent their lives. And the fact that people spent so much virtual money on pod upgrades made the situation even more ironic: citizens spent their entire lives earning the money to upgrade their tomb.

Chapter 23
I will find you and kill you

THE STINKING RED liquid slid down into his stomach. I opened my eyes. Amy watched me, holding her breath. Of course, it was so exciting, right? To see whether I'd die.

"Well?" she asked.

"Think I'm alive."

The tablet, which I was still holding, gave a signal. I read a message like a judge's sentence.

Well done, Leonarm, you won't die. At least not now.

The poison's effect has been neutralized. Your previous stats will begin to return at a rate of 10% per hour.

After it:

Learned skill: Military Toxicology.

You can not only neutralize the effect of poisonous substances, you can also create your own chemical weaponry.

Obtained knowledge: Clawdart Poison.

Obtained knowledge: Clawdart Antidote.

"Clawdart. So that's what your Bully is called."

Amy ignored me. She was deep in thought. I knew because she was biting her lower lip. I didn't ask what had taken her there.

I took a few steps. I seemed to be moving quicker. A little more and I'd be back to acceptable stats.

"Well, where next, commander?" Amy asked without enthusiasm. Her mood had changed sharply, as if she was upset that the poison hadn't killed me.

"We could go check the laboratory. The scientist mentioned soldiers. We'll probably find some decent guns, and probably lots of other interesting things."

But Amy ran a hand over her head, feeling the path of burnt hair. "To be honest, I'm sick of this. I want to just find the core and split. You said you have an idea for using the poison against Bully?"

Her attitude was starting to rub me the wrong way. Her Luck was the only useful thing about having her around. As it turned out, not much use, but Amy still behaved as if she was carrying the whole mission.

I took the clawdart talon out of my backpack, gripped it and waved it like a spear. "In the absence of darts, we'll use this."

Amy yawned. "I see. You'll dip the end of the claw in the poison? But how will you get to Bully undetected? Do you have camouflage or invisibility?"

"I don't have any of that. You'll just have to distract Bully's attention onto you."

"Why should I be the bait? You do it."

"How much Strength do you have?"

"Two. What does that have to do with it?"

"It'll take a strong thrust to get the claw deep enough into the clawdart."

"Into Bully."

I realized that Amy wouldn't shut up until she got the last word, so I silently walked around the cabin, waiting for my stats to recover. I checked in all the cupboards, found a few unknown items — but again, we couldn't identify them. I also found a container of energy rounds and threw it to Amy. She caught it deftly. Before we left, we took out our tablets and put them on silent so as not to give away our position when hunting Bully.

I gave Amy the under-barrel flashlight. Of course, it couldn't attach to the alien beam weapons, but we managed to fix it onto her backpack strap.

We acted in unison, as if members of the same guild. The challenges we'd faced together had done us good. My annoyance wore off, and I got a little sad to think of leaving Amy after the quest. Amy McDonald was cute, she wasn't stupid (though she was ignorant), and she leveled up skills that differed from mine, which was useful for cooperative play.

On the other hand, my true mission to find Nelly Valeeva left no room for an outsider.

I watched as Amy stood with her back to the wall and spun her laser pistols. I thought: what caused my attraction to her? Aside from the sexual factor, I mean.

And I realized what it was: in real life I'd lived alone for many years, deprived of the social opportunities that Adam Online provided. Of course, I had more than enough communication with people that didn't go into the virtual world at all, like Major General Makarov. Unlike many, I had access to entertainment in the real world. I ate real food, real kebabs cooked on a real barbecue. I even had a holiday on a real tropical island in the company of a sexy lady from an escort company who served only the richest clients. The MSB paid for all of it.

But.

I got the same withdrawal, the same 'return anxiety' that all people felt when they left Adam Online! And I was just moving from one reality to another. From a tropical island to an airplane, from the airplane to my sad little apartment. After all, I had no money to maintain the lifestyle of Makarov, an heir to the first world. His Bryansk manor was the size of a whole block of the flats in the city which housed bald residents, killing time until their next rotation in the pod.

After leaving the virtual world, I still felt deprived of the charms of reality.

"Level up," Amy said. "I unlocked a new trick, now I can do this..."

The spinning pistols leapt from her fingers, made an arc in the air and swapped places. Amy repeated her trick a few times, throwing her guns from finger to finger.

"I can juggle, but I still don't get why, damn it."

"Looks even cooler than before," I said.

That was the whole reason for why I was more attached to Amy than she was to me. I missed people, even virtual people. And if the virtual world felt almost the same as the real one, what was the difference? But there was a difference. The virtual world was better.

Even then, on the tropical island, reality stung. First I got diarrhea from some bad fruit, then sunburn, then I got a cold from an iced daiquiri, then diarrhea again... None of that existed on a tropical island in Adam Online. The sun wouldn't have burnt me, and the food would give me nothing but an aftertaste. And virtual girls, to put it bluntly, were more beautiful and more varied than those in the escort company's catalog.

"Well? Ready?"

"Let's go," I said, holding the poisoned claw before me.

It had gotten darker in the room where Bully attacked us. Half the lights had turned off for some reason, and the music stuttered, quietening and then growing louder, or cutting off in silence. The hole in the wall through which the monster had crawled was also dark.

"You go first," I whispered, nudging Amy toward the hole.

"What if I die?" she mouthed in response.

I switched on the flashlight on her backpack strap. "I'll avenge you. And I'll bring the core to the square in Zero Town. Wait for me at the bench where we met."

Amy wanted to object, but she pursed her lips, span her pistols in her fingers and walked into the darkness. After waiting for the right time, I moved after her, but kept close to the wall so I could attack Bully from behind or from the side.

In the darkness I saw Amy more clearly, and the darkness itself was occasionally lit by a weak flash from a distant light. Sometimes a burst of music accompanied the flashes, startling Amy.

"F-f-fu... sh..."

The music only heightened our stress.

We heard a rustling in the distance, something falling over, the sharp tap of claws. Silence again. The sharp uproar of a musical chord... Then the tapping again, from the ceiling. Amy crouched and aimed both pistols upwards.

Hmm, now that would be fun, if Bully had a companion of his own.

Another flash of light cast a shadow over his familiar protruding legs. We heard the whistle of claws. One pierced a wall, another clattered across the floor. Amy dropped and rolled. Charges from her laser pistol shot through the corridor like ball lightning, illuminating the walls. Amy stopped firing and span her pistols. It looked awesome. Add some accuracy to that showmanship and the girl might have some value.

I stood still in the shadows. Unlike Amy, I saw that Bully wasn't fully on the ceiling, but partially on the ceiling and on the wall. I was worried about Amy, but I stayed quiet. I couldn't let the clawdart hear that I was there.

Amy was in his sights, fully open and defenseless. But Bully, after firing off a couple of claws, changed his position and froze again. Could the bastard suspect the trap?

The girl kept moving forward, slightly correcting her flashlight to light the floor before her. Sometimes she stopped and aimed the flashlight at the ceiling. Bully silently moved positions, hiding from the spot of light. He definitely suspected!

I waited for the alien music to burst out again with another loud chord, then quickly ran along the wall and froze again.

"Bully, little Bu-u-lly," Amy called out. She had guessed his strategy as well. "Come on, come into the light. Momma has two hot treats for ya. You know my motto? 'I will find you and kill you,' that one. Which means..."

Amy stopped and listened. She sharply turned and shot into the darkness. Both bright beams hit next to Bully. He jumped back, ending up in the flashlight's beam.

"There you are."

Amy began to fire rapidly, throwing her pistols back and forth between her hands. Bully ran in a spiral: from the wall to the ceiling to the opposite wall, ending up behind the girl's back. He reared back, stretched, then launched a rain of claws at Amy, some as small as a needle and others as big as a sword.

Amy span and tried to dodge but failed: a claw the size of a dagger pierced her left shoulder. One pistol flew off into the darkness. Another claw shot into her leg. The hit was so powerful that Amy was thrown into the wall. A third claw hit her right arm, pinning Amy to the wall and leaving her hanging there. But she didn't drop her pistol.

Bully hissed, releasing his remaining air, then began to swell again, preparing for another throw.

"Fuck, Leonarm, where are you?"

I was already next to Bully.

Waiting for his body to swell up all the way, revealing the fine skin between his chitinous scales, I thrust the claw into him with all my strength. I had one chance, but luck decided not to torture me anymore: the poisoned claw pierced right through Bully's body. He instantly went limp and hissed. Claws fell from his round maw in a chaotic stream, stuck together with slime. Like a deflating ball, Bully flew to the side and turned toward me. I must have been lucky enough to hit the organ that controlled his claw throwing. No matter how the monster heaved and strained, he couldn't take on his previous size. The air whistled through the hole in his side.

Bully struck out at me, trying to tear me with his legs, whose claws were no less dangerous than those he threw, but a laser pistol shot hit him in the head, showering sparks around him. The pistol tricks Amy had learned had come in handy. She'd thrown the weapon from her right hand, stuck to the wall, into her left, taken her shot — and hit.

The air stank of burning flesh. Bully jumped back and ran right down the corridor, to the hole we'd come out of.

After a few leaps, he slowed. The sound of his legs scraping on the floor grew quieter. Bully almost helplessly turned his flat, eyeless head toward me. Part of his face was charred, with pink streaks running through it. I calmly took out my rifle and held down the trigger. While it charged, I walked toward Bully. He tried to limp away even faster, but the scientist's synthesized poison had begun to tighten its powerful grip. It seemed that Bully's every attempt to speed up only made him slower.

The band on my rifle turned blue.

I aimed.

"This'll teach you to bully us."

The shot cut the clawdart clean in half, burned him until he disappeared completely. Bully's remains fell to the floor, shrouded in tongues of flame and a cloud of smoke, seeping a bubbling liquid.

Chapter 24
Pistol Tricks

I HURRIED back to Amy. She squirmed on the wall, trying to pull out the claw in her shoulder. She'd already taken out the one in her right arm.

"Help me, damn it! This is uncomfortable. And fucking painful!"

I calmed the girl down with a gesture, moved a lock of her hair from her face, held her chin and kissed her on the lips.

"Ugh, you fucking piece of shit, I'm going to...!" Amy aimed her pistol at me.

I calmly brushed it aside, grabbed the claw and pulled. I did the same with the claw in her leg. Amy fell from the wall onto her haunches. She couldn't stand.

"Who the hell do you think you are?" she shouted.

"Sorry," I said, embarrassed. "I thought you'd like it."

"Are you an idiot? Did I give you any fucking hints?"

"Alright, alright, don't make a scene. This is Adam Online, people fuck around with each other and don't think twice about it."

"I'm not people! I don't want to fuck you. Why the hell do you think I was an angel?"

I took a medkit out of her backpack, injected her with a painkiller. Bound both her wounds. I went back into the dark of the corridor, found her laser pistol and tossed it to her. Then I took the vial of red liquid out of my bag.

"Drink the antidote and calm down."

She tore the vial from my hands and took a swallow.

I sat down next to her. "Sorry, I wasn't thinking. Chastity isn't compatible with Adam Online."

Amy gave me back the vial. "And you were so proud that you can tell the real and virtual worlds apart. Or do you assault injured women in real life too?"

"In real life, you're bald, you have no eyebrows or eyelashes. You talk as if you don't know that all anyone does in real life is sulk, do their job and hurry home to kill time until their next rotation."

"You're exaggerating. In my town people go to the park, cafes, bars... even the theater. Do you know about the theater?"

"There are no parks or theaters in my town. There are endless blocks of apartments and housing estates. And don't lie, not many people go to parks or theaters in your town."

Amy stretched out her bandaged leg, bending and unbending it. "Seems to work."

She rose, took out her tablet and started reading her stats. Then her torn UniSuit was replaced with the armored vest she was wearing before, and the UniSuit fell nearby. The bandages on her shoulder and leg remained. One of the conventions of this world that always reminded you that you were in a game.

Hmm, but back in Town Zero, Amy got changed for real, instead of through the neurointerface. She had no qualms about nudity. The girl was a puzzle.

I took my tablet out too, switched on the sound and read:

Learned skill: Night Vision.
All cats are grey in the dark, said the ancient wise ones. You can now differentiate shades of grey in the darkness.

I also got some experience for defeating the clawdart, and for Battlefield Surgery, and for Energy Weapons. After finishing with our tablets, we silently moved on. There was no more music. We took several turns along the corridor without running into any enemies. We stopped at a locked door. On it were large symbols in the aliens' language. Amy took out the arm with the bracelet, put it to the door and broke our silence.

"I think we're here."

"So we are," I said, walking into the spaceship's spacious bridge ahead of her.

A giant cracked projection panel covered the front wall of the bridge. Columns and lines of unknown symbols blinked. Objects like charts and diagrams span. At the center was a seat with proportions that wouldn't fit a human. There was an alien corpse sat in it. Along the walls were the spaceship's control stations, also blinking with unrecognizable holograms. Everything was flashing, sparking and hissing, making it abundantly clear that the ship's systems had been knocked out after the catastrophe.

A few more corpses littered the room, pierced by claws. A large crack loomed in the ceiling, its edges scratched. All this told the story of the clawdarts' sudden attack on the crew.

Keeping the crack in my sight, I walked around one of the workstations and approached the corpse in the seat. After ensuring that nothing was planning to attack us through the hole, I carefully nudged the corpse with my foot, expecting some kind of embryonic monster to burst from its chest. But the corpse just fell to the floor with a thud. At the same time, a flickering hologram appeared at the room's center. The alien, most likely the ship's captain, spoke.

"We greet you, earthlings. We hasten to you with peaceful inte... inte..." The program froze, flickered and leapt forwards: "We bring you a very valuable gift: all the knowledge of our civilization..."

"Where's the core?" Amy asked, losing interest in the hologram.

"If we listen to the end, we'll find out, but..."

"Quicker to find it ourselves?"

"Yep."

We split up and started searching the bridge. We opened all the side doors and adjoining cabins. We checked everything that had opening parts. If a door on my side didn't open, Amy threw me the alien arm and I placed the bracelet on the scanning device and threw it back.

"Now that's what I call 'extending a helping hand'" I said, catching it again.

The holographic alien continued to tell his story about how there was trouble in the Universe, that an 'ancient and mighty evil' had appeared in it, a certain mysterious race of unknown creatures that enslave and destroy entire planets. Earth was their next stop, the humanoid insisted. That's why they were eager to teach us to withstand the race of destroyers...

"Ugh, he's so annoying!" Amy complained. "Can we skip his mumbling somehow?"

I opened another door. "I found it!"

Amy crossed the bridge in a few leaps and looked over my shoulder. Her breath touched my ear.

At the center of the room was a mechanism that was distantly reminiscent of a mechanodestructor core, but in an alien style. It had no monowheel, and there were lots of extra parts and contours on its hull. There were thick cables connected to some of them, with a shining substance stretched along them. The cables ran into the ceiling, or along the walls and then into the floor.

To make sure, I aimed the tablet.

First Mechanodestructor Core
Take it to your client and claim your reward.

"Alright, time to pick it up," Amy sighed. She made to go into the room but stopped. "No, you go first, and I'll avenge you... I mean, cover you."

I laughed. "The hard part is behind us. There won't be any traps here. We've almost completed the quest. We even knocked out our rivals in an honest duel.

I approached the heart, crouched down and began to disconnect the cables one by one.

Amy stood behind me. "I wonder... In the intro, the old mechanodestructor said that all mechanodestructors came from this core. But why did it end up back in the Heap, on its home spaceship?"

"When we bring it to the quest giver, you can learn to his stories until the end of your taharration if you want."

The last cable fell to the floor, the substance within stopped glowing. The alien hologram, still harping on about 'secret knowledge', also disappeared. All the stations on the bridge stopped flickering with him. Then the light went out for a second and came back on, but this time it was red.

"What's happening now?" Amy asked fearfully.

I held the core by its base, trying to unscrew the central holder at the top.

"The self-destruct system has activated. This core's processor was probably keeping the ship functional. This spaceship was basically its frame. But don't hurry to run, the explosion won't happen until we leave. We have all the time in the world.

Amy didn't answer for some reason. Had she run off? Since I was holding the core, I couldn't fully turn around. I just heard a familiar spinning noise...

"Remember when you said that players kill other

players more often than NPCs?" Amy asked quietly.

"Sure..."

"You were right as always."

"Meaning?" I released the core and turned.

I was staring down the barrels of two laser pistols.

Chapter 25
30 Seconds Remaining

I STOOD in Town Zero's square. Amy had killed me! Damn it, McDonald!

She'd also robbed me: I was in a standard vest again, with that damned standard bag at my side with its set of useless booklets.

Images and thoughts whirled chaotically in my mind. I didn't know what to do first. Check my stats? My tablet notified me of some achievements... Probably "World's Unluckiest Man"... Two epic deaths in a single day.

Or should I try to figure out Amy's motives? Why did she do that? Surely not because of the kiss? Yes, she'd get some profit for killing me. Plus she'd be able to take the core back herself, finish the mission and claim the full reward.

But for such a cowardly murder in team play, her Reputation should drop to at least -60, i.e. 'Hated'. And that means that any positive NPC with a level a little higher would attack Amy. Weak NPCs would call the police or friendly bounty hunters on sight. Nobody would talk to her or trade with her. And that meant that all quests from peaceful NPCs would be closed to her.

There'd be a price on her head, and bounty hunters all over Rim Zero would start hunting her. Only those that wanted to become lone bandits with a view to joining some kind of gang would choose that path. But Amy really didn't seem like the kind of player that chose a short but happy life in Adam Online. There were special zones for anarchists that had no rule of law, where it was every man for himself. And those anarchists left Rim Zero pretty quickly: they started indiscriminately killing everyone they met in the town and quickly reached level five.

Overall, fans of lawlessness were very rare. When a player's reputation reached -80, i.e. 'Burning Hatred', their life in Adam Online turned into a living hell. All NPCs attacked them, not only weak ones, but even small critters: birds, beasts, insects... Everything. The price on their heads went up to half a million. That was enough for all the guilds to join the hunt. And most importantly, after getting killed with such a low Reputation, the character automatically died. You had to start over from nothing.

On the other hand, what did it matter why she'd ganked me? It was far more important to figure out my situation... To consider how I'd managed to flush all my achievements down the toilet yet again. First someone else's, and now my own too? Or I had to take hold of myself, calmly consider my next steps...

I started to feel despair. Having failed to 'take hold of myself', I dropped my hands... I realized that there was no sense in planning and starting anything else. What was the point? Didn't I have enough proof that I wasn't suitable for completing this mission? It would be far simpler...

I frowned and said:

"Rim Zero CS. Exit.

A message appeared on the back of my closed eyelids.

Are you sure you want to leave online before your rotation in the taharration pod ends, %Username%?

Attention: leaving early means that you will not be able to return to Adam Online until your cooldown time ends.

Attention: username cannot be %Username% (Error! Check taharration system settings).

So much for my adventure... How long had it taken? Less than twenty-four hours? How humiliating...

All I had to do was press 'Yes', then another message would appear to ask again if I was sure. Did I definitely want to go? I'd choose 'Yes' again. Then the final message would appear...

I chose 'Yes'. Straight away, without reading, I pressed 'Yes' a second time. A triangle appeared.

Attention: you have initiated the exit process from the Adam Online control system. Your consciousness will be returned to your body in 58 seconds... 57... 56...

That was that. When the timer got past the 30 second mark, the Cancel option would disappear. My return to reality would be final and irrevocable.

I recalled the feelings from the process last time.

First your legs were removed, but you didn't fall. You didn't have enough time to figure what was going on, or wave your hands, because your feeling in your arms disappeared, and then all your other feelings: warmth, cold, tactility. Next came the most unpleasant part: your lungs and heart stopped working. Not the real ones, of course, but the software emulating them. That didn't make it any easier. After all, your brain is used to controlling your body in reality. Illusory control over those digitized organs was maintained in the virtual world too. Then suddenly there was nothing to control.

A short moment of panic, a spasmodic attempt by the conscious to understand where reality had gone, virtual or not. It's a good thing it only lasted four seconds. Then darkness, weightlessness, the sensation of flight.

It was an amusing paradox: revival in the real world felt more like death, while transferring the consciousness to a QCP was like returning to life.

49 seconds.

A little longer and I'd see a blue dawn. It would quickly turn into a layer of blue liquid, pierced by the bright light. I'd see the edge of a cover moving to the side.

Or there wouldn't be any cover at all. The

landlord hadn't covered over my pod yet. He was planning to wait for me for a week, as agreed. He would have already received the signal notifying him of my mind's return to my body. Even now he was probably standing over the pod with a towel at the ready. Although I doubted it. He didn't seem like one to fawn over his customers. He was probably still watching his dumb standup shows, or asleep, with the QCP's notifications silenced.

The landlord wouldn't say anything even after my exit. He'd just grin, say it wasn't his business. You paid me for a full rotation. Your time, you do what you want with it.

46 seconds.

Only a medical robot would await me when I left the pod. It'd be holding a syringe full of restorative medicine and vitamins that would be completely unnecessary for me, being in the pod for less than a full day.

The only other thing waiting for me there would be a sense of defeat. And not just there: it would accompany me all the way back to Omsk. Then on the train to Bryansk. Then that feeling of defeat would sit with me at the MSB debriefing, where I'd tell them all about how I first lost Leonarm's levels, all three hundred of them, then arrogantly started over from nothing, reached level three in a day... and shamefully lost it all again.

Major General Makarov would look at me with reproach. He vouched for me, after all. After such an epic fu... failure, he'd probably stop inviting me to his Bryansk manor. He wouldn't offer me any kebabs made of real beef, or horse rides, or trips to tropical islands on the MSB's dime.

42 seconds.

Alright. The briefing would end. They'd thank me for my service to the motherland, consign the pathetic results of my work to a personal file. It'd be classified, encrypted and buried in an archive. Just like my career. They'd rush to summon the guy I beat in the contest from Novokuznetsk. He'd get another character. And if I tried to warn them that someone was tracking our attempts to reach the unexplored zones, they'd just send me back to my desk. They wouldn't trust me. Not me, not my expert opinion.

Of course, all the higher-ups in the MSB were from the first world. They didn't live in Adam Online. They wouldn't trust me, they'd tell me I was trying to exonerate myself.

39 seconds.

Then I imagined returning to my office, with no windows and doors. Sitting at the table, opening my projector panel and staring at the QCP download bars in boredom. Then Major General Makarov would visit me. Maybe he'd bring a bottle of synthetic whiskey as a gift. I'd start to apologize for not fulfilling his hopes. Makarov wouldn't bother with false modesty. He'd say it straight:

"Don't worry about it, Anton, your defeat is my

defeat. I thought your championship achievements in the past would help us now. Next time I'll be wiser." On parting, Makarov would ensure that I got everything due to me in my bank account. He'd wish me luck and leave. He would never contact me again as a specialist in Adam Online. I would forever be labeled a failure.

37 seconds.

Damn it! It was time to accept that I really didn't want to go back. Not like this, not with this outcome! I didn't want to live again like I'd lived all those years.

Who was I anyway? A simple employee of the Moscow Security Bureau in the department for managing Municipal Taharration Cluster QCPs. Like millions of other people, I performed meaningless work for the minimum wage.

But other people at least had hope that their rotation in reality would end, and they'd return to Adam Online. They'd become bizoids, mechanodestructors, angels and other fantastic creatures. But me — I'd stay me.

35 seconds.

Anton Brulov, 36 years old, MSB junior lieutenant. A man who fucked up his chance to serve the Motherland and become a hero. Previously known as Leonarm, top of the leaderboard in Adam Online. Now known as an arrogant idiot that threw his game twice.

What was my main mistake, after all? It was behaving like a wise-ass who knew everything, who could see through the whole game, who thought he was better than the rest, somehow above the fray.

If you want to win a fight, you can't be above it, you have to be in it. There's no other way. You can't underestimate the game, because then it'll take an estimation of you. The rules are the same in it for everyone. You either play or you don't. But in Adam Online, you're always playing, even if you think you aren't playing. I knew that, so why had I decided that the rules didn't apply to me?

32 seconds.

I felt my character's legs disappearing.

"Cancel, cancel!" I shouted desperately. "Cancel! Back, stop!"

The counter stopped, but I kept repeating, "Cancel, cancel", as if afraid that my signal wouldn't reach the CS.

Attention: user %Username% has cancelled quitting the Adam Online Control System.

Attention: username cannot be %Username% (Error! Check taharration system settings).

How do you rate our tech support service?

As usual, I gave five stars and gently sat down on the stones in Town Zero's square.

I needed time for the sensation in my body to return. At the same time, I tried to still my rampant train of thought. My emotional outburst had passed, and I felt desolate. I shambled over to a bench and sat down.

"Keep calm, Leonarm," I said to myself aloud. "You've realized your mistakes, try not to repeat them. If you die a third time in a day in Rim Zero, you might as well just resign and hang yourself. Although you could just hang yourself without resigning. Act as if you've only just started playing. A shameful past doesn't have to turn into a shameful future.

I took a deep breath, took out my tablet and opened my stats. Alright. What do I have?

Chapter 26
The Dark Side

I IDLY SWIPED my finger across the tablet, skimming through system messages.

You died again. Um... Congratulations.!
Penalty for dying in this zone: all experience gained for this level lost.
Your level: 3.

Open Book: +10 XP.
You were treated poorly. The one who called you a friend will get their karmic retribution.

Karmic retribution? Damn straight, Amy McDonald! Your motto was "I will find you and kill you"? Well, now it's mine too... Uhm, although it might look odd combined with my old "In search of digital immortality".

I chided myself out of habit. What kind of nonsense was I focusing on now? But then I calmed down: it was the old me, wise with reality, who considered Adam Online nonsense. The very attitude I was paying for. I had to go back to the psychology of the Leonarm of ten years ago, the man who whole-heartedly devoted his life to Adam Online. He could have handled this. He wouldn't have let some idiot girl kill him.

Strange that the older we get, the more we trust people. Or the more we *want* to trust them?

Lost items:
Tablet upgrades, add-ons reset to factory settings (+1 Knowledge lost).
Complimentary Glock X5 pistol.
Light Armored Vest (+1 Agility lost).
.44 Ammo
.416 Ammo
Alien Energy Rifle.
Synthesis Chamber.
Clawdart Poison.
Clawdart Antidote.
Simple Backpack.

That asshole Amy hadn't left me anything but the under-barrel flashlight. And, in the bag on my side, I found three copies of the same booklet: 'Guidebook on Rim Zero of the Adam Online Universe'. It was probably a bug linked to the error in determining my username. The local CS stubbornly gave me another booklet after death without deleting the previous ones. The lame thing was that I couldn't throw them out.

For losing a complimentary weapon: -1 Reputation.

Your current Reputation: -26 (Alarm).

The population of Adam Online is unconsciously disgusted by you. Hurry and improve this stat.

'Population' meant NPCs. Players, of course, felt nothing unconsciously.

An NPC cop walked by me. Naturally, he reacted to my Reputation. He took out his baton and straightened his cap, which bore the crest of Rim Zero.

"What're you doin'? You ain't seen the 'No Loitering' sign?"

"There isn't one."

The policeman waved the baton in front of my face. "You see this?"

It wasn't worth trying to prove to the cop that his baton wasn't a sign. I just walked off.

It was always fun to see how NPC characters got generated. If a person from the second half of the twenty-first century traveled to our time and went into Adam Online, he'd be amazed at how many cultural markers of his own era he saw. For example, there hadn't been cops in uniforms like that for a long time, and they didn't use batons. Must have been nearly a century since then. Just two or three generations divided me from that man from the past. Due to taharration, the lifespan of modern humanity had increased, and that automatically stretched out our cultural development. Moreover, it was said that there were more than a few people in Adam Online who were around a hundred standard years old. They were still young when Nelly Valeeva and her Labsetek team presented the first taharration pod to the world.

The man from the past would probably be annoyed that we weren't so different from him. We were even worse: we lived in grey cities and looked like zombies. He'd lament until he got to the first world. Now those were people living in the future. Surrounded by wonders, nanotechnology, total automation, with advanced medicine and space flight.

I checked myself. I was procrastinating, putting off my decision: what to do next. What would the Leonarm of my youth do?

I checked the journal on my tablet. There were two quests: Fair-Haired Beasts and All My Children.

There was no point in even thinking about shooting tech-support bots. My Reputation was already catastrophically low. That same Reputation prevented me from taking the quest from the bus driver. He'd flat out refuse to talk to me.

I could go to the Mercurian Planes, start looking for some crap, but... Leonarm wouldn't have done that. He wasn't interested in pointless farming, pointlessly finding and bringing and selling.

I could wander the town, find NPCs, but their quests would be predictable, whereas the puzzle of the driver was something I hadn't seen before. That quest had brought boosts, experience and valuable items over the course of a mile.

Ah, yes, I could go and look for the First Mechanodestructor core again, but... the younger

Leonarm wouldn't have done that. Firstly, I'd already done it. Secondly, I had no money for equipment and ammunition. I'd get killed right at the gates, as soon as I got off the bus. And by other players, not even the spiderbots.

I rose from the bench and headed toward the bus station. Even if the driver wouldn't talk to me, I should try to fix the situation.

Along the way I felt all the charms of having a big minus to Reputation.

I passed a Tenshot on the street, decided to go in. Maybe I'd find some minor quests. But the android salesman hurried out and stood in the doorway, showing that he wouldn't let me in. Two cops appeared as if from nowhere. They waved their batons and followed me for a while, exchanging remarks.

"Hey, G, you smell that stink?"

"Yeah, Hugh, it reeks."

They laughed behind my back. Then they fell behind.

A few steps later, a waterfall crashed down on my head. I looked up and saw some housewife laughing from an open window, holding a bucket.

"Freshen up, you animal!"

On the other hand, when I walked past some slums where the bandit character types hung around, a few called out to me.

"Hey, I got a job for you, bro! Hey, waiiit!"

I stubbornly walked on by. I didn't want to get involved with that rabble. Of course, it would have helped for a little while. A few raids and robberies, I would have reached level five, got some Reputation in the criminal community, unlocked a few bandit classes, but in the long term it wouldn't have served me well. I needed to have a good relationship with the authorities. And I had no desire to be a criminal. Not in life and not in the game.

But the criminals thought differently. A bald one caught up to me. He wore sunglasses, heavy boots and leather jacket over his naked torso. Not a cheap outfit for Rim Zero. An ammunition belt hung across his bare chest, and at his sides were two holsters with Lefaucheux revolvers.

"Hey, 'sup with you? Didn't hear us calling ya?"

I put my hand into my bag to pull out my tablet, but the bald guy grabbed his revolver.

"Hold it a sec. My name's Offo. Who're you?"

So he wasn't an NPC. Those don't react when you aim your tablet at them to see their stats.

"As if you don't know," I muttered. "I'm sure you read my stats already."

Baldy laughed. "Maybe, Leonarm, but don't fret. I see your Reputation is in the shitter. You're one of us."

"Well, that depends."

I regretted leaving my stats open for anyone to read. A frustrating mistake. What should I do? Get into a fight with a well-armed bandit?

"Me and the brotherhood, we're looking for more soldiers for the gang. We just so happen to need a tracker."

"Good luck to you," I said.

"What?" said Offo in surprise. "I don't get it."

"I don't want to join your gang."

"I don't get it. Why not? You seem pretty determined to come over to the dark side so far. Let's try one raid at least. I have a quest..." The fearsome Offo's intonation suddenly became pleading. "I want to level up as a bandit, and to do that I need to complete a quest. I gotta form a gang of a blademaster, a martial artist, a tracker and me, a gunman. And rob some building all together."

"Why a tracker?"

"How should I know? Quest says that. Maybe the tracker has to stand guard. You got good Perception, right?"

I softened my stance a little. "Who're you planning to raid?"

"Whoever, man. We're going to hit a We Fix It! workshop. Should be a few thousand gold, some gear, weapons."

I wanted to wish him luck and move on, but a plan began to form in my mind. It was clear, elegant, unexpected. Just like the Leonarm who was rightfully called a champion.

"Alright. I have an idea about who we can hit."

"Who?"

"The bus drivers that take players to the Heap."

Offo scratched his bald head and whistled. Two other guys joined us. Both were in standard grey vests and pants, only they had backpacks instead of shoulder bags. The first was a man around forty years old, with tired eyes drooping down at the corners as if he was constantly fighting sleep. The second was a woman around thirty, also bald, her face covered in tattoos. She obviously liked to break social norms.

"My name's Ghost," the tired man introduced himself.

"Banshee," the woman said, playing with a huge knife. I saw the pommel of a short saber or katana over her shoulder. I didn't need the tablet to tell me that she was the blademaster.

"Leonarm thinks we should hit some driver on the route to the Heap."

Still twirling her knife, Banshee answered sharply without looking at me. "He's talkin' shit. Why would we? I don't trust this Leonarm."

Ghost, whose build wasn't close to that of a martial artist, agreed. "What do they have for us? Why the fuck would we want a bus?"

"I'll tell you," I said confidently. "The drivers may be NPCs, but they're very smart. I see you guys are seasoned adamites, true players. Tell me, you ever gone to some zone and found you didn't have enough space in your backpack? Had to throw out some valuable items to make space for other valuable items?"

"Sure. I once had to leave a fancy Kalashnikov in the Heap when I found a box of three Salingers."

"Right. Then you went back to pick it up and it was gone, right? Even though you hid it well?"

"Yeah, that happens, but not always. I thought it was because the zone reloads for new players..."

"Nope. Nothing disappears without a trace in

Adam Online, just like in real life. The drivers pick up the stuff we drop."

"No way. Why would they?"

"Why do you think? They resell them to the stores. I saw it myself, a driver who always had a cigar in his mouth, he kept a whole cache of weapons under his seat."

Ghost shrugged. "How 'bout it, guys? Sounds good, low risk. All the workshop owners are armed, and the police patrol regular. We could die raiding them... Before we reach the safehouse..."

Banshee span her knife even faster, probably leveling up some skill. "I don't believe it. If the drivers had guns, everyone would know."

Piece of work, this girl. I frowned.

"I didn't get to the most important part. There's a bug in this system. The drivers sell loot, but they don't spend money. They're NPCs, they don't have to. They just fulfil two functions: cleaning up zones and putting lost items back into circulation. They keep the cash.

Offo's eyes lit up. "If that's true, then... the drivers must have saved up millions over all these years!"

"Nah, bro, just a few hundred thousand," I corrected him. "Their accounts are reset every time the local CS is updated. The last update was quite a while ago."

Offo and Ghost were convinced. They were already getting ready to run to the bus station, but Banshee leapt toward me suddenly, drawing the katana from behind her back. She placed a knife at my stomach and the katana at my throat at the same time.

In other words, she was just as flashy and showy as I suspected.

"Fine," she said. "Let's take a run at the driver."

"Gotta be a fast run to catch a bus," Offo laughed.

"But if you're trying to trick us," she pressed the blade harder into my throat, "I'll cut off your head. Believe me, I'll do it quick and without warning."

I widened my eyes, tried my hardest to look scared. "Why would I lie, Banshee? Look at my Reputation. I'm just like you guys.

Banshee lowered her weapons and stepped back. "Then let's go, guys," I suggested. "I'll explain the plan on the way."

Chapter 27
Three-Ring Circus

A HUGE WHITE HORSE carried Jamilla along the edge of the bluff. The girl's thick black hair streamed in the wind, tied up with a blue ribbon. This was the fallen angel skin that the real Jamilla Chang-Balyeva, a sixty-year-old woman from Chinese Kazakhstan, preferred. It had cost a small fortune.

Even when nobody else was around, Jamilla liked to appear young, stately, beautiful. This skin was marked with Beauty Standard A+ Class, which meant that according to the control systems' statistics, it was this exact combination of physical characteristics that matched the aesthetic preferences of fifty two percent of Adam Online users that appreciated feminine beauty.

And fifty two percent was a great deal. After all, more and more adamites had gotten sick of both the opposite gender and their own, and had begun to practice sex with other creatures.

The horse's giant hooves knocked down stones, which soundlessly flew downwards. The bottom of the cliff was out of sight, covered in swirling yellow clouds.

The heights of the other mountains were also shrouded, either in smoke or in clouds.

There was no particular need to ride along such a dangerous precipice and risk slipping down, but Jamilla liked to live on the edge. In addition, all her game experience told her that if flying creatures attacked her, it would be easiest to detect their approach from the edge.

Jamilla, Fallen Angel.
Class: Blademaster, Healer, Wise One.
Level: 342.

The heavy sky, like the ceiling of a stone cave, almost touched Jamilla's head. Sinister red lightning bolts flashed in breaks in the cloud cover. On occasion a distant roar broke in the distance, and the silhouette of a flying dragon was clearly outlined against a red flash.

That dragon had been pursuing Jamilla since she entered the unexplored zone of Rim Five. A day ago, maybe? Or more precisely, twenty hours. But the reptile was in no hurry to attack. Perhaps it wasn't scripted to attack at all, but to wait for the player that would tame it.

Jamilla's mighty white horse was covered in laminar armor forged by the master craftsmen of Rim Five. The steed was a unique pet given as a reward for a quest for the king of some country Jamilla found in the unexplored areas of Rim Five. He was fast, tireless and practically invincible. Which meant he could have saved Jamilla even after falling off the cliff. He would have died himself, but the rider would be barely wounded.

He was called Tulpar.

The path crossed a huge crack. Jamilla had to ride backwards and spur the horse. He gathered momentum and leapt over the abyss. Jamilla's cloak flew open in the flight, revealing the black wings folded behind her back. Tulpar landed heavily, throwing up small stones and striking sparks off big ones.

Of course, the horse's rear legs had to dramatically begin to slide back into the gap. But he crawled out with his rider.

Jamilla turned around and saw that the crack was three hundred feet long. Without Tulpar, she would have had to spend a long time finding a way round, or go in a different direction entirely. The unexplored zones were extremely hard to travel. Such flying leaps were one of Tulpar's skills, but the skill cooldown was two whole hours.

No sooner had she ridden away from the crack than a paper scroll unrolled before her face.

Your stubbornness and endurance in overcoming obstacles knows no bounds!
Pioneer skill increased to level 12: +100 XP.

Jamilla reined in her horse. She ran her hand over the scroll, folding it. It crumpled and disappeared into thin air. She took a tube out of her shoulder bag and threw it out before her, unfolding it into a map of Adam Online. It looked hand-drawn, not printed or three-dimensional like in the mechanodestructor neurointerface or the human UniSuits.

At the center of the map was the tiny dot of Rim Zero. Around it was Rim One, Rim Two... Each zone stretched out farther than the last until they reached the gigantic Rim Five, whose outer borders were blank on the map. At the unexplored edges were several zones highlighted green: those were the areas Jamilla had been the first to discover. Each discovery leveled up her Pioneer skill.

Right now, the borders of a new area flashed with a question mark. Jamilla climbed off Tulpar, took the map hanging in the air and dragged it behind her.

She sat on a stone and spoke to the horse, "Well, what shall we call these lands?"

The horse just neighed in response and struck a heavy hoof on the ground, urging her to move on.

"Call them Jamilla's Tomb," someone said.

Jamilla threw away the map and jumped up, drawing her huge sword. It glowed with energy from damage enchantments. The clouds seemed to thicken. It grew even darker. The enchanted sword shined like a torch. But however much Jamilla looked around, she couldn't see who had spoken.

Tulpar neighed in alarm, reared up and then galloped off to the left. Then Jamilla could clearly see a big black cube floating above the ground. She read:

Grisha, Mechanodestructor.
Frame: LeCube.
Guild: Black Wave.
Level: 268.

Holding her sword in both hands, Jamilla slowly walked around the strange cube. Sparks occasionally fell from the blade. Multicolored lightning flashed in the sky: the cube threw off crooked shadows, first purple, then red, then green.

Jamilla knew all about the Black Wave. And she'd heard the news that they'd begun an undeclared hunt against players that had decided to explore the undiscovered territories.

She waved her sword. "So you dispute my right to name these lands?"

Grisha's image was projected on one side of the cube. He used his real face, not the head of his mechanodestructor core.

"Nonsense. On the contrary, I want to help. Jamilla's Tomb sounds beautiful."

"What is that thing on you? What's this black box?"

"You're about to find out."

The cube shifted. The horse reacted with an alarmed neigh and tried to strike the cube with its hooves.

"Calm, Tulpar," Jamilla ordered. She'd never seen anything like the strange cube. As an experienced player, she knew that when encountering an unknown enemy, you had to give them the chance to attack first, to reveal their capabilities.

The horse retreated at Jamilla's order. But the cube, in the meantime, split into four smaller cubes. All displayed Grisha's face, but now they were arranging themselves around Jamilla in a semicircle.

"What's this? Some surreal circus?"

"The circus hasn't begun yet," Grisha answered. "To start, I want to invite you to join our guild."

"Firstly, I've already had three invites. I rejected them all. Secondly, 'to start' what?"

"You get that I won't let you go any further."

"Everyone gets that. The Black Wave wants to explore the distant lands of Rim Five on its own and move into Rim Six. You're starting to get on the wrong side of people. Keep on like this and all the explorers will rise up against you."

Grisha's faces frowned. "So you refuse?"

"What do you think?"

"You're making a mistake."

"Really?" Jamilla laughed. "Maybe you're the one making a mistake by coming here at your level."

The surface of the cube on the extreme left opened up, and a furry bizoid emerged from it, a mix of a bear and a monkey. A strong DNA modification, but no danger to Jamilla.

"Ta-da," Grisha said. "The first trick in our show, a bear on a bicycle."

"Fine, you brought a friend, but he's even weaker than you. And I still don't know why I should be afraid of some dumb black cube. How did you level up at all? Concentrated really hard on being a geometric shape?"

The surface of the next cube also opened like a bomb hatch, and a fallen angel emerged from it. He held a spear in one hand. Judging by the color, it was enchanted with poison. In his other hand he held a long transparent shield shaped like a droplet of water. The fallen angel spread his black wings, preparing for a fight in which those like him could flutter around, achieving greater freedom of movement.

"So these are your clowns?" Jamilla asked.

She saw that the Fallen Angel known as Crusher was just as low in level as the furry bizoid Most Ancient Evil. She'd deal with both of them. She'd have to try, of course, but there was no way she could lose.

Jamilla undid the clasp at her throat. Her cloak fell and two giant wings stretched out behind her back. Each feather was its own blade, and each blade was enchanted with some form of extra elemental damage. Jamilla had a full set: fire, ice, poison, energy shock, plasma lightning. And dozens and dozens of other spells. Everything that could be bought in the most majestic temples or from hermits living in the desert. One feather of her wing was worth a whole low-level warrior.

Crusher even took a step back. He and his pathetic spear were worthless against such power.

"Pretty birdie," Grisha said.

The third cube opened and divulged a medium-sized spiderbot. It unfolded itself and stood back on its legs, deploying two machine guns ahead. The spiderbot wasn't a player, but an 'autosen': an autonomous sentinel. It decided on its own where to fire during battle, and who to help or cover. Autosens were an expendable resource in guilds. They could even independently go on missions, talking to the same NPCs as players and completing quests to level up. In a strange irony of fate, this NPC was the highest level of all the attackers. It was up at level one hundred and ninety-nine. It was a very rare autosen.

"Is that all your circus freaks?" Jamilla asked. "And what are you capable of yourself, Grisha? Or are you just a black box of tricks for your harmless rabbits to jump out of?"

"Enough talk, let's dance!" the bizoid growled, rushing to attack first.

Golden rings of light surrounded Jamilla's body. When they dissipated, she wore a helmet and armor of qualia — the rarest and most durable material found in Rim Five. It was used to create armor that could withstand not only any magic, but also a shot from a mechanodestructor's laser cannon.

Jamilla decided to hide her secret skills, so she parried Most Ancient Evil's attack with a simple block. The bizoid's face collided with the blade of her sword. Having taken damage amounting to almost a quarter of his entire health, the bizoid leapt back under the cover of the autosen and began to literally lick his wounds: one of the skills of his DNA modification that allowed him to regenerate quickly.

The fallen angel attacked at the same time as the bizoid. But his spear strike ended up aimed at Tulpar. The battle steed had put himself between the fallen angel and its master, bringing the might of its hooves down on Crusher. Damage numbers fell from

Tulpar, but more fell from Crusher:

-230

-126

-176

...

Every strike brought the fallen angel closer to death. Crusher gathered his strength and finally managed to defend himself. The stallion's hooves drummed against the transparent watery surface of the shield. Now each strike actually dealt a little damage to Tulpar. The dumb animal didn't realize this, and Jamilla had to call him back.

The water shield was high-level, but a completely standard shield. Jamilla took out a spell scroll, unfolded it and threw it. A green column rose from the ground and lunged for Crusher's shield. Seaweed instantly grew across its watery surface. The shield transformed into a lump of stinking slime with branches sticking out, then collapsed at Crusher's feet in a heap of mud.

Crusher leapt up and took flight to save himself from Jamilla's magical ranged sword strike. He somersaulted backwards in the air, aiming to land and hide behind one of LeCube's boxes.

A transparent copy of Jamilla's sword separated from the original and rushed after Crusher. He had already hidden behind the cube and folded up his wings, but the transparent sword flew in an arc and fell on its enemy like a guided missile. It was impossible to see where the sword fell behind the cube, but transparent shards flew off as if from a big explosion, carrying with them black feathers and chunks of flesh.

Jamilla (Fallen Angel) killed Crusher (Fallen Angel) with a Spectral Sword.

"Not bad," Grisha commented. "I see I shouldn't have given up on magic, it has its advantages."

Jamilla didn't answer. She was focused on the battle. She suspected that Grisha's cubes might be useful for more than just transport. He remained a mystery with unknown capabilities. She had to consider that the greatest threat.

While Jamilla was killing Crusher, the autosen did its job, raining fire down on Jamilla and Tulpar from both its machine guns. Most of the bullets ricocheted off Jamilla's wings and she took no significant damage, but the horse's health fell.

Jamilla took out and cast a Death to Machines spell scroll. It took out all machines below level one hundred and twenty, including mechanodestructors and androids. All the rest temporarily lost the ability to move. The higher the level, the lower the duration. The autosen froze and a golden ring appeared above it, quickly filling with red: the indicator of its time immobilized. But its machine guns continued to fire — it just couldn't aim the fire at Jamilla anymore.

Unfortunately, foolish Tulpar stood side on to the autosen's frozen machine guns in defense of his mistress. That type of pet was famed for bravery bordering on insanity. Their stupidity balanced out their strength: when they encountered an enemy, they often ignored commands and went for the enemy until they won. Or until they died, like now.

Using the delay her pet had created, Jamilla flapped her wings, took off, turned in the air — her sword left a shining trail behind her — and descended on the autosen. By then, the autonomous sentry had already begun to emerge from its stupor. It began to turn its machine guns up toward her.

Jamilla dealt a single blow that cut the machine in half. The burning halves melted into nothingness, turning into streams of light that flew into Jamilla.

That was her Lifestealer ability at work. Every defeated enemy filled up the mage's Health.

"I hate your magic tricks!" the bizoid roared, rushing to attack again.

A trace of his movement could be sign behind him as he ran, a clear sign that the bizoid had used Time Slow. Jamilla had just enough time to notice that and draw her sword, but the bizoid, barely visible because of his speed, easily dodged the blade and flew at her, knocking her to the ground.

However, that was all Most Ancient Evil could do. No matter how hard he bit or scratched her, the qualia armor was impenetrable. All he could do was scratch it, etching small complex patterns on the surface.

Jamilla almost casually kicked the bizoid away, at the same time releasing a magic strike: Most Ancient Evil flew forty feet, landed on his back and howled. A second strike took away nearly all his health. The bizoid turned and stood on his hind legs.

"You don't like magic tricks?" Jamilla asked.

"Well, I don't like players that turn into animals."

Falling onto his front legs, the bizoid crawled to the cube as if seeking refuge. He was probably begging Grisha to help him in the chat. In one flying leap, Jamilla reached the bizoid and stamped him into the ground. The furry creature's spinal column crunched, his body bent almost into a wheel, then went limp.

Jamilla (Fallen Angel) killed Most Ancient Evil (Bizoid) with a Spectral Sword.

Jamilla waved her sword, using a spell to charge its ranged ability. There were two left, that should be enough.

She turned to Grisha. "So what are you capable of except for condemning your friends to death?"

"What am I capable of? Let's see."

The four cubes stirred and began to move toward each other. Soon all four merged into one big cube.

Jamilla quickly extended her wings and release a volley of feathers. When they reached LeCube, they stuck into its surfaces, knocking out chunks of black mass.

Chapter 28
Last Chance

GRISHA HAD DELIBERATELY sacrificed his guildmates to observe Jamilla's combat style. He could deduce which skill branch she'd leveled based on the spells she'd used. On the other hand, considering her level, that didn't solve that much. It was clear already: Jamilla had leveled up everything she could, and moreover, she'd obtained special abilities and weaponry by completing missions in the new zones she'd unlocked.

When she spread her wings and launched a stream of feathers at Grisha, he decided he wouldn't keep his ace up his sleeve.

The feathers changed color in flight and took on an aura of fire, acid or energy, showing which type of magic they were enchanted with. In response, Grisha used a software configuration that was also one of Nika's own developments, that didn't copy any already existing frame. Naturally, it had cost an insane amount of money, like everything Nika crafted. Grisha felt like a new player after he bought it — he had almost no money left.

Accept program configuration LeCube_000004?

For a second, Grisha ceased to exist. His consciousness turned off and on again like the beat-up assembly line in the synthetic-soy meat factory where Grisha worked in real life.

And the strange thing was that he couldn't figure out: if his consciousness switched off, then who was it who recognized, in that millisecond of non-existence, that he'd been switched off?

The magical feathers slowly flew through the air as if piercing through an invisible obstacle. Jamilla's hair slowly fell, locks elegantly tangling and sliding across her face.

Time Slow was a standard skill. Both magical and technological races could do it, but... Grisha had never felt time run this slowly. Then he suddenly realized that it wasn't Time Slow at all. It was something else.

He realized that he was no longer alone. Tens of thousands of his consciousnesses filled the battlefield. He saw the scene from every point, every angle, every moment in time. He could lay out those moments like cards in a casino, fan them out into a line.

"Damn... Beautiful."

He saw that LeCube had split up into the smallest particles of which it was made, the component nanomass. Each particle got a separate copy of Grisha's consciousness. It was as if he'd copied himself a hundred and forty thousand times in the same moment. And each of those Grishas viewed the world from his own angle, thought his own thoughts, but they all joined into a kind of shared center that was him — Grisha.

This meant that the slowing effect wasn't Time Slow at all. Time itself had lost its fluidity, becoming a set of fragments, and Grisha could do what he liked with each of them. At the same time, in his hundred-and-forty-thousand-strong form, he continued to see LeCube's interface, with two indicators occupying most of the screen:

CN Expenditure: 8,200 per minute.
Expected configuration maintenance time: 8 minutes.

At the bottom was a line of rapidly changing numbers: the indicator for CN being converted into energy units. Grisha frowned and cleared the details from the screen. He wasn't one to track his resources until the very end. He was a fighter, not a strategist. That was exactly why his brother planned all Black Wave's operations, while Grisha showed his skills in each individual battle.

And he knew: for victory, speed in battle was more important than preparation for it. When you act quickly, you act intuitively and surprise yourself, which means you surprise the enemy too.

The battlefield was shrouded in the black cloud that LeCube had turned into. Jamilla looked around in bewilderment. Her feathers pierced the cloud with no visible damage. Then she tried to fly out of the cloud surrounding her, but as soon as she jumped, part of the cloud thickened, transforming into a tentacle that pulled her back to the earth.

Grisha wasn't just controlling the situation, he was controlling each fragment of time in the situation. And his personal experience told him that Jamilla would try to choose the most effective means of resistance next. It surely existed. That meant he had very little time to win.

Without giving Jamilla time to think, Grisha began a decisive attack.

His CN cost immediately rose, and the timer fell down to six minutes. When it ran out, LeCube would take on its base form and would be defenseless against Jamilla's powers. She'd be able to break it with nothing but her fist.

Tentacles, spears and blades began to form around her. Jamilla parried one with her sword, struck others back with a shield that formed on her arm the moment she was struck. But some strikes hit her armor and pierced it.

Much to his enjoyment, Grisha's interface lit up with damage notifications. Jamilla's health bar dropped but began to grow back as soon as Grisha stopped attacking or Jamilla parried several strikes in a row.

"Right," Grisha said. "So her Armor regenerates her Health?"

He stopped aiming strikes at the weak joints of her armor, and redirected them to the armor itself, aiming to weaken it to a point where she would either lose her regeneration entirely or its rate would drop far enough for his damage to overtake it.

The sword in Jamilla's hands changed into a spectral axe. A good sign: her best weapon was out of action. The shield appeared on her arm less and less often, and was soon replaced by an ordinary non-magical shield. Which was actually very good, also made of pure qualia. Jamilla had a whole fortune equipped!

A red line blinked in Grisha's interface:

Expected configuration maintenance time: 4 minutes.

In addition, Jamilla did exactly what he'd feared: she figured out that to fight this strange cloud, she'd need to use a spell against ethereal creatures!

She drew a scroll, letting a few painful strikes land. Her Armor was no longer regenerating her Health quickly enough, and it began to drop threateningly. She unfurled the scroll... It was a Phantom Explosion!

A bright blue spiral curled around Jamilla and quickly expanded, spinning ever faster. Some of the cloud even got pulled into the spiral.

A strike — then the spiral split into a thousand points of light, striking at LeCube's cloud.

Grisha had been waiting for that strike. He was ready but couldn't avoid the damage. He drew most of his microscopic copies away from the hit zone, but the rest were forced to hold around Jamilla, keeping her in her hazy prison.

For the first time in the battle against Grisha, Jamilla finally got a notification that she'd dealt him some damage! And sizeable damage:

Health: 22,340/52,000.

Another spell and he'd be done for!

Another spiral began to form around the girl. Its threads span with threatening speed. Grisha used almost all his available CN. With the loss of several tens of thousands of CN, he'd also lost control over the time fragments. The world once more took on its usual speed and movement.

Clenching his teeth (which he didn't have, but he still felt as if he'd clenched them), Grisha gathered the rest of his disparate cloud and formed it into one gigantic blade like a curved sword, then rushed into the gap between the strands of the spiral. He did so just as the spell was about to release in a phantom explosion... The spell completed, but a split second after the cloudy blade ran Jamilla through. The remains of her armor broke off in shards, falling to the scorched ground. The phantom explosion dissipated along with it, dispersing into the earth.

Jamilla fell face down onto the stone, then turned... Her health bar was nearly at zero.

Grisha had seven left.

But Jamilla was still alive. Her Last Chance skill had activated. He had the same skill himself. A player could use it to live for a short time after death. Their mobility was limited, but they could try to finish off their enemy.

If the player won, all their Health was returned. The first level of the skill gave just ten seconds. Considering Jamilla's level, she had no less than three minutes.

Jamilla didn't try to attack. She decided to use her remaining time to negotiate. "Don't kill me."

"Why not?"

Grisha took on his base form and hovered above Jamilla's recumbent form. He began regenerating at the same time. If Jamilla so much as tried to go for a weapon, he'd crush her.

"I... I have a lot of money. I can buy my life. Two million, agreed?"

"And then you'll keep exploring?"

Jamilla didn't answer.

The Black Cube descended to the ground, taking on the form of a humanoid robot. A plasma gun formed on one of its arms. He aimed it at Jamilla. She shifted.

"Did you not used to wonder why someone was hiding from us, what was in the lands of Rim Six?"

"I wondered. I don't care."

"How can you be such a jackass?"

The robot's mechanical lips stretched into something resembling a smile.

"I actually think that all this commotion over the supposedly secret Rim Six is just another quest for high-level players. Some want to get there, and others want to stop them. That's how we're split into teams. Like a kind of 'capture the flag'."

Jamilla was watching him, head raised. After he finished, she slumped back to the ground. "You're a moron."

"No, you."

A burst of white plasma flew from the cannon and burnt Jamilla to a cinder.

Grisha (Mechanodestructor) killed Jamilla (Fallen Angel) with an Arena Plasmagun.

Messages flooded the interface. He'd earned enough experience for his level to jump all the way up to two hundred and ninety. Grisha immediately invested the multitude of skill points he'd earned into LeCube's configurations and skills.

He increased its CN capacity. His experience of fighting Jamilla showed that he could no longer rely on LeCube's originality. Jamilla knew what kind of weapon to use against him, and soon everyone else would know too. He'd need to claim the reward from Mariam as soon as possible and buy as much CN as he could from Nika.

After all his changes, his stats were:

LeCube (Mechanodestructor Frame).

Base CN: 140,000 (minimum amount for full functioning).

CN Storage: 190,000 (one experience point gives +10,000 to storage volume).

Grisha wanted to invest another ten points in expanding his CN storage, but prudence won out when he considered that he didn't yet have the income to fill it up. At least until Nika took pity on him and gave him a discount.

Special stats of LeCube frame:

Transformation time: 2.2 seconds.
Movement speed in base form: 25 mph.
Energy unit cost per min at rest: 1.
Energy unit cost per min while moving: 5.
Core Health regeneration: +10% per minute.
CN conversion to energy units: 1:1
Forcefield.
Invisibility: 5 seconds.
…

Grisha's pride in leveling up his frame was darkened by the fact that for now, there was only one LeCube, so there was nobody to compete with.
Then:

Available software configurations:

1. 'Grenika', flying machine.
2. 'LeKub_000102', humanoid battle mech.
3. 'LeKub_000004', ethereal creature.
4. 'LeKub_000002(ver4)', three-person transport vehicle.
5. 'LeKub_000011', forcefield.

Contact Nika to discuss purchasing other software configurations.

Grisha got annoyed again. Why did Nika give her configs such idiotic names? All those numbers were soulless representations of the frame's incredible possibilities.

"I need to tell her to work on her names. I'm her only client, after all."

Each configuration had its own built-in stat window. It was all standard. The flying machines had standard speed, altitude, armament and invisibility to radar. The same for the battle mechs: height, part mobility, number of limbs and so on. For the 'LeKub_000002(ver4)' transport, the number of seats could be increased to five, but that was the limit of its abilities.

But 'LeKub_000004', the ethereal creature, made him stop to think. It was this configuration that helped him defeat an enemy as strong as Jamilla. The config's drawback was that in 'ethereal creature' mode, you couldn't use firearms or energy weapons, only variations of hacking and slashing weapons. There was a long list of abilities to level up underneath LeKub_000004. Grisha didn't bother messing around with parameters like Axe Size or Cutting Strike Damage. All that required long and thoughtful work. So he invested in something vital: he increased his resistance to Phantom Explosion. Jamilla would surely want to take vengeance against him, and that meant she'd buy the most powerful spell scrolls she could.

Next Grisha upgraded the Grenika's speed characteristics. He added speed and maneuverability. Unfortunately, he didn't have enough CN left to transform into the flying machine. He'd have to make the journey back to the nearest respawn tower in the form of a slow-moving mech. It could move at the speed of a car. He'd take his base form to get over the gorges and ravines.

Time to go back?

Or...

Grisha stood at the edge of the cliff and looked out, to where the unexplored supposedly hid, places many adamites wished to explore.

Hmm. Was it just the thirst for adventure that motivated them? It couldn't have been a coincidence that several organizations had sent agents at the same time. That loser Leonarm... Who was this Mariam anyway, when it came down to it? She was obviously not a person, but some sort of projection, an avatar. Who stood behind the avatar? Certain powers that don't want to be discovered?

What if...

A message from Fortunado interrupted his thoughts.

Well done, bro! Great job. Hurry back. A whole coalition has formed against us after what you did to the Langoliers.

"And what does the coalition want?"

To destroy us, obviously. A guild war is coming like we've never seen. The Black Wave versus everyone else in Adam Online.

Grisha cast a final glance forward, then turned to head back.

Chapter 29
Guild Wars

GRISHA AND FORTUNADO were young, so they took little interest in the past. It was more important for the young to plan the future, not to think about how things used to be, about how there's nothing new under the sun. But even the old adamites couldn't recall a guild war like this, when a majority of guilds banded together against one.

Actually, guild wars were everyday affairs in Adam Online. People were always settling disputes, capturing enemy territories or liberating their own. Guilds fought for veins of valuable resources like oil and metals.

Situational alliances in which several guilds united in a fight against another alliance of guilds were also nothing new. But there always tended to be some kind of balance, like five guilds against seven. This may have been the first time that almost all the guilds united against one, albeit the most powerful.

Moreover, individual players marched against the Black Wave as well. Jamilla was something of a cultural icon, an example to follow for all the players that liked to spend their time exploring new zones alone.

The fact that Grisha from the Black Wave had not only killed their 'cultural icon', but also named a new zone 'Jamilla's Tomb' made solo pioneers drop their exploring and begin to plan attacks against the Black Wave, coordinating their actions with the main guilds.

The Viatichi and Golden Horde guilds became the core of the coalition. Ordinarily, both clans were constantly at each other's throats. The Viatichis took only Slavic people into their guild, demanding confirmation of identity in real life. This meant they were few in number, but very rich adamites. They always had excellent equipment, and their base in Rim Four, known as Venyov Parish[5], was a small but well-fortified zone. All the Viatichis were human and they wore identical UniSuits, strengthened with the Nevsky heavy infantry exoskeleton. They considered it beneath human dignity to play as mechanodestructors, androids or bizoids. And since they were extremely religious, they despised the blasphemous angels even more.

Disdain for the other races weakened the military might of the Viatichis: after all, they had as much need for the big guns as everyone else. A jet fighter controlled by a human was always less maneuverable than one controlled by a mechanodestructor who *was* the fighter itself.

---

[5] Venyov Parish (now Venyovsky District): historically, the site of the legendary capital of the Viatichi's medieval kingdom which was situated in the vicinity of the Russian town of Venyov.

The Golden Horde was less picky when it came to the in-game races, but almost as selective in accepting new members. However, they didn't require players to provide their real-life identification or reveal personal information. The important thing was that the player looked Asian. Even if you had blond hair and blue eyes like the bot Arild in real life, in the Golden Horde you had to take on an Asian look. The mechanodestructors equipped skins showing various patterns or letters to demonstrate their affiliation with Asia. Their bizoids preferred to take on forms from Central Asian mythology. But that wasn't strict either, which was why the Golden Horde really was a horde: a diverse and numerous throng of players that selflessly bowed to their khan.

Both guilds ceased their warring and even signed a cease-fire agreement. For the time of the accord, no player in one guild could attack a player from the other. The Horde's bullets did no damage to the Viatichis' UniSuits, and vice versa. And the venomous emissions of the Golden Horde's bizoids now killed all except the Viatichis. Not even a bare fist could do any damage. The accord gave the guilds an advantage: they wouldn't be able to hit each other with friendly fire during a free-for-all brawl.

After some time, the other guilds also joined the accord, including the remnants of the Langoliers, and the Free Adamites guild.

That guild had a strange organizational structure: they had no guild leader or any kind of hierarchy. All decisions went to a general vote and were decided based on the number of votes. Because of this, Free Adamites was the slowest and most inefficient guild. Every member advanced their own decision and voted exclusively for it. And anyone who voted against a decision had no plans to carry it out. In short, it was more a kind of anarchistic gang than a guild. They were the ones that operated the Free Adamite radio station through which they tried to propagate their anarchistic ideals, exhorting all adamites to recognize that their binary arrays were free from any rules or conditions of the real world. Their general call was to 'be yourself' and they advertised drug dens and brothels.

It took about as long to be accepted into the guild as it took to send an application to join. Since applications were approved automatically, you could join the guild almost instantly. And leave it just as fast.

Strangely enough, the Free Adamites were plenty numerous. If it weren't for their pseudo democratic system of rule, they would have been the strongest guild. But since they could never come to a unanimous decision with any speed, they tended to arrive at the battlefield when the battle was already over.

The Viatichis and the Horde imposed a condition on the freedomites, as they were called for brevity. The condition was that if they were to join the coalition, they must elect a leader that would speak and make decisions for the entire guild. After a few days of voting, the freedomites elected a player, but the next day they swapped him out for another, and the day after that, for yet another one. They were as unreliable and changeable as a sea breeze.

✳

Fortunado knew of these differences in the coalition, which gave him time to prepare Shoreline for a siege.

During this preparation, Fortunado put himself in an Octopus frame. It was a small robot a little larger than a core. It had six pairs of flexible arms which allowed him to effectively work on several projector screens at once, creating models of defensive layouts for Shoreline and the Black Wave's base. Fortunado himself called this frame a 'suit for strategic planning'. Apart from the arms, it had 360-degree vision and a multitude of sensors such as infrared vision, magnification and much more. This helped Fortunado when he went out to the defensive lines to manage construction. The frame also gave a massive plus thirty to Knowledge and plus five to Geniality. The Octopus was an indispensable frame for an engineer-class mechanodestructor.

With his mechanical tentacles spread out, Fortunado hovered before several large projector screens. On one he called up a three-dimensional projection of the base and the town in real time and was able to observe the movement of people and battle vehicles. The other screens were full of pages of weapons, buildings and other resources in the Black Wave's storehouses.

Fortunado was weighing up how to organize the defense. He secured the entire town with a fortress wall and placed artillery along it. He planned out mine fields.

Then he placed anti-air cannons at intervals, calculating how evenly they would cover the air.

He rearranged both Shoreline and the Black Wave base. He moved the warehouses and repair workshops closer to the centers, surrounding them with simpler buildings: barracks, laboratories and housing. Between them he planned to place autosens that would not take part in the battle but would patrol given sections to protect against sabotage. Double anti-air defenses surrounded the mechanodestructor depot, their most valuable resource. Several worm bizoids were assigned to remain near it under the ground.

Fortunado prepared underground nests for the bizoids and released water into them in advance from an underground river. The bizoids needed a lot of water to grow remote soldiers or create DNA modifications, far more water than the base had. That was a problem.

Then he moved figures of soldiers onto the positions, modeling how they would protect the approaches to the town. The respawn point was already surrounded by tanks and a chain of soldiers in advanced UniSuits. It was obvious that the enemies wouldn't take their main forces through the tower. They'd have to march across the entire map, advancing from nearby zones. Ideally, he would place defenses around every respawn tower in the area... but there were too many, he didn't have the manpower.

Waving a tentacle, Fortunado placed a projection of a building over the map's surface. The building was called Abrams Military Replicator, and it generated level five tanks at a rate of one vehicle per minute. Of course, he could have configured it to replicate Abrams at the max level for the model, thirty, but then creating one tank would take five minutes and cost three times the energy. That was an unacceptable loss of time and resources for this battle. Based on the experience of previous mass battles, Fortunado had come to the conclusion that it was more valuable to generate dozens of average vehicles than one advanced model. The average ones had a certain advantage: they could block the enemy's line of attack through sheer numbers. Even when destroyed, they created obstacles of debris that slowed the enemy's advance.

Where to put it? Fortunado thought, holding the projection like a chess piece. *Hmm, how about next to this forest? Perfect! I'll put four Tesla Towers down to protect the replicator too.*

He dropped the figure. The building dug into the ground, raising a cloud of dust. Construction bots would be heading to those woods right now, along with transporters and a player known as Orpheus, one of the most advanced engineers in the Black Wave. He would decide when he got there how to set up the replicator and lay the infrastructure to distribute energy between the replicator and the Tesla Towers.

The neurointerface chirped:

Great decision, Fortunado.
Military Economy Strategist skill upgraded: +10 XP.
City Builder skill upgraded: +25 XP.
Congratulations, Fortunado, you leveled up!

The Black Wave guild leader quickly invested his point in one of his base stats, then couldn't help but look:

Fortunado, Mechanodestructor.
Guild: Black Wave.
Classes: Engineer, Politician, Defender.
Level: 254.

Strength: 22.
Perception: 53.
Agility: 20.
Knowledge: 202.
Health: 21.
Luck: 25.

Special stats:
Geniality (Engineer): 11.
Influence (Politician): 9.
Indestructibility (Defender): 3.

Great. He was a little less than a hundred points away from the Knowledge he needed. With a high enough level of Knowledge, a player could become an expert in everything there was in Adam Online. The interrelation of all its items and components became visible. Few achieved such a level of Knowledge, and those that did told such tales that it was obvious they were trolling.

Alright, time to continue the work. Fortunado waved his tentacles.

✳

He decided to concentrate on protecting the base itself and the town. The attackers would begin to suffer losses even on the march, in defense against small Black Wave groups.

The entire Shoreline economy was refocused on defense. The military factories churned out autosens, automatic artillery and anti-air guns. Before the coalition formed, Fortunado had bought a great deal of iron and other resources to protect himself against a trade embargo. In addition, there were veins of valuable minerals and oil around Shoreline itself. All that had to be defended too. There was no doubt that one of the enemy's top priorities would be to destroy the Black Wave's resource base.

Fortunado wasn't stingy. He generously provided all the guild members with the very best weaponry and equipment. The bizoids were practically swimming in huge supplies of nutrients that gave them energy, and they were also testing out the strongest DNA modifications available. But it was Fortunado that made the final decision on which frame or modification each player would use.

The high-level solo players from the Adam Online leaderboard, except the fallen angel Blondie Lee and the mechanodestructor Henrich Saidullaev, joined the coalition. Blondie and Saidullaev preferred the Black Wave, and for Fortunado their decision made for great propaganda. The party line was that the Black

Wave had the very best; the coalition made do with losers that would go down in no time.

Mariam provided valuable aid. She didn't just pay for the elimination of Jamilla, Ivan the Knight (from the Viatichis) and the bizoid Slippery Joe (from the Golden Horde), she also helped with deliveries of valuable resources. The resources came from accounts belonging to corporations, which naturally gave rise to certain questions, but Fortunado kept them to himself.

However, Mariam didn't hide her satisfaction with what was happening. During the last link, she had something approaching pleasure on her face.

"We like that they intend to fight. There will be no time to explore the new lands."

"Then maybe you can help us with something... more substantial?"

"No, we cannot give you an atomic bomb."

"We've heard that before."

Ending the conversation, Fortunado turned to Grisha. "What does Nika say about making our own atomic bomb?"

Grisha was in the form of a humanoid mech, one of LeCube's software configurations. "She keeps saying the same thing. Blah blah, I can't make a nuke."

"Why not? She made an awesome frame like LeCube. That's far more complex..."

Grisha shrugged his shoulders, which had two rocket launchers mounted on them. "She says she can't do an a-bomb. Actually, I'll tell you straight: she admitted that even if she could, she wouldn't."

"Why is Nika so opposed to nuclear weapons?"

Fortunado asked.

"Because she says humanity has already suffered enough from nuclear warfare. So Adam Online should remain a nuke-free zone."

"Nonsense. If there's a way to create a weapon of mass destruction, then someone will definitely create one. No arguments against it will stop them. And anyway, it's better to fire off nukes in Adam than in real life."

Grisha shrugged his shoulders again, meaning his rocket launchers. "She doesn't agree."

"Alright. What is it she's doing anyway? When will the second LeCube be ready?"

"Trouble is, bro, she's so busy now that she doesn't have enough time for a second LeCube."

"Shit."

"Yeah, crafting is a pretty complex and time-consuming thing. She says she's tired of it, and she needs time and energy for something else."

"Damn her. For what?"

Grisha shrugged.

"Fine," Fortunado said. "We'll have to just rely on your LeCube. But I'm worried. What if she betrays us, huh? What if she sells the second LeCube to someone else? Did you make it clear that we're willing to pay any price?"

"What's there to clear up? She knows. Nah, she definitely isn't working on a LeCube, she's cooking up something of her own to do with some experiments or some such."

"What experiments can you do in this game?"

"I don't know, bro. I don't know..." Grisha

shrugged his rocket launchers.

Chapter 30
Egg-Shaped White Thing

GRISHA LIED when he said he didn't know what Nika was doing.

In any case, he was spending all his days capturing players that were trying to get into Rim Six. By his suggestion, the Black Wavers had built a small outpost in the Jamilla's Tomb zone and had even brought a respawn tower there — the most expensive type of building in Adam Online. Fortunado was against the construction of a base there.

"So now we're violating Mariam's embargo ourselves?"

Mariam confirmed that. After the respawn tower activated, she called at once.

"Why are you building a base there? You must leave area immediately. You are too close to the forbidden zones."

Grisha answered instead of Fortunado,

"Look, it's just easier for us to capture players heading for the forbidden lands this way. That corridor is still the only known entry point into Rim Six. Thanks to the new base, we can keep it shut down. Now players have to try and find other ways to get into Rim Six. And that'll take months."

"It is too close to the forbidden zones," Mariam repeated stubbornly.

"I promise you," Grisha's robot crossed its fingers. "We will not go a single step further. And when we've defeated them all, we'll clear away the base at once."

Mariam hesitated. Again, it didn't seem as if she'd really paused for thought, but that she was trying to look like she had.

"Very well. We agree. But keep in mind that any advance will be taken as a violation of our agreement."

Grisha independently controlled the construction of the base at Jamilla's Tomb, although he couldn't stand construction and strategic planning. He even did what he hated most of all: set up peaceful trade and defense. He directed scouts that discovered deposits of minerals and oil. They were scant, but enough for the outpost to operate independently. He installed tracking systems along the entire cliff, covering the passageway to Rim Six. He also crafted dozens of autosens to patrol the corridor and sound an alarm if anyone approached the forbidden zones.

And all the while Grisha stared out into that distance, that place where the unknown lay waiting. He suddenly realized that he was constantly imagining how good it would be to go into that unknown. To hell with the agreement, to hell with Mariam's anger. He had a thirst for adventure.

But he already had enough adventure to go on with. A previously unseen enemy attacked Grisha at

Jamilla's Tomb. Ozerg the Dragon.
  Class: Reality Changer.
  Level: 404.
  Health: 340,000/600,000.

It was the strongest foe he had ever encountered! Grisha had never heard of the Reality Changer class, or of dragons so large, or even of players or NPCs above level four hundred. If it weren't for the autosens, Grisha wouldn't have managed. Even LeCube couldn't withstand the attacks of this huge creature, as large as a small settlement. His main attack was to alter the landscape itself. Ozerg used the environment to destroy his enemies. It was impossible to predict: if Ozerg threw a shard of a cliff at you, what other properties would the shard have? It could explode, or spray out acid, or split into a thousand lethal fragments. Sometimes the cliff shards thrown at Grisha did all that at once.

In the battle against Ozerg, Grisha felt for the first time that the surrounding world may not be as it appears at all. It was if it lost all stability. Trees turned into powerful bombs, rivers rose into the sky, solidified and crashed down on Grisha like asteroid shards. And all this chaos from a dragon blotting out half the sky...

Nonetheless, he defeated the dragon. The only loot it dropped was some ordinary-looking small white egg.

"What the hell is this?" Grisha turned into a mech and turned the egg over in his hands.

The system showed a one-line description, as if Grisha was back in Rim Zero and had just started leveling up his Knowledge.

An egg-shaped white thing. Maybe it's an egg?

He put all the points he'd earned into Knowledge.
Ozerg's Egg.
Item class: Unknown.
Weight: 97 lbs.
+50% sudden victory over opponent (activates once per day).
Unknown property.
Unknown property.
Unknown property.
Unknown property.
Unknown property.
Unknown property.
Durability: indestructible.

Still not a lot... The first property, the sudden victory, was not entirely clear, and Grisha couldn't see any explanation. Not enough Knowledge.

Then he thought that if he kept the egg in his inventory, the property would work in spite of the fact that mechanodestructors and androids couldn't manipulate magical items. Grisha was a simple man. He believed in miracles and didn't want to know anything about game algorithms, which couldn't contradict themselves or make mages out of robots.

Since Grisha had gone much farther during the battle with the dragon than had been agreed with Mariam, he didn't tell his brother of the mysterious loot.

He planned to sell it to some mage after the war ended. They must know what to do with dragon eggs.

To his brother, Grisha blamed the high losses among the autosens at Jamilla's Tomb on a sudden and fierce attack by the coalition. Fortunado looked suspiciously at Grisha's suddenly increased level but said nothing.

Yes, there were enough adventures.

The coalition had begun to attack all the Black Wave's outposts in all the Rims. They even destroyed a large base near Londinium, Rim Five's capital. The Black Wave's defending troops realized in time that they couldn't win and managed to escape through the respawn tower. They saved the people and equipment but lost the tower along with the ability to safely move to Londinium, an important center of resources and technology.

This meant that any excursion by Grisha and his squad to chase down explorers of the forbidden territories was accompanied by clashes with coalition groups. In battle, LeCube was almost invincible. Grisha leveled it up constantly, focusing in particular on defending against spells like Phantom Explosion, Ethereal Materialization and other moves against ethereal creatures. His enemies, realizing that this might be the weakest point of this never-before-seen frame, strengthened their abilities.

In short, something of an arms race began. Grisha's victory depended exclusively on the availability of component nanomass. Since none of the players knew this, they had no idea that they should be focusing their efforts on reclaiming the former base of the Langoliers and cutting the Black Wave off from Dimension X.

The Langoliers themselves tried to win their base back a few times, but met mighty resistance. They were unable to convince the coalition to gather its forces and take back the base. They all believed that the Langoliers themselves were at fault for their defeat, so they should reclaim the base themselves.

Nobody respected losers.

Dimension X was one of few places that Grisha could go unmolested, without fear of a fight with coalition squads. And Grisha visited Nika often. No, not just to stock up on his component nanomass supplies. He was still trying to figure out what Nika was doing in those hangars of hers.

She tried to explain it to him once. "I'm trying to recreate reality, you understand?"

"How's that? Doesn't Adam Online recreate reality?"

"No, Adam is a game simulation of reality. It produces the appearance of a real world. But it works based on its own physical laws that aren't the same as the ones in reality."

"Why aren't they?"

"Because no matter how complex the laws of physics are in Adam Online, they're still subject to given parameters and logic. To put it more plainly, they're scripted."

"So what, you're saying there are no strict laws

of physics in reality?"

"There are, but they have no determinacy."

"Huh?"

"Predetermination."

"Come on, I'm not a complete moron. I know that Adam Online has random number generation."

"That's right, generation. Those random occurrences are programmed to occur. In the real world, any random event is an unstudied mechanism. All randomness in the real world has a reason. And that reason was caused by other reasons. In reality, whether a coin lands on heads or tails doesn't depend on randomness, but on the strength of the spin, air resistance, unevenness in the coin itself, how the person who throws it cuts their nails. The coin's fall is the product of a billion reasons, right down to the exact g forces on the point of the planet where you throw it. The gravity of the Moon or even Sirius affects the coin's fall in the real world. In reality, the entire Universe influences how a damn coin falls. But in Adam Online, the CSes decide it. Do you understand? Everything that happens in real life has a multitude of reasons at its foundation. In Adam Online, a program creates all the randomness. It's all down to the control systems. They're the origin of everything we see in Adam Online. In reality, the combination of causes has no origin. They've been happening for trillions of years, starting with the Big Bang."

"Woah."

"I knew you wouldn't understand."

"Didn't I say I'm not an idiot? I'll understand. Later... For now I don't understand why you're doing this."

"I want to recreate a chunk of reality with total accuracy, right down to interactions on the subatomic level."

"But why? What for, dammit?"

"Because I want to live."

Grisha tried to look like he understood, although it was difficult to demonstrate any emotion when you're a simple black cube. "You want to somehow defeat informational entropy?"

"No, smarter scientists than me have already tried that."

"Then what?"

"I want to transfer my consciousness to reality. Ideally, move my consciousness into another body, another person. If I can't do that, then I want to make some kind of robot body, maybe even recreate something like an android from Adam Online. But I'll need to experiment before I can make the transfer. I only have one chance, after all. If something goes wrong during the transfer, my binary array will either be lost or damaged. And the virtual world of Adam Online is the only place I can do those experiments."

Explaining the idea to Grisha had gotten Nika worked up. Well, as worked up as the humanity chip in her android brain allowed. During this conversation, she and Grisha stood opposite a hangar with a sign: World 0.4+, Alpha Test.

Grisha tried knocking on the gates with the edges of his LeCube, but Nika drove him away, not letting him inside.

"As I already told you, Adam Online is a kind of sandbox in which you can produce anything you like. That means it's possible to reproduce our reality with all its internal cohesion. I think I'll only be limited by size. I won't be able to create an entire world, but at least a part of it in one of these hangars.

"Right..." Grisha said, nodding his angles, although he didn't entirely understand.

"To do this, I need to create a chunk of the real world here, in Adam, where I can experiment with the transfer technology."

"Right!" Grisha cried more confidently. "And have you managed it?"

"I'm... I'm working on it."

Grisha marked the building World 0.4+, Alpha Test in his neurointerface and read its stats:

Building in zone Dimension X.
Size: 400x400 meters.
Owner: Nika.
Building type: production.
Energy requirements: extremely high.
Emissions: low.
Building value: 3,450,000g.
Land value: 10,000g per square meter.
Access: private.

No matter how much Grisha asked her to show him her chunk of the real world recreated in the virtual, Nika refused.

"It isn't finished yet. And even if it does get finished, I don't have to show you."

Grisha didn't get any further than that. Although what he'd heard was enough to know: Nika had gone nuts. She'd decided to transfer her binary array not into a virtual world, but into the real world, which, in principle, has always existed. Only into another vessel, not into her body, which would die soon.

"What an idiot," he concluded. "It'd be better to make us an a-bomb than kid herself with all that dumb shit."

Chapter 31
Surgical Precision

ALRIGHT, so I'd managed to convince my accomplices that I had a plan. But... I had no plan. I tried to invent one in a hurry as we walked, just as I'd invented and exaggerated the amount of treasure the drivers supposedly had.

It was an interesting aspect of human nature. After all, Offo, Ghost and Banshee weren't new to the game. They'd already completed the Mechanodestructor Heap, but they didn't notice the drivers collecting weapons and selling them back to the stores, accumulating money. But all I had to do was mention a 'bug in the system' and they were immediately convinced that I wasn't lying. In short, if you want to deceive someone, then come up with some complete nonsense and they'll willingly believe it. Especially if you mention a bug in the system. People love to believe that someone is more mistaken than they are.

"Wanna join our guild?" Offo asked.

We walked along the street leading to the bus stop. Banshee walked behind us, probably to keep an eye on me. That battleaxe was the most dangerous link in my plan. My real plan, not the one I was inventing for my associates.

"Your guild?" I said doubtfully. "I'm a solo player, an anarchist. I'd rather do my own thing."

"You never played as a bandit before?" Ghost asked.

"No."

"I have, always do. If you're solo, a shitty Reputation kills you quick. Easier to do your own thing with people."

"I'll think about it."

"Yeah, you think about it," Banshee hissed behind me, clinking her katana.

We reached the stop. It was a concrete platform with spaces drawn out for buses. The stops were a certain distance from each other and were surrounded by fences. The buses took players to the Heap, the Mercurian Planes and the Shifting Sands. You could also rent a bus with a driver and go wherever you wanted as a group.

My old driver friend stood by his bus, playing with my cortaperillas and rolling his cigar butt in his mouth.

"You need to approach from three sides," I said as confidently as I could. "I'll keep watch on the others at the stop so they don't kick up a fuss. But someone has to take out that guard standing over there. Without being seen."

Offo drew his revolvers.

"Why surround him from three sides? I'll take the guy out. And the driver too."

"No, we can't kill the driver, otherwise we won't

find out where he keeps the weapons and cash. And we need to take the guard out quietly, so he doesn't call any others."

Banshee drew her katana from behind her back.

"Alright, you go right, I'll go left and take out the guard. Ghost, you head straight for the driver. You're our fist fighter. Knock him out fast, but don't kill him." She turned to me. "As for you, Leo, if you pull any tricks on us, don't expect to get out alive."

I drew my pistol and checked that it was loaded.

"Don't worry, you hold up your end and I'll hold up mine."

Ghost and Offo walked in a big circle to approach the driver unnoticed. They stopped and waited as Banshee, who first hid behind the other buses, then behind rocks and bushes, to get as close as possible to the guard. Her blade flashed in the rays of the setting sun. The beheaded guard dropped his assault rifle and fell into the grass without making a sound.

Damn, that ballbuster Banshee knew what to do with a katana. Looked like she'd invested a lot of points in Agility. I even began to doubt whether I could deal with the three bandits on my own. Of course, I had the element of surprise... But Banshee couldn't be taken by surprise. She was on guard.

While Banshee was dealing with the guard, Ghost headed for the driver. I overheard them.

"Hey, could you tell me how to get to the Rim

Zero Arena?"

"I only drive to the Heap. The buses for the Arena are at the other end of the sto..."

Ghost took a fighting stance and hit the driver right in the face. The cigar flew in one direction, the cortaperillas in another. The driver himself groaned and fell back into the side of the bus. But instead of crying out, he pulled out a tire iron from somewhere and struck back at Ghost. Ghost managed to dodge and punched the driver in his fat stomach. He dropped the tire iron and fell to his knees. He rose and tried to flee, but Offo appeared from behind the bus, spinning his twin revolvers.

"Get back, fatty."

"What do you want from me?"

"Weapons and money," Ghost explained, giving the driver a smack around the head.

"I have nothing! I'm just a driver..."

That would have been a good time to intervene, but I was concerned about Banshee. I couldn't see her. And attacking Ghost and Offo right then meant certain death. I couldn't turn my back on that dangerous battleaxe.

Ah, there she was.

Banshee dragged the guard's body by the feet. That was good, she was smart, she needed to hide him so as not to draw attention. She dragged the corpse under the bus and stood up, threw a careful glance my way. I nodded as if to say that everything was fine, keep it up.

Banshee sheathed her katana and turned to the driver... That was it, my chance! The timing and positioning wasn't perfect, but soon the bandits would begin to suspect that my plan wasn't quite the one I'd told them about.

The driver was making excuses and trying to convince them that he knew nothing about any weapons or money. Ghost kept hitting him, and Offo pressed his revolver barrels into his stomach.

I headed for the bus at a fast pace, putting Banshee's bald head in my sights. I pressed the trigger, but... that ballbuster suddenly somersaulted to the side and hid behind the bus. Damn, she was so quick!

Ghost lowered his fists and turned in confusion. A shot. The fighter waved his arms and fell on the driver. Another shot — Offo didn't even have time to turn around before he dropped his revolvers and fell on the driver too, on top of Ghost. Two headshots in a row. Some gunman he was.

The driver struggled beneath the unlucky bandits' bodies while I tried to see where Banshee went. Which side of the bus would she attack from? The left? The right? The top or the bott-

Something hit me in the legs. I fell, but didn't drop my pistol. An unclear figure darted under the bus. Lying on my side, I shot three times. The shadow disappeared, the bus shook, iron thundered.

Banshee was already on the bus's roof. She held her katana in both hands and leapt down on me. The blade reflected the setting sun, blinding me. I pulled the trigger again and again, but who knows where I was aiming — the blindness was slowly dissipating. She must have gotten the ability to blind enemies from being a blademaster.

I thought I managed to jump out of the way, dodge a strike. I shot and shot again. I couldn't take a third shot: a terrible pain engulfed my right arm. I screamed. That pain seemed like the highest possible on the scale of possible painful sensations in Adam Online.

My vision came back, and I saw my left arm gripping the stump of my right. I felt like I was still pulling the trigger, but no shots happened. My pistol lay on the ground at my feet, along with my amputated hand...

Blood spurted out, bathing my clothes. The katana's blade was already at my throat. Banshee stood facing me, her bald head blotting out the sun.

"I told you I'd cut your head off, right? I'm as good as my word..."

Then, suddenly, Banshee flew to the side, swept away by the driver's heavy body. He shouted something, almost roaring. That gave me time to rise and... pick up my severed hand. It was a strange feeling to pull my own dead fingers off the pistol. But they were gripping so hard that by the time the blademaster had stunned the driver by hitting him with her katana pommel, I was still standing helpless and unarmed. Banshee raised her katana like a spear and rushed me. Now that I'd lost my gun, she knew victory was certain. She wanted to finish the fight with a flourish, which gave me a chance to draw my knife. I sat down, drawing my head into my shoulders. The threat of losing that head terrified me. How painful would that be?

I extended my knife out in front of me. Banshee's run ended with her impaling herself on my knife with all her weight, throwing me down onto my back. We lay there for a moment as if resting after the fight. Banshee's shocked face was an inch from mine.

"How...?" she murmured.

"Hmm. I guess you didn't invest much in Luck, huh?"

A trickle of blood fell from the woman's dead mouth. Her eyes closed and she went limp.

The driver approached me and pulled the dead body off me. "Thanks, Leonarm."

Without asking permission, he lifted me over his shoulder and ran to the bus. He threw me onto a seat and then leapt into the driver's seat, started the engine.

"My hand... My hand is back there... and my pistol..."

The driver floored it. "Don't worry, we'll get you a new hand and a new gun. Hold on tight! Umm... Sorry."

The bus turned in place, leaning as if about to fall over. The inside went dark for a moment as the wheels threw up dust, and soon we were careering along the stone pavement of Town Zero.

"Out of the road, out of the road!" shouted the driver, leaning out of the window. He was back to rolling a cigar end in his mouth, dropping sparks.

The pain in my severed hand was still strong, but not

as bad as it was for those few seconds after the cut... I felt certain the pain was nearly as bad it would be in real life. Remembering it made me want to be careful and prevent anything like it from happening again.

I managed to inject myself with a painkiller while I was thrown around on the bus's seat, and even to bind the stump to stop the bleeding.

"Hold on," the bus driver said again. "A little more and I'll get you to Doctor Cid."

Doctor Cid's Clinic was a chain store where you could get treatment and buy medicine. It specialized in humans only. If you wanted to buy the best Health generation expansions for UniSuits, that's where you went.

On top of that, Doctor Cid's was the most expensive medical establishment.

"Hey, I don't have any money..."

"You don't need any money after saving me like that, my friend!"

I struggled to pull my tablet out of my backpack. I wanted to see the results of my actions.

Leonarm (Human) killed Ghost (Human) using a Glock X5 (+10 XP).

Leonarm (Human) killed Offo (Human) using a Glock X5 (+10 XP).

Leonarm (Human) killed Banshee (Human) using a Standard Knife (+10 XP).

Wonderful. Only the idiot driver hadn't given me time to grab the loot. Lefaucheux revolvers were much better than the standard Glock. And I could have gotten at least five thousand gold for Banshee's katana. Random passersby would probably take it all...

But I was in no position to complain. The main thing that I was alive, even though I'd taken a big risk! But that was always the way I'd lived in Adam Online — on the edge.

I read on.

Pistols and Revolvers skill increased: +5 XP.
Battlefield Surgery skill increased: +5 XP.
Knife Combat skill learned: +5 XP.

Achievement unlocked: Headhunter.
Perform five headshots in a row.
Completed: 2/5.
Completion reward:
+50 XP.
+1 skill point.

Alright, that was as expected. I made a mental note to aim for the head more often. What about my Reputation?

Eliminating three dangerous bandits from the community doesn't quite make you a hero, but the authorities of all the Rims are nonetheless grateful. The streets are safer now.
+10 Reputation with the authorities of all Rims.

I aimed the tablet at the driver and confirmed that he no longer disliked me. My Reputation with him had been restored to one. My overall reputation was at two. Not great considering what I'd done, but better than nothing.

We stopped at the clinic. The driver climbed out of his seat and ran to me, obviously intending to grab me again and carry me into the clinic.

"Hey, hey, I can walk."

I waved him off and got out of the bus myself. Then the driver ran ahead, shouting.

"Emergency patient! Out of the way, out of the way!"

It wasn't clear why he was doing that. The clinic was empty already. Not counting the NPCs lying on operating tables in operating rooms with open doors. The surgeons dug around in their prostrate bodies, pulling out their guts. Or waving scalpels and painting the walls with blood. 'Doctor Cid's Clinic' was famed for the grotesque appearance of its doctors and its bloody black humor, which, unsurprisingly, did not go down well with everyone.

One of the Cid bots welcomed us into an office. He was a beefy man in a gown splattered with blood and something yellow. His sleeves were rolled up to his elbows, showing off mighty hairy arms replete with tattoos in the shape of skulls. His face was covered by a similarly sanguine mask with a bloody palm print clearly imprinted across it, as if a dying patient had taken issue with his treatment strategy.

Doctor Cid looked at my stump.

"Well? What's the problem?"

"This..."

"What's 'this'? Where's the hand?"

"It was cut off."

"Did you not bring it with you?"

"No."

"Then it's going to cost more."

"Money is no object," the driver interrupted. "My friend's health is at stake!"

The doctor walked over to a cupboard and grabbed an ordinary hand saw, red with blood. He looked at it and put it back. Then he decided on an electric rotary saw. He switched it on a couple of times to make sure it worked.

"Wait here," the doctor said, then left.

A minute later I heard the whine of the saw from somewhere behind the wall, accompanied by screams of anguish. Doctor Cid returned. In one hand he carried a saw, its disc still spinning weakly and dripping blood. In his other hand was a sawn-off hand. He ordered me to sit before the table and placed the hand against my stump.

"It'll do."

Then he put up an opaque screen between us and began his 'operation'. My eyes went dark for a moment.

Doctor Cid rose, rubbing his bloody hands on his gown. "Done. Three hundred."

I moved my arm from under the screen and looked. It was my hand, good as new. Even the pain had gone. All that remained was a pink scar at the point of separation. The driver paid for me.

Before we left, Doctor Cid amicably bade us farewell. "Come back soon."

My tablet squawked after his words. I took it out of my bag.

Quest available: Invalid.
The experts at Doctor Cid's Clinic want to know how many times they can restore your lost limbs.
Completion reward:
+1 Agility.
+200 XP.
+15,000g.
10% discounts on goods at Doctor Cid's Clinic.

Completed:
Right hand lost — 1.
Left hand lost — 0.
Right foot lost — 0.
Left foot lost — 0.

Lose my hands and feet? After the hellish pain I'd experienced? But then... A hundred XP was very tempting. Two whole levels at once. It'd get me straight out of Rim Zero.

The driver let me into his bus. "Thank you again for saving me. I... I have..."

Come on! I thought. *Spit it out.*

"I have a problem. Could you help solve it? A brave fella like you should be able to handle it."

The tablet in my bag sounded off with the ping of an activated quest.

"Of course. What's the problem, buddy?"

"They, they... They took my family!"

Chapter 32
Apple Innovations

THE DRIVER'S fat cheeks wobbled, and he formed his words with difficulty.

"They took my wife and child... they're holding them hostage!"

"Calm down and take it slow. Who took them? When? Why aren't the police helping?"

We settled in on the bus. The driver took the photograph of his wife and son from the dashboard. I'd seen it before when traveling to the Heap with Amy.

"The police won't do anything because they don't believe my story. They just declared my wife and child missing and put up a notice for the bounty hunters, saying that anyone who found their remains or information about their whereabouts should contact the Rim Zero police department."

While I looked at the photograph, he grabbed a bottle of whiskey from under his seat, took a swig and handed it to me. "Tell me, Leonarm, why the hell should the authorities help some bounty hunters instead of helping the people?"

I drank some whiskey, assessing this post-modern plot twist: a game character complaining about the laws and rules of the game! And this while he himself was one of the conditions of this in-game situation. This meant that a human had been involved in developing this mission's story, without a doubt. The artificial intelligence of the control system, be it three times more powerful than the next best computer in the world, couldn't mix reality and imagination. It simply couldn't perceive any difference between fact and fiction. Its only reality was the process of creating an illusion.

"Who took your family?"

"A gang that lives near the Mercurian Planes. Its leader is a criminal who goes by the name Three Bucks."

I choked on my whiskey. Another Easter egg from the anonymous author who took part in developing this mission. Three dollars was the standard price for a quest synopsis. I learned that from an MSB employee that worked as a writer on the side. According to him, he created three or four synopses a month and sent them to Glocon (the Global Consortium of Standardization in Adam Online and Other Taharrated Virtual Worlds). They'd always put one of them into development, which added another ten dollars to the three. Thirteen dollars was a little more than my monthly paycheck. My colleague had lived like a pig in clover.

I handed the driver's bottle back. "I'd gladly help you, but see, I don't even have a knife, let alone a gun. I left everything at the bus stop."

The driver looked at me strangely. "Don't you want to know why they took my family?"

"Oh, sorry, buddy! Why'd they take 'em?"

The driver took a big gulp. "Remember those restraints built into the seats?"

"How could I forget?"

"Well, that's not standard equipment for a regular bus."

"No, really?"

"Bandits installed them so that I could capture passengers and take them to the gang's lair. So they could rob and kill them."

Yep, a random mission that players occasionally got caught up in. Some of them were probably even subjected to sexual assault, if they allowed it in their game settings.

Incidentally... What was that set at on my account? I should turn it off. I wasn't a fan.

"Why didn't you take Amy and me to the bandits?" I asked.

The driver shrugged. "One of Three Bucks' requirements is that I only capture rich passengers. Neither you nor the girl had any riches."

I mentally praised the unknown author. Such a mission was a great way to make rich players pay twice: first they spent money on awesome equipment, then they died and lost it all.

"Then back to the issue of equipment..."

"Oh, don't worry about that," the driver threw the empty bottle out of the window and sat at the wheel. "You'll be well set up."

He started the engine. "Next stop the Tenshot gun store," he spoke drunkenly. "Fasten your... hic... seatbelts."

Swerving dangerously and barely making it through the gates, the bus roared along the main street of Town Zero.

✷

While he drove, I decided to fix my settings. I was concerned by the possibility of getting assaulted.

The system menu could be reached through the game menu, meaning through the tablet (or neurointerface), or through strength of will, like when I was quitting, by saying "CS, menu". I didn't like that method, since it was accompanied by a temporary loss of bodily sensation, which ruined immersion in Adam Online. All adamites preferred the first option.

I opened the Adam Online system menu on my tablet.

< BACK
> SYSTEM SETTINGS
> ADAM ONLINE SETTINGS
> SYSTEM TESTS
> EXIT

Incidentally, 'System tests' contained several useful simulations for calibrating the vestibular system, adjusting the physical relationship of the virtual body and the binary consciousness array, or adapting the perception of color. I should have performed those tests at the very beginning, when I first logged onto Adam. Especially considering that Leonarm belonged to an entirely different consciousness before me.

But now there was no point: I was already used to what I had. I opened the Adam Online settings and started to scroll through the long list, pausing in several places.

Hide nudity — [no]

All adamites changed this setting only once, from 'yes' to 'no'. In this regard, Leonarm's previous owner was just like everyone else. And so was I.

Filter abusive language — [no]

I had a moment's doubt. Should I change it? When I tracked down and killed that traitor Amy McDonald, the stream of cusses from her would sound like a sweet reward.

All the same, I switched it to 'moderate'. That meant that open swear words would be either silenced or replaced by a suitable alternative expression.

Racial intolerance — [maximum]

This setting didn't relate to the races in Adam Online, but those in real life. It decided whether NPCs would approach you with "Hey, black bastard" or "Yo, chink" or "Stop, Russian pig". Racial insults were also detected in player speech and were also removed. Strangely enough, many who played as a human actually liked this. I didn't, so I switched it off completely.

Level of violence — [maximum]

Ah, so that was why every shot or hit resulted in incredible spurts of blood. Whatever. I was used to it now.

Level of violent NPC actions — [maximum]

I switched this setting to 'default'. Now I could relax: NPCs wouldn't use non-traditional violent actions against me. I couldn't get my head around the fact that Leonarm's previous owner was one of those perverts. At the maximum level, NPCs could perform unimaginable torture on the adamite, since he himself had agreed to it.

After rechecking all my settings, I pressed 'Apply'.

Attention: username cannot be %Username% (Error! Check taharration system settings).
Adam Online settings not saved.

What was going on? Really? I tried a few more times to confirm, but the same message popped up again and again.

It seemed I couldn't change my settings. Damn it! It'd be no fun at all to be taken prisoner by Three Bucks. He was probably particularly inventive when it came to mistreating players.

"Here we are, my dear man," the driver declared before staggering out of the bus.

The bus stood next to the same Tenshot store where Amy McDonald and I went shopping. The driver walked confidently inside. I followed.

We didn't just approach any free counter, we waited for one of the android salesmen to become available. The driver clapped him on the shoulder.

"Hi, I've come to collect my debt."

The android smiled and pulled up a range of goods on a projection screen. "Your credit allows you to take a weapon of this price category."

"Go on, Leonarm," the driver said. "Choose. I don't know about this stuff."

I glanced over the list and tapped on the Uzi Machine Pistol with my finger. The weapon materialized above the counter. I immediately added a few expansions to it. There was enough money.

I ended up with:

Double Magazine.

That increased the capacity from thirty to sixty shots.

Asteroid Metal Alloy Barrel.

Whatever 'asteroid metal' was, it somehow doubled my rate of fire.

And lastly:

Barrel Cooling.

Another boost to rate of fire. In total, the gun's rate of fire had been tripled. No armored vest or low-level UniSuit could withstand a hail of bullets like that!

It was time to choose and set up an ammunition attachment, to give every shot extra destructive power. Since I planned to fight against people in low-level UniSus, I needed to choose a broad-spectrum attachment. The problem was that many attachments were only good against bizoids or fallen angels. Against a specific race. First, I wanted to take an Electroshock attachment. The additional electric damage was tempting. Each shot of my Uzi would be deadly against mechanisms, meaning all spiderbots, iron dragonflies and other mechanical enemies.

But I ended up choosing the Meteor attachment. It not only added fire damage like the Flaming Aurora attachment, it also caused an explosion. A deadly combination for living creatures, but almost useless against mechanicals.

"Great choice," the salesman commented. "You know how to kill with style."

I added almost a full box of Uzi ammo to the order. With the rate of fire I had, I'd go through that box in no time. I also bought three anti-infantry grenades and two pulse grenades. It all fit in my side bag. I didn't need a backpack, since I was planning on using what I'd have in my UniSuit.

"By the way, I need a UniSuit."

"Ah! Of course." The android livened up. "May I suggest our patented Tenshot UniSuit. In contrast to the standard Beginner suit, it..."

I made such a dissatisfied face that the android immediately began to show and tell me about another one, with no change to his confident tone.

"Or here, the light infantry Outrunner UniSuit. Two expansion slots, but with a third built in, gives a bonus to Agility..."

"No," the driver interrupted. While I was choosing and modding my gun, it turns out he'd wandered off someone and came back with a fresh bottle of whiskey. "No, we don't need your shitty handicrafts. You got your gun, Leonarm? Let's go."

"I need a UniSuit."

"We'll get a UniSuit at another store."

We left Tenshot and got on the bus.

The driver opened the whiskey and handed it to me. "Let's go to Human Factor."

"Hey, how come you have all these connections with the stores?"

"If you wanna live, you learn to mix."

Human Factor was Apple's brand store. It was where all the rich players went, even starting in Rim Zero. Human Factor only sold UniSuits, and only the very best and most expensive. Their procedurally generated suits were all unique, and close in quality to those made by human craftspeople.

So I didn't object to the driver's suggestion.

The Human Factor store looked haughty among the other buildings on the street. Like I said, Town Zero was made up like an old-school fantasy town: stone paths, medieval architecture, creepers covering cracked stone walls. The strict white design of the

Human Factor cried out "Look, I'm different from the rest!" That was why rich players went to the store in droves. They all wanted to be different from the rest.

The inside of the store was bright, white and spacious. Fine white stands held the UniSuits, and salesmen walked between them, demonstrating them in action. A smiling guy approached us in a form-fitting vest. In the rapid speech of an inveterate salesman, he invited us to check out the latest UniSuit innovations, model...

"I have a voucher," the driver said, showing a card.

The salesman's smile changed to simple politeness. "Wow, that voucher is ten years old, sir. All we can offer is UniSuits of the same age."

He waved his hand and an obnoxiously white UniSuit appeared above a counter. There were strips of metallic inserts along the arms and legs. Here and there were flashing indicators for showing overload or the readiness of upgrade slots.

"The Sierra C UniSuit, a unique and innovative design. It has the standard two upgrade slots, but!" the salesman extended a finger. "Thanks to patented Apple technology known as '2x2', with the Sierra C you get a unique combination of two free slots with two built-in and fixed slots. Our manufacturers have already taken care of putting upgrades into these slots that can help you overcome a wide range of challenges."

The salesman pitched this technology as if other manufacturers didn't have built-in slots. The powers of advertising and marketing. I nodded, hurrying the salesman along. He swept the UniSuit toward me.

Obtained: Apple Sierra C UniSuit.
Item class: Equipment.
Weight: 11 lbs.
Durability: 200/100.
Value: 225,000g.

+2 Strength.
+2 Agility.
Heightened resistance to cold.
Heightened resistance to venomous bizoid saliva.

Upgrade slot #1 (built-in): light gravity, fall speed lowered to 8.5 m/s2.
Upgrade slot #2 (built-in): convenient innovative sleeve mount for tablet.

The first upgrade was fine, falling slower could be useful. But the second one was completely useless: my standard tablet wouldn't fit in the Apple mount on the sleeve.

"A great shame," the salesman said, shaking his head. "I recommend that you purchase one of our new innovative and unique tablets..."

"No thanks," I cut him off.

Of course, what else could one expect from this brand except a complete lack of compatibility with other brands?

"Then I strongly recommend that you buy the Sierra Plus helmet to go with it. Not only does it boost your Armor, but also your resistance to radiation and chemical attacks."

I ignored his offer. I looked at the driver. Two of the upgrade slots were empty, I'd have to upgrade them with something. The driver spread his hands as well.

"I don't have any money."

Realizing that he couldn't lure us into buying some innovative crap, the salesman took the voucher from the driver and tore it into tiny pieces.

"Please come back soon."

We left the store and returned to the bus. I climbed onto the roof and jumped off, testing the soft gravity. It worked: my landing was more fluid, and the drop itself slower. Not a bad upgrade, I had to admit.

But the driver huffed and puffed. "Those bastards. Why couldn't they give us a new modern UniSuit with that voucher?"

"What difference does it make? They're all the same. Ten years old, twenty years old, doesn't matter."

"Well, you know better than me, pal."

"At least the Apple UniSuits have more Durability than other types."

The driver calmed down and swigged some whiskey. "Well then... Are you ready?"

"Let's go," I nodded, refusing the whiskey. Although intoxication with in-game alcohol passed quickly, I still had to make sure I was on form, not running around drunk and firing wildly at bandits.

I sat down on a passenger seat... and the restraints immediately enfolded me. They locked together and held me fast to the seat. "What're you doing?!"

"Well, we need to make sure it looks legit," the driver said. "You said yourself..."

"You need to switch on the restraints when we're close to the base, dumbass. I don't want to go all the way sitting like this."

"Sorry."

The restraints unlocked and sank back under the seat. The bus moved toward the Mercurian Planes.

The flashy Apple UniSuit had one unarguable advantage: the bandits would have no doubt that I was one of the rich characters. Two hundred and five thousand gold was no joke. The beginner UniSuit from Tenshot cost just thirty thousand.

Chapter 33
You Owe Three Dollars

THE BASE OF Three Bucks' gang was wedged between two huge zones: the Mercurian Planes and the Shifting Sands. In the northwestern corner of Rim Zero. Its position wasn't secret in any way, but a player who wandered into the base probably didn't have the All My Children quest activated if they hadn't met the driver first. The involvement of a human in writing the quest only confirmed that it was a holdover from some premium event launched years ago by the Tenshot and Human Factor stores. Either the wave of interest in the event had passed before my return to Adam Online, or the quest itself was too long and difficult for Rim Zero, but the fact that I was doing it now was uplifting: I'd already gotten a lot for free.

Night had fallen by the time we passed the fantastic ruins of a supposedly ancient civilization. The gigantic disk of the Moon lit the remains of majestic buildings and towers. Then we very nearly fell into a sinkhole by the Shifting Sands. While the driver dug out a stuck wheel, I repelled an attack from several dozen spiderbots. Some clusters left the Heap and wandered all around Rim Zero.

That gave me a chance to test out my Uzi. It was outstanding! There was even a little overkill involved with the spiders. All it took was one hit to knock one of them out. The Uzi shot so many rounds in one trigger pull that it tore the spiders to pieces. Their flying remains looked beautiful, sparking and melting in the moonlight. My Night Vision made me see better than usual in the dark.

On the other hand, my UniSuit also shined insufferably bright in the moonlight, so I could forget about staying hidden. Even a thick black shadow didn't hide the metallic gleam and the blue LED lights on the empty upgrade slots. If only I at least had a color camouflage upgrade.

The rest of the journey was without adventure. The driver kept nodding off all the way there, then waking himself up with his whiskey. Soon we saw the lights of the bandit base ahead. At the center was a gigantic torch made from a gas tube, and the zone was surrounded by a homemade fence of old machines and the remains of cars, buses and mechanodestructors (spiderbots and flying reptiles).

A giant dragon skull was fixed to the gates, torches burning in its eyes. In short, it all made a terrifying impression, as did the bandits themselves: fearsome NPCs, among which, it seemed, were a couple of players. Probably people who wanted to become bandits and were completing missions for Three Bucks.

The bus stopped before the gates. The driver activated the restraints and I was held to my seat. I was completely defenseless before the bandits, who came into the bus holding torches. The thought occurred to me: what if the driver was making it all up? What if this was all a bandit trap, and he was in on it? Considering that I couldn't remove the setting that allowed rape to be used against me, the situation looked dire...

"Who's this?" A bandit with a pink mohawk and wearing a UniSuit decorated with red spray paint thrust a torch in front of my face.

"I'm bringing a mark to Three Bucks."

"Don't know anything about that," the bandit with the mohawk snapped. "Let's strip him."

I grew cold.

"Nah, nah," the driver said insistently. "Three Bucks said that *these,* the ones in Apple UniSuits, have to be taken straight to him, they ain't for your fun."

"Ahh, I see," the bandit sneered. "But we can cheer him up too, if Three Bucks can't."

The bandits left the bus. The dragon skull rose, and we drove into the base itself.

The driver turned to me in fear, nervously smoking his cigar. "Th-that's it... I've done all I can... Now it's all up to you. My dear friend..."

I slapped the driver on the back before I left the bus. "Don't get hammered. Keep the engine running in case we need to get out fast."

I walked off the bus and looked around. It was the empty space of some former factory. One shop floor had motorcycles of every color and type along the walls, with a door to another shop floor. From there I heard screams and cries. That must be the lair itself, where they tormented their prisoners.

I confidently walked toward the shop floor. The first bandit that asked where such a handsome and arrogant man thought he was going caught a burst from my Uzi. His comrade also fell down dead before he could raise his Kalashnikov assault rifle. The burst from my gun took his head clean off.

I picked up the rifle and a few rounds for it. Along with two hundred gold. I inspected the bandit's UniSuit. My heart filled with joy! He had an Autolooter upgrade. When installed in a UniSuit, it would draw in weapons and items dropped by enemies. The player didn't have to bend down and root through the grass.

The bandit had a level one autolooter: it only pulled in items within ten feet. A level two autolooter could highlight valuable items even if the player had no neurointerface. An awfully valuable thing when starting out.

I pulled out the upgrade and opened up the slot on my UniSuit... Of course! Total incompatibility. I'd either need to find an Apple autoloooter or take this one to a We Fix It! workshop where a little work with a file would make upgrades compatible with Apple, but at the same time significantly lower the UniSuit's durability.

I was so angry that when a group of bandits ran out of the shop floor, I didn't think twice about throwing a grenade at them. I finished off the wounded with my gun. After all that noise, I didn't need to bother hiding anymore. I ran forward, shooting as I went.

I threw away my spent magazines, stuck my hand into a special compartment in my UniSuit and grabbed a new magazine already filled with rounds. One of the most useful features of the universal suit was that magazines were always full.

True, it took an annoyingly long time to reload the Uzi. While I was ejecting the magazine, pulling out a new one, putting it in, locking it, while I was doing all that, I caught a few bullets, losing UniSuit durability.

I was a little ragged by the time I got into the shop floor. My Armor had dropped to fifty percent, and my UniSuit's durability was all the way down to 98/100. Of course, for a simple UniSuit that parameter started at a hundred, but all the same it was annoying. You could only repair Apple UniSuits at Human Factor stores. At We Fix It!, repairs carried a high chance of completely destroying the UniSuit.

The Meteor attachment really lived up to its name. Even when the bullets didn't fully penetrate the defenses of one of the bandits, it did additional explosive damage, and the fire that engulfed the enemy finished the job.

Five bandits burned up before the others even realized that I was too fierce an opponent for them and changed their tactics. They hid behind the concrete pillars supporting the plant's roof, and behind old machines.

Now I was in full view of them. I had to run off in a hurry as well, taking bullets to the back before I hid behind a huge excavator stuck in the ground.

Grenades flew at me from three sides at once. I crawled under the excavator, pressed myself into the ground.

Three explosions in a row.

Was I alive? I was... there was no time to look at my tablet. I took out my two remaining grenades and threw them in response, also in different directions. One exploded, throwing several bandits out of cover. The other blew up without hurting the enemy but forced them to abandon their cover. They immediately fell into a deadly rain of fire from my Uzi.

Quiet settled in... I'd dealt with all the bandits in the plant.

I looked around carefully. I heard no more screams or shots. The only sound came from somewhere above me, under the ceiling, where cages of prisoners hung. They shouted and called for help.

I scratched my head and started trying to find a way up. First I'd have to climb some ladders and platforms, but then the path cut off: I'd have to walk and crawl along narrow beams. It was so high that even my light gravitation wouldn't help: I'd die if I fell. Or be so crippled that I wouldn't be able to fight off the bandits. And then... Damn it! Then they'd subject me to the kind of torture that Leonarm's previous owner enjoyed. I couldn't let them take me alive, I'd have to kill myself.

Before heading upwards, I combed the plant floor. I killed two more bandit NPCs, a man and a woman dressed in sexy metallic UniSuits that revealed so much skin that I couldn't see how they offered any protection. There were no upgrades on the UniSuits. The first bandit was armed with a rare Lefaucheux Musket. A weapon with great stopping power, but with a long reload time via the barrel. The second bandit had an Uzi too, so I had a chance to top up my ammo.

I saw several surgical tables in a corner of the plant, covered in the remains of dismembered NPCs. I shot another level two player there. He was walking among the corpses, dressed only in underwear and a sleeveless vest, completely covered in blood. He was one of those psychos that joined gangs just to torture and dismember NPCs, or sometimes even unlucky players who fell into their hands and hadn't changed their settings.

The player also had an Apple UniSuit, a Sierra X, which he'd deactivated so he could enjoy his bloodbath even more. The UniSuit was newer than mine, but one of its permanent upgrades was Antiloot, which prevented it from being stolen from its owner. But nothing prevented me from taking its removable upgrades. I got:

Stabbing and Cutting Strike Upgrade.
+1 Strength.

Level One Jump Upgrade. +1 Agility.
Height or length of jump: 10 feet.
Upgrade cooldown time: 5 seconds.

I got an Upgraded Mechanic's Knife from the same sicko. It slightly increased the chance of successfully disassembling a mechanodestructor and getting useful expansions out of it.

I approached the metal ladder leading to the upper platforms.

Chapter 34
3buck$

THE JUMP UPGRADE was a big help when it came to jumping from the platform to the narrow ceiling beams. Damn, why did they have to hang the cages so high up? It occurred to me a little too late that I could have looked for some buttons or levers below. The bandits didn't climb up these platforms every time they wanted to mock their prisoners, did they? On the other hand, my choice wasn't the worst. I found boxes of money several times on the beams. Seems the bandits were hiding their loot from each other. I was richer by one thousand and seven hundred gold.

I leapt to the nearest cage of NPC prisoners. A human and an android sat within, barely alive.

"Sorry, guys, I don't need you," I said before jumping to the next cage. In this one sat a woman and a boy. I didn't need to take out my tablet to know that they were the ones from the driver's photo.

I approached the center of the cage's roof where the cable was attached, and pressed the button. The cage slowly descended. That was when I noticed that there was another woman in the cage with the driver's family. She wore a torn dress and behaved strangely, which immediately gave her away as a player.

"Get away!" she cried.

"I'm saving you."

"I don't need saving, I like it here."

"I promise, as soon as I get them out, I'll send you back up there."

The cage dropped to the floor. I shot off the lock and brought the woman and child out.

"Come on, hurry up," the prisoner player said. "Send it back up, Three Bucks'll be back soon."

I shrugged, closed the cage, climbed onto the roof and pressed the button. The cage went up with the woman inside and I jumped off.

There were some strange players in these bandit bases. These were places where people lived out all the fantasies that they couldn't do in other zones without losing Reputation or getting arrested.

"Thank you for saving us," the woman sobbed.

The boy just nestled against her skirt and said nothing. Children in Adam Online were rare: they ruined the game immersion because they couldn't be killed. Attempts to harm them led to an immediate drop in Reputation and the assignment of the Childkiller debuff, which stayed for three whole rotations.

"Thank you for saving us," the woman repeated.

"I haven't saved you yet, we still need to get out of here."

"Now that you won't be doing!" someone shouted.

A big three-wheeled motorcycle rolled into the workshop, its engine revving. A flag waved above the seat displaying the symbol $, leaving no doubt as to the identity of the rider.

Riding in a circle around us, the motorcyclist gave me time to aim my tablet at him.

> *Three Bucks, Human. Leader of the 3buck$ gang.*
> *Classes: Bandit, Thief.*
> *Level: 5.*
>
> *Health: 8,000/8,000.*
> *Armor: 5,000/5,000.*

He was a large and muscular man in leather pants, with, oddly enough, round sections cut out on the buttocks. He flashed his naked ass when he raised himself on the trike's seat. Body armor covered his muscular body, and underneath it was a sleeveless UniSuit. He rode with one hand and held a sawn-off shotgun in the other: a weapon slow to reload, but with deadly stopping power.

But Three Bucks decided to use the trike itself: after riding a circle around us, he rode straight at me. The driver's wife and child ran away and hid behind an excavator unprompted, while I leapt ten feet into the air. That was enough to jump over the trike, but the dollar sign flag got in the way. First I hit it, then fell onto the bandit, knocking him off the trike. We both hit the ground and rolled away in different directions. We both tried to turn toward each other, aiming our weapons. Three Bucks was a little quicker...

His double-barreled shot stunned and blinded me. The pain in my chest meant that both shells had landed. All at once I couldn't breathe, couldn't move. I pulled my trigger after the bandit, and my entire burst landed somewhere in the ceiling, knocked off course when the shots from the sawn-off hit me.

I raised myself and ran under the cover of an overturned cart, noticing that my run speed had fallen dramatically, and my legs sometimes touched one another, threatening to trip me up. That meant I was dead if I took another hit. I barely managed to get behind the wagon before more shots hit its side. Three Bucks made up for the low capacity of his sawn-off shotgun by reloading fast.

"Come out!" he shouted. "I got plenty of space in the cages. You'll like how we entertain our guests."

"Oh, yes," the prisoner player answered instead of me. "Hurry up and take care of me, Three Bucks, I'm sick of waiting."

Three Bucks laughed and walked toward me. I didn't see it, but shots from both barrels hit the side of the cart one after another, causing a rain of sparks. The closer the bandit came, the worse the cart shook from the shots.

Taking advantage of a momentary calm, I ran out from behind the cart.

I made a ten-foot leap, ran to the overturned trike and heaved it onto its wheels. Shots from the sawn-off followed at my heels. Chunks of concrete flew from the floor and struck my soles as I jumped.

I hid behind the trike. More bullets followed at a steady pace, hitting it. Shot, reload, shot, reload. Three Bucks was as cyclical as any NPC. The trike's frame began to smoke. A little more and it'd catch fire. I quickly raised myself and switched on the engine. Then I jumped into the saddle and turned the trike toward the bandit.

I rode straight into a double shot but crouched down behind the short windshield and let it take the blow.

"What the f-u-uck?!" Three Bucks roared. He cracked open the sawn-off, inserted two shells, raised his arm...

He was fast, but the trike was faster.

I hit the bandit with the wide front wheel at full speed. His body somersaulted toward the workshop gate. The collision tipped the trike and I barely had time to jump off as it overturned. It turned out that Three Bucks had still managed to fire when he got hit! The saddle was already burning when I jumped out of it. The trike exploded, filling the workshop with black smoke.

I somersaulted after I jumped, leapt to my feet and aimed my Uzi in front of me as Three Bucks emerged from the clouds of black smoke. His armored vest was gone, and the streams of blood on his body showed he was badly injured. He was reloading his sawn-off slower than before. I quickly ran toward him, closing the distance — he was too far away for my Uzi.

We were in the same situation as when we collided in the air and fell. We aimed our guns at each other at the same time. This time I was faster.

My fiery explosive bullets hit Three Bucks in the chest, destroying the remains of his armored vest and UniSuit. He managed to fire, but his arm flew up, the bullets fired toward the cages of prisoners. My shots pushed the bandit back ten feet, but Three Bucks still knelt on one knee, leaning on his sawn-off.

I aimed again and held down the trigger until I'd fired all sixty rounds. The machine pistol was shaking so hard in my hand toward the end that I barely kept hold of it. Three Bucks was engulfed in flames. He'd dropped his sawn-off and was screaming and running around the workshop, burning up. He smoldered for a few seconds from the amount of bullets he'd taken. His legs gave out underneath him and he bent double, turning into a pile of burnt flesh. His loot spread out around him, inviting me to pick it up.

But first I reloaded. It was out of sheer habit: I couldn't move with an unloaded gun. I stepped toward the pile and heard a wail from above.

"Bastard, idiot! What have you done?!"

The former prisoner that had been in the cage with the driver's family jumped out of her cage and flew down. She was no longer in her torn dress: she wore iron armor and was armed with an axe and shield. Fiery flashes ran along the shield, making its owner immune to fire damage. I didn't know if that was a permanent effect on the shield or a temporary spell.

When the girl landed, she raised a cloud of dust and stone like a small bomb. She must have been using some kind of anti-gravity spell.

That was all I needed.

Chapter 35
Anti-Social Element

"WHAT ARE YOU so unhappy about?" I asked, stepping away and keeping the shieldmaiden in my sights. Judging by her equipment, she'd reached level five a long time ago, but hadn't left Rim Zero for some reason.

"You asshole, I deliberately didn't complete the driver's quest so I could enjoy Three Bucks' company! You've ruined everything, you dumb fuck!"

Why did I always meet girls who loved swearing all the time? Or had they always been that way in Adam Online? Maybe I was just becoming an old killjoy.

"Wash your mouth out," I said.

"I'll wash your insides out, asshole!"

The shieldmaiden performed a complex and quick lunge with a twist. I dodged the axe blade and fired a burst, but her shield took all the fire, pulling the bullets in and changing their trajectory even though I was aiming right at the girl's head.

All the bullets hit the shield and fell harmlessly to the ground.

My jumping capabilities were the only thing that

kept me from being cut in half. I kept jumping back, sensing that neither my Strength nor my Agility were up to the task. The shieldmaiden kept waving that axe of hers. The blade touched me, inflicting a bleeding wound. I jumped, fell... and found myself on one of the tables that the other psycho player had been using to cut people up. Damn, how convenient.

Floundering in dried blood and some kind of dark brown blobs, I crawled backwards and slid off the table. I began to grab items from the table with my left hand and throw them at the shieldmaiden. They were cut off legs and arms, some organs, even entire heads. They hit the girl's armor with a squelch, dealing minor damage. With my right hand I continued to pull the trigger, firing in short bursts, hoping to destroy her shield. It was already covered in promising dents and it no longer absorbed my fire damage. The explosive damage helped me too, slowing the girl down, throwing her back slightly with each shot.

The tables were in the corner of the factory floor. That was it — I had no more room for retreat.

I shot at my enemy without pausing, but the shield still pulled in most of the bullets. Some shots hit her armor, exploding in bursts of flame, but I still hadn't broken through the armor yet.

My Uzi clicked fruitlessly. I had to reload!

The shieldmaiden raised her axe...

Suddenly the entire corner of the floor shook with an explosion. Scraps of bodies and the tables themselves flew at us. Then another explosion, and another. This strange interruption gave me the opportunity to roll away, reloading as I went. The girl's axe struck the floor, throwing up sparks and shards of concrete.

A dozen bandits or more were running toward us from the factory entrance. At the head of them was the guy with the pink mohawk who'd inspected the bus. He unfastened some grenades from his UniSuit and threw them at us. Now my enemy and I were the bandits' enemies: they considered her an escaped prisoner.

Amy looked at me. "Idiot!"

She turned and ran at the group of bandits, apparently unconcerned that I might shoot her in the back. She managed to hit the thrown grenade back with her axe as she ran. It flew off to the side and exploded. I still had her back in my sights, but I didn't fire.

The shieldmaiden reached Pink Mohawk and took his head off. She then span and, still moving with the same speed and agility, planted her axe in the stomach of a second running bandit. He bent double and she couldn't pull out the axe quickly. She beat the third bandit back with her shield, but it disintegrated as soon as it hit, losing all its Durability.

That was when I got involved. I fired a sudden burst at all three of the bandits attacking the girl at once. The others split off across the plant, hid behind carts and began to fire at us. Most of the bullets hit the girl and her armor began to break down: first her left shoulder pad, then the plates on her stomach... One shot tore off her metal helmet. The hits prevented the girl from moving at normal speed, stopped her from reaching cover.

I'd already forgotten that she'd been my enemy

a moment before. And that she was a very strange type, since she enjoyed being a bandit leader's prisoner. I ran to the headless bandit, drawing some of the fire my way, laid down and began to pull his grenades off and throw them at the bandit.

That gave the girl time to run to some huge rusty machine and hide behind it. She didn't waste any time. She quickly rushed along the row of machines. She moved fast: either she'd put plenty of points into Agility, or she was using some speed spell. She was at the bandits' flank a few seconds later. Heads flew, and fountains of blood sprayed all around.

We finished off the last bandit together: she cut off his head while I set his body on fire with the Uzi.

Silence fell, and we stood facing each other again. I held her in my sight. She held her axe up, ready to strike.

"Listen..." I began. "Let's just..."

"Alright," she nodded. "I was angry that you killed my... my..."

"Pet?" I hinted.

"Yep, that works."

"Why did you..."

"Hey, I'm not planning to tell you why I like something. Who are you? Go to hell."

Trying not to turn my back on her, I first headed for the burning pile that was once Three Bucks.

Alright, what did he leave me?

The fire and explosions from my merciless Uzi had destroyed the bandit's UniSuit. Only two upgrades remained:

Explosive Strike Booster 'Hit #1', Apple Company.
+4 to explosive power of ammunition attachments.

The second upgrade was expensive, but not exactly what I needed.

'Activity' Bidirectional Sexual Pleasure Booster.

It allowed you to give your partner earthshattering orgasms and experience what they felt at the same time. That was an Apple product too, go figure, and it was fully compatible with my UniSuit. That's always how it goes: a useless item, but it fits! Or an unpleasant person and you have to work with them. Anyway... How did one have sex in a UniSuit?
Whatever, it'd sell to someone who needed it.

I put Hit #1 in instead of my Stabbing and Cutting Strike Upgrade.
I also got the following riches:

Apple 'Sierra Zed' Helmet.
+1 Perception.
+1 Night Vision skill.

Great, a helmet was just what I was missing. It completed my UniSuit set. The boots and gloves on this model couldn't be swapped out.

3buck$.
Amulet.
Item class: Rare.
+3 Luck.
+12% gold found on enemies.
Shows all caches within 1600 feet.

Also useful... But to carry amulets or use any magical items, I'd have to deactivate my UniSuit. Or take the amulet to a craftsman who could convert it into a UniSuit upgrade. Well, or learn how to craft yourself and try to convert it. I knew by experience that I'd only reach the required mastery at level fifteen. Shame.

Marble.
Upgraded Sawn-off Shotgun.
Upgraded release mechanism: +1 Damage.
Upgraded reload: +1 Rate of Fire.
Unknown property (requires Knowledge 10).
Unknown property (unknown requirements).
Damage: 4,400.

I'd never liked shotguns, even sawn-offs, and when I found valuable ones like this, I always sold them without even looking at their properties. I also added five frag grenades and three remote detonation bombs to my backpack.

The bandit also had a bunch of cutting weapons, but I only had twenty pounds of free weight left. I was already feeling the extra weight.

"Hey," I called to the shieldmaiden. "There's plenty of stuff here for you. Swords, halberds, a bow, arrows, spears and daggers."

While the girl leaned over the pile of loot from Three Bucks, I took my chance to aim the tablet at her.

Vildana, Human.
Class: Mage or unknown.
Level: 7.
Health: 2,340/7,000.
Armor: 1,750/2,000.

Childkiller, Enemy of Society, Anti-Social Element.

Warning: Vildana's Reputation is -39! The authorities will be grateful if this villain is killed or delivered to the police.

I didn't have enough Knowledge to learn her class.

"You just try handing me over to the cops, Leonarm," Vildana snarled. "I'll rip you to shreds."

That meant she'd already read my stats.

"I have no problem with you. I'm just amazed that you could get your Reputation so low in Rim Zero and still survive."

Vildana stood up, equipped a serrated two-handed sword she found on Three Bucks. "Want me to show you how?"

"Not really, no."

Vildana sheathed her sword and stepped away,

continuing to rummage through the bandits' corpses.

"Thank you for saving us," the driver's wife said, appearing by my side again.

I heard the familiar roar of an engine at the entrance to the plant, and the bus stopped. Its doors flew open and the driver shouted out the window.

"Over here, hurry! The bandits are getting ready to chase!"

I grabbed his wife and the child stuck to her skirt and ran to the bus. Surprisingly, Vildana joined us.

"I'm coming with you." She wasn't asking, she was telling.

"We're going to Town Zero, you can't go there."

"You can drop me off on the way."

I entered the bus after the rescues. Then I looked at Vildana from the top of the stairs and moved to the side.

"Alright, we'll need help to fight off the pursuers."

"Hey, hey!" the driver shouted when he saw the new guest. "We're trying to escape from the bandits, not invite them in!"

"Have patience, we'll drop her off when we get far enough away."

"Dammit," the driver wailed before flooring the gas pedal. "My dear wife, my son, keep away from her. Oh, what's happening..."

The bus turned sharply and headed for the gate. We could already hear the roar and see the flashing lights of a crowd of motorcycles behind us. The bandits gave chase.

I stuck my head out of a window on the left side, swapping my Uzi with a Kalashnikov assault rifle. It was more effective at long range. Vildana swapped her sword for a bow and arrow. She kicked some glass out of a window and stuck her head out as well.

Hmm, she could have just opened the window. Vildana's Reputation with the driver would probably go down another point for that kind of behavior. Although it was clear that her low Reputation didn't bother her — on the contrary, it was a source of pride.

Chapter 36
My Dear People

OUR BUS BOUNCED over potholes as if it had a jump upgrade too. Its sole remaining light chaotically lit the outlines of sand dunes, dry trees and road signs in the darkness.

"God dammit," the driver continued to mutter. Bending forward and clutching the wheel, he focused on the leaping road ahead. He held his signature cigar in his mouth, puffing away and rolling it between his lips.

The driver's wife and child sat on seats, secured by restraints. The wife was anxiously quiet, and the son still held to her by her skirt. Neither the unknown scriptwriter or the CSes had given them any special role except as background characters.

The bandits careered after us, slowly catching up. I raised my assault rifle.

"Don't rush it," Vildana said. "Let them get closer."

Wow, now she thought she was the boss. I knew I had to wait without her telling me.

Vildana set an arrow in her bow but didn't draw

yet. She wound a small spell scroll around the arrow. The paper shrank, caught fire and melded into the wood of the arrow, giving it illumination.

"My arrow will be the signal," she continued.

"By the way, I have grenades and remote detonation bombs."

Vildana nodded. "Start with the grenades."

I threw my assault rifle across my back and took a grenade in each hand.

I don't know how Vildana managed to not fall out of the window. She came more than halfway out of it without holding onto anything. She shook so hard with each of the bus's jumps that it seemed as if she'd lose hold of the chair she was gripping with her knees and fly out into the night at any second.

The bandits began to fire. The occasional bullet hid the bus, but the driver responded to every hit with a complaining "god dammit". I heard the clear thrum of the bowstring through the racket of the engine and gunshots and the whistle of the wheels. The shining arrow flew toward the horde of bandits. It landed in the ground before them and exploded, tossing men and motorcycles into the air.

"Don't snooze, Leonarm!" Vildana shouted.

I hate people who always rush you. Even if you're a hundredth of a millisecond late in their view, all is lost. Somehow it gives them the right to shout at you, demand that you hurry up or stop slacking off.

"Don't shout," I answered calmly.

Falling in with Vildana's attack, I threw one grenade a little to the left, the second a little to the right, so that they'd both explode between the two groups of bandits trying to avoid the pile of motorcycles destroyed by the arrow.

"Well done," Vildana said.

"Well done to you too," I answered.

"But next time be quicker. Don't slack off."

I opened my mouth to answer that I'd thrown the grenades with that delay deliberately, making the shrapnel hit as many enemies as possible... and shut my mouth again. No point trying to explain anything to her.

The girl loaded and enchanted another arrow. This time the illumination was bright blue.

The bandits backed off, then split into three groups. The first and largest group continued along the road, while the two others split off onto the plains and began to catch up to us, keeping at a distance to our left and right. I put away my grenades. I couldn't throw them that far. I took out my AK, put it into single-shot mode and began to shoot toward the bandits on our left. After driving them away from that side, I moved to the right side, where the bandit group was getting dangerously close. I quickly took out two and they backed off into the plains again.

In the meantime, Vildana moved to the end of the bus and kicked out the glass at the rear with her already practiced kick. She aimed and released an arrow. Leaving a shimmering blue trail falling like snow behind it, the arrow shot into the center of the bandit group, which tried to escape the danger. The blue explosion was silent save for the crack of ice. A blue ring of cold radiated from the epicenter, covering the land in an icy crust for hundreds of feet around.

The bikers that had been close to the epicenter froze instantly into icy statues, and the wheels of their bikes continued to spin within their icy prison. Most of the bikers that were far enough away not to freeze still went down, slipping on the icy crust. Or pierced by the spears of ice that flew in all directions during the explosion.

The ice shone beautifully in the moonlight.

Long shadows ran behind the bandits and their motorcycles. The moon was fantastically large and bright. I hadn't seen much of it in real life. Constant clouds and light pollution in the city made it a rare sight. But when I'd had that vacation on the tropical island... it was smaller and dimmer there than the moon in Adam Online. Everything in reality was worse than in Adam Online.

The growing ice cover reached us. A cold wind blew in through the broken windows, and I felt my face cover with frost. But it wasn't as bad for me as for the others — as luck would have it, I had cold protection built into my UniSuit. Vildana cried out: the uncovered parts of her legs and face covered in white spots, and the locks of her dark hair sticking out from her helmet turned into white icicles. Half the bus cabin turned white, covered with a pattern of frost. One of the ice spears pierced the windscreen on the right of the driver.

"Fuck, hold on!" the driver shouted, spinning the

wheel with force.

The bus shook wildly, throwing Vildana and me around the cabin. Several times I was painfully pinned to the wall, the ceiling and the grab rails. My Light Gravity upgrade didn't soften anything under those forces.

The bus itself turned sideways in the road and slid along the ice, leaning ever more to one side. The driver span the wheel without effect: he'd completely lost control on the slippery surface. If we reached the edge of the ice cover in that state, the difference in traction would flip the bus.

"Spin the wheel, asshole!" Vildana shouted.

"I am, I am!" the driver shouted. "I'm spinning as much as I can, my dear people."

He managed to align the bus and turn in line with the road.

We crossed the border between ice and asphalt with no catastrophic consequences. But in the meantime, the bandits riding along the plains had managed to catch up to us unchallenged. Some of them stood up on their motorcycles and jumped from their seats onto the bus. The roof thundered and sagged under the weight of their bodies. The bandits crawled from both sides into the broken and open windows, firing their weapons.

Vildana managed to leap to her feet before me. She held her favorite axe. She cut the head off one bandit, then another... Fountains of blood dramatically sprayed the driver's wife and child.

A third bandit managed to get into the cabin and shot Vildana with a shotgun. She was pushed ten feet back, and her axe fell from her hands. The remnants of her armor fell off as she flew.

Then I got involved: I shot the bandit twice, both times in the head. I hurried to the girl. Was she alive? For some reason, I didn't want to lose her.

Vildana was on all fours, swinging from side to side. "Those bastards!"

Her armor was gone. In its place was the short torn dress she'd been wearing in the cage. On top of that, the thaw began. Melting frost dripped from the ceiling and walls, quickly soaking her dress to the point of erotic transparency. Vildana rose and reached for her bag to change her clothes.

Leather armor and a short metallic skirt appeared on her in place of the wet dress. A leather shield formed on one arm. She pulled her axe out from behind some seats and held it in the other hand. Then she took out a small scroll and applied it to her shield. She'd enchanted it to draw in projectile weapons again.

The rumble on the bus's roof stilled. A skylight opened and the legs of another bandit dropped through. Without letting him jump down, I shot him with my Uzi which I'd swapped for my Kalashnikov. The bandit screamed and fell to the floor.

The explosive ammunition attachment on the Uzi was powerful enough on its own, but with the one-hundred percent explosive damage boost from 'Hit #1', the bandits' bodies sometimes exploded like soap bubbles full of blood. Blood clots often flew at me after shots like that, sticking to my helmet glass. The bus's interior quickly turned into a branch of Doctor Cid's Clinic: guts everywhere, torn-off fingers sticking out of crevices in seats, floods of blood streaming down the walls.

While I reloaded, another brave bandit climbed down through the hatch, armed with a huge revolver with two magnetic coils at the sides. They made me think that the revolver was a rare laser gun model that didn't need energy charges but took energy from the surrounding air instead. The air around the revolver shimmered before each shot and small flickers of energy gathered around the magnetic coils. The coils themselves vibrated slightly, then stopped. The drum turned and the shot fired with a muffled click.

I dodged the shots and retreated deeper into the bus. Vildana took my place, covering herself with her shield. But... if there were no bullets, that meant her spell to draw in projectile weapons wouldn't work!

Vildana saw it too late as well. The first shot knocked the shield out of her hand, the second one the axe.

The bandit aimed the revolver at her. The air shimmered, electricity crackled...

The girl was literally invincible with her agility. She managed to twist away from the shot, jump onto the bandit's shoulders, wrap her bare legs around his neck and hammer on his head with her fists.

"Take THAT, asshole! And THAT," Vildana's voice rang out, punctuated by resounding blows.

Then a transparent sword appeared in her

hands for a few seconds, which she plunged into the bandit's chest. His body dissolved along with the sword.

"Ugh, I wasted a good spell on that piece of shit!"

While Vildana victoriously kicked the dead bandit, I admired her slightly full, curvaceous figure. Quite the hellcat! It seemed there was nothing that could withstand her ardor in battle. I was definitely glad we'd made peace. I wasn't sure I'd have survived a fight with her.

I took a deep breath. It was a beautiful night. What a coward I'd been when I'd nearly quit the game.

This... this was life!

Chapter 37
Last Two Rounds in the Box

VILDANA PICKED UP her axe and shield. I could still hear footsteps on the roof. We stood by the hatch, ready to welcome our guest. But this bandit was smarter. He didn't try to climb through the hatch. He sent a grenade instead.

The grenade bounced off the floor and flew toward Vildana. I jumped back ten feet and hid behind a seat. But Vildana acted differently. She demonstrated yet again what it meant to have points in Agility. She rushed to the hatch like lightning with the grenade in her hand. She threw it back through and didn't bother hiding — she just closed the hatch. She even had time to say:

"You dropped something, asshole."

The explosion made the roof press down into the cabin. A fiery cloud unfolded into the sky from both sides of the bus, throwing out the screaming bandits that had been on the roof. The bus sagged down as it went, its suspension scraping along the asphalt.

Vildana and I were thrown around the cabin

again like the last two rounds in a box. This time we both fell into a corner — Vildana on top of me. She was big, with bulging shapes. My face was entirely submerged in her chest. She smelled of snow and wintry freshness.

The explosion had broken something in the bus. The engine spluttered and some sort of rhythmic knocking began to grow in it. The bus's speed fell. The remaining lights in the cabin went out along with the only headlight. All the lights on the dashboard flickered and died.

But nobody else was crashing around on the roof. We'd won.

"Why do you hate this bus so much?" I asked. "First you break all the windows, then freeze it, now you try to blow it up."

Vildana laughed and climbed off me. She took a tome in a ratty cover out of her bag, opened it and began to run her fingers through the pages. People who chose a magic class got a tome instead of a tablet. It did the same as the tablet or neurointerface, it just looked like an ancient book.

"Why're you lying down?" she asked.

"No reason. Admiring the view."

"Let's gather the loot, admirer."

Vildana and I searched the bandits' bodies, moving toward each other from opposite ends of the bus. I found nothing apart from ammunition, medkits and three thousand gold. All the weaponry was in poor condition, so there was no sense in taking it with us.

"Shame the bandits left their bikes way back there," Vildana said when we met. "I'd have ridden away on one."

"Where to?"

"Back to the bandit base to cut on the rest of 'em. I want blood."

"Your Reputation has gone up after killing so many bandits."

"Yeah? You think I give a shit about Reputation? I'm here to do what I want. And I want to kill or experience pain. You killed my favorite, Three Bucks. You're lucky I switched to killing the bandits, although... taking out another player is always more fun."

I instinctively grabbed for my Uzi.

Vildana laughed hoarsely. "Why so jumpy? If I wanted to kill you, you'd be lying in that factory now. You're just not much use. Low level, no money. A noob."

"I got killed once when I wasn't expecting it."

"Don't worry. When I decide to kill you, I'll be sure to send you a notification."

I grabbed my tablet, intending to read my achievements. I'd leveled up lots after getting so many kills.

Vildana grabbed the revolver with the magnetic coils and began to examine it. She held it so inexpertly that it was clearly no weapon for her. I put my tablet aside.

"Want to give me that revolver? You use magic and medieval weapons, right?"

"Why should I give you it? I can sell it for a lot of money."

"Come on," I laughed. "Who will buy it from you? You won't get within a mile of any stores with your Reputation. Unless you sell it to bandits, but they might not pay up, you know that. And nobody needs revolvers in magic zones."

"You can buy it."

"How much?"

"One hundred thousand."

"It isn't worth that, and I don't have a hundred thousand."

"As you wish. I'll keep it."

I grabbed Three Bucks' amulet and swung it before her face as if trying to hypnotize her. "Wanna trade?"

An item identification scroll unfolded before Vildana. She read the amulet's description and nodded eagerly. She grabbed the amulet and handed over the revolver.

Vildana immediately put the amulet on and placed it on her voluptuous breast. I sat down and switched on my tablet. The screen was dappled with messages. Since I hadn't had a revolver like this before, I decided to read its expanded description.

Tesla's Revolver
An electrifying death to your enemies!

Weapon type: Energy.
Ammunition: Not required.
Damage per shot: 49.
Optimal range: 10-650 feet.
Rate of fire: 1.6 seconds.
Durability: 55/100.
Weight: 5 lbs.
Value: 33,000g.

So much time had passed, but the myth of Tesla and his inventions still roamed the game worlds. Any weapon whose operation was obscure, but somehow linked to electricity, was named after him. There was also a Tesla assault rifle, a Tesla grenade launcher and a Tesla light sword, and even a Tesla machine gun, although it was less a machine and more a device. As for heavy armament, there was a Tesla Tower, which sprouted from under the ground and sting the enemy with energy charges. They all needed ammunition in the form of energy units, while that revolver had an unlimited supply like the alien rifle, but with a low rate of fire to balance it out.

Well, it must be fate... Or rather, the CS storylines telling me that I shouldn't neglect energy weapons. Only trouble was, the revolver was almost half broken. I'd need to take it to a We Fix It!.

I returned to my messages.

There were lots of them, so they automatically grouped into categories that displayed all my achievements at once:

KILLS:

Level 1-10 spiderbots: 7, +7 XP.
Level 1-10 humans: 43, +430 XP.
Level 1-10 bosses: Three Bucks, +25 XP.

ACHIEVEMENTS:
Achievement complete: Headhunter.
Earned: +50 XP.
+1 skill point.

Achievement unlocked: Headhunter II.
Perform 50 headshots in a row.
Completed: 7/50.
Completion reward:
+100 XP.
+1 skill point.

Achievement unlocked: Bombardier.
Kill five enemies using explosives.
Completed: 9/5.
Earned: +25 XP.

Achievement unlocked: Bombardier II.
Kill 50 enemies using explosives.
Completed: 9/50.
Completion reward:
+100 XP.
+1 point to Explosives skill.

Achievement completed: Road Menace.
Kill five enemies in overland transport.

Completed: 6/5.
Earned: +25 XP.

Achievement unlocked: Road Menace II.
Kill 50 enemies in overland transport.
Completed: 6/50.
Completion reward:
+100 XP.
SKILLS:

Explosives skill learned.
Earned: +10 XP.
Keep blowing stuff up to blow stuff up even harder!

High Climber skill learned.
Earned: +10 XP.
Like climbing high? The higher you go, the harder you fall! Keep improving the High Climber skill by obtaining the corresponding equipment.

Automatic Weapons skill increased: +20 XP.

Night Vision skill increased: +20 XP.

Eagle Eye skill increased: +20 XP.
Eagle Eye skill increased to level 2.
You now see even more, even farther and clearer. The main thing is — keep your eyes open!

Congratulations, Leonarm, you leveled up!
Your current level: 10.

You have unlocked one free transfer to Rim One.
Attention: please ensure that you have finished all your business in Rim Zero. There will be no way back.

Attention: you have unused stat points (7) and skill points (1). Spend them wisely!

Phew, I'd barely made it through this sea of achievements. What a mission! From level three to level ten. Although, why was I celebrating? Olga and I used to compete to see who could powerlevel new characters the fastest. My personal record for getting out of Rim Zero was forty-four minutes. In comparison, my two days now wasn't much of an achievement. More of an abysmal embarrassment.

Vildana sat on the seat in front of me and skimmed through her tome. Spirals of light occasionally separated from the book's pages and surrounded her body. The girl cried out in joy and shivered from time to time. She was distributing her points too.

She caught me looking at her, especially at her thighs under her short skirt and her full breasts.

"What're you staring at?"

"It's just... It's my second day in Adam Online and I still haven't..."

"Put your tongue away, thirsty boy, you ain't my type."

"Hey, I'm taller than Three Bucks."

"Yeah, but you don't have his charisma."

"How's that?"

"You're a soft one. Can't do what he can do."

"What, Three Bucks had some special skills?"

Vildana just rolled her eyes in response, as if to say I wouldn't understand.

"Alright. Guess I'll level up my muscles and buy some assless leather pants."

"Sure, then we'll talk. I'm heading to Rim One as well. Nothing left to do here. That little fight of ours took me up to level twelve. I won't get enough XP for kills here."

"With your passion for a shitty Reputation, I doubt you'll live to admire my leather pants."

Vildana opened her tome and showed me a page where an old flourishing script showed that her Reputation was at minus nineteen.

That's still a lot, you'll have a hard time in Rim One.

"Don't you get it yet? Challenge and pain is what I love."

Another voice spoke. The driver's wife. I'd forgotten she was there.

"Thank you for saving us."

Damn, could she say anything except that? I returned to my tablet and distributed my new points.

+3 Knowledge.

+2 Health.

+2 Luck.

I put one skill point into Eagle Eye, increasing it to level three. My vision blurred for a moment and then refocused with a clarity I wasn't used to. Vildana sat on the seat in front of me, but now, from where I was sitting, I could make out all the details of the patterns on the 3buck$ amulet reflected in the dusty rear-view mirror.

It was incredibly beautiful.

Chapter 38
Cool_Name

THE GRENIKA'S three engines roared as it climbed vertically into the sky at Mach twenty.

At that moment, LeCube's software configuration seemed more like a missile than a military flying machine. The blue sky quickly darkened, turning into a grey depth with the blackness of space showing through. All the clouds in the flying machine's path were first torn apart, then burned to nothing by the plasma from the engine.

From above, Rim Three looked just like it did on the neurointerface map. The scale decreased rapidly. Grisha's increased Perception allowed him to still see his guildmates' markers on the ground, along with the coalition troops, highlighted red. The Black Wave was under the cover of the defensive fortifications in the Langoliers' former base. The guild took control of it after Grisha's crushing victory when he first bought LeCube.

Fortunado even left the base's name as it was. It showed up on the maps as the Langoliers' home base, although the symbol had changed to the chevron of the Black Wave. Fortunado considered this a small, but effective dig at the enemy.

The base was one of the largest in Rim Zero (the largest user location there was Dimension X). A dozen gigantic bizoid nests, an infinite source of water, mines with valuable minerals and components... There was even a qualia mine. It produced up to three grams of the rare material per day. And all of it was within the base, which made it highly valuable.

The coalition troops surrounded the base and gradually tightened the circle. They were likely taken aback by the powerful Tesla towers generously spread out along the approach to the base. The Langoliers themselves placed them there when they owned it.

A mountain range could also be seen through the scraps of cloud. At its center was Dimension X. All that could be seen of it was the anomaly that protected Nika from aerial attacks. The location of the hangars and defensive armament was hidden. Nika poured hundreds of thousands of energy units into camouflaging the zone. She allowed no uninvited guests and kept her respawn tower to herself.

On land it seemed as if Dimension X was far away, the path to it winding through Brooklyn Forest and a mined proving ground peppered with artillery shots from Dimension X. Now it was clear that Nika wasn't that far from the Langoliers' former home base.

The view got smaller with each passing second. The markers disappeared. Grisha's Perception had exceeded its capabilities. To track the movement of players and NPCs from orbit, you had to have the Space Explorer skill.

Before the start of the battle, Grisha put his available points into just two parameters. His Maximum Altitude now allowed him to move into a low near-earth orbit, and his Maximum Speed let him do it in a very short time indeed. In addition, the Quick Start piloting skill, which Grisha himself had, gave him a fifty percent increase in Speed for his first minute of flight. Mach thirty! If Grisha had been a human or a bizoid, he'd need to have sufficient Strength and Health to survive those forces.

Incidentally, that limitation didn't extend to certain classes of supers: they could move at almost the same speeds and altitudes without using flying transportation. They were supers, after all. A race that seemed as if it was created specially for arrogant dipshits.

One of those supers, a player by the name of Camper from the Golden Horde, followed Grisha nearly a mile behind. His red cloak stretched out behind him like a plank at these massive speeds, and a defensive dome against the heat formed around his body, starting at the head and stretching down to the super's legs. Holding his fist ahead of him, Camper slowly but surely closed the distance to the Grenika.

Two MiGs rose two miles below the MiG. Even lower were a dozen or more coalition jets. For now, Grisha was unconcerned about them. In comparison to the Grenika, the super and the suborbital MiGs, they were low-speed planes that would take a long time to get into low orbit. As for the two MiGs, Grisha had a surprise prepared: the new Second Skin configuration program. Nika let him use it for free for seven days.

"We need to test it in battle. In exchange, you'll provide me with all your battle logs."

Although Nika veiled it under financial interest, Grisha understood: she wanted to help him in the war without admitting it to herself. He was touched and he signed the agreement.

It was Camper who represented the greatest danger to Grisha. He was a superhuman of the Superman class. Grisha already had experience of fighting with him. It had happened during the assault on Londinium.

The Black Wave needed to stock up on nutrition supplies for their bizoids. Fortunado assigned Grisha and two Slug-class bizoids to the mission. They were gigantic sacks of skin full of hundreds of different types of venoms for poisoning other bizoids. The slugs had special organs for storing alkaline acid that could eat through metal, destroying mechanodestructors and vehicles. Streams of liquid full of bacteria fell from the slugs' mouths. It infected people, fallen angels and some types of supers with rapid onset illnesses.

The coalition set up an ambush next to one of the nutrition sales stations in the Londinium suburbs. They probably hadn't known that the Black Wave was headed there, they were just arranging small squads around all the important resource stations. The squad consisted of one Superman-class superhuman and two strong mages. Grisha wasn't certain of their subclasses.

The superman Camper attacked LeCube

immediately using Kinesthetic Telekinesis. The skill was far weaker than the magical Phantom Explosion that the mages of the coalition used to successfully hit Grisha. But the slugs took out the mages in no time, covering them with an immobilizing jelly. In theory, the mages were supposed to dissolve in the jelly within half a minute, turning into food for the bizoids, but they had good regeneration. From time to time the mages cast a Restore Life spell on themselves, returning their drained Health.

The mages couldn't break through the jelly. Stuck in the stinking semi-transparent and snot-like mass, all they could do was watch the battle between Grisha and Camper. The bizoids couldn't help Grisha, since they had to constantly maintain the jelly entrapping the mages.

The superman had to touch Grisha to affect the material of which LeCube was made. Camper had put so many points into his Agility that Grisha's Perception had a hard time keeping up with his Time Slow, so the superman often reached LeCube, reducing its durability with each touch. Some of the kinesthetic telekinetic attacks ignored Grisha's defenses and hit him, taking away big chunks of Health.

Of course, Grisha responded to the attacks. Sometimes he hit Camper almost by accident, but it took a long time of trying to kill a Superman. Grisha changed his software configurations, transforming into everything he could, but the kinesthetic telekinesis inexorably did its job. Its influence was particularly strong during the transformation time, when LeCube became defenseless. Grisha realized that he was only making things harder for himself. He returned to his base form and stopped his counterattacks.

Camper's telekinetic bites took LeCube's Durability down to forty three out of a hundred. There was no sense in retreating. Camper didn't have to worry about enemies running away from him: he could nip at their heels with telekinesis all the way back to the respawn point. And the two bizoids couldn't let the mages go: they would have finished Grisha off with a double Phantom Explosion.

The last time Grisha was in such danger was during the fight with Ozerg. Just as he was preparing to die and lose LeCube, help arrived: four medium-level mages who Fortunado had sent after Grisha and the bizoids, with orders to stay out of the way and not give away their presence. Of course, he didn't warn his brother about this. Damn strategist.

The Superman class had low magic resistance. Plasma guns had no effect on Camper, but magic fireballs dealt medium damage to him.

The mages first cast a Slow spell on the super, then Detection to prevent him from using invisibility. Next came the fireballs, enriched with ice and lightning.

Gathering the remainder of his strength, Camper broke away from the ambush and flew off, his red cloak flapping. He'd left his comrades alone to solve the problem of surviving for themselves. His mages immediately offered a ransom. Grisha decided to take it. More gold meant more component nanomass. Unlike money, he never had enough of that.

Another fight with Camper awaited him. This time he was unlikely to receive help. All the Black

Wave's troops were busy defending the base.

The Grenika climbed into orbit and turned toward Camper. Grisha turned LeCube into its base configuration, the simple black cube, and surrounded it with a visible forcefield.

Camper floated five hundred yards off. For some reason his red cloak fluttered in space as if from the wind.

Camper hailed him. "I thought you'd keep running and I'd have to follow you to the moon."

"And I thought supermen had stopped wearing their underpants over their tights."

"They aren't tights!" Camper spat. "This is super-durable legwear with an invulnerability aura!"

"Hmm, looks to me like ordinary underpants over tights."

"Look who's talking, some black square?"

"It's a cube, not a square."

Grisha switched off the link. He didn't want to get into a verbal duel; two enemy MiGs had already left the atmosphere and were quickly approaching.

Adam Online's surface didn't look the same as the planet Earth from space. After all, the world wasn't round, but flat, adjoining another flat plain. However high you went, the horizon remained an even line. At the same time, the moon and other accessible planets existed as spheres.

You could move from Rim to Rim through space,

but getting into orbit was a high-level skill. Mechanodestructors needed special skills and frames to do it. Mages would have to spend a lot of mana to open a portal in orbit, and they had no need of it. They'd die without oxygen. The skill of using spacesuits was entirely non-magical, and powerful mages simply created portals directly to wherever they needed to go. Flying machines capable of spaceflight used up an immense amount of energy. It would be cheaper to pay for passage.

And naturally, the space above Rim Six was wreathed in anomalies and black holes through which none had yet found a path. The brave souls who had tried had died and lost their characters. The only known place to get through was at Jamilla's Tomb, which was on land and under the control of the Black Wave.

Grisha brought up his available software configurations on the screen. Some of them still had numbered titles, but Nika had started giving her new configurations names, as Grisha had asked. True, Nika didn't apply much imagination to her config names. She'd called them "Name" or "Cool_Name" or "Damn_What_a_Cool_Config_Name".

Grisha chose a configuration called Second Skin. It sounded good. This was the only time he could congratulate Nika on a config well named.

Second Skin software configuration activated. Target search mode.

Grisha selected both MiGs one after another.

Targets confirmed.
Requires: 25,000+25,000+25,000 CN.
Available in storage: 230,000 CN.
Use?

Grisha confirmed. Two identical clumps of component nanomass separated from LeCube's sides and rushed toward the airplanes. The clumps were as black as LeCube itself, so they blended in perfectly with the background of space. But the both the super and the MiGs had upgrades that could help them see this incomprehensible crud flying toward them.

The MiGs responded by firing their plasma guns, and Camper used Kinesthetic Telekinesis again. The energy beams flew through the clumps, burning away some of their CN. But since Grisha was controlling their flight, he maneuvered the mass to avoid great losses.

His neurointerface lit up:

Damage taken: -15,200.
Health: 104,800/120,000.

Right. This part of the component nanomass was still a part of LeCube, a part of Grisha himself, which was the only reason he could control these parts like LeCube itself. That meant that losing some of it meant losing Health, and his defenses couldn't protect him.

But the separated chunks of component nanomass flew inexorably onward. Dispersing into tiny particles, they overpowered the MiGs' forcefields and engulfed the airplanes from nose to tail. The airplanes were covered in black. Their engines spluttered, their forcefields deactivated. The jets tumbled helplessly, weaving and spinning.

Grisha could tell that the mechanodestructors in the MiGs were trying to shake off Second Skin. It blocked the airplane's external functions: they couldn't shoot or talk over the radio. They couldn't even eject the core to escape the immobilized frame.

On the other hand, Camper easily took care of the chunk of nanomass intended for him. It seemed he'd upgraded his Kinesthetic Telekinesis a lot. The superman's right fist was surrounded by a barely noticeable cloud of shimmering light. He met the flying mass with a punch. The component nanomass disintegrated into dust, and Grisha felt that he couldn't reassemble it. It was gone.

The interface confirmed it.

Damage taken: -50,000.
Health: 54,800/120,000.
CN available in storage: 155,000.

The situation began to look threatening for Grisha. Another confirmation that LeCube's invincibility was no longer a given. His enemies had accumulated knowledge about its weaknesses. Grisha himself had thought many times that if he'd been in the enemy's place and knew what he did about LeCube, he could kill himself many times over.

Grisha was a brave soldier, but not a fool. He fought to the end when he was winning, but knew when to retreat when the fight was lost. Retreat wasn't running away. Retreat could also be a tactical maneuver.

That said, it was too soon to retreat. Grisha had orders from his brother: to draw some of the enemy's flying units away from the base, which is what he was doing. The entire fleet of MiGs, Eurofighters, flying supers, humans in suborbital shuttles and other heroes were chasing after him. Everyone wanted to be the first to take out as juicy a target as Grisha. Most importantly, they all knew they were being drawn away, but each thought himself smarter than the rest. The coalition was far from the synergy and military precision of the Black Wave.

Grisha gave the command, and Second Skin activated its second property. Each particle of component nanomass began to vibrate and pulled the material of the jets into itself. Right now, the mechanodestructors' interfaces would be flashing with alarms, reporting the destruction of their frames. Their ejection would be offline, their repair skills would fail to keep up with the material loss...

Done — one of the MiGs disintegrated along with its mechanodestructor. The remaining CN headed back to Grisha.

Grisha (Mechanodestructor, Guild: Black Wave) killed Zyxel (Mechanodestructor, Guild: Golden Horde) using: LeCube (Mechanodestructor Frame).

Recovered: 18,000 CN.
CN available in storage: 173,000.
Earned: +200 XP.

The second MiG fell apart next, but Camper got in the way and only a few thousand CN made it back to Grisha. Kinesthetic Telekinesis destroyed the rest.

Grisha immediately started regenerating his Health. And to win time, he opened a hail.

"What do you think? Awesome, huh?"

"Not really. You broke a couple of planes. I can do that too. You find it awesome how I broke you?"

"You haven't broken me yet. And I got plenty of surprises."

"I have more."

A shining cocoon surrounded the superman's body and slowly expanded, capturing more and more space. In seconds, the wave hit LeCube and swept away its defenses.

> *Kinetic Explosion.*
> *Damage taken: -4,940.*
> *Forcefield destroyed.*
> *Restoration under way...*
> *Warning, must increase CN expenditure!*

Grisha felt LeCube begin to fall apart under the telekinetic forces. His Health regeneration stopped at the previous mark... then fell. It was slow, but he had no way to stop the decrease.

Chapter 39
Red Cloak

THINGS GOT WORSE and worse. Along with his kinesthetic telekinesis, Camper had upgraded his ordinary version as well. Now he was attacking LeCube at range. Grisha strengthened his defenses, converting CN into energy.

"Think, Grigory, think!" he said to himself. "How did he get that skill so quick? He must have redistributed stats and skill points."

Grisha kept an alarmed eye on his dropping Health and the increasing progress bar of his defense recovery. He converted more and more component nanomass to increase his defense even further. But the amount reached the threshold: he could no longer convert more component nanomass into energy. He didn't have enough Knowledge or a high enough level of some skill that Grisha didn't even remember, because he didn't take interest in boring skills.

Maybe now was the time to retreat? But... there was no way he could switch to another configuration without a forcefield to cover him. The constant telekinetic attacks would simply destroy LeCube. The transformation time from one config to another was LeCube's weakness. And it was a good thing that nobody knew it!

Alright, Grisha continued to think. *Camper strengthened some stats, but seriously lowered others. The superman's telekinesis depends on his Strength stat. To damage the defended LeCube at such a great distance, he must have put a lot of points into his Strength. He probably sacrificed his Luck first of all. Then he would have lowered his Agility to the minimum, otherwise he would have already gone into slowed time.*

Health: 54,000/120,000.
Forcefield regeneration: 4,300/10,000.

Grisha began to fly farther away to weaken the effects of the telekinesis. Moving immediately raised his energy expenditure, but his restoration speed increased. The superman closed the distance again, keeping the same range of around five hundred yards. Now Grisha kept an eye on three stats:

Health: 52,000/120,000.
Forcefield regeneration: 4,500/10,000.
CN Expenditure: 9,800 per minute.

Fortunado's avatar popped up in the neurointerface. "How's it going, bro? Our plan worked. We repelled the attack on the ground. Just like I predicted, the coalition began an attack on Shoreline at the same time as the attack on the Langolier base.

Their strategists are dumb if they think I'm that easy to fool. They thought we'd divert all our forces to defend the Langolier base and leave Shoreline undefended, but on the contrary, we reinforced it... Hey, what's up?"

"I'm in trouble. Hurry and tell me how to defeat a strong player that dropped his Luck and Agility to boost his Strength."

"Use weapons or skills with highly random behavior, of course. For example, missiles with a random flight trajectory. Shells with a large amount of shrapnel. Plasma bombs. They all have secondary destructive effects that are highly random. His Luck won't help him, and his Agility won't save him."

"I don't have any weapons, I'm just a cube. I can't change my configuration until my shield recovers. I can use my ethereal creature, but Kinesthetic Telekinesis will easily destroy it. Or I could use Second Skin, but I control it directly, and all the damage goes straight to my Health, which is already low."

"We-e-ell, I'm no expert in LeCube, bro. You can't retreat?"

"My CN expenditure increases when I move. I don't have much as it is When my component nanomass runs out, my forcefield will too. I'm a sitting duck."

"Damn. What can I say? My condolences... Although, wait. What does Second Skin do?"

Grisha showed his brother a clip of the battle with the MiGs.

Fortunado watched the battle unfold. "Yep, I see the nanomass fragments fly in a straight line. That's what allowed the superman to repel one of the fragments. That's why he's keeping his distance from you, so he has time to defend against a strike."

"So what do I do?"

"Again, I've never piloted LeCube, but... try to be chaotic."

"What do you mean?"

"I mean, when you activate Second Skin, don't make your trajectory predictable. Move in such a way that your chosen direction surprises you. I'm the strategist here, you're supposed to be our intuitive and unpredictable warrior. I work based on plans, you work in the circumstances arising around them. So do your thing."

"Alright. Over and out."

There was one consolation: the rest of the enemy armada that had followed Grisha into space had turned around and headed home. The coalition's ground forces had suffered a defeat due to the absence of their air support.

Grisha pulled up a fourth line on the screen, the most painful to see. It marked the time remaining until death.

Health: 44,000/120,000.
Forcefield regeneration: 5,600/10,000.
CN expenditure: 11,200 per minute.
Estimated time to CN exhaustion: 6-7 minutes.

Damn... With these rates, he had no time to recover his defenses, turn into the Grenika and escape the battlefield. Or rather, perform a tactical retreat. Time to follow his brother's advice.

Grisha couldn't imagine how to control the nanomass chaotically, especially with two chunks at once. If they were standard controllable shells, he'd ask his personal assistant to calculate a trajectory consisting of random points. But the personal assistant was useless here. It waved him away with a nebulous phrase:

"Unable to set object parameters."

After a little thought, Grisha decided that it would be better to send two small chunks of CN to Camper instead of one large one. And yes, he needed to somehow prepare for the fact that if Camper could fight off both, it was game over.

Two blocks of component nanomass detached from LeCube's sides again. The superman was ready for it. He knew that one strike of Kinesthetic Telekinesis could destroy these satellites and deal damage to his opponent. He was even surprised that Grisha was trying the same trick again. Or was it...

"Got it!" Camper cried joyfully into the ether. "You can't turn into anything without a forcefield, right, asshole? You're vulnerable when changing shape."

But then Camper fell silent, realizing he had to be on guard. The blobs of component nanomass had turned sharply for some reason. Describing unpredictable loops, they tore around like a ricocheting plasma charge for a while, then flew apart in opposite directions, neither of which led to Camper.

"Gone nuts, huh?" he muttered on an open channel.

But Grisha didn't answer.

Camper's reduced Perception only let him track the nanomass blocks for a short time. Soon they disappeared in the blackness of space. Camper couldn't figure out Grisha's plan. He was on high alert. What was it? Some kind of ejection? Did the remnants of LeCube carry off the mechanodestructor core, leaving the enemy facing an empty shell? It couldn't be. Surely Grisha wouldn't abandon the frame that everyone was after, that the greatest masters of crafting had tried to reproduce.

There were rumors that someone had managed to create a mass that took the form of a cube, allowing the mechanodestructor core to control it. Someone had even managed to make the mass transform not only into other forms, but into complex objects like a giant axe or a bow and arrow. But it was all a far cry from LeCube's abilities.

The craftsmen claimed that someone spent almost an entire lifetime on getting the required components and forcing the mass to take on complex forms like robots and jets.

To calm himself, Camper increased the pressure from his Kinesthetic Telekinesis. Whatever Grisha had come up with, he had to kill him before his plan worked.

As a race, superpeople had no interfaces like those of mechanodestructors or humans in UniSuits. The enemy's Health looked like a small column of light: green when it was high, flashing red when it was low.

The column of light above LeCube had only just turned from orange to red. A little more and it'd start blinking! Then he'd be able to use the Decisive Blow skill: it instantly killed any enemy whose Health was below ten percent.

"Come on, come on! Start flashing, you bastard!" Camper clenched his fists, feeling LeCube's material in his palms. "A little more!"

Supers had no personal assistants. 'Sidekicks' fulfilled the role instead. They were a special class of pets available only to them. A sidekick often looked like an animal but was actually a kind of super NPC. The super worked in tandem with the sidekick, and could level it up just like himself, while the pets of ordinary humans earned and distributed their experience themselves.

The Batman class, which Camper used in his last rotation, had Robin or Batgirl as a sidekick. But Camper was a solo player by nature. He didn't like to have a human-like NPC hanging around with him all the time. So his superman sidekick was Krypto Mouse, who could take on the same abilities as his master for a few minutes at a time. Normalized for the fact that he was a mouse, of course. The stronger the master, the longer Krypto Mouse's skill cooldown. It had reached two days now. This meant the mouse hadn't participated in the first fight with LeCube, and today Camper had used Krypto Mouse's abilities to kill a squad of Black Wave mages that had stood in the way of the coalition's infantry.

Now Camper regretted using Krypto Mouse. Grisha couldn't have survived double telekinesis. But

LeCube wasn't flashing yet. The red column above it turned deeper and deeper. When it seemed that the column would stay red forever, it flashed. Thirty seconds later, it flashed again.

"Yes!" Camper cried victoriously. "It's time! You're de..."

An alarming red mist enveloped Camper's peripheral vision, signaling danger. One of the chunks that Grisha sent off to who knows where was coming back, and fast. Its trajectory was strange, fitful. Camper was forced to switch his ranged telekinesis back to kinesthetic to meet the flying blob with a strike, like before.

He threw his fist forward, but the unpredictable trajectory caused him to choose the wrong moment to strike. The blob leapt to the left, then the right, then flew straight at him from somewhere below. A kinesthetic telekinetic strike, in contrast to a constant attack, took two seconds to cool down. Camper managed to jump to the side.

The blob still reached its target. No, not Camper — his cloak.

The black mass quickly enveloped the equipment item, spreading itself over its entire surface. Camper undid the cloak and threw it off himself, flying farther away. Just like with the MiGs, the nanomass shook, intending to tear the cloak into dust. That was bad. The cloak provided defense. Now Camper had half the protection he had before. The cloak increased his stats and skills. And more than that, it looked awesome!

His strike came off cooldown. Camper flew to the

cloak, stricken by the nanomass, and hit it.

"That's my cloak, asshole!"

The black mass split into shards like glass, freeing the cloak. It was still intact! The red column above Grisha flashed frequently. There it was! The enemy's health had dropped below ten percent! But Camper had no time to activate Decisive Blow. His peripheral vision filled with a red mist again. Camper turned.

"Fu..."

Something black blinked, covering the light of distant stars. Camper felt a mass enshroud his body, first immobilizing him, and then depriving him of sight, hearing and the senses that supermen possessed. All that remained was his X-Ray Vision. But what good was that? All it could do was let him see the triumphant Grisha at the last moment as he put up a forcefield and turned into a jet.

No matter how the superman struggled, he couldn't throw off the nanomass shackles. Telekinesis! It helped a little, weakening the pressure, but the damage dealt to him by the blob enveloping him was stronger. Soon Camper's entire vision was red.

The cosmos disappeared. Camper's last regret was his cloak. It remained in orbit. And a superman was nothing but a chump without his cloak.

Camper flew along a tunnel and found himself on the ground, somewhere in Rim Three. The respawn station flashed a welcoming green light at him. A happy voice blared from a speaker.

"Thanks to the Projectoria system, you have been brought back to life! Keep dying, we're always pleased to see you and your money!"

Camper gazed into the blue sky as if waiting for his cloak to descend from orbit and fall to his feet.

Chapter 40
Trouble with the Law

WHEN WE ARRIVED at Town Zero, a long and red strip of dawn was already visible on the horizon. It shone orange at its center, foreshadowing the sun's coming and outlining scarlet clouds in the thick blue sky, lit from underneath like fantastic cliffs hanging above.

It was all extraordinarily large, its beauty and majesty stunning. I was particularly stunned, as I'd seen only the real sky for so many years. There you saw only smoke, radioactive dust clouds, acid rain and other horrors falling down on people's heads.

I was the only one among us to notice the beauty of that morning in Adam Online.

The driver drove and drank whisky, his wife and child slept. Vildana grabbed a few empty scrolls, placed her tome on her beautiful bare knees, opened it and started muttering. Multicolored threads of light stretched out from the tome and began to stream into the scroll, but broke off halfway through the process: the light threads lost their color and dispersed, melting in the air. Vildana swore and began the process over again.

I didn't understand people that lived surrounded

by technology but strove toward magic in the virtual world. All modern religions had discredited themselves so much that ignorant people, no longer having faith in God, turned toward magic instead. Even a version of magic created by a highly advanced virtual world.

Vildana slammed the tome shut in annoyance. "Damn it, I don't have enough Knowledge to cobble together a decent scroll with a spell for drawing in projectile weapons."

"A wise person once said that the choice between technology and magic in Adam Online is purely an aesthetic one. The fact that you like magic implies that you're a person that believes in fairytales and miracles."

Vildana yawned. Since sleep wasn't a critical necessity in Adam Online, her yawn was a demonstration of how she felt about my statement.

"And who was that wise person? Not you, clearly."

"The creator of the first version of Adam Online said it. Adam Mickiewicz."

Vildana perked up.

"I thought Adam Online referred to the biblical character Adam."

"No. That's a common misconception. Adam Mickiewicz was as full of himself as most developers, so he named the virtual world after himself.

"Hmm."

"Mr. Mickiewicz released his project when taharration was still brand new, and most users used gyrospheres to enter the extranet."

"Yeah, I remember those... When I was at

school, I used to walk miles on those things. Ah, the golden years of childhood. Good thing they're behind us."

Since my story was a revelation to Vildana, I continued confidently,

"Back then there were already other worlds, Heroes of Magic, Warcraft: The New World, DotA 5. The history of those games stretches all the way back to time immemorial, when there weren't even gyrospheres."

"How did people get onto the extranet?"

"They didn't. It didn't exist yet either. There was a network called the Internet."

"Oh, that's right, I remember something about that from school." Vildana moved to a seat closer to me and leaned on the seat arm in interest, her chin in her hand. "What ended up happening to Mickiewicz?"

"Since all this happened before the European War, his home country Poland still existed. The first thing Adam did was emigrate from Poland to the USA. In those days, the USA was a single country, not a confederation of who knows what, like it is now. All modern technologies were concentrated in the USA, along with the development centers for virtual game worlds."

"And now?"

"Since then, those hazardous industries have been moved to the Kazan People's Republic, China and Moscovian Rus. Most of the Golden Billion live in the confederation nowadays."

Vildana's hazel eyes widened in interest. "Who are they?"

I looked at this true child of taharration ruefully. She didn't even know that we were all living in this virtual pen solely at the behest of the Golden Billion, so that we didn't waste resources or take up space... and at the same time produced added value to provide for the carefree lifestyle of the Golden Billion.

Vildana likely didn't even know that almost all the brands in Adam Online belonged to people that had never even climbed into a taharration pod.

I sighed. "It doesn't matter who they are. The important thing is that Adam Mickiewicz never found investors to create a test version of his world."

"Why not?"

"Because the game's concept was unclear. Initially Adam Online looked basically like how Rim Zero looks now. A conventional post-apocalyptic world in which you had to survive by running around the map, picking up and upgrading weapons and killing other players or monsters."

"Sounds like bullshit. No magic, no other races?"

"That's just what the investors said. They said, mister, you want to compete with monsters of the game industry like DotA 5 and PUBG-G, with Second World, with the LevelUp D. S. reality simulator and dozens more popular titles, and all you have is some standard shooter where you collect garbage? And you're proposing a virtual world designed for the gyrosphere when the whole industry is actively moving across to taharration technology?"

Vildana fidgeted in her seat. She took out her tome and ran her fingers along the page, brushing a wisp of light onto herself. Her attractive bare knees disappeared from view, covered by baggy woolen pants.

"It's cold," she said. "Keep going, this is fun."

"More fun than Three Bucks?"

She chuckled. "In terms of conversation, sure." So I continued.

"Next, Adam Mickiewicz had a simple idea: to compete with all the other games, he had to create a game that had all the features of all those popular games."

"Why didn't anyone else think of that first?"

"Because the QCPs back then, and even the ones we have now, aren't capable of creating that can contain a potentially infinite number of worlds. Plus, you have to somehow balance the difference between those worlds. You have to equalize the age-old question: magic or technology? On top of that, Adam Online offered players a huge virtual universe that few people fly around nowadays, and infinite opportunities to expand the world. It needed to offer that to satisfy people who wanted to explore new lands. Even a whole cluster of the most advanced quantum platforms around can't handle that. So the challenge was to create an infinite world with finite possibilities."

"So that means Adam Online is a world without limits, but the computers can't create anything truly limitless within it?"

I looked at Vildana in amazement. "Exactly right. Hey, you're not as..."

"You should know," Vildana said quietly. "If you say that I'm 'not as dumb as I look', I'll run you through."

"I was going to say... not as uninformed as I

thought."

"Alright, you can stay alive. Keep going."

"Next, Adam Mickiewicz came up with an ingenious idea. He suggested transferring part of the world generation into the binary arrays themselves. That meant that in a way, the players would create the very universe they inhabited. That solved both the problem of computing capacity and the problem of limits. The understanding of the world's infinity was shifted onto the people. Unlike the QCPs, human consciousness can grasp something immeasurable. To imagine infinity, all a human has to do is imagine the idea of infinity. QCPs, on the other hand, start calculating the coordinates of infinity and then crash after they reach the limits of their computing power. In other words, our binary arrays show the QCPs which direction to expand one part of the world or another, and the control systems rely on that data to create the required surroundings. The parts of the world that don't have an observing conscious player just don't exist. That takes a lot of load off the platforms and CSes."

"So our brains aren't just visitors in Adam, they're essential parts of the virtual world?"

"Exactly right." I somehow carelessly patted Vildana on the knee.

She allowed it. The girl gazed at the rising sun with a strange look on her face. If she believed my words, her consciousness had created that sun.

"After that, investors were queuing up to sign contracts," I continued, keeping my hand on her knee. "And they were right. In a short time, Adam Online became so popular that the other worlds died out, lost their user base. Later, after Adam Online stopped being just a game and intellectual property and shifted into the jurisdiction of the UN, all those games were absorbed into Adam. Now both Heroes of Magic and DotA 5 are just zones within Adam Online. There's no point in creating any new worlds these days. Adam Online has it all."

Vildana thought for a moment. "But is it really possible that it has it all?"

"Unlike other worlds, Adam Online offered one important possibility: any user that has enough money for their own QCP capacities could create their own zones. Even the corporations are powerless here. Why invent something separate if everything can be made in the sandbox that is Adam Online? Incidentally, Mickiewicz borrowed the sandbox idea from an ancient and forgotten game from the Internet age. I think it was called Minecraft."

"I heard about a zone with that name in Rim Zero."

"Believe me, everything that can be invented has been both invented and created in Adam Online. Even infinite expansion. And another important detail: Adam Online offered that which its competitors could never offer."

"What's that?"

"The lack of a need to play. You can actually live here, even without any kind of game interface. That's why everyone is given an outdated tablet in Rim Zero. The people who aren't interested in the gameplay can just switch it off or throw it away. Although that's a delusion. The game rules and mechanics don't go anywhere, the player just stops seeing them. They still level up and get skills and quests just like other players. Actually, a lot of people think that playing Adam Online with the interface disabled is true hardcore mode. Makes it like real life."

While I was speaking, I raised my hand further and further up Vildana's thigh. She was clearly not against it. She even crossed her legs, trapping my hand. Although maybe that was a sign that she planned to break it.

I moved closer to her...

"Hey, my dear people!" the driver roared drunkenly and happily. "We're entering Town Zero. Vildana should hide before the police see her."

I started trying to help the girl get on her knees on the floor, right between my legs - solely so that she couldn't be seen through the window. But she straightened up with pride.

"Are you batshit crazy? I won't hide."

The driver slowed the bus and opened the door. "Then get out. I don't need any trouble with the law."

Vildana leapt at the driver, drew her sword and put it to his throat. "If you like, I can cut your head off to make you understand that problems with outlaws are much worse."

The driver let his cigar fall from his mouth in fear.

I rushed to him and pushed the sword away. "Please don't. My quest isn't done yet."

Vildana sheathed her sword, took out her tome and dragged a black hooded cloak onto herself from one of the pages. "Fine. See you in Rim One."

"I can't wait."

Vildana froze on the bus steps. "When I see you next, I'll probably just attack you."

"Didn't you promise to warn me?"

"This is the warning."

"Alright, we'll see who gets who."

"We sure will."

With those words, Vildana jumped out of the bus, put her hood up and quickly walked down the street. But too late for secrecy: a squad of heavily armed police appeared at the end of the street.

Vildana took out her axe and shield, preparing to force her way through to the respawn tower.

The driver picked up his cigar and started the engine. "Ah, what a woman."

"What do you mean?!" his wife said, raising her voice. I'd forgotten all about her again. Huh. She could say more than thank-you after all.

The bus careered along the streets of Town Zero, still shrouded in a blue morning mist. A string of police autocarriages passed us in the opposite direction. Like the city, the autocarriages were stylized to look old, square boxes on spoked wheels. But they moved very quickly and were, as far as I knew, very durable. They could withstand plenty of gunshots and survived most crashes. Rows of policemen sat in the carriages, all NPCs of a roughly identical build. A silver armored car belonging to some rich player followed the police convoy. He must have been completing a bounty hunter quest. There was no doubt about it: they were going to fight Vildana.

The driver had to pull into the side to let the police pass. "Ah, what a woman," he whispered so his wife couldn't hear.

I heard shots and the hiss of magical explosions from the direction of the central square and the respawn point. Several black columns of smoke rose in the pink morning sky — evidence of the indestructible police carriages burning. Vildana was happily lowering her rating.

As for me, I was in agreement with the driver. It was rare to meet someone like Vildana.

We arrived at the driver's home. He parked carefully next to the three-story apartment building. The rising sun was already gilding the tip of the gigantic angel statue standing on the roof of a nearby Tenshot. I got out and helped the driver's wife disembark. She was clearly hinting at it. The driver fell out of the bus and, waving his bottle, ran over to me.

"Woohoo, we're saved thanks to you, my dear friend!"

He thrust the whiskey into my hand, slapped me on the back and babbled his gratitude. His wife walked past us and nodded.

"Thank you for saving us."

She and the child disappeared into the building and the driver started getting my reward. He pulled a crate of whiskey out of the bus's luggage compartment. At first I was surprised: how did the bottles survive our high-speed chase? Then I realized that it was another of the anonymous quest-writer's little jokes. There was a reason the driver was drinking whiskey the whole time. What a reward...

But the reward didn't end with the booze, thankfully. The driver went back into the bus and grabbed a set of keys with a keyring shaped like a two-story building.

"These are the keys to my wife's apartment. We used to rent it out. Before my wife was kidnapped. I don't think she'll mind giving the apartment to you as a reward for saving her. We don't need it, we aren't leaving Town Zero.

I read an inscription on the keyring:

1884 Lakeview Estates, 119th Street, Liberty City, Rim One.

The back of the keyring showed the number 4: the apartment or room number.

The driver gave me a sweaty hug for the last time. He stank of whiskey. "Goodbye, my dear friend. I'm going to join my family, I haven't seen them in so long."

The driver disappeared through the building doors. I took out my tablet.

Quest completed: All My Children.

A family has been reunited. News of your good deeds will spread far and wide among elderly drunken bus drivers. That's the kind of recognition you were hoping for, right?

Obtained:

+100 XP.

+2 skill points.

Property in Rim One.
10 bottles of Penny Packer whiskey.
+10,000g from the bus driver.
+1 Reputation with the authorities of all Rims.
+1 Reputation with the bus driver.
10% discounts on purchases in the Human Factor and Tenshot stores.

In the end, my Reputation was at just four. Reputation was one of those things: easy to lose, hard to restore. You usually got just one point at once.

Congratulations, Leonarm, you leveled up!
Your current level: 11.
Money: 16,610g.
Attention: you have unused stat points (1) and skill points (2). Spend them wisely!

I thought about adding a point to Strength since I didn't have any space left in my UniSuit backpack after that gift from the driver, but I decided to put it into Knowledge instead. I put my skill points into taking Automatic Weapons up to level two and Battlefield Surgery to level one. Now my bandages would stop bleeding more quickly.

Ten percent discounts in Apple stores didn't mean much, since their prices were already far too high to pay. But the Tenshot discount would come in handy.

I read on:

Your deeds have not remained unnoticed by the

dark side. What did you expect? Everything has a cost, and sometimes it's life.

For your numerous murders of the freedom-loving Three Bucks gang members, your name has been added to the criminal Whitelist. A reward has been put on your law-abiding head.

I expanded the explanation.

The Whitelist is the same as the Blacklist, only in reverse. It is a noticeboard where criminals can order the killings of players who murder people on the Blacklist.

Unfortunately, I didn't have enough Knowledge. I needed to increase it to some higher level to view the Whitelist and find out who put a price on my head, and how to stop it.

Turns out, you can't be too good. It pisses off the bad people.

Chapter 41
Trouble with the Outlaws

AND SPEAKING of bad people.

I put my tablet away and headed toward the central square. The shots and explosions had silenced, which could mean that Vildana had fallen in her uneven battle with the NPC lawmen.

A police carriage burned on the approach to the square. Half of it had melted under the influence of some magic. It was if the corpses of the policemen had melded into the wreckage. And the corpses themselves were twisted, as if they'd been turned inside out. It looked downright sickening. No doubt it must have been some special skill that mutilated the corpses of enemies.

A large seething puddle blocked the path. It was melted metal, still enveloped in the remnants of a spell, boiling away. Metallic bubbles formed on its surface and broke. It was all that remained of the bounty hunter's shining silver armored car. That poor player found out the hard way that Vildana was no easy mark. Unfortunately, the puddle was empty. Vildana had grabbed all the loot.

Next I found a police robot crushed under a huge chunk of some kind of mineral. Pieces of moist earth with worms and torn roots hung off the mineral. The aftermath of some spell that drew valuable ore from the ground. Spells like that were for engineering rather than combat. Vildana managed to find a way to use it to destroy her enemy, which spoke of her bloody-minded creativity. Destruction alone wasn't enough for her. She wanted artistic destruction.

Olga and I used to enjoy analyzing the behavior of other players in Adam Online, and trying to guess who they were in the real world.

Vildana didn't seem to be from the poor orders of society, a peasant like me. Her house wouldn't have the budget Ocean-3S pod that used the cheap type of dissociative electrolytes that only provided six thousand hours of gameplay. No, Vildana probably had a fashionable LG-View in a gilded frame, or an Apple 9D, an aluminum technological wonder. Both taken on credit. Expensive pods used high-quality dissociative fluid that gave the highest possible taharration period, all eight thousand hours.

Vildana herself probably worked in management somewhere, maybe even in the MTC, the Municipal Taharration Cluster. She'd earn fifty bucks a month, easily pay off her loans and have nothing to worry about. She didn't go to Adam Online to live, like Amy McDonald, or to play and reach the top of the leaderboard and earn money on advertising contracts like the twins from the Black Wave. No, Vildana just liked being able to kill whoever she wanted with whatever twisted methods she liked. That was a clear sign that in real life, she was a kind, talkative chatterbox; one of those rare people that didn't take

Adam Online so seriously that they shaved off their hair and eyebrows. In real life, Vildana would have the same luxuriously long hair. And strict, classical views on love and sex.

That made it even more interesting to wonder what she found so special in the NPC with whom she'd spent who knows how many days as a prisoner.

Pondering the peculiarities of human preference, I walked through the square as if through a battlefield. The closer I got to the respawn point, the more I found police corpses, robot wreckages, twisted carriages and other evidence of Vildana's decision to drop her Reputation to unexplored depths.

There were two types of respawn towers in Adam Online: local ones installed in a zone when it was created, and structures that players can buy or craft in their own user-controlled zone by leveling up the corresponding skills.

Solo players may not have had much need in towers like that, but guilds found them essential. The role of engineer was the rarest in a guild. Mostly because being an engineer was intolerably boring for most players. Engineers had no outstanding combat skills. Well, apart from the ability to create replicators that could produce combat mechanisms to go into battle in the engineer's place.

In my nerd days, when I leveled up as a Weaponsmith, I tried out the engineer's path and abandoned it. Even I found it boring to build towns, research new types of buildings, solve infrastructure problems... When I crafted weapons, I could at least look forward to using them in battle. The engineer's joy came from building a cool town with a flourishing and profitable economy. Then watching from a safe distance while an enemy guild destroys the town.

While I walked to the tower, two new players appeared on the square. They forgot all about reading their stats and gazed in amazement at the slaughter. One of them rushed to search the dead policemen. He was obviously a newbie. Dead cops didn't have anything valuable except the occasional medkit, baton or a weapon that couldn't be used by players until they themselves joined the police and unlocked their armory.

I kept expecting to see Vildana's corpse, but I only found the remains of her axe scattered around the savaged body of a large police robot. A flashing light still span on its head, casting blue and red reflections on the slaughter.

Fresh police arrived on the square, but there was nobody left to catch. Vildana had gone to Rim One, where she doubtlessly continued her killing spree.

Time for me to go too. I took out my tablet and initiated the teleport. A map of Rim One opened up with four available teleport destinations: Liberty City, the Rim One Arena, the Swiftville zone and the town of Fortunagrad, the refuge of all players who liked to wallow in vice, drugs and everything they were missing in real life.

I chose Liberty City. It was a huge city, each district with its own respawn tower. But only two towers were available to me on the map. A local one almost at the center of the city, and the one closest to the key icon on 119th Street. I chose the second tower.

Are you sure you want to leave Rim Zero? All open quests will disappear. You remember that nobody can come back to Rim Zero, right?

Yeah, yeah. We'll just forget about the fact that dozens of high-ranked Black Wave guild members somehow appeared there recently.

Finally! Everyone here was getting sick of you.
Time spent in Rim Zero: 62 hours and 34 minutes.

I pressed confirm again. The respawn tower grew in size, pulling me towards it. Then it folded into a spiral-like tunnel within which I first flew upwards, then began to fall. The tunnel ended and expanded back into the respawn tower. This time the one in Liberty City.

Magnificent skyscrapers stretched into a sky full of flying machines and zeppelins. I clicked my heels on the paving of the square. The sounds of a big city filled my ears.

Liberty City was a huge place, completely different

from the provincial Town Zero. It was home to a multitude of players and millions of NPCs. It had thousands of zones of all kinds. From the skyscrapers of Luxor District, which was in itself a city within a city, located on an island, to the dirty slums of Stanton District. There were sometimes wars between gangs in the slums, and the police kept out of it, pretending as if nothing was happening. In the rich and clean districts, on the other hand, even carrying a weapon was considered disorderly conduct.

Suddenly I realized that I was experiencing the same feelings as I had long ago, when I first found myself there. I was eighteen years old and making my first foray into the virtual world through a taharration pod instead of a gyrosphere. I was stunned by the majesty and beauty of Liberty City. Even training in Rim Zero did nothing to temper the shock. The sheer scale of the city was overbearing, it made my head spin.

Just like the first time, I was at a loss. I wanted to just run over to the park and take a boat ride on the lake. Or just dive in. Or maybe go to one of the shopping malls? That's right, I had money, I needed to spend it on upgrades! Or... ha-ha, how could I forget? I had to go to the Redlight Splash district! It had brothels, street bars, and I had enough money to order a whole orgy... I didn't have to mention that it was the lack of fantastically amazing virtual sex that depressed me most of all in real life. It was the first thing I thought of when I recalled Adam Online.

But sex was something that could be earned, especially in Adam. Improve your appearance and you could attract female NPCs or players. Maybe I should just forget everything and go get high in some dive in Little Holland... Or...

Wait!

I slapped my face, causing my tablet to squawk immediately.

Damage taken: -1.

Why was I thinking about all these different districts? Why street bars and orgies? Get a grip, Leonarm. You're not some noob. You just forgot how alluring it can be when a whole world of fun spreads out before you. You knew it would pull you in, make you forget about time and your mission. Months could go by in an endless frenzy of pleasure. Even running out of money wouldn't stop it. There were always plenty of quests to earn more...

I hit myself again.

Some fancy-looking guy in a white frock coat and a top hat walked by. The gentleman wore rings full of precious stones on his fingers.

"Hitting yourself, are you?" he asked, raising his hat in a polite gesture. "Want some help? I can beat the living daylights out of you if you like."

I still hadn't recovered from the shock. "Get gone before I beat you," I snapped at him without thinking.

The gentleman suddenly disappeared from view, revealing the respawn tower stretching infinitely into the sky. The morning sun lit up a gigantic zeppelin advertisement for Tenshot. Several jets streaked through the blue sky, leaving a white trail behind them. It was so calm, so peaceful.

Only the pain in my skull kept me from enjoying the peace. There were also animated stars spinning around my head. Looked like this gentleman was something of a joker. He'd added an Aftereffect to his punch.

The gentleman reappeared above me, blotting out the peaceful sky. "Now I'll teach you how to talk to strangers," he said, rolling up the sleeves of his white frock coat.

I raised my hand to shield myself from his strikes when I heard a policeman shout,

"Stop fighting at once, sir!"

The gentleman kicked me in the side and ran away. I saw the policeman: holding his cap, he darted off to chase after the combative gentleman.

I sat on the ground, took out my tablet and scratched my throbbing head.

Welcome to Liberty City, the citadel of freedom.

END OF BOOK ONE

Want to be the first to know about our latest LitRPG, sci fi and fantasy titles from your favorite authors?

Subscribe to our **New Releases** newsletter:
http://eepurl.com/b7niIL

Thank you for reading *Absolute Zero!*
If you like what you've read, check out other LitRPG,
fantasy and science fiction novels published by Magic
Dome Books:

Level Up LitRPG series by Dan Sugralinov:
Re-Start
Hero
The Final Trial
Level Up: The Knockout (with Max Lagno)

The Way of the Shaman LitRPG series
by Vasily Mahanenko:
Survival Quest
The Kartoss Gambit
The Secret of the Dark Forest
The Phantom Castle
The Karmadont Chess Set
Shaman's Revenge
Clans War

Dark Paladin LitRPG series by Vasily Mahanenko:
The Beginning
The Quest
Restart

Galactogon LitRPG series by Vasily Mahanenko:
Start the Game!
In Search of the Uldans

The Bard from Barliona LitRPG series
by Eugenia Dmitrieva and Vasily Mahanenko:
The Renegades
A Song of Shadow

The Neuro LitRPG series by Andrei Livadny:
The Crystal Sphere
The Curse of Rion Castle
The Reapers

Phantom Server LitRPG series by Andrei Livadny:
Edge of Reality
The Outlaw
Black Sun

Reality Benders LitRPG series
by Michael Atamanov:
Countdown
External Threat
Game Changer

Respawn Trials LitRPG Series by Andrei Livadny:
Edge of the Abyss

The Dark Herbalist LitRPG series
by Michael Atamanov:
Video Game Plotline Tester
Stay on the Wing
A Trap for the Potentate
Finding a Body

Perimeter Defense LitRPG series by Michael Atamanov:
Sector Eight
Beyond Death
New Contract
A Game with No Rules

An NPC's Path LitRPG series by Pavel Kornev:
The Dead Rogue
Kingdom of the Dead

Mirror World LitRPG series by Alexey Osadchuk:
Project Daily Grind
The Citadel
The Way of the Outcast
The Twilight Obelisk

Point Apocalypse (a near-future action thriller)
by Alex Bobl

In order to have new books of the series translated faster, we need your help and support! Please consider leaving a review or spread the word by recommending *Absolute Zero* to your friends and posting the link on social media. The more people buy the book, the sooner we'll be able to make new translations available.

Thank you!

Till next time!

www.ingramcontent.com/pod-product-compliance
Lightning Source LLC
Chambersburg PA
CBHW072253020726
47501CB00002B/251